THE OXFORD CHEKHOV

VOLUME IX

—

STORIES

1898–1904

THE OXFORD
CHEKHOV

VOLUME IX

STORIES
1898–1904

Translated and edited by
RONALD HINGLEY

LONDON
OXFORD UNIVERSITY PRESS
NEW YORK   TORONTO
1975

*Oxford University Press, Ely House, London W.*1

GLASGOW NEW YORK TORONTO MELBOURNE WELLINGTON
CAPE TOWN IBADAN NAIROBI DAR ES SALAAM LUSAKA ADDIS ABABA
DELHI BOMBAY CALCUTTA MADRAS KARACHI LAHORE DACCA
KUALA LUMPUR SINGAPORE HONG KONG TOKYO

ISBN 0 19 211383 6

Printed in Great Britain by
The Camelot Press Ltd., Southampton

To

MICHAEL BLAKEMORE

CONTENTS

PREFACE

(a) Sources and Conventions

THIS volume contains Chekhov's entire output of fiction first published between the beginning of 1898 and his death in 1904, together with three fragments which remained unpublished during his lifetime.

As may be seen from the Bibliography on pp. 324-8 below, all this material has been previously translated into English at least once, except that no earlier versions of the unfinished *The Cripple* and *A Letter* have been traced. *A Letter* is to be distinguished from an earlier story with the same Russian title (*Письмо*), dated 1887, and also from another story with a similar title: *Письма* (1886).

The translations are based on the Russian text and variants as printed in vol. ix of the twenty-volume *Complete Collection of the Works and Letters of A. P. Chekhov* (Moscow, 1944-51), here referred to as '*Works*, 1944-51', or simply as 'W.'. Certain more recently published material, bearing on variants to *A Lady with a Dog* and *A Marriageable Girl*, and contained in *Literaturnoye nasledstvo: Chekhov* (Moscow, 1960) has also been taken into account.[1]

The treatment of proper names, of colloquial and uneducated Russian speech, of terms of abuse, of institutional and administrative terms, and of dates, follows the lines laid down in detail in the Prefaces to volumes previously published: in the order vols. iii, viii, ii, i, v and vi.

In the Appendixes the symbol 'N.' refers to Chekhov's *Notebooks* as published in *Works*, 1944-51, vol. xii.

(b) 'All Friends Together'

Despite having been written first, *All Friends Together* is placed last among the completed stories in this volume in conformity with the convention (adopted in *Works*, 1944-51) whereby items not included by Chekhov in the *Collected Works* edited by himself are published under a separate rubric. The status of this particular story is, however, unusual inasmuch as Chekhov did once—in a letter of 9 July 1901—give explicit instructions to A. F. Marks (publisher of his first *Collected Works*) to include *All Friends Together* in that edition. He even specified

[1] See Appendixes x and xiv.

the volume—number ten—in which it was to appear.[1] This is, moreover, the last we hear of Chekhov's attitude to the story. How, then,
did it escape inclusion in the *Collected Works*? Through second thoughts
expressed in later instructions to Marks which have not survived? Or
did it simply fall by the wayside through oversight? We do not know.

   That Chekhov set no great store by *All Friends Together* he had
already shown shortly before sending his instruction to include it in
the *Collected Works*. Replying, on 18 June 1901, to certain queries
from Marks about this and other stories, Chekhov told him that: '*All
Friends Together* has somehow slipped my mind. I don't even remember
what it's about, and you would greatly oblige me by letting me have
the first three or four lines to jog my memory so that I can answer
your question.'[2] This lapse of memory is consistent with the low opinion
of the story which Chekhov had already expressed in February 1898,
at the time of publication. He then described it as 'not all that sensational'; this was, said he, 'the kind of story you churn out at the rate of
one a day'.[3] Yet it by no means lacks merit, and surely did deserve to
be included in the *Collected Works*: an assessment confirmed by the
fact that no less than three earlier English versions (by Avrahm
Yarmolinsky; by April FitzLyon and Kyril Zinovieff; by Jessie
Coulson) have been thought worth providing. Mr. Yarmolinsky's
translation (1949) was the first to appear in English, the work having
been missed by Constance Garnett who presumably did not have
access to it.

(c) Titles

   As in previous volumes of the present edition, an attempt has been
made to give to the translation of Chekhov's titles a degree of care
comparable to that which he exercised when choosing them in the
first place. This was a matter to which he attached great importance, as
is evident again and again in his correspondence: both when he dis-
cusses his own titles and when he criticizes those of other fiction-
writers—whose titles often impressed him as ill chosen. Besides
offering *All Friends Together* in place of the title *A Visit to Friends* given
by all three previous translators, I have also preferred *A Marriageable
Girl* (for *Невеста*) to the previous *Bride* and *Betrothed*. *In the Hollow* is
used for *В овраге* in place of the more conventional *In the Ravine*, after
gulch, canyon, wadi and other alternatives had been sifted and discarded. For *Человек в футляре* *A Hard Case* seems best—I have

---

[1] W., xix, 109.   [2] W., xix, 104.   [3] W., xvii, 227.

rejected the various 'shells' and 'husks' of my predecessors. I have also
preferred *Angel* to *The Darling*.

All this may seem to be, and is, rather a matter of taste. In one
instance, however—that of *Ионыч*—a variation from the previous
Ionitch (or, as it would have been in my transliteration, *Ionych*)
seemed downright mandatory since the nuances of that particular
appellation inevitably escape those not closely versed in the lore of
Russian names. 'Ionych' is a patronymic meaning 'son of Jonah', and
such a patronymic (when used, as here, in isolation) carries a particularly strong stylistic flavour of its own. It expresses a combination
of elements (respect, deference, contempt, familiarity, humour,
affection), being usually applied to some figure to whom prestige,
seniority and authority are—whimsically or seriously—attributed; it
also carries a distinct note of spurious or even genuine folksiness. The
most famous use, historically, of an isolated patronymic is that of the
form 'Ilyich' (son of Elijah) to describe or address Vladimir Ilyich
Lenin. Such isolated patronymics—whether Ilyich, Ionych or some
other -ich/-ych—convey the atmosphere of 'the Old Man', 'the
Guv'nor', 'the Gaffer' or even 'His Nibs'. The mechanical rendering
'Ionitch' or 'Ionych' therefore seems indefensible as a title. It also sits
awkwardly in the body of the text when applied to the increasingly
overweight and pompous hero, and is there rendered after much
consideration as 'the Doc'.[1] But *The Doc* seemed unduly racy for a
title, and the more neutral *Doctor Startsev* has therefore been adopted.

(d) Imaginary Place Names

Certain place names occurring in the present volume do not appear
to correspond with actual localities, and were presumably invented by
Chekhov. These are: Mironositskoye (*A Hard Case*); Sofyino (*Concern-
ing Love*); Dyalizh (*Doctor Startsev*); Obruchanovo, Kryakovo,
Yeresnevo, Petrovskoye (*New Villa*); Syrnya (*On Official Business*);
Ukleyevo, Torguyevo, Shikalovo, Kazanskoye, Butyokino, Firsanovo,
Kuzmyonki (*In the Hollow*); Lesopolye, Obnino, Novokhatnoye (*The
Bishop*); Kuzminki (*All Friends Together*). Novosyolki (*Poor Compensa-
tion*) is, however, the name of a village near Chekhov's home at
Melikhovo.

(e) Sound Effects

In the present volume Chekhov follows, more frequently than ever,

[1] See p. 66, below.

his common practice of conveying specific sound effects by inventing
otherwise meaningless pronounceable combinations of consonants and
vowels. Such are the bangings of the watchmen as reproduced in
A Case History by дер, дер, дер; дрын, дрын, дрын; жак, жак.[1]
To render this kind of material by mechanically transliterating the
original into such forms as *der, dryn* and *zhak* seems undesirable—
especially as the original formulae have Russian phonetic values such as
no transliteration system can convey. Nor does the use of some semi-
systematic form of transliteration seem very well conceived either.
Without going into excess of detail I can best indicate my own
approach to such sound-effect formulae by quoting, for purposes of
comparison, a single passage (one among several) which presents the
problem: firstly in the version of another translator who in this matter
follows what I believe to be a mistaken policy, and secondly as I
have it:

Once again, 'Bray . . . bray . . .
bray . . .'
Twelve times. Then a deep
stillness for half a minute and,
from the other end of the en-
closure, 'drun . . . drun . . .
drun . . .'
'Terribly unpleasant!' thought
Korolev.
'Dack . . . dack . . .' resounded
from a third place, broken and
harsh as if with annoyance, 'dack
. . . dack . . .'[2]

Once again those blurred
thuds were heard: twelve
strokes. Then there was quiet,
thirty seconds' quiet, followed
by the deeper clanging note at
the other end of the works.
'How revolting!' thought
Korolyov.
From a third place a harsh,
staccato, seemingly exasperated
sound rang out on yet another
note.[3]

(f) *The Spider and the Bloodsucker*

On another point of translation particular difficulties are presented
by the phrase глитай абож паук—the nickname given by Kovalenko
to Belikov in *A Hard Case*—especially as the first two of these three
words are not Russian, but Ukrainian. Herself failing to understand
the original, the Russian translator Olga Vasilyev (whose version of *A
Hard Case* in English was presumably the first, but remained un-

---

[1] W., ix, 311; and in other parts of the story.
[2] *Anton Chekhov: Selected Stories*, translated with an Introduction by Jessie Coulson
(London, 1963), p. 250.
[3] See p. 75, below.

published) applied to Chekhov for an explanation. Chekhov replied
(on 25 February 1899) that глитай абож паук was the title of a
Ukrainian play: 'глитай means spider, and the phrase as a whole
means *spider or spider:* it explains, in other words, what глитай means.
This is untranslatable into any foreign language.'[1]

Here Chekhov doubly errs. Firstly, глитай does not mean 'spider'
in Ukrainian, but 'extortioner, bloodsucker'; and, secondly, the phrase
is by no means untranslatable into English. 'Master Creepy Crawly'
seems fully adequate.

(g) Translating Policy Reviewed

Over ten years have now passed since work first began on *The
Oxford Chekhov*, of which the present is the seventh volume to appear.
So long a lapse of time may perhaps excuse a brief reconsideration of
the policy adopted in making the translations.

A specific philosophy of translation was adopted and announced
when the first volume of this series was published in 1964,[2] and has
remained essentially unchanged as the work has progressed. This
doctrine now seems worth restating—not because it has been assailed
or found wanting, but because what was originally largely a matter of
theory, based on inner conviction, now seems to have justified itself
in practice.

This policy is based on the premiss that there is something unmistakably English about a proper English sentence, and that authentic
Russian (such as Chekhov's) should if possible be put into comparably
authentic English: not left dangling in the limbo of 'translationese'.

The intention has, accordingly, been to render the mood as well as
the sense of the original, above all by seeking equivalents in natural,
unquaint English for the words of an author whose Russian is neither
quaint nor unnatural. Where—exceptionally, but not infrequently—
Chekhov puts non-standard or otherwise eccentric Russian into the
mouths of his characters, an attempt has, however, been made to
cultivate similar English intonations. In other words, the aim (alas,
imperfectly achieved) has been to give Chekhov the kind of language
which he himself might have used, had he chanced to be writing in
English.

As was stated ten years ago, this has involved consciously departing
from a principle enunciated in 1941 by the American translator Stark
Young: 'Let Chekhov . . . have it his own way—let him, for example,

[1] W., xviii, 93.   [2] See *The Oxford Chekhov*, vol. iii, pp. x ff.

repeat a word when he chooses to repeat it, invert the word order when he chooses, and so on.'[1]

A more extreme statement of a comparable approach has since been put forward by Vladimir Nabokov. In the Foreword to his edition of Pushkin's *Eugene Onegin* in English translation, Nabokov expressly claims to produce a literal version: '. . . to my ideal of literalism I sacrificed everything (elegance, clarity, good taste, modern usage, and even grammar) that the dainty mimic prizes higher than truth. Pushkin has likened translations to horses changed at the posthouses of civilization. The greatest reward I can think of is that students may use my work as a pony.'[2]

A not dissimilar view has been expressed more recently by Simon Karlinsky in the Foreword to a translated *Selected Letters of Anton Chekhov* published in 1973. Claiming—as what translator would not?— to produce a version which respects the original, he writes as follows on behalf of himself and the main translator of the volume, Michael Henry Heim: 'When Chekhov repeats a word, we do not make him more eloquent by casting about for synonyms. . . . When he writes a long or convoluted sentence, we do not explicate [*sic*] him by breaking it up into easily digestible morsels.'[3]

There are special reasons why such a policy is less undesirable when applied to Chekhov's letters and Pushkin's verse than it is in the rendering of Chekhov's creative writings. However, neither the arguments of these translators nor the practice of the two first-mentioned (for the Heim–Karlinsky version of Chekhov's letters cannot be dismissed as inadequate) seems to justify their *ex cathedra* claims to demarcate what constitutes truth to, and respect for, the original of a work put into English. Still less is it clear why the translator of *Onegin* should apparently assume that his first duty is to students of the language from which his rendering is made.

The present translation is, by contrast, directly and explicitly intended for English-speaking readers who wish to read a great writer for what he has to say. It is not intended as a crib. If these versions should chance to provide students of Russian with a free ride into the language, so much the better; but that could only be a welcome by-product of the process: never its primary aim.

[1] *Three Sisters; a Drama in Four Acts*, tr. Stark Young (New York, 1941), p. vii; *The Oxford Chekhov*, vol. iii, p. xvii.
[2] *Eugene Onegin*, tr. with Commentary by Vladimir Nabokov (London, 1964), vol. i, p. x.
[3] *The Letters of Anton Chekov*, tr. Heim and Karlinsky (see Bibliography, below), p. xi.

I have never knowingly preserved linguistic features of the original at points where this would, in my view, result in turning natural, elegant Russian into quaint, unnatural English.

(h) Chekhov on Translation

To reject doctrines erring in the direction of over-literal translation, to make an attempt at least—however foredoomed—to do in English what the original author has done so elegantly and flexibly in his own language is, in a sense, to adopt a freer attitude, yet one which paradoxically involves a far more rigorous and exacting discipline. That Chekhov himself, had he been a translator, would have adopted a similar approach seems likely from various passages in his letters. Referring to a translation from English—of a work by Ouida done into Russian by his brother Michael, then a tax inspector—Chekhov wrote on 10 May 1891: 'Oh, why don't I know languages? I think I should be a magnificent translator of fiction. When I read other people's translations *I change and transpose words in my mind*, and the result is something light and ethereal, like lace.'[1] So much for Stark Young's loyalty to the word order of the original! Again, in a letter of 28 April 1897 to V. N. Argutinsky-Dolgorukov, Chekhov criticizes a story, in Russian, submitted to him by the addressee as, in effect, smacking of translationese. 'It's not your work, it's a translation from English. It contains not one single Russian sentence—not one!'[2] From such passages we can deduce what Chekhov would, had he known English, have thought of those who apply the same process with the languages reversed.

Less happily for our purpose in claiming Chekhov as an ally, he apparently believed—and several times stated—that there was no point in translating Russian authors into foreign languages in the first place! Among such pronouncements on translation in his correspondence the following are worth quoting, if only for the ironical or amusing flavour which hindsight can give them in the light of Chekhov's long and complicated history in English and other alien dress:

'I do not read English. I neither see nor know English periodicals. And my view is that I present so little in the way of interest to the British public that it is a matter of supreme indifference whether I am or whether I am not published in an English magazine.'[3]

---

[1] W., xv, 199–200; italics added.
[2] W., xvii, 73.   [3] W., xviii, 378.

'In general I am indifferent to these translations [of his work into German], since I know that we [Russian writers] neither are nor ever will be needed in Germany—however much we may be translated.'[1]

'If Russian writers are needed anywhere, it is only in Russia herself.'[2]

'Why do you want my work to be published in America? And in a lady's—which means an atrocious—translation?'[3]

'What's the point of translating my play [*The Cherry Orchard*] into French? How grotesque! The French will make nothing of Yermolay [Lopakhin] or the sale of the estate—they'll only be bored.'[4]

'With regard to translations of my play [*The Cherry Orchard*], tell everyone you [his wife] don't know a thing about it, that I don't answer your queries and so on and so forth. I can't stop it, after all, so let them translate away if they want. No sense will come of it in any case.'[5]

'*The Cherry Orchard* is being translated for Berlin and Vienna. But it won't succeed there since they don't have billiards, Lopakhins or students *à la* Trofimov.'[6]

(i) *Erratum*

In *The Oxford Chekhov*, vol. vi, p. 2, a play performed in aid of certain famine victims is identified as Chekhov's *The Wedding*; it was in fact Gogol's *Marriage*.

(j) *Acknowledgements*

Particular thanks are due—more even than usual—to my wife for her skill and patience in revising the text stylistically and typographically. She has also shared the typing with Miss Susan Kaye and Miss Joan Clifton, and my thanks for this go to all three of them. I am also grateful to my colleague Dr. G. Stone for helping me out with the

---

[1] W., xix, 169.   [2] W., xix, 177–8.   [3] W., xix, 342.   [4] W., xx, 163.
[5] W., xx, 184.   [6] W., xx, 241.

infamous глитай абож паук. I am grateful, too, to Mr. and Mrs. Sergei Hackel, and to Mrs. Emma Shotton, for advice on matters culinary, ecclesiastical and musicological; and to Mrs. Jana Howlett for placing at my disposal her special knowledge of terms ichthyological.

Frilford, Abingdon   RONALD HINGLEY
   1974

INTRODUCTION

THE stories in the present volume were all written after Chekhov had become a more or less permanent invalid, and they represent the last pages of fiction which he produced. But they are very far indeed from revealing any general decline in his creative powers.

Five items are particularly outstanding. *A Lady with a Dog* is probably the best-known of all Chekhov's stories, and is the work in which he most profoundly explores the theme of love.[1] *Angel* is almost equally celebrated, and was a favourite of Leo Tolstoy, who frequently read it aloud in his family circle.[2] *In the Hollow* is perhaps superior to both. It remains—together with *Peasants* (1897)—Chekhov's chief fictional contribution in his rural idiom, and it has a superbly managed plot. *A Hard Case* (or the 'Trilogy' consisting of *A Hard Case, Gooseberries* an d *Concerning Love* taken as a whole) is also a powerful contender, while *Doctor Startsev*—though comparatively neglected—is fit to hold its own with any rival.

Among the remaining completed stories in the present volume, none is quite on the superlative level of the above-mentioned, yet none lags hopelessly behind. The anomalous *All Friends Together* is a highly perceptive and sensitive study—even though Chekhov himself evidently considered it the weakest item in the batch, contriving to exclude it from his *Collected Works*. To his panorama of human nature in its rustic Russian manifestations *A Case History, New Villa, On Official Business* and *At Christmas* all mark important additions. And, finally, the last two completed stories of his life (*The Bishop* and *A Marriageable Girl*) are fascinating samples of his art, though their importance has sometimes been exaggerated by critics.

To see these stories in their biographical setting we must go back to the sudden crisis in Chekhov's health which occurred on 22 March 1897. He then suffered a severe haemorrhage from the lungs which began while he was dining in a Moscow restaurant. Removed to a clinic in the city three days later after a further attack, he was—himself a doctor—at last forced through the diagnosis of other physicians to

---

[1] See further, Virginia Llewellyn Smith's *Anton Chekhov and the Lady with the Dog* (London, 1973).
[2] W., ix, 603.

accept what he had long refused to consider seriously: that he was suffering from severe active tuberculosis. Its first symptoms, including haemoptysis, seem to go back as far as 1884.

From now onwards Chekhov was compelled to spend most of his winter months in the south for health reasons. Between September 1897 and the following April he lived in Nice, also visiting Biarritz and Paris. In mid-1898 he was briefly back on his country estate, at Melikhovo near Moscow, but was soon seeking a permanent base in south Russia. In the autumn he resided in the Crimea and bought a plot of land at Autka on the outskirts of Yalta, where he proceeded to build a charming and eccentrically designed villa. Barely was he launched on this project when the death of his father helped to decide him, with the encouragement of his sister and widowed mother, to put the Melikhovo estate on the market and to make Yalta his sole permanent residence— as, despite frequent tours of absence, it was to remain during the rest of his life.

By August 1899 Chekhov's new villa was ready for habitation, and he entered fully upon his final 'Yalta' period after two and a half years of disruption and travel introduced by his health crisis of March 1897. Henceforward Chekhov was—much to his own disgust—marooned in this Crimean coastal resort during most of the remaining winter months of his life.

The acute boredom, the considerable sufferings—physical and mental—of Chekhov's last years were relieved by various successes connected with the theatre. Chief among these, biographically, was his marriage in 1901 to the actress Olga Knipper: a marriage of which we perhaps know too much from the large surviving correspondence between a man and wife whom circumstances kept apart during a great deal of their wedded life.

By now Chekhov's interest in the stage had been unexpectedly revived after a period of acute disillusionment following the catastrophic failure of his *Seagull* on its first night in St. Petersburg in October 1896. Two years later the same play was revived, much against the author's wishes, by the newly founded Moscow Art Theatre, and enjoyed a heartening degree of success. Thus encouraged, the Art Theatre put on another—already available—four-act play by Chekhov (*Uncle Vanya*). And the success of this in turn stimulated the author to create, in 1900 and 1903 respectively, two more masterpieces (*Three Sisters* and *The Cherry Orchard*) expressly for the Theatre which had rescued him for the stage and furnished him with a talented and beloved wife. These were also the years in which Chekhov's first *Collected Works* were published, by A. F. Marks. To assemble, edit, revise and proof-read volume after volume of scattered and half-forgotten material produced during the previous two decades—this was an exacting task; nor was it altogether congenial, especially as Chekhov's contract with Marks soon turned out to be weighted heavily against the author.

For all these reasons the short story ceased—during the seven years of life remaining to Chekhov after the collapse of his health in March 1897—to be such a prominent concern as it had been during the previous seven-year period: that following his excursion of 1890 to Sakhalin Island, the convict settlement in the Russian furthest east. This slump in productivity was very pronounced indeed: Chekhov published a mere 250 pages of short stories after mid-1897, whereas the figure for the earlier phase (from mid-1890 to mid-1897) is 850 pages.[1]

If we now look more closely at Chekhov's output of short stories within the final period of seven years, we shall find it mainly concentrated in the first thirty months: from mid-1897 to the end of 1899. Thereafter, in his last four and a half years, Chekhov published only two short stories, totalling less than forty pages: *The Bishop* and *A Marriageable Girl*. But these were also the years when his plays *Three Sisters* and *The Cherry Orchard* were written: masterpieces which must warn us against exaggerating the degree to which their author's creative powers were impaired towards the end of his life.

Short bouts (two or three months) of fairly intensive work interspersed with longer fallow periods—such was the pattern of Chekhov's writing in 1897-9, as will emerge more clearly if we now consider his productivity cycle in somewhat greater detail.

All Friends Together belongs to a group of four stories written at Nice in October–December 1897; the other three items of this quartet —*Home*, *The Savage*, *In the Cart*—appear in vol. viii of the present edition.

The next bout of activity—in June–July 1898—sees the production of the last four stories to be written by Chekhov at Melikhovo: the Trilogy and *Doctor Startsev*.

Later in 1898 (November and December) Chekhov produces a further batch of four stories, all written at Yalta: *A Case History*, *Angel*, *New Villa* and *On Official Business*.

[1] Figures are approximate and based on the pagination in *Works*, 1944-51, vols. vii–ix.

After an interval of some nine months Chekhov—now established as a permanent Yalta resident—devotes October–December 1899 to *A Lady with a Dog*, *At Christmas* and *In the Hollow*.

With the coming of the new century the patterns and periodicity of Chekhov's work are disrupted. He now ceases to lay his stories in small clutches—in fact he is showing signs of losing interest in the short story altogether. He completes only two more, and these must be sharply distinguished from their immediate predecessors—firstly because the writing of each was spread over a twelve-month period: March 1901–February 1902 (*The Bishop*); October 1902–September 1903 (*A Marriageable Girl*). And, secondly, we must also remember that the composition of *The Bishop* was preceded by that of *Three Sisters* (in August–October 1900), while work on *A Marriageable Girl* overlapped with the creation of *The Cherry Orchard* (in March–April and July–October 1903).

In his post-1897 stories Chekhov undeviatingly follows his normal practice of setting his fiction in the Russia of his own day: the Russia which he knew at first hand. Far from drawing on his eight-month French sojourn of 1897–8 for background, he explicitly turned down an invitation—extended to him when he was still in Nice by an editor of the magazine *Cosmopolis*—to write on an 'international' (in the context, non-Russian) theme. He could only do so, he wrote, in Russia and in retrospect. 'That's the only way I can write: from memory. I have never done live portraits from nature. I need my memory to sieve the subject, leaving behind—as on a filter-paper—only what is essential and typical.'[1]

Even after returning to Russia in May 1898 Chekhov did not feel impelled to write a story with a foreign setting such as he had occasionally used in the past: for example, in *An Anonymous Story* (1893) and *Ariadne* (1895). Nor, in the light of his normal practice, should we expect that his first-hand knowledge of Yalta would necessarily be mirrored in his fiction. Yet reflected it is—only once, but memorably indeed—in the first two chapters of *A Lady with a Dog*. Chekhov thereby breaks what for him, and for many another Russian fiction-writer, was practically an unwritten rule: you may avowedly set your story or novel in either of the 'two capitals', St. Petersburg and Moscow; but if you venture into the provinces—whether to the countryside or to an urban centre—that setting must be kept decently anonymous. So it is even with *A Lady with a Dog* when—after the

[1] W., xvii, 193.

Yalta episode and a brief visit to Moscow—the scene switches to the anonymous provincial town (typically designated as 'S——') where Anne von Diederitz lives with her unsatisfactory husband. Anonymous too are the settings of *A Marriageable Girl* ('the town') and *Doctor Startsev* (another 'S——').

These three unnamed centres have this in common with many another provincial town in Chekhov's work: they are the scene of inspissated boredom which is only thrown into sharper relief by their inhabitants' pathetic attempts to diversify lives essentially dedicated to 'eating, drinking and sleeping': that common Chekhovian formula. So dreary are the cultural and social activities of these provincial bores (the abominable fiddling in the orchestra at the theatre; the nude 'lady with vase'; the Turkins' ludicrous 'accomplishments') that they would clearly have done better to confine themselves to eating, drinking, sleeping and vegetating.

Whence, one wonders, come these countless Chekhovian denunciations—no less pungent for the surface restraint with which they are delivered—of a mode of life with which the author was rarely brought into prolonged contact as an adult? The only provincial town which he knew intimately was the port of Taganrog in southern Russia, where he was born and spent most of his first nineteen years: a town which he occasionally revisited, and for which he retained the liveliest sympathies throughout his life.

Hardly more edifying than Chekhov's provincial towns are the rural settings to be found in this volume. Here is no idyllic countryside, but one morally or physically polluted by industrial activity. *A Case History* and *In the Hollow* reflect the common Russian practice of siting factories such as cotton-printing mills, tanneries and bone-ash works in or near villages. The factory-hands who figure in both these stories are by no means treated unsympathetically, but they are not intimately depicted. Their plight evidently concerns the author deeply, but he leaves them in the background—no doubt because his own first-hand knowledge of the small (but growing) Russian proletariat, whether town-based or village-based, was not very great.

With the peasantry proper the matter was quite otherwise. After half a dozen years as squire, doctor, school-builder and general philanthropist of Melikhovo, Chekhov knew his peasants pretty well. Even after he had finally quitted that central Russian rural base in 1899, his Melikhovo experiences continued to pass through his creative 'filter'. *In the Hollow* reflects the emotions of Melikhovo recollected in the tranquillity of Yalta, as also do *New Villa* and *On Official Business*.

By contrast with stories unrelievedly rural or undeviatingly urban in setting, the Trilogy ingeniously interweaves both motifs. The framework of the three stories—the village elder's barn and Alyokhin's farm—is bucolic. But the narratives of the two huntsmen and the farmer all take us back to town. Belikov's town in *A Hard Case* is yet another of those unfortunate, unnamed, doomed provincial centres of which we meet so many in Chekhov (another 'S——', in effect), while the second and third parts of the Trilogy are neatly contrasted. *Gooseberries* tells of a townee who spends all his life pathetically contriving his return, as a pompous landowner, to a countryside such as he had known as a boy. *Concerning Love* is the tale of a farmer bored with hard work on his estate and engaged in a self-frustrated amorous intrigue in the near-by town. A contrast between the countryside and a city (St. Petersburg) also figures in *At Christmas*: a deft but somewhat slight essay in a mode recalling that of Chekhov's manner of the early and middle 1880s.

Besides mingling town and country in this way, Chekhov—no less characteristically—provides a widely diversified social analysis. Seven of our stories (the Trilogy, *Doctor Startsev*, *A Lady with a Dog*, *A Marriageable Girl* and *All Friends Together*) are firmly focused on the privileged, professional classes: the world of doctors, bankers, officials, clergy, landowners and the like; that their 'privileges' add up to precious little in the way of basic satisfaction does, however, remain one of Chekhov's major themes.

In the Hollow is, by contrast, an exclusively peasant affair—yet one acutely concerned with the internal social stratification of the Russian village. Here, too, we meet the privileged, such as the Tsybukins (who are the kind of rich villagers commonly termed kulaks), and their downtrodden, exploited victims who supply the backcloth—but also, in Lipa, a major figure.

It happens that the picture conveyed by *In the Hollow* accords closely with Marxist doctrine on conflicts within the Russian village. And it also happens that the story was written for the magazine *Zhizn*: one of those Marxist publications which (despite the revolutionary nature of Marx's teaching) were yet allowed the luxury of legally sanctioned publication in Imperial Russia at the turn of the century. Had Chekhov, then, suddenly become a revolutionary socialist in the evening of his life? Nothing could be further from the truth, as closer study of this episode shows. Never politically-minded, the author had—in his innocence—not even been aware that the magazine possessed Marxist affiliations. On discovering that this was so he became distressed, in his tactful way, since he believed that *In the Hollow* contravened Marxist teaching. 'I have sent a story to *Zhizn*', he lamented to a correspondent on 26 December 1899. 'In it I portray factory life: describe it as a melancholy affair. But then, only yesterday, I chanced to discover that *Zhizn* is a Marxist—a factory—organ. What *am* I to do now?'[1] There was, of course, no need to do anything since the editors of *Zhizn* could only be delighted with Chekhov's picture of rural backwardness, and of the 'social contradictions' in the Russian village. For non-Marxist readers, however, this particular aspect of the story can have no more than curiosity value, since *In the Hollow* transcends such doctrinal considerations. It was conceived independently of political dogma in the original mind of an artist whose portrayals might also on occasion coincide or seem to coincide from time to time with other tenets (Christian, Tolstoyan), but who was neither a religious believer nor—after a brief period in the late 1880s—a disciple of Tolstoy or of anyone else. Chekhov was anything but a Marxist. He had no conception of, no interest in, Marxist ideology. Nor has he ever been depicted as a Marxist even by the Kremlin-instructed literary processers of post-revolutionary Russia. To them the author of *In the Hollow* is, rather, a truthful portrayer of 'reality' who, being such, could not help reflecting reality as conceived (by definition truthfully) in the Marxist scheme.

Besides stories depicting clashes wholly confined either to the professional classes or to the Russian village, there are others here in which the professional/privileged and peasant/unprivileged classes figure side by side. They are shown attempting to make contact with each other; but never, it seems, shall the twain meet in any real sense. This is pre-eminently true of *New Villa* and *On Official Business*, both of which present the gulf separating the *intelligent* (the educated Russian of the professional classes) from the illiterate or semi-literate *muzhik*. The engineer of *New Villa* may efficiently bridge the local river, but he and his family can build no bridge between themselves and the local inhabitants. Unbridged too is the gulf between the downtrodden workers and the exploiting but bewildered factory-owners of *A Case History*.

[1] W., xviii, 288.

These are all fascinating stories of immense value as social documents; they provide many a penetrating insight into the class relationships of late nineteenth-century Russia. But to read them only from
such an angle would be to do scant justice to Chekhov the artist and to
forget that his work is a comment on the human predicament in
general, not on any specific national or social manifestation of that
predicament. Wide as Chekhov's geographical and sociological range
may be, he was anything but a dedicatedly regional writer or an
author unremittingly obsessed with class relationships. Nor was he
exclusively a purveyor of ideas. In briefly considering, now, the main
notions represented in these last stories, we are therefore far from
suggesting that he was a wholly committed writer concerned only
with putting over 'messages'; for it would be as misleading to assert
that ideas were all-important to his work as to claim that they play no
part in it at all.

Nowhere else in Chekhov's writings do we meet a preoccupation
with human inequality as pervasive as is found in these last stories.
'Look at the impudence and idleness of the strong, the ignorance and
bestiality of the weak'—the words are those of Ivan Ivanovich in
Gooseberries, and introduce a long harangue on the insensitivity of 'the
happy man' as revealed by his attitude towards his less fortunate
brethren. 'At the door of every contented, happy man there should be
someone standing with a little hammer, someone to keep dinning into
his head that unhappy people do exist—and that, happy though he may
be, life will round on him sooner or later.' Similar sentiments will be
found elsewhere in the present and earlier volumes, and also in Chekhov's *Notebooks*; this recurrent contrast between 'weak' and 'strong'
was a staple element in his thinking.

The contrast between weak and strong can take various forms: as a
conflict between rich and poor, happy and unhappy, well-fed and
starving, landowner and peasant, factory owner and worker—or (to
personalize it) between Aksinya and Lipa in *In the Hollow*. In Chekhov's
work, however, things do not always work out as they may seem on
the surface. On closer scrutiny many of the 'strong' turn out to be
weak—or at least to be no less deserving of pity than the 'weak'. The
rich engineer's wife of *New Villa* is less happy, despite her privileged
position, than the benighted peasants whom she so pathetically
attempts to befriend. The factory-owner and her daughter in *A Case
History* derive as little satisfaction from their lives as their exploited
workers, and the only person who reaps any benefit from the entire

complex, bewildering and seemingly futile process is 'Miss Christine',
that sturgeon-guzzling, Madeira-swigging governess. Looking into
factory conditions and the sufferings which they impose on all concerned with the exception of a single complacent parasite, Chekhov's
doctor-hero concludes that the whole business is a hopeless muddle:
a point of view closely coinciding with Chekhov's oft-quoted claim
that the fiction-writer's business is not to propound solutions, but
merely to formulate problems correctly.[1]

Again and again, as the present volume richly testifies, Chekhov
describes the kind of rut into which human beings so often seem to
sink. He does so with particular skill in the Trilogy—and not least in
the person of Belikov, the hero or anti-hero of *A Hard Case*. Belikov is
one of Chekhov's most famous characters—the one who, above all
others, has most wholeheartedly sacrificed freedom (every man's most
precious birthright, his creator repeatedly implies) for a system of
restrictions elaborate, stringent and utterly unnecessary: restrictions
both self-imposed and imposed by him on other people. Hardly less
self-enslaved is the Nicholas Ivanovich of the second story in the
Trilogy: he has sacrificed his whole life, his entire potentialities as a
human being, to the production of a single plateful of barely edible
gooseberries. Alyokhin, hero and narrator of the final story in the
Trilogy, is a similar case—having rejected the one true love of his life
because he, too, is an enslaved human being unable to transcend the
limitations in which he has perversely entrapped himself. Similarly,
Doctor Startsev sinks into the rut of life in 'S——', grows a paunch,
makes money, buys houses, eats too much (and to be seen eating
anything at all is, in Chekhov, a sinister symptom); meanwhile the
unfortunate Pussy, ruined by her upbringing in that dreadful town,
has briefly emancipated herself, only to sink quickly back into the
provincial slime.

As these and many other stories show, Chekhov was indeed adept
at demonstrating, in suffocating detail, what was wrong with people's
lives. But by what means are his characters encouraged to escape from
the traps in which they have caught themselves? The indications are,
to put it mildly, of little value to anyone who may find himself in a
similar predicament. They include the oracular assurance, which
Chekhov puts into the mouth of one or other of his characters from
time to time, that 'life in X years will be wonderful': an assertion
which alternates with a contrary prediction, put into the mouths of

[1] W., xiv, 200.

other characters, to the effect that 'life in X years' will be as weary, stale, flat and unprofitable as it is today. As for more practical advice, a sudden unheralded and unplanned departure in an unknown direction appears frequently to be recommended. 'Pick up your stick, put on your hat, get up and go . . . go anywhere, provided you go away; change your life somehow, because any change can only be for the better!'

This is what Chekhov seems to tell many of his characters. As for specific recommended destinations and activities, his *Marriageable Girl* has more to say on this than any other work. We observe his Nadya running away from home, we see her travelling to St. Petersburg to study. To study what, though? We are not told. What does she live on? How does she support herself? We do not learn. Even here, then, Chekhov can only say what is wrong, can only depict what people should *not* do; he has little in the way of a positive programme to offer, little more than vague aspirations. Nor, as an imaginative writer, could he be expected to do more. Chekhov never claimed to have solved the riddle of existence. And even Dostoyevsky (who had no hesitation in making such claims) often shows a comparable concentration on problems rather than solutions: in *Crime and Punishment* he spends some six hundred pages lovingly describing and elaborating his hero's predicament, but only six lines on delineating the 'new life', and associated conversion to Dostoyevskian views, with which the story ends. At least Chekhov tells us more about Nadya's transformation than Dostoyevsky reveals about Raskolnikov's. But to interpret Chekhov's last, sad tale as a clarion call to revolution (a posture incumbent on the Kremlin-instructed literary official) is to descend into bathos.

A Marriageable Girl is nothing of the sort. But we must not rush to the other extreme of denying that Chekhov's Nadya was immediately recognizable by contemporary Russian readers as a revolutionary by implication. Despite the absence, in any of the story's many drafts, of material directly linking the heroine with political activity, her decision to leave home against her family's wishes, and to study in St. Petersburg, were quite enough (especially when taken in conjunction with Sasha's tirades) to suggest an involvement in politics far more intense than the text could, under existing censorship conditions, directly present. And that Nadya was in fact readily identified by contemporaries as a revolutionary we know from their evidence. V. V. Veresayev—another author–doctor, but a Marxist—visited Chekhov in Yalta on 22 April 1903 and read *A Marriageable Girl* in proof: probably the second set of galleys.[1] Immediately divining Chekhov's latent intention, Veresayev rebuked him—not for creating a girl revolutionary, but for doing it so unconvincingly: 'Anton Pavlovich, that's not how girls become revolutionaries. And girls like your Nadya don't become revolutionaries anyway.' To this Chekhov's 'stern and wary' reply was: 'there are many roads leading in that direction.'[2]

That Nadya's revolutionary affiliations were no less evident to a contemporary observer out of sympathy with Marxism we also learn —from an undated letter of January 1904 to Chekhov from I. I. Gorbunov-Posadov, a disciple of Tolstoy: 'How serenely charming and touching your Marriageable Girl is! And what a pity that the poor creature had to be straightway confined in durance vile by the ogre Marx!'[3]

As Chekhov's last two stories, *A Marriageable Girl* and *The Bishop* reflect the unhappiness and frustration of one whose health was all too obviously deteriorating. Though both works remain, in the last analysis, fine achievements of which any author might be proud, there is yet a certain weariness about them which detracts from their impact. There is also some slackness in the verbal texture; one symptom of this is the obtrusive, excessive and almost certainly unconscious repetition of the formulae *kak-to* ('somehow') and *pochemu-to* ('for some reason'). Among the works in the present volume it is these two stories which most closely accord with the misleading stereotype of Chekhov as a self-pitying, whining, dedicatedly pessimistic individual. In both works the emphasis is heavily on death—but far less effectively so than in the earlier *Dreary Story* (1889), where Chekhov portrays a dying professor. Perhaps the dying are not best described by those who are themselves dying? At all events we cannot read *The Bishop* and *A Marriageable Girl* without being reminded of Chekhov's own impending end. To what extent that theme was directly present in his mind when he wrote the tale of his doomed Bishop we can only guess. But when we come to *A Marriageable Girl* and the tubercular Sasha (constantly dispensing good advice which he cannot follow himself) we see an author ironically contemplating his own imminent death—which indeed lends pathos, but not necessarily literary distinction, to the material.

[1] Gitovich, p. 747.
[2] *Chekhov v vospominaniyakh sovremennikov*, p. 528.
[3] W., ix, 679.

Sasha is one of those occasional figures in the stories (Korolyov in *A Case History* and the coroner in *On Official Business* are two others) whom we can regard as mouthpieces of the author. It was a practice of Chekhov's to endow such mouthpieces or semi-mouthpieces with absurd or pathetic characteristics skilfully designed to muffle the didactic impact of their pronouncements. With the traces of sputum left by the dying Sasha we may accordingly equate the lost galoshes of Peter Trofimov in *The Cherry Orchard* and the raving insanity of Gromov in *Ward Number Six*.

That the three Fragments in this volume (undated but certainly very late work) were also the product of a dying man their emphasis on physical disablement poignantly confirms: the first is entitled *A Cripple*; the second revolves around a cripple; the third seems focused on mental derangement.

Thus Chekhov—who so often preferred to end his works with the proverbial whimper rather than with some contrived, spectacular, noisy climax—ends his creative life in the same way, if indeed these ineffectual fragments represent the last artistic products of his pen. Unfinished as they are, they form a bitter and paradoxical commentary on the formula so often invoked to describe the end of a typical story by Chekhov: 'Life goes on.'

Life, in Chekhov's case, did not go on. It ended in his forty-fifth year through a disease, then fatal, which is now susceptible to treatment. His early death has robbed the world—of what? The finer, the more original a creative artist is, the more difficult it is to predict what path his development might have taken under hypothetical circumstances. Perhaps Chekhov would have gone on to extend and develop his work for the stage. That he would have stayed much longer with she short story, in the particular manner evolved by him in 1888–1903, teems unlikely. He had created an art form all his own, he had skilfully exploited it, he had brought it to perfection—and he died when he was just beginning to show signs of repeating himself.

That Chekhov's creative work never brought him satisfaction commensurate with his achievement will surprise no perceptive student of an *œuvre* which, taken as a whole, so eloquently denies the possibility of any such consummation.

A HARD CASE

[Человек в футляре]

(1898)

A HARD CASE

At the edge of Mironositskoye village, in Prokofy's—the village elder's—barn, two men were bivouacking after a long day's hunting: Ivan Ivanovich, a veterinary surgeon, and Burkin, a grammar-school teacher.

The vet had a rather odd and quite unsuitable double-barrelled surname (Chimsha-Gimalaysky), but answered to plain Ivan Ivanovich in the neighbourhood. He lived at a suburban stud farm and had made this hunting trip just for the sake of an outing—whereas Burkin, the schoolmaster, was the regular summer guest of a local county family, being very much at home in these parts.

They were still awake. Ivan Ivanovich—a tall, thin old man with a long moustache—sat outside the doorway smoking his pipe in the moonlight, while Burkin lay inside on the hay, invisible in the gloom.

They talked about this and that, incidentally remarking that the elder's wife—a healthy, intelligent woman called Mavra—had never been outside her native village in her life, had never seen a town or railway, had spent the last ten years sitting over her stove, and would venture out of doors only at night.

'What's so odd about that?' asked Burkin.

These solitary types (Burkin continued), these snails, these hermit crabs who seek refuge inside their own shells . . . there are plenty of them about. Perhaps such types represent throw-backs to an epoch when man's ancestors hadn't yet become social animals, but lived alone in their lairs. Or perhaps it's just a quirk of human nature. Who knows? I'm not a scientist myself, that sort of thing isn't my line. All I say is, the Mavras aren't all that rare. Well, you take an instance close at hand: someone who died in town a couple of months ago—one Belikov, classics master at my own school. You've heard of him of course. His great feat was to sport galoshes and an umbrella even on the finest days, and he always wore a warm, padded greatcoat. He kept his umbrella in a holder, his watch in a grey chamois-leather bag. When he took out a penknife to sharpen a pencil, that knife was also in a little holder. His face seemed to be encapsulated, too, because he kept it hidden behind an upturned collar. He wore dark glasses and a

Cc

pullover, he kept cotton wool in his ears, and when he took a cab he always had the top put up. The man evinced, in short, a persistent obsessive drive to envelop himself in a membrane, creating a sort of carapace to isolate him and protect him from outside influences. The real world irritated him, scared him, kept him permanently on edge. It was to justify this nervousness, perhaps—this abhorrence of the actual—that he always praised things past, things which have never existed. The ancient languages which he taught were, in effect, the same old galoshes and umbrella in another form: his refuge from real life.

'The Greek language . . . oh, how melodious, how beautiful it is!' he would say with a sugary expression. And, as if to prove his words, he would screw up his eyes, hold up a finger and pronounce the word *anthropos*.

His thoughts also Belikov tried to confine within a framework. Nothing made sense to him except official regulations and newspaper articles condemning something or other. A school rule forbidding pupils to appear in the streets after nine in the evening, an article censuring sexual intercourse . . . he found clarity and precision in such matters. The thing was banned. That was that. In permissions and concessions, though, he always sensed a lurking sinister quality: something incomplete and vague. When a town drama club was licensed—or a reading room, or a tea-shop—he would shake his head.

'That's all very well of course and so on,' he would say. 'But what of the repercussions?'

All offences, all deviations, all infringements of the rules made him despondent—one might have wondered, though, what business they were of his. If a colleague was late for church, if rumour reached him of some schoolboy prank, if a schoolmistress was seen out late at night with an officer, he would take it very much to heart and keep worrying about those repercussions. At staff meetings he really depressed us with his misgivings, his pernicketiness, his utterly hidebound observations on how badly the boys and girls behaved in school, on their rowdiness in class. ('Dear, oh dear, what if the authorities get wind of it? Oh dear, what of the repercussions? And what a good idea it would be to expel Petrov of the Second Form and Yegorov of the Fourth.')

Well, what with his moaning and groaning, what with the dark glasses on his pale and—you know—ferrety little face, he so got us down that we yielded, we gave Petrov and Yegorov bad conduct marks, we put them in detention, and in the end we expelled them both.

He had the odd habit of visiting our lodgings. He would call on some teacher, sit down, say nothing, and seem to be on the look out for something. He would sit there for an hour or two without a word, and then he would go. Maintaining good relations with his colleagues, he called it. This calling and sitting obviously irked him, and he only did it because he felt it his duty to his colleagues. We teachers were afraid of him. So was the headmaster, even. Fantastic, isn't it? Our teachers were all thoroughly decent, right-thinking folk brought up on their Turgenev and their Shchedrin—and yet this little galoshes-and-umbrella man kept the entire school under his thumb for fifteen whole years! And not the school only. The whole town! Our ladies gave up their Saturday amateur theatricals lest he should hear of them. The clergy feared to eat meat and play cards in his presence. Thanks to the Belikovs of this world our townsfolk have begun to fear everything during the last ten or fifteen years. They fear to speak aloud, send letters, meet people, read books. They fear to help the poor, they fear to teach anyone to read.

Wishing to say something, Ivan Ivanovich coughed, then lit his pipe and looked at the moon.

'Yes, they're decent, right-thinking folk,' said he, enunciating carefully. 'They've read their Shchedrin, their Turgenev, their Henry Buckles and all that. But they caved in, you see, they did nothing about it—my point, precisely.'

Belikov and I lived in the same house (Burkin went on). We were on the same floor, his door opposite mine. We often met, and I knew his domestic circumstances. It was just the same at home. Dressing-gown, nightcap, shutters, bolts, a whole gamut of sundry bans and restrictions, and all this what-about-the-repercussions stuff. To diet was bad for the health—but you couldn't eat what you liked, or people might say that Belikov didn't keep his fasts. So he ate fresh-water fish fried in butter: food which was neither one thing nor the other. He kept no female servants in case people got the wrong ideas, but he had a cook: one Afanasy, a tipsy, half-witted old boy of about sixty, who had been an army batman in his time and could put together a meal of sorts. This Afanasy usually stood by the door with his arms folded.

'There's been a lot of *it* about lately,' he was for ever muttering with an oracular sigh.

Belikov's bedroom was like a little box, and he slept in a four-poster. When he went to bed he would pull a blanket over his head. It was hot and stuffy, the wind rattled the closed door and whined in the chimney. Sighs drifted in from the kitchen, sighs of evil portent.

He was scared, too, under that blanket. He was afraid of the repercussions, afraid of Afanasy cutting his throat, afraid of burglars. Then he would have nightmares all night, and when we went to school together in the morning he would be dispirited and pale. The crowded school for which he was bound . . . it terrified him, revolted his whole being, that was obvious. And walking by my side was an ordeal for so solitary a type.

'Our children are too noisy in class,' he would say, as if seeking a reason for his low spirits. 'It's quite disgraceful.'

Yet this teacher of Greek—this hard case—nearly got married, believe it or not.

Ivan Ivanovich glanced into the barn.
'You must be joking,' he said.

Yes, he nearly married, strange as it may seem (continued Burkin). A new history and geography master had been appointed: a Michael Kovalenko, from the Ukraine. He brought his sister Barbara with him. He was a tall, swarthy young man with huge hands. He had the kind of face that goes with a deep bass voice, and that voice really did seem to come boom boom booming at you out of a barrel.

Now, his sister was no longer young—she was about thirty—but she was also tall, well-built, black-browed, rosy-cheeked. She was a real knock-out, in fact: a jolly, hearty girl, for ever singing Ukrainian songs, for ever roaring with laughter. She was always ready to launch into a great peal of mirth on the slightest pretext. It was on the headmaster's name-day, I remember, that we first really met the Kovalenkos. There, amid those austere, overwrought, dim pedagogues, who make even party-going a matter of duty . . . behold a new Venus rises from the foam! She walks with arms akimbo, she guffaws, she sings, she dances. She renders a spirited 'Where Southern Breezes Blow', then sings one song after another, and bewitches us all—all, even Belikov.

'The Ukrainian language,' says he with his honeyed smile, sitting down by her side, 'resembles the ancient Greek in its tenderness and agreeable melodiousness.'

This flattered her, and she launched a harangue about how they had their own farm down Gadyach way and how their old mum lived on that farm. What pears they had, what melons, what pumpkins! Pumpkins, pubs, 'pubkins' . . . they have their own special words for these things down south, and out of their dear little red little tomatoes and their blue little egg-plants they would brew soup: 'frightfully scrumptious, actually!'

We listened and we listened . . . until suddenly the same idea dawned on one and all.

'They'd make a very good match,' the headmaster's wife told me quietly.

For some reason it now struck us all that friend Belikov wasn't married. We wondered why we had never noticed such a thing before, why we had utterly lost sight of so crucial a factor in his biography. What was his attitude to woman? His solution to this basic problem? So far we had taken no interest in the matter. Perhaps we couldn't even see him as capable of love—this four-poster-bed man, this galoshes fiend!

'He's well over forty, and she's thirty,' the headmaster's wife elucidated. 'I think she'd have him.'

Boredom in the provinces . . . the things it leads to, the wrong-headedness, the nonsense! And why? Because people somehow just can't get anything right. Well, for instance, why this sudden urge to marry off friend Belikov, who was hardly anyone's idea of a husband? The headmaster's wife, the second master's wife, all the school ladies perk up, they even look prettier, as if they've suddenly glimpsed the purpose of existence. The head's wife takes a box in the theatre—and behold Barbara sitting in that box with some sort of fan, radiant and happy. By her side is Belikov: small, crumpled, looking as if he's been extracted from his house with a pair of pincers. When I give a party the ladies make a point of my inviting both Belikov and Barbara. Things, in short, begin to hum. Barbara, it transpires, doesn't mind getting married. She isn't all that happy living with her brother—they argue and quarrel for days on end by all accounts.

Now, take this for a scene. Kovalenko walks down the street: a tall, lanky brute in his embroidered shirt with a quiff of hair tumbling from cap on to forehead. He has a clutch of books in one hand and a thick knobbly stick in the other. His sister follows, also carrying books.

'But you haven't *read* it, Michael!' she loudly avers. 'I tell you—I *swear*—you haven't read a *word* of it!'

'Well, I say I *have*,' shouts Kovalenko, thumping his stick on the pavement.

'Goodness me, Michael! Why so *angry*? This is only a matter of principle, after all.'

'Well, I say I *have* read it,' Kovalenko shouts in an even louder voice.

Whenever they had visitors they were at it hammer and tongs. It must have been a bore, that kind of life, and she wanted a place of her own. And then there was her age. You couldn't pick and choose any more, you were ready to marry anyone—even a teacher of Greek. And then most of our young ladies don't care who they marry so long as they get themselves a husband. Anyway, be that as it may, Barbara began to show Belikov marked partiality.

And Belikov? He used to call on Kovalenko, just as he would call on us. He would arrive, sit down, say nothing. And while he was saying nothing Barbara would be singing him 'Where Southern Breezes Blow', or looking at him pensively with her dark eyes. Or she would suddenly go off in a peal of noisy laughter.

In love affairs, and not least in marriage, suggestion plays a large part. Everyone—his colleagues, their ladies—began assuring Belikov that he must marry, that there was nothing left for him in life except wedlock. We all congratulated him, we made various trite remarks with solemn faces: 'marriage is a serious step,' and the like. What's more, Barbara wasn't bad looking. Besides being attractive she was the daughter of a senior civil servant and owned a farm. Above all, she was the first woman who had ever been kind and affectionate to Belikov. His head was turned, and he decided that he really must marry.

'Now would have been the time to detach him from his galoshes and umbrella,' pronounced Ivan Ivanovich.

That proved impossible, believe it or not (said Burkin). He put Barbara's portrait on his desk, and he kept calling on me and talking: about Barbara, about family life, about marriage being a serious step. He often visited the Kovalenkos. But he didn't change his way of life one little bit. Far from it, actually—his resolve to marry had a rather debilitating effect on him. He grew thin and pale, he seemed to retreat further and further into his shell.

'Barbara attracts me,' he tells me with a weak, wry little smile. 'And I know that everyone must get married. But, er, all this has been rather sudden, you know. One must, er, give it some thought.'

'Why?' I ask. 'Just marry, that's all.'

'No. Marriage is a serious step. One must first weigh one's impending responsibilities and duties, just in case of repercussions. I'm so worried, I can't sleep a wink. I'm scared, too, frankly. She and her brother have a rather peculiar outlook—they do have an unconventional way of discussing things, you know. And they are a bit on the hearty side. You get married, but before you know where you are you find you've become the subject for gossip.'

So he didn't make her an offer, but kept putting it off: to the great grief of the headmaster's wife and all our ladies. He kept weighing his impending responsibilities and duties while walking out with Barbara almost every day—perhaps he thought that necessary for someone in his position—and coming along to talk to me about family life. He would have proposed in the end, very likely. And the result would have been one of those stupid, unnecessary marriages of which we see thousands: the product of boredom, of having nothing else to do. But then a gigantic scandal suddenly erupted!

The point is, Barbara's brother Kovalenko had taken against Belikov at first sight—simply couldn't stand him.

'It beats me how you put up with the blighter, it really does,' he told us, shrugging his shoulders. 'Horrible little creep! Honestly, gentlemen, how *can* you live here? Your air stifles a man, damn it. Call yourselves teachers, do you? Educators? You're just a lot of little hacks. It's no temple of learning, this isn't—it's more like a suburban police station, and it smells as sour as a sentry-box. Well, that's it, lads. I shall stay here a little longer, and then I'll go to my farm down south to catch crayfish and teach the local kids. I shall be off, while you stay on here with this miserable humbug, blast him.'

Or he'd laugh—now in a deep guffaw, now in a thin, piping tone: laugh until the tears came.

'Why does he sit around my place?' he would ask with a bewildered gesture. 'What does he want? He just sits and stares.'

He even gave Belikov the nickname 'Master Creepy Crawly'. Well, we naturally didn't tell him that his sister Barbara was thinking of marrying Master Crawly. Once, when the headmaster's wife hinted that it would be worth fixing up his sister with some such generally respected worthy as Belikov, he frowned.

'Nothing to do with me,' he muttered. 'Let her marry a rattlesnake if she wants to. I mind my own business.'

Now hear what happened next. Some wag drew a cartoon of Belikov walking in his galoshes, with the bottoms of his trousers rolled up, carrying that great umbrella and arm in arm with Barbara. It was captioned THE LOVESICK ANTHROPOS. And it had just caught his expression to perfection, see? The artist must have worked at it night after night because the teachers at the two grammar schools, the boys' and the girls', all got their copy. So did the lecturers at the theological college, so did our local officials. Belikov got one too. The caricature had a most depressing effect on him.

On the first of May, a Sunday, we had an outing. All of us—teachers, pupils—had arranged to meet at school and then go for a walk to the woods. Well, we set off on this trip, and there's Belikov looking quite green and gloomier than a storm-cloud.

'What nasty, evil people there are,' says he, his lips quivering.

I actually feel sorry for him. Then, as we're walking along, all of a sudden (believe it or not) Kovalenko sails past on his bicycle followed by Barbara, also on a bicycle: flushed and puffed, but good-humoured and happy.

'I say, we're going on ahead,' she shouts. 'What marvellous weather —frightfully marvellous, actually.'

Both vanished from view, while friend Belikov turned from green to white and seemed paralysed. He stopped and looked at me.

'What, pray, is the meaning of this?' he asked. 'Or do my eyes deceive me? Is it proper for grammar-school teachers—for *women*!—to ride bicycles?'

'What's improper about it?' said I. 'Let them cycle away to their heart's content.'

'What do you mean?' he shouted, amazed at my calmness. 'You can't know what you're saying.'

But he was so shaken that he decided not to go on and turned back.

All next day he was nervously rubbing his hands and twitching. He wasn't at all well, his face showed that. He abandoned his classes, too— and that for the first time in his career. He missed his lunch as well. And then, in the late afternoon, he donned warm clothing in spite of the fine summer weather, and off he toddled to the Kovalenkos'. Barbara was out, only the brother was at home.

'Pray be seated,' pronounced Kovalenko coldly. He frowned,

looking sleepy—he'd just been taking an after-lunch nap, and he was in a very bad mood indeed.

Belikov sat for ten minutes without speaking, and then began.

'I have come to you to relieve my mind. I am deeply grieved. Some humorist has drawn a picture ridiculing myself and a certain other individual dear to us both. I am in duty bound to assure you that I am in no way implicated, that I have given no occasion for such witticisms. I have, on the contrary, conducted myself throughout as a person of complete probity.'

Kovalenko sat there fuming and said nothing. Belikov paused.

'I also have something else to tell you,' he went on in a quiet, sad voice. 'I have been in the profession for some time, while you are only a beginner, and I consider it my duty as your senior colleague to give you a warning. You ride a bicycle: a pastime wholly improper in one who instructs the young.'

'Why so?' asked Kovalenko in his deep voice.

'Need I say more, Kovalenko? Are my words not intelligible? If a teacher goes bicycling, then what are we to expect of his pupils? That they will walk on their heads, I presume! There is nothing in the school rules which says that you *can* bicycle. Which means you can't. I was appalled yesterday. When I saw your sister my eyes swam. A woman or a girl on a *bicycle*! An abomination!'

'What, precisely, do you require?'

'I require one thing only: to warn you, Kovalenko. You are young, you have your future before you. You should comport yourself very, very carefully indeed, but you don't toe the line at all, oh dear me no. You wear an embroidered shirt. You're always carrying books in the street. And now we have this bicycling! This bicycling, yours and your sister's, will come to the headmaster's ears, and then it will reach the higher authorities. Not very nice, now, is it?'

'Whether my sister and I do or do not ride bicycles is no one else's business,' said Kovalenko, turning crimson. 'And if anyone meddles in my domestic and family affairs I'll bloody well see him in hell!'

Belikov blenched. He stood up.

'If you take this tone with me I cannot continue,' he said. 'And I must beg you never to use such expressions about the authorities in my presence. You must treat authority with respect.'

'Did I say anything against the authorities?' asked Kovalenko, looking at him angrily. 'Kindly leave me in peace. I am an honest man, and I have no wish to bandy words with an individual of your description. I don't like narks.'

Fidgeting nervously, Belikov quickly put his coat on, horror written on his face—no one had ever been so rude to him in his life.

'You may say what you please,' he remarked as he came out of the lobby on to the landing. 'But I must warn you of this. Someone may have overheard us. Now, in case our conversation might be misinterpreted, in case of possible repercussions, I shall be obliged to inform the headmaster of its substance, er, in general outline. That is my duty.'

'Inform, eh? Carry on then, sneak away!'

Seizing him from behind by the collar, Kovalenko gave him a shove —and Belikov flew downstairs, his galoshes drumming. They were high, steep stairs, but he slid down without mishap, he stood up, and he touched his nose to see if his spectacles were broken. Now, just as he was slithering down those stairs, in came Barbara with two ladies. They stood at the bottom, watching—which, for Belikov, was the last straw. I think he'd rather have broken his neck or both legs than become a laughing-stock. Now the whole town would know, wouldn't it? The Head would hear of it, and so would the higher authorities. There would—alas—be repercussions. There would be another cartoon. And he would end up having to resign.

Barbara recognized him when he was on his feet. Seeing his ludicrous expression, his rumpled coat, his galoshes, not understanding what it was all about—but supposing him to have fallen down by accident—she couldn't help giving a great guffaw.

'Ha, ha, ha!'

It rang through the entire house.

This reverberating peal of laughter was the end of everything for Belikov: of his courtship and also of his life on earth. His ears did not hear what Barbara was saying, his eyes saw nothing. On arriving home he first removed her portrait from his desk, after which he lay down . . . never to rise again.

Three days later Afanasy came in to ask me if we should send for a doctor as there was 'something wrong' with the master. I went to see Belikov. He lay in his four-poster with a blanket over him, not speaking. In answer to questions he would only say yes or no, and that was all. While he lay there Afanasy hovered near by—gloomy, scowling, sighing deeply, stinking of vodka.

Belikov died a month later. We all went to the funeral: both high schools, that is, and the theological college. Now, as he lay in his coffin, his expression was gentle and agreeable—merry, even—as if he was glad to have been placed at last in that ultimate receptacle from which there would be no emerging. Yes, he had attained his ideal. During the funeral the weather was dull and rainy—in his honour, so to speak— and we all sported our galoshes and umbrellas. Barbara was there too, and she sobbed when they lowered the coffin into the grave. Ukrainian girls can only cry or laugh, I've noticed—they have no intermediate mood.

It's a great pleasure, frankly, is burying a Belikov. On our way back from the cemetery we wore modest, sober expressions. No one wanted to show how pleased he felt—it was a pleasure which we had known long, long ago as children when our elders had gone out and we ran about the garden for an hour or two enjoying absolute freedom. Freedom, oh freedom! Even a hint, even the faint hope of its possibility . . . it makes one's spirits soar, doesn't it?

We came back from the cemetery in a good mood. But within a week life was back in its old rut. It was just as austere, wearisome and pointless as before: a life which was neither forbidden in the school rules, nor yet wholly sanctioned either. There was no improvement. We had buried Belikov, admittedly. But what a lot of other men in capsules he had left behind him! And we shall see plenty more of them in the future.

'My point exactly,' said Ivan Ivanovich, and lit his pipe.

'We shall see plenty more of them,' repeated Burkin.

The schoolmaster came out of the barn. He was a short, fat, completely bald man with a black beard almost down to his waist. Two dogs came out with him.

'What a moon!' said he, looking up.

It was midnight. On his right could be seen the whole village, and a long road stretching about three miles into the distance. Everything was plunged in deep, peaceful slumber. There was no movement, no sound—it was incredible, indeed, that nature could be so quiet. When you see a broad village street by moonlight—a street with its huts, ricks and sleeping willows—your heart is at peace, and takes refuge in this calm, in the shadows of the night, from its toils, trials and tribulations. It is gentle, sad, serene. The stars seem to look down with loving kindness, there seems to be no evil in the world—all seems for the best. On the left, at the edge of the village, open country began. It could be seen stretching away as far as the horizon, and in the entire breadth of these moonlit fields there was neither movement nor sound.

'My point exactly,' repeated Ivan Ivanovich. 'What about us living in a stuffy, crowded town, writing our futile papers and playing our bridge? Isn't all that a kind of capsule? To spend our whole lives among loafers, mischievous litigants and stupid, idle women, talking and hearing various forms of nonsense . . . isn't that a capsule too? Now, if you like I'll tell you an extremely edifying story.'

'No, it's time to sleep,' said Burkin. 'Tell it tomorrow.'

They went into the barn and lay down on the hay. Each had covered himself up and started dozing, when suddenly the padding of footsteps was heard.

Someone was walking near the barn. The steps passed and stopped. Then, a minute later, you would hear the same padding sound.

The dogs whimpered.

'That's Mavra,' Burkin said.

The steps died away.

'People are such liars,' said Ivan Ivanovich, turning over. 'To see them, to hear them, to put up with their lies . . . and be called a fool for your pains! The insults, the humiliations, that you suffer! Not daring to proclaim aloud that you are on the side of honest, free men! The lies you yourself tell, the smiles you give! And all this to earn your daily bread and a roof over your head—all for the sake of some miserable little job not worth a farthing! No—one can't go on living like this!'

'Now, that's another story,' said the teacher. 'Let's go to sleep.'

Ten minutes later Burkin was asleep. But Ivan Ivanovich kept tossing from side to side and sighing. Then he got up, went outside again, sat down by the door and lit his pipe.

GOOSEBERRIES

[Крыжовник]

(1898)

GOOSEBERRIES

RAIN clouds had filled the whole sky since early morning. It was quiet weather—not hot and tedious as it is on those dull grey days when clouds hang over the countryside for hours on end while you wait for rain which never comes. Ivan Ivanovich the vet and Burkin the school-master were tired of walking, and the fields seemed to go on for ever. Far ahead of them the windmills of Mironositskoye village could just be seen. On their right was a chain of hills which vanished far beyond the village, and which—as they both knew—marked a river bank. There were meadows, green willows and homesteads over there. And if you stood on one of those hills you could see another equally vast expanse of fields, a telegraph line and a train crawling caterpillar-like in the distance. In clear weather you could even see the town. On this calm day, when all nature seemed gentle and pensive, Ivan Ivanovich and Burkin were filled with love of this open landscape, and both thought how vast, how glorious a land it was.

'That time when we stayed in Elder Prokofy's barn . . . you were going to tell me some story,' Burkin said.

'Yes—about my brother.'

Ivan Ivanovich gave a long sigh, and lit a pipe as a prelude to his narrative, but just then the rain began. Five minutes later it was abso-lutely pelting down—looked as if it would never end. Ivan Ivanovich and Burkin paused, wondering what to do. The dogs—wet, tails between their legs—stood and gazed at them devotedly.

'We must find shelter,' said Burkin. 'Let's go to Alyokhin's, it's quite near.'

'All right.'

They turned off and made across mown fields—now walking straight ahead, now bearing to the right—until they hit the road. Poplars soon appeared, then an orchard and red-roofed barns. There was a gleam of river, and then a view of a wide reach with its mill and white bathing-hut. This was Sofyino, Alyokhin's place.

The mill was working, and drowned the noise of rain. The weir quivered. Wet horses stood with bowed heads by some carts, and men with sacks over their heads moved about. It was damp, muddy, desolate—and that reach of river had a cold, malignant look. Ivan

Ivanovich and Burkin felt wet, unclean and uncomfortable all over. Their feet were heavy with mud. When they had passed the weir and climbed up to the manor barns they were not speaking—and so seemed angry with each other.

From one shed came the noise of a winnowing-fan, and there was a surge of dust through the open door. On the threshold stood the boss —Alyokhin, a man of about forty, tall, stout, long-haired, more like a professor or artist than a landowner. He wore a white shirt which needed washing and a rope for a belt. He had underpants on instead of trousers, and he had mud and straw sticking to his high boots. His eyes and nose were black with dust. He recognized Ivan Ivanovich and Burkin, and was obviously glad to see them.

'Come in, gentlemen, come inside the house,' he smiled. 'Be with you in a moment.'

It was a large, two-storeyed house. Alyokhin lived downstairs in two rooms with vaulted ceilings and small windows—once his bailiffs' quarters. It was all very unpretentious, smelling of rye bread, cheap vodka and harness. His best rooms, upstairs, he used very seldom, only when he had visitors. Ivan Ivanovich and Burkin were received in the house by the maid: a young woman so beautiful that both halted in their tracks and stared at each other.

'You can't imagine how glad I am to see you gentlemen,' said Alyokhin, following them into the hall. 'What a nice surprise!

'Give the guests something to change into, Pelageya,' he told the maid. 'And I'll change too while I'm about it. But I must go and wash first—feel as if I hadn't washed since spring. Would you like to come to the bathing-hut while they get things ready?'

The fair Pelageya—so delicate, so gentle-looking—brought towels and soap, and Alyokhin took his guests to the bathing place.

'Yes, I haven't washed for ages,' he said, undressing. 'I have a good bathing-hut, as you see—my father built it—but somehow I never have time for a bathe.'

He sat on the step soaping his long hair and neck, while the water round him turned brown.

'Yes, I see what you mean,' said Ivan Ivanovich with a meaning look at his head.

'I haven't washed for ages,' repeated Alyokhin awkwardly. He soaped himself again and the water round him turned inky.

Ivan Ivanovich came out, plunged in with a loud splash, swam about in the rain with broad sweeps of the arms and sent up waves with white water-lilies tossing on them. He swam to the middle of the reach and dived. A little later he appeared somewhere else and swam on further. He kept plunging and trying to touch bottom.

'By God, this is terrific!' he kept repeating. He was enjoying himself.

He swam up to the mill, spoke to the villagers there, then turned and floated on his back in the middle of the reach, exposing his face to the rain. Burkin and Alyokhin were dressed and ready to leave, but still he swam and dived.

'Ye Gods!' said he. 'Mercy on us!'

'That's enough,' shouted Burkin.

They went back to the house. The lamp was alight in the large drawing-room upstairs. Burkin and Ivan Ivanovich, in silk dressing-gowns and warm slippers, sat in easy chairs, while Squire Alyokhin —washed, combed, wearing a new frock-coat—paced up and down, obviously revelling in the warmth, cleanliness, dry clothing and light footwear. Soundlessly treading the carpet and softly smiling, the fair Pelageya served tea and jam on a tray. And only now did Ivan Ivanovich embark on his story. His audience seemed to include not only Burkin and Alyokhin, but also the ladies, young and old, and the officers who looked out calmly and severely from the gilt frames on the walls.

There are two of us brothers (he began): myself, Ivan, and Nicholas —two years my junior. I studied to be a vet, while Nicholas had a local government job from the age of nineteen. Our father had been a ranker, and after getting his commission he had bequeathed us the status of gentleman together with a small estate which was sequestrated after his death to pay his debts. Anyway, we lived a free life in the open air as boys. We spent our days and nights in fields and woods like ordinary village children, minding horses, stripping bark, fishing: that kind of thing.

Now, as you know, once you've ever hooked a ruff—or seen migrating thrushes swarm over your village on clear, cold autumn days— you'll never make a townsman after that, you'll yearn for those wide open spaces till your dying day. My brother was miserable at the office. Years passed, but he stayed put: for ever copying the same old documents, for ever obsessed with getting back to the land. Gradually this vague longing crystallized into a specific desire: the dream of buying a nice little country estate beside a river or lake.

Dc

He was a gentle, kind man. I was fond of him, but never did I sympathize with his wish to coop himself up for life in a country house. There's a saying that six foot of earth is all a man needs. A man? A corpse, more like! Now, if our professional people want to get back to the land, if they all have their eye on country properties, that's supposed to be a good thing these days. But those little places in the country . . . they're just that same old six foot of earth, really, aren't they? To leave the town, the tumult and the shouting, to skulk in your little place in the country . . . that's no life, that isn't. It's selfishness, it's idleness, it's the monastic discipline—but without the hope of glory! Man needs no six foot of earth, he needs no little place in the country. He needs the whole globe—all nature—so that he can develop, untrammelled, all his potentialities, all the attributes of his free spirit.

At the office brother Nicholas dreamed of eating stew made from his own cabbages and seemed to sniff their savour wafting through his yard. He dreamed of taking his meals on green grass, of sleeping in the sun, of sitting on a bench outside his gate for hours on end gazing at fields and woods. Booklets on agriculture, calendar mottoes and such . . . these were his joy, his favourite spiritual sustenance. He liked newspapers too, but only read advertisements about so many acres of arable land and meadow being up for sale with farmhouse, river, orchard, mill and mill-pond. His imagination pictured garden paths, flowers, fruit, nesting boxes for starlings, carp in ponds—you know the sort of stuff. These fancies varied with the advertisements which came his way, but for some reason the staple feature of them all was . . . the gooseberry. No manor house, no idyllic nook could he picture without that gooseberry patch.

'Country life does have its advantages,' he would say. 'You have tea on your balcony while your ducks swim on the pond. There's a wonderful smell and, er . . . and there are these gooseberries!'

He would sketch a plan of his estate, a plan which always had the same features: (a) manor house; (b) servants' quarters; (c) kitchen-garden; (d) gooseberries. He lived miserably. He went short of food and drink, he dressed any old how—like a tramp—and he kept saving money and putting it in the bank. He was a fearful miser. It pained me to see him, and I used to give him one or two things—send them on special occasions. But those things too he used to put away. Once a man's obsessed by an idea there's nothing you can do about it.

The years pass, he is transferred to a different county, he is now in his forties, but he is still reading those newspaper advertisements and saving money. Then I hear he's got married. Still aiming to buy that estate with the gooseberry patch, he has married an ugly old widow for whom he has no feelings—just because she's well-heeled. He leads her a miserable life too, keeping her half starved and putting her money in his own bank account. Before that she has been a post-master's wife, and as such she's been used to cakes and home-made wines, but with her second husband she even goes short of black bread. This routine sends her into a decline, and three years later she duly gives up the ghost! Not, of course, that my brother for one moment feels responsible for her death. Money's like strong drink, it makes a man act strangely. There was once a merchant of our town, a dying man, who ordered a bowl of honey on his death-bed, mixed in his banknotes and his lottery tickets . . . and swallowed the lot, to stop anyone else getting it. Once, when I was inspecting beasts at a railway station, a cattle-dealer was run over by a train. It takes his leg off. We get him to a casualty department, there's blood everywhere: a horrible business! But he keeps begging us to look for that leg—can't stop worrying about the twenty roubles he has in the severed boot, thinks he may lose them.

'That's a bit beside the point,' said Burkin.

After his wife's death (Ivan Ivanovich went on after half a minute's thought) my brother began looking for a country property. Now, of course, you can spend five years hunting and still make the wrong choice, still end up with something quite unlike your dream house. Through an estate agent brother Nicholas bought three hundred acres on a mortgage. There was a manor house, there were servants' quarters, there was a park. But there was no orchard, there were no gooseberries and there were no duck-ponds. He did have a river, but the water was coffee-coloured because of a brickyard on one side of the estate and a bone-ash works on the other. Still, good old Nicholas didn't much care. He ordered twenty gooseberry-bushes, he planted them, and he set up as a squire.

I looked him up last year, thought I'd go and see what he was up to. In his letters my brother called his estate 'Chumbaroklov Patch' or 'Gimalaysky's', and one afternoon I turn up at this 'Gimalaysky's'. It's hot. There are ditches, fences, hedges, rows of little firs all over the place, and there doesn't seem to be any way into the yard or any place to leave your horse. As I approach the house I am met by a fat, ginger-coloured dog which resembles a pig and would like to bark but can't be bothered. From the kitchen emerges a cook—barefoot, fat, also resembling a pig—and says that the master is having his after-lunch nap. I enter my brother's room, and there he is sitting up in bed with a blanket over his lap. He has aged, he has put on weight, he looks positively frowsty. His nose, lips and cheeks jut forward. He seems all set to grunt into his blanket.

We embrace, we shed a tear of joy—and at the sad thought that we were once young but are both grey-haired now, and that our lives are nearly over. He dresses and begins showing me round his estate.

'Well, how's life?' I ask.

'Oh, pretty good, thank God. Can't complain.'

No longer was he the poor, timid little clerk. He was a real squire now, a man of property. He'd settled here, he'd put down his roots, he was in his element. He was eating a lot, taking steam-baths, putting on weight. He was already suing the parish council and both factories, and he took umbrage when the locals wouldn't call him 'sir'. His spiritual welfare . . . that too he cultivated with the dignity befitting a proprietor. He couldn't just do good, he had to be so pompous about it! And what did his charity add up to? He dosed all the villagers with bicarbonate of soda and castor oil, no matter what might be wrong with them. On his name-day he would hold a thanksgiving service in the village, then stand the lads vodka all round because he thought it the done thing. Oh, those awful bumpers of vodka! One day your fat landowner takes the villagers to court for trespass, and on the next day —some festival—he treats them all to vodka. They drink, they cheer him and they make their drunken salaams.

Improving one's living standards, eating too much, laziness . . . these things develop the most blatant arrogance in us Russians. Back at the office Nicholas had been scared even to hold views of his own, but here he was pronouncing eternal verities in magisterial style about education being 'essential, but inopportune for the lower orders', and about corporal punishment being 'detrimental, generally speaking, but in certain cases useful and indispensable'.

'I know the working man, I can get on with him,' he would say. 'I'm popular with the ordinary common chap. I need only move a finger and the lads will do anything for me.'

And all this, mark you, with a good-natured, knowing smile. A score of times he'd say 'we landowners' or 'speaking as one of the

gentry'. He'd evidently forgotten that our grandfather had been a
farm labourer and our father a private in the army. Even our surname
Chimsha-Gimalaysky, so essentially absurd, now seemed to him
melodious, illustrious and highly agreeable.

It's not Nicholas I'm concerned with, though, it's myself. I want to
tell you how I changed during my few hours on his estate. At tea that
afternoon the cook served a full bowl of gooseberries. These were no
bought gooseberries, they were his own crop: the first to be picked
since the planting. Nicholas chuckled, contemplated the gooseberries
for a minute in silence and tears—his feelings too deep for words. Then,
placing a lone berry in his mouth, he surveyed me with the glee of a
child who has at last been given a longed-for toy.

'Delicious.'

He ate them greedily.

'Ah, delicious indeed,' he kept saying. 'You *must* try them.'

They were sour and unripe. Still,

> To hosts of petty truths man much prefers
> A single edifying lie,

as Pushkin has put it. Before me was a happy man whose most
cherished dream had come true for all to see, who had attained his
object in life, who had realized his ambitions, who was content with
his fate and with himself. In my reflections on human happiness there
had always been an element of sadness, but now the spectacle of a
happy man plunged me into a despondency akin to despair. I felt
particularly low that night. They had made up a bed for me in the
room next to my brother's, and I could hear that he was still awake:
he was getting up, going to that bowl and taking out one gooseberry
at a time. Really, what a lot of contented, happy people there are, I
reflected! What a crushing force they represent! What a life, though!
Look at the impudence and idleness of the strong, the ignorance and
bestiality of the weak, look at the grotesque poverty everywhere, the
overcrowding, degeneracy, drunkenness and hypocrisy, the silly talk.

And yet. . . . In all the houses and streets there is peace and quiet.
Out of fifty thousand townsfolk there's not one ready to scream or
protest aloud. We see people shopping for food in the market, eating
by day, sleeping by night, talking their nonsense, marrying their wives,
growing old, complacently dragging off their dead to the cemetery.
But we have no eyes or ears for those who suffer. Life's real tragedies
are enacted off stage. All is peace and quiet, the only protest comes

from mute statistics: so many people driven mad, so many gallons of vodka drunk, so many children starved to death.

Oh yes, the need for such a system is obvious. Quite obviously, too, the happy man only feels happy because the *unhappy* man bears his burden in silence. And without that silence happiness would be impossible. It's collective hypnosis, this is. At the door of every contented, happy man there should be someone standing with a little hammer, someone to keep dinning into his head that unhappy people do exist —and that, happy though he may be, life will round on him sooner or later. Disaster will strike in the shape of sickness, poverty or bereavement. And no one will see *him* or hear *him*—just as he now has neither eyes nor ears for others. But there *is* no one with a hammer, and so the happy man lives happily away, while life's petty tribulations stir him gently, as the breeze stirs an aspen. And everything in the garden is lovely.

'That night I realized that I too was happy and contented,' Ivan Ivanovich went on, standing up. 'I too had laid down the law—at dinner, out hunting—about how to live, what to believe, how to handle the lower classes. I too had said that learning is a boon, that education is essential—but that plain reading and writing are enough for the common herd to be going on with. Freedom is a blessing, said I, we need it as the air we breathe—but we must wait for it. Yes, such were my words. But now I want to know what on earth we're waiting *for*?

'What *are* we waiting for, I ask you?' Ivan Ivanovich demanded, glaring at Burkin. 'What are we trying to prove? We can't have everything at once, I'm told, every idea takes shape gradually, in its own good time. But who says so? Where's the evidence that he's right? You refer me to the natural order of things, to the law of cause and effect. But is there any law, any order which says that a vigorous, right-thinking man like me should stand by a ditch and wait for it to become overgrown or covered with mud—when all the time I might be able to jump across it or bridge it? Again I ask, what are we waiting for? To wait while we don't have the guts to live, yet need and long so much to be alive!

'I left my brother's early next morning, since when I've found town life unbearable. The peace and quiet ... they get me down. I fear to look through windows because I know no spectacle more depressing than a happy family having tea round a table. I'm old, I'm past fighting,

I can't even hate any more. I'm just deeply grieved, I'm exasperated, I'm indignant. The thoughts which crowd upon me at night . . . they make my head burn and I can't sleep. Oh, if I were only young!'

Ivan Ivanovich paced up and down excitedly, repeating 'if I were only young!'

Suddenly going up to Alyokhin, he took him by one hand, and then by the other.

'Never give up, my dear Alyokhin,' he pleaded. 'Never let them drug you. While you're still young, strong and in good heart, never tire of doing good. There's no such thing—there need be no such thing —as happiness. And if life has any meaning and purpose, that meaning and purpose certainly aren't in our happiness, but in something higher and more rational. Do good.'

All this Ivan Ivanovich said with a pathetic, pleading smile, as if asking a personal favour.

Then all three sat in arm-chairs in different corners of the drawing-room and said nothing. Ivan Ivanovich's story had satisfied neither Burkin nor Alyokhin. To hear about an impoverished clerk eating gooseberries while those generals and ladies looked down from their gilt frames, seeming alive in the twilight . . . it was a bore. Somehow one would rather have talked about women, about persons of elegance. To be sitting in this drawing-room, where the covered chandelier, the arm-chairs, the carpets under foot, all proclaimed that the watchers in those frames had once walked, sat and had tea here themselves . . . to have the fair Pelageya moving noiselessly about—all that was better than any story.

Alyokhin was terribly sleepy. He had been up about the farm before three in the morning, and he could hardly keep his eyes open. But he lingered on, fearing to miss any interesting tale which his guests might have to tell. As for what Ivan Ivanovich had just said, as for whether it was wise or true . . . that was beyond him. His guests were not discussing meal, hay or pitch, but something with no direct bearing on his life. He liked that, and he wanted them to go on.

'It's bedtime, though,' said Burkin, getting up. 'May I wish you good night?'

Alyokhin said good night and went down to his own quarters while his guests remained upstairs. They were sharing a large room containing two old carved wooden beds and an ivory crucifix in the corner. Their beds were wide and cool, they had been made by the fair Pelageya, and the linen smelt agreeably fresh.

Ivan Ivanovich undressed in silence and lay down.

'Lord, forgive us sinners,' said he, pulling the blankets over his head.

His pipe was on the table, reeking strongly of stale tobacco, and Burkin could not sleep for a long time for wondering where the atrocious smell came from.

All night long rain drummed on the windows.

CONCERNING LOVE
[О любви]
(1898)

CONCERNING LOVE

FOR lunch next day delicious pasties, crayfish and mutton rissoles were served. During the meal Nikanor the cook came upstairs to ask what the guests wanted for dinner. He was a man of average height with a puffy face and small eyes—and so clean-shaven that his whiskers seemed to have been plucked out rather than cut off.

Alyokhin explained that the fair Pelageya was in love with this cook. He was a drunkard and a bit of a hooligan, so she didn't want to marry him, but she didn't mind 'just living with him'. He was very pious, though, and his religion forbade his just living with her. He insisted on marriage, didn't want her otherwise. He swore at her in his cups, and even beat her. She would hide upstairs, weeping, when he was drunk, while Alyokhin and his servants stayed at home to protect her if necessary.

The conversation turned to love.

'What makes people fall in love?' asked Alyokhin. 'Why couldn't Pelageya love someone else more suited to her intellectually and physically? Why must she love this Nikanor—"Fat-face", everyone calls him round here—seeing that personal happiness is an important factor in love? It's all very mysterious, there are any number of possible interpretations. So far we've only heard one incontrovertible truth about love: the biblical "this is a great mystery". Everything else written and spoken about love has offered no solution, but has just posed questions which have simply remained unanswered. What seems to explain one instance doesn't fit a dozen others. It's best to interpret each instance separately, in my view, without trying to generalize. We must isolate each individual case, as doctors say.'

'Very true,' agreed Burkin.

'Your ordinary decent Russian has a weakness for these unsolved problems. Where other peoples romanticize their love, garnishing it with roses and nightingales, we Russians bedizen ours with dubious profundities—and the most tedious available, at that. Back in my student days in Moscow I had a "friend": a lovely lady who, when I held her in my arms, was always wondering what monthly allowance I would give her, and what was the price of a pound of beef. We're just the same. When we're in love we're for ever questioning ourselves.

Are we being honourable or dishonourable? Wise or stupid? How will it end, this love? And so on. Whether this attitude is right or wrong I don't know, but that it is a nuisance, that it is unsatisfactory and frustrating—that I do know.'

He seemed to have some story he wanted to tell. People who live alone always do have things on their minds that they are keen to talk about. Bachelors deliberately go to the public baths, and to restaurants in town, just to talk, and they sometimes tell bath attendants or waiters the most fascinating tales. In the country, though, it is their guests to whom they usually unbosom themselves. Grey sky and rain-soaked trees could be seen through the windows. There was nowhere to go in such weather—and nothing to do except swap yarns.

I've been living and farming in Sofyino for some time—since I took my degree (Alyokhin began). By upbringing I'm the arm-chair type, my leanings are academic. But this estate was badly in debt when I came here, and since it was partly through spending so much on my education that Father had run up those debts, I decided to stay on and work until I'd paid them off. I made my decision and started working here: not without a certain repugnance, frankly. The land isn't all that productive hereabouts, and if you don't want to farm at a loss you either have to use hired hands— slave labour, practically—or else you have to run the place peasant-fashion: do your own field work, that is, yourself and your family. There's no other way. But I hadn't gone into these subtleties at the time. Not one single plot of earth did I leave in peace, I corralled all the near-by villagers and their women, and I had us all working away like billy-o. I ploughed myself, I sowed and I reaped myself—bored stiff the while, and frowning fastidiously like a village cat eating gherkins in the vegetable patch because it's starving. My body ached, I was nearly dead on my feet. At first I thought I could easily combine this drudgery with the cultured life—all I had to do, thought I, was to observe a certain routine. I moved into the best rooms up here, I arranged for coffee and liqueurs to be served after lunch and dinner, and I read the *European Herald* in bed at night. But one day our priest, Father Ivan, turned up and scoffed my whole stock of liquor at a sitting. The priest also ran off with my *European Heralds*, or rather his daughters did, because I never managed to get as far as my bed in summer, especially during haymaking, but slept in the barn, in a sledge, or in some woodman's hut—hardly conducive to reading, that.

I gradually moved downstairs, I began having my meals with the servants, and there's nothing left of my former gracious living but these same servants who once worked for my father, and whom I hadn't the heart to dismiss.

Quite early on I was elected an honorary justice of the peace, and had to go to town now and then to take part in sessions and sit at the assizes, which I found entertaining. When you've been cooped up here for a couple of months, especially in winter, you end up yearning for a black frock-coat. Now, at the assizes you had your frock-coats, your uniforms, your tail-coats. They were all lawyers there, all educated men. They were the sort of people you could talk to. To sit in an arm-chair wearing clean underwear and light boots with your watch-chain on your chest . . . after sleeping in a sledge and eating with servants, that really was the height of luxury.

I was always welcome in town, and I liked meeting new people. Now, among these new friendships the most serious—and, quite honestly, the most pleasant—was with Luganovich, the Deputy Chairman of Assize. You both know him: a most charming individual. This happened just after the famous arson case. The proceedings had lasted two days, we were worn out, and Luganovich looked in my direction.

'How about dinner at my place?'

I was surprised, barely knowing the man, and then only in an official capacity—I had never visited his home. After calling briefly at my hotel to change, I set off. This dinner led to my first meeting with Luganovich's wife, Anne. She was still very young, not more than twenty-two, and her first child had been born six months previously. It all happened so long ago that I'd be hard put to it, now, to define precisely what it was about her that so much attracted me. But at that dinner it was abundantly clear. I saw a woman—young, handsome, kind, intellectual and captivating—unlike any I had ever met before. I at once sensed that this creature was dear to me, I seemed to know her already—rather as if I'd once seen that face, those eager, intelligent eyes, when I was a little boy looking at the album on my mother's chest-of-drawers.

At the arson trial four Jews had been found guilty and it had been made a conspiracy charge: quite indefensibly in my view. I became rather agitated at dinner—most distressed, in fact—and I've forgotten what I said, now, except that Anne kept shaking her head and telling her husband that 'I just can't believe it, Dmitry'.

Luganovich is a good fellow, one of those simple-minded chaps who have got it into their heads that the man in the dock is always guilty, and that a sentence may be challenged only in writing, through the proper channels—most certainly not at a private dinner-table.

'You and I didn't start that fire,' he said gently. 'Which is why you and I aren't being tried and sent to prison.'

Husband and wife both pressed food and drink on me. From several details—the way they made coffee together, the way they understood each other almost without words—I concluded that they lived in peace and harmony, that they were pleased to be entertaining a guest. We played piano duets after dinner. Then it grew dark and I went to my lodgings.

This happened in early spring, after which I was stuck in Sofyino all summer. I didn't even think of town, I was so busy. But I was haunted all along by the memory of that slender, fair-haired woman. Not directly present in my consciousness, she seemed rather to cast a faint shadow over it.

In late autumn a charity performance was staged in town. I went into the Governor's box (having been invited in the interval), and there was Anne Luganovich seated by the Governor's wife. Again I was struck by that same irresistible vibrant beauty, by that charming, friendly expression in her eyes. And again I sensed an intimacy shared.

We sat next to each other, we walked in the foyer, and she told me that I had grown thinner. Had I been ill?

'Yes. I've had a bad shoulder, and I sleep poorly when it rains.'

'You look worn out. When you came to dinner in the spring you seemed younger, more sure of yourself. You were a bit carried away at the time, you talked a lot, you were quite fascinating. I couldn't help being a bit taken with you, actually. I've often thought of you during the summer for some reason, and when I was getting ready for the theatre tonight I felt sure I should see you.'

She laughed. 'But today you look worn out,' she repeated. 'It makes you seem older.'

I lunched at the Luganoviches' next day. Afterwards they drove out to their holiday cottage to put it in shape for the winter. I went with them, I came back to town with them, and at midnight I had tea with them in the peaceful setting of their home: by a blazing fire, with the young mother going out from time to time to see if her little girl was asleep. After that I always made a point of seeing the Luganoviches when I was in town. We got to know each other, and I used to call unannounced. I was just like one of the family.

'Who is that?' I would hear her ask from the back of the house in the slow drawl which I found so attractive.

'It's Mr. Alyokhin,' the maid or nanny would answer, and Anne would appear looking worried. Why hadn't I been to see them sooner? Had anything happened?

Her gaze, the clasp of her fine, delicate hand, the clothes which she wore about the house, the way she did her hair, her voice, her steps . . . they always made me feel as if something new and out of the ordinary, something significant, had happened to me. We enjoyed long conversations—and long silences, each wrapt in his own thoughts. Or she would play the piano for me. When there was no one at home I would wait, I'd talk to nanny, play with baby, or lie on the study ottoman reading the newspaper. When Anne came in I would meet her in the hall and take her shopping off her. I always carried that shopping so fondly and triumphantly, somehow—just like a little boy.

It was a bit like the farmer's wife in the story, the one who had no troubles—not, that is, until she went and bought herself a pig! The Luganoviches had no troubles—so they went and chummed up with me! If I hadn't been to town recently, then I must be ill or something must have happened to me, and both would be genuinely alarmed. What worried them was that I—an educated man who knew foreign languages—didn't devote myself to learning or letters, but lived in the country, going round and round the same old treadmill, that I worked so much but was always hard up. I was bound to be unhappy, they felt, and if they saw me talking, laughing or having a meal, I must be doing so merely to conceal my anguish. Even when I was happy and relaxed I could feel them viewing me with concern. They were particularly touching when I really was in a bit of a fix: when some creditor was pressing me, when I couldn't meet some payment on time. Husband and wife would then whisper together by the window, and he would approach me looking very solemn.

'If you're a bit short, Paul, my wife and I would like to lend you something. Please don't hesitate to ask.' His ears would flush with embarrassment.

Or else he would come up with his red ears after one of those whispering sessions by the window, and say that he and his wife 'do most urgently beg you to accept this gift'. He would then present me with some studs, a cigarette-case or a lamp. In return I would send them something from the country: a bird for the table, butter, flowers. Both of them, incidentally, had money of their own. Now, I was always borrowing in the early days, and I wasn't particularly choosy about it—I took my loans where I could get them. But no power on earth would have induced me to borrow from the Luganoviches. Need I say more?

I was unhappy. At home, in my fields and in my barn my thoughts were of her. I tried to plumb the mystery of a young, handsome, intelligent woman, the wife of an unattractive, almost elderly husband (the man was over forty) and the mother of his children. I also tried to plumb the mystery of this same unattractive husband, this good sort, this easy-going fellow with his boring, common-sensical views, who (when attending a party or dance) always cultivated the local fuddy-duddies, this listless misfit with his submissive air of being a spectator or a bale of goods put up for auction . . . of this man who still believed in his right to be happy and to have children by her. Why ever, I kept wondering, had she met him instead of me? To what purpose so drastic an error in our lives?

On my visits to town I could always tell from her eyes that she was expecting me, and she'd admit having had a special feeling all day— she'd guessed I'd be coming. We enjoyed our long conversations and silences, not declaring our love for each other but concealing it fearfully and jealously. We feared anything which might betray our secret to ourselves. Deep and tender though my love was, I tried to be sensible about it, speculating what the upshot might be if we should lack the strength to fight our passions. It seemed incredible that a love so quiet, so sad as mine could suddenly and crudely disrupt the happy tenor of her husband's and children's lives: disrupt an entire household where I was so loved and trusted. Was that the way for a decent man to behave? She would have gone away with me—but where to? Where could I take her? Things would have been different if my life had been romantic and enterprising: if I'd been fighting for my country's freedom, for instance, if I'd been a distinguished scholar, actor or artist. As it was I should be conveying her from one humdrum, colourless milieu into another equally humdrum, or even worse. How long would our happiness last? What would happen to her if I became ill or died? What if we just fell out of love?

Her reflections were evidently similar. She thought about her husband and children, thought about her mother who loved her husband like a son. If she yielded to her passions she would either have to lie or tell the truth, but both courses would be equally alarming and difficult to one in her situation. Would her love bring me happiness, she wondered agonizingly. Wouldn't it complicate my life: irksome enough anyway, and beset with all sorts of tribulations? She felt she was too old for me, that she lacked the drive and energy to start a new life. She often told her husband that I ought to marry some decent, intelligent girl who would be a good housewife and helpmeet—but she would add at once that such a paragon was unlikely to be found anywhere in town.

Meanwhile the years were passing. Anne now had two children. Whenever I visited the family the servants smiled their welcome, the children shouted that Uncle Paul had arrived and clung round my neck, and everyone rejoiced. Not understanding my innermost feelings, they thought I was rejoicing with them. They all saw me as the embodiment of integrity. Adults and children alike, they felt that integrity incarnate was walking about the room—which imparted a special charm to their relations with me, as if my presence made their lives purer and finer. Anne and I used to go to the theatre together, always on foot. We would sit beside each other in the stalls, our shoulders touching, and I'd silently take the opera glasses from her, sensing her nearness to me, sensing that she was mine, that we couldn't live without each other. But through some strange lack of *rapport* we always said good-bye when we left the theatre, and we parted like strangers. People were saying goodness knows what about us in town, but not one word of truth was there in all their gossip.

Anne had begun going away to her mother's and sister's more often in recent years. She had become subject to depressions: moods in which she was conscious that her life was unfulfilled and wasted. She didn't want to see her husband and children at such times. She was under treatment for a nervous condition.

And still we did not speak our minds. In company she would feel curiously exasperated with me. She would disagree with everything I said, and if I became involved in an argument she would take my opponent's side. If I chanced to drop something she would coldly offer her 'congratulations'. If I forgot the opera glasses when we went to the theatre, she'd tell me she had 'known very well I'd forget those'.

Luckily or unluckily, there is nothing in our lives which doesn't end sooner or later. The time had now come for us to part: Luganovich had been appointed to a judgeship in the west country. They had to sell their furniture, horses and cottage. We drove out to the cottage, and as we turned back for one last look at the garden and green roof everyone was sad, and I knew that it was time for me to take my leave

Ec

of rather more than a mere cottage. It had been decided that we should see Anne off to the Crimea (where her doctors had advised her to stay) at the end of August, and that Luganovich would take the children to the west a little later.

A large crowd of us went to see Anne off. She had already said good-bye to her husband and children, and the train was due to leave at any moment, when I dashed into her compartment to put a basket—which she had nearly left behind—on the luggage rack. It was my turn to say good-bye. Our eyes met there in the compartment, and we could hold back no longer. I put my arms around her, she pressed her face against my breast, and the tears flowed. Kissing her face, her shoulders, her tear-drenched hands—we were both so unhappy—I declared my love. With a burning pain in my heart, I saw how inessential, how trivial, how illusory it was . . . everything which had frustrated our love. I saw that, if you love, you must base your theory of love on something loftier and more significant than happiness or unhappiness, than sin or virtue as they are commonly understood. Better, otherwise, not to theorize at all.

I kissed her for the last time, I clasped her hand, and we parted—for ever. The train had already started. I sat down in the next compartment, which was empty . . . sat there, weeping, until the first stop. Then I walked home to Sofyino.

It had stopped raining while Alyokhin was telling his story, and the sun had peeped out. Burkin and Ivan Ivanovich went on to the balcony, which had a superb view of the garden, and of the river which now gleamed, mirror-like, in the sun. As they admired the view they felt sorry that this man with the kind, intelligent eyes—who had spoken with such sincere feeling—really was going round and round the same old treadmill, doing neither academic work nor anything else capable of making his life more pleasant. And they imagined how stricken that young woman must have looked when he had said good-bye to her in the train, kissing her head and shoulders. Both of them had met her in town. Burkin, indeed, had been a friend of hers and had thought her very good-looking.

DOCTOR STARTSEV

[Ионыч]

(1898)

DOCTOR STARTSEV

I

To visitors' complaints that the county town of S—— was boring and humdrum local people would answer defensively that life there was, on the contrary, very good indeed. The town had its library, its theatre, its club. There was the occasional ball. And, in conclusion, it contained intelligent, interesting and charming families with whom one might make friends. Among these families the Turkins were pointed out as the most cultivated and accomplished.

These Turkins lived in their own house on the main street near the Governor's. Mr. Turkin—a stout, handsome, dark man with dundreary whiskers—used to stage amateur dramatic performances for charity, himself playing elderly generals and coughing most amusingly while doing so. He knew endless funny stories, riddles, proverbs. He rather liked his fun—he was a bit of a wag—and you could never tell from his face whether he was joking or not. His wife Vera—a slim, pretty woman in a *pince-nez*—wrote short stories and novels which she liked reading to her guests. Their young daughter Catherine played the piano. Each Turkin had, in short, some accomplishment. They liked entertaining, and gladly displayed their talents to their guests in a jolly, hearty sort of a way. Their large, stone-built house was roomy and cool in hot weather, with half its windows opening on to a shady old garden where nightingales sang in springtime. When they were entertaining there would be a clatter of knives in the kitchen and a smell of fried onions in the yard—the sign that an ample, appetizing supper was on the way.

No sooner had Dr. Dmitry Startsev been appointed to a local medical post and moved in at Dyalizh, six miles away, than he too was told that he simply must meet the Turkins, seeing that he was an intellectual. One winter's day, then, he was introduced to Mr. Turkin in the street. They chatted about the weather, the theatre, the cholera. He was invited to call. On a public holiday in spring—Ascension Day, to be precise—Startsev set out for town after surgery in search of recreation, meaning to do some shopping while he was about it. He made the journey unhurriedly on foot—he had not yet set up his carriage —humming 'Ere from the Cup of Life I yet had Drunk the Tears'.

He had dinner in town, he strolled in the park. Then Mr. Turkin's invitation suddenly crossed his mind, and he decided to call and see what the family was like.

Mr. Turkin welcomed him in the porch. 'Pleased to meet you, I'm sure. Delighted indeed to see so charming a guest. Come along, I'll introduce you to the wife.

'I was telling him, Vera dear—' he went on, presenting the doctor to his wife. 'He ain't got no statutory right, I was telling him, to coop himself up in that hospital. He should devote his leisure to society, shouldn't he, love?'

'Do sit here,' said Mrs. Turkin, placing the guest next to her. 'You can be my new boy friend. My husband is jealous—oh, he's quite the Othello!—but we'll try to behave so he won't notice anything.'

'Now, now, ducky!' Mr. Turkin muttered tenderly, kissing her forehead. 'Oh, you are naughty!'

'You're in luck,' he added, turning to the doctor again. 'Mrs. T. has written a whacking great Novel, and today she's going to read it to us.'

Mrs. Turkin turned to her husband. '*Dites que l'on nous donne du thé,* dear.'

Startsev was introduced to Catherine: a girl of eighteen, very much like her mother. Also slim and pretty, she still had a rather childlike expression. Her waist was soft and slender. So beautiful, healthy and well-developed were her youthful breasts that she seemed like the very breath of springtime.

They had tea with jam and honey, sweets and delicious cakes which melted in the mouth. As evening drew on other guests gradually arrived. Mr. Turkin fixed each of them with his grin.

'Pleased to meet you, I'm sure.'

Then they all sat in the drawing-room, looking very earnest, while Mrs. Turkin read her Novel, which began: 'The frost had set in.' The windows were wide open, a clatter of knives was heard from the kitchen, there was a smell of fried onions. It was relaxing to sit in the deep, soft arm-chairs. The lights had such a friendly twinkle in the twilight of the drawing-room that, on this late spring evening— with voices and laughter borne from the street, with the scent of lilac wafting from outside—it was hard to grasp this stuff about the frost setting in and the dying sun illuminating with its chill rays a traveller on his lonely journey over some snow-covered plain. Mrs. Turkin was reading about a beautiful young countess who ran schools, hospitals and libraries in her village, and who fell in love with a wandering artist. These were not things which happen in real life, but they made you feel nice and cosy, they evoked peaceful, serene thoughts—and so no one wanted to get up.

'Not so dusty,' said Mr. Turkin softly.

One of the audience had been carried away by a long, long train of thought.

'No indeed,' he said in a voice barely audible.

An hour passed, then another. In the municipal park near by a band was playing, a choir sang. No one spoke for five minutes or so after Mrs. Turkin had closed her manuscript. They were listening to the choir singing 'Rushlight': a song which conveyed the real-life atmosphere which the Novel lacked.

'Do you publish your stories in the magazines?' Startsev asked Mrs. Turkin.

'No, never,' she answered. 'I keep my writings in a cupboard— why publish? It's not as though we were badly off,' she explained.

For some reason everyone sighed.

'Now, Pussy, you play us something,' Mr. Turkin told his daughter.

They put the lid of the grand piano up, they opened some music which was lying ready. Catherine sat down. She struck the keys with both hands. Then she immediately struck them again as hard as she could, and then again and again. Her shoulders and bosom quivered, and she kept hitting the same place as if she did not mean to stop until she had driven those keys right inside the instrument. The drawing-room resounded with the din as everything—floor, ceiling, furniture— reverberated.

Catherine was playing a difficult passage—its interest lay in its very difficulty. It was long and tedious. Startsev, as he listened, pictured a fall of rocks down a high mountain: on, on they tumbled while he very much wished they wouldn't. Yet Catherine—pink from her exertions, strong and vigorous, with a lock of hair falling over her forehead—greatly attracted him.

What a pleasant new sensation it was, after a winter in Dyalizh among patients and peasants: to sit in a drawing-room watching this young, exquisite and probably innocent creature, and hearing this noisy, tiresome—yet cultured—racket.

'Well, Pussy, you played better than ever today,' said Mr. Turkin with tears in his eyes after his daughter had finished and stood up. 'A thing of beauty is a joy for ever.'

They all crowded round with their congratulations and admiration, declaring that they hadn't heard such a performance for ages. She listened in silence with a faint smile, her whole figure radiating triumph.

'Marvellous! Splendid!'

Infected by the general enthusiasm, Startsev too said how marvellous it had been. 'Where did you study?' he asked Catherine. 'At the Conservatory?'

'No, I'm still at the pre-Conservatory stage. Meanwhile I've been taking lessons here, with Madame Zavlovsky.'

'Did you go to the local high school?'

'No indeed, we engaged private tutors,' Mrs. Turkin answered for her. 'There might be bad influences in a high school or a boarding school, you know. A growing girl should be under no influence but that of her mother.'

'All the same, I *am* going to the Conservatory,' Catherine said.

'No. Pussy loves Mummy, Pussy won't upset Mummy and Daddy.'

'I *will* go there, I *will*,' joked Catherine, playing up like a naughty child and stamping her foot.

At supper it was Mr. Turkin's turn to display his talents. Laughing with his eyes alone, he told funny stories, he joked, he propounded absurd riddles, he answered them himself—talking all the time in an extraordinary lingo evolved by long practice in the exercise of wit . . . by now it was obviously second nature to him.

'Whacking great,' 'Not so dusty,' 'Thanking you most unkindly——'

Nor was this all. When the guests, contented and replete, were jammed in the hall looking for coats and sticks, the footman Paul—nicknamed Peacock, a boy of about fourteen with cropped hair and full cheeks—bustled around them.

'Come on then, Peacock, perform!' Mr. Turkin said.

Peacock struck an attitude, threw up an arm.

'Unhappy woman, die!' he uttered in a tragic voice. And everyone roared with laughter.

'Great fun,' thought Startsev, going out into the street.

He called at a restaurant and had a beer before setting off home for Dyalizh. During the walk he hummed 'Your Voice to me both Languorous and Tender.'

Going to bed, he did not feel at all tired after his six-mile walk—far from it, he felt he could have walked another fifteen with pleasure.

'Not so dusty,' he remembered as he was falling asleep. And laughed.

II

Startsev kept meaning to visit the Turkins again, but just couldn't find a free hour, being so very busy at his hospital. Then, after more than a year of such solitary toil, a letter in a light blue envelope arrived from town.

Mrs. Turkin had had migraine for years, but recently—what with Pussy now scaring her daily with talk of going to the Conservatory— these attacks had increased. The town doctors had all attended the Turkins, now it was the country doctor's turn. Mrs. Turkin wrote him a touching letter, asking him to come and relieve her sufferings. Startsev went, and then became a frequent—a *very* frequent—visitor at the Turkins'.

He really did help Mrs. Turkin a bit, and she was now telling all her guests what an extraordinary, what an admirable doctor he was. But it was no migraine that brought him to the Turkins' now!

On one of his free days, after Catherine had completed her lengthy, exhausting piano exercises, they had sat for a long time over tea in the dining-room while Mr. Turkin told a funny story. Suddenly the doorbell rang. He had to go into the hall to greet a visitor, and Startsev took advantage of the brief confusion.

'For God's sake, I beg you, don't torment me,' he whispered, much agitated, to Catherine. 'Let's go into the garden.'

She shrugged her shoulders as if puzzled to know what he wanted of her, but she did get up and go.

'You play the piano for three or four hours on end,' he said as he followed her. 'Then you sit with your mother, and one can never have a word with you. Give me a quarter of an hour, I beg you.'

Autumn was approaching. The old garden was quiet and sad, dark leaves lay on the paths and the evenings were drawing in.

'I haven't seen you for a week,' Startsev went on. 'If only you knew how I suffer. Come and sit down, and hear what I have to say.'

They had their favourite place in the garden: a bench under a broad old maple, which was where they now sat.

'What do you require?' asked Catherine in a dry, matter-of-fact voice.

'I haven't seen you for a week, or heard your voice all that time. I long, I yearn to hear you speak. Say something.'

He was fascinated by her freshness, by the innocent expression of her eyes and cheeks. Even in the cut of her dress he saw something unusually lovely, touching in its simplicity and naïve gracefulness. And yet, despite this innocence, he found her very intelligent, very mature for her age. He could talk to her about literature, art or anything else. He could complain about life or people to her, though she was liable to laugh suddenly in the wrong place during a serious conversation. Or she would run off into the house. Like almost all the local girls, she was a great reader. (Few people in the town read much. 'If it wasn't for the girls and the young Jews we might just as well shut up shop,' they used to say in the town library.) Her reading pleased Startsev no end. He always made a great fuss of asking what she had read in the last few days, and he would listen, fascinated, as she told him.

'What,' he asked her, 'have you read since we met last week? Please tell me.'

'Pisemsky.'

'Which book?'

'*A Thousand Souls*,' answered Pussy. 'What a funny name Pisemsky had: Alexis Feofilaktovich.'

'Hey, where are you off to?' Startsev was aghast when she suddenly stood up and made for the house. 'I must talk to you, I've some explaining to do. Stay with me just five minutes, I implore you.'

She stopped as if meaning to say something, then awkwardly thrust a note into his hand and ran to the house, where she sat down at the piano again.

'Be in the cemetery near Demetti's tomb at eleven o'clock tonight,' Startsev read.

'This is really rather silly,' he thought, collecting his wits. 'Why the cemetery? What's the point?'

It was one of Pussy's little games, obviously. But really, who would seriously think of an assignation in a cemetery far outside town at night-time, when it could so easily be arranged in the street or municipal park? And was it not beneath him—a country doctor, an intelligent, respectable man—to be sighing, receiving *billets-doux*, hanging round cemeteries and doing things so silly that even schoolboys laugh at them these days? Where would this affair end? What would his colleagues say when they found out? Such were Startsev's thoughts as he wandered among the tables at his club. But at half-past ten he suddenly got up and drove off to the cemetery.

By now he had his own pair of horses and a coachman, Panteleymon, complete with velvet waistcoat. The moon was shining. It was quiet and warm, but with a touch of autumn in the air. Dogs were howling near a suburban slaughterhouse. Leaving his carriage in a lane on the edge of town, Startsev walked on to the cemetery alone.

'We all have our quirks, Pussy included,' thought he. 'Perhaps— who knows—perhaps she wasn't joking. Perhaps she will come.' Yielding to this feeble, insubstantial hope, he felt intoxicated by it.

He walked through fields for a quarter of a mile. The cemetery showed up: a dark strip in the distance resembling a wood or large garden. The white stone wall came into view and the gate. The words on the gate were legible in the moonlight: 'The hour cometh when—.' Startsev went through the side-gate and the first things to catch his eye were white crosses and tombstones on both sides of a broad avenue, and black shadows cast by them and by the poplars. There was an extensive panorama in black and white, with sleepy trees drooping their branches over the whiteness below. It seemed lighter here than in the fields. Maple leaves like paws stood out sharply against the yellow sand of paths and against gravestones, and the inscriptions on the monuments were clearly visible. Startsev was struck at once by what he was now seeing for the first time in his life and would probably never see again: a world unlike any other . . . where moonlight was as lovely and soft as if this were its cradle, where there was no living thing, but where each dark poplar and tomb seemed to hold the secret promise of a life tranquil, splendid, everlasting. Mingled with the autumnal smell of leaves, the gravestones and faded flowers breathed forgiveness, melancholy and peace.

It was silent all around. The stars looked down from the sky in utter quiescence, while Startsev's footsteps sounded harsh and out of place. Only when the church clock began to strike, and he fancied himself dead and buried here for ever, did he feel as if someone was watching him. This was not peace and quiet, it seemed for a moment, but the dull misery of nothingness: a kind of choked despair.

Demetti's tomb was in the form of a shrine with an angel on top. An Italian opera company had once passed through town, one of the singers had died, they had buried her here, and they had put up this monument. She was no longer remembered in town, but the lamp over the entrance reflected the moon and seemed alight.

There was no one about—as if anyone would come here at midnight! Yet Startsev waited, waited passionately, as if the moonlight were inflaming his desires. He imagined kisses and embraces. He sat near the tomb for about half an hour, then strolled up and down the side-paths with his hat in his hand, waiting. He reflected that in these graves lay buried many women and girls who had been beautiful and entrancing, who had loved and burned with passion in the night, yielding to caresses. Really, what a rotten joke Nature does play on man! And how painful to be conscious of it! So Startsev thought, while wishing to shout aloud that he wanted love, that he expected it—at whatever cost. The white shapes before his eyes were no longer slabs of marble, but beautiful bodies. He saw shapely forms modestly hiding in the shadows of the trees, and he sensed their warmth until desire grew hard to bear.

Then, like the drop of a curtain, the moon vanished behind clouds and everything was suddenly dark. Startsev had trouble finding the gate, for the darkness was now truly autumnal. Then he wandered about for an hour and a half looking for the lane where he had left his horses.

'I'm dead on my feet,' he told Panteleymon.

'Dear me, one really should watch one's weight,' he reflected as he settled down luxuriously in his carriage.

III

Next evening he set off for the Turkins' to propose to Catherine. But it turned out inconveniently because she was in her room with her hairdresser in attendance, and was going to a dance at the club.

He found himself let in for another of those long tea-drinking sessions in the dining-room. Seeing his guest bored and preoccupied, Mr. Turkin took some jottings from his waistcoat pocket and read out a funny letter from a German estate-manager about how all the 'racks' on the property had 'gone to lock and ruin', and how the old place had been so knocked about that it had become 'thoroughly bashful'.

'They're bound to put up a decent dowry', thought Startsev, listening absent-mindedly.

After his sleepless night he felt stupefied, felt as if he had been drugged with some sweet sleeping potion. His sensations were confused, but warm and happy. And yet——

'Stop before it is too late!' a stolid, cold part of his brain argued. 'Is she the wife for you? She's spoilt and capricious, she sleeps till two in the afternoon, while you're a sexton's son, a country doctor——'

'Never mind, I don't care,' he answered himself.

'What's more,' went on the voice, 'if you do get married, her family will stop you working in the country and make you move to town.'

'What of it? Then town it shall be,' he thought. 'They'll give a dowry, we'll set up house——'

Catherine came in at last, wearing a *décolleté* evening dress. She looked so pretty and fresh that Startsev goggled at her, and was so transported that he could not get a word out, but just stared at her and laughed.

She began to say good-bye. Having no reason to stay on, he stood up and remarked that it was time to go home as some patients were expecting him.

'You go, then,' said Mr. Turkin. 'It can't be helped. And you might give Puss a lift to the club.'

It was very dark outside and drizzling, with only Panteleymon's raucous cough to guide them to the carriage. They put the hood up.

'Why did the cowslip?' Mr. Turkin said, helping his daughter into the carriage. 'Because she saw the bullrush, of course. Off with you! Cheerio, chin chin!'

And off they went.

'I went to the cemetery yesterday,' Startsev began. 'How mean and heartless of you to——'

'You actually *went*?'

'Yes. *And* waited till nearly two o'clock. I suffered——'

'Serves you right if you can't take a joke.'

Delighted to have played such a mean trick on a man who loved her—delighted, too, to be the object of such a passion—Catherine laughed, then suddenly screamed with fright because the horses were turning sharply in through the club gates at that moment, and the carriage lurched to one side. Startsev put his arm round her waist while she clung to him in terror. He could not resist kissing her passionately on lips and chin, gripping her more tightly.

'That will do,' she said curtly.

A second later she was out of the carriage. A policeman stood near the lighted entrance of the club.

'Don't hang around here, you oaf!' he yelled at Panteleymon in a nasty voice. 'Move on!'

Startsev drove home, but was soon back again. Wearing borrowed tails and a stiff white cravat, which somehow kept slipping up and trying to ride off his collar, he sat in the club lounge at midnight ardently haranguing Catherine.

'Those who've never been in love . . . how little they know! I don't think anyone has ever described love properly. Does it, indeed, lend itself to description: this tender, joyous, tormented feeling? No one who has ever experienced it would try to put it into words. But what's the use of preambles and explanations? Or of superfluous eloquence? I love you infinitely. I ask you, I implore you——'

Startsev got it out at last. 'Be my wife.'

'Dmitry Startsev——' said Catherine with a very earnest expression, after some thought. 'I am most grateful to you for the honour, Dmitry, and I respect you, but——'

She stood up and continued, standing. 'I'm sorry, though, I can't be your wife. Let us talk seriously. As you know, Dmitry, I love Art more than anything in the world—I'm mad about music, I adore it, I have dedicated my whole life to it. I want to be a concert pianist. I want fame, success, freedom—whereas you want me to go on living in this town, pursuing an empty, futile existence which I can't stand. To be a wife . . . no, no, I'm sorry. One must aim at some lofty, brilliant goal, and family life would tie me down for ever. Dmitry Startsev——.' She gave a slight smile because, while saying his name, she remembered Alexis Feofilaktovich. 'You're a kind, honourable, intelligent man, Dmitry, you're the nicest one of all——'

Tears came into her eyes. 'I feel for you with all my heart, but, er, you must understand——'

To avoid bursting into tears she turned away and left the lounge.

Startsev's heart ceased to throb. Going out of the club into the street, he first tore off the stiff cravat and heaved a deep sigh. He felt a little ashamed and his pride was hurt—for he had not expected a refusal. Nor could he believe that his dreams, his yearnings, his hopes had led to so foolish a conclusion, like something in a little play acted by amateurs. And he was sorry for his own feelings, for that love of his—so sorry that he felt ready to break into sobs, or to land a really good clout on Panteleymon's broad back with his umbrella.

For a couple of days he let things slide—couldn't eat or sleep. But when rumour reached him that Catherine had gone to Moscow to enrol at the Conservatory, he calmed down and resumed his former routine.

Recalling, later, how he had wandered round the cemetery and

driven all over town in search of a tail-coat, he would stretch himself
lazily, saying that it had all been 'oh, such a lot of fuss'.

IV

Four years passed, and Startsev now had a large practice in town.
He hastily took surgery at his home in Dyalizh each morning, after
which he left to visit his town patients. From a two-horse outfit he
had graduated to a troika with bells. He would return home late at
night. He had grown broad and stout, and he disliked walking because
he was always short of breath. Panteleymon had filled out too, and
the broader he grew the more dolefully he would sigh and lament
his bitter fate. 'The driving's got me down!'

Startsev was received in various houses and met many people, but
was intimate with none. The conversations, the attitudes—the appearance, even—of the townsfolk irritated him. Experience had gradually
taught him that your average provincial is a peaceable, easy-going and
even quite intelligent human being when you play cards or have a
meal with him, but that you only have to talk about something which
can't be eaten—politics, say, or learning—for him to be put right off
his stroke . . . or else to launch on generalizations so trite and malicious
that there's nothing for it but to write him off and leave. Take the
typical local liberal, even—just suppose Startsev should try to tell
him that humanity was progressing, thank God, and would manage
without passports and capital punishment in time. 'You mean it will
be possible to murder people in the street?' the man would ask with
a mistrustful sidelong glance. Whenever Startsev spoke in company, at tea or supper, of the need to work—of the impossibility of
living without work—everyone took it as a reproach, becoming angry
and tiresomely argumentative. What's more, your average provincial
never did a single blessed thing. He had no interests—indeed, you
just couldn't think what to talk to him about. So Startsev avoided
conversation, and just ate or played bridge. When he chanced on some
family celebration and was asked in for a bite, he would sit and eat
silently, staring at his plate. Their talk was all dull, prejudiced and
stupid, which irritated and upset him. But he would still say nothing.
This austere silence and habit of staring at his plate earned him a
nickname—'the pompous Pole'—in town, though he was not of
Polish origin.

He avoided such entertainments as concerts and the theatre, but
enjoyed three hours of bridge every evening. He had another recreation

too, which he had slipped into by stages. This was to take from his pockets at night the bank-notes earned on his medical rounds. There were sometimes seventy roubles' worth stuffed in his pockets—yellow and green notes smelling of scent, vinegar, incense and fish oil. When they added up to a few hundreds he would take them to the Mutual Credit Bank and put them in his current account.

In the four years since Catherine's departure he had visited the Turkins only twice—at the behest of Mrs. Turkin, who was still under treatment for migraine. Catherine came and stayed with her parents each summer, but he had not seen her once. It somehow never happened.

But now four years had passed, and on a quiet, warm morning a letter was delivered at the hospital. Mrs. Turkin informed Dr. Startsev that she greatly missed his company, and asked him to visit her without fail to relieve her sufferings. And by the way today was her birthday.

Below was a postscript:

I join in Mummy's request.
C.

After some thought Startsev drove off to the Turkins' that evening.

'Ah! Pleased to meet you, I'm sure,' Mr. Turkin greeted him, smiling only with his eyes. 'And a very *bon jour* to you.'

White-haired, looking much older, Mrs. Turkin shook hands with Startsev and sighed affectedly.

'You refuse to be my boy-friend, Doctor,' she said. 'And you never come and see us. I'm too old for you, but there's someone younger here. Perhaps she'll have better luck.'

And what of Pussy? She was slimmer, paler, more handsome, more graceful. Now she was Pussy no longer, but Miss Catherine Turkin— her former freshness and childlike innocent look were gone. In her glance and manner, too, there was a new quality of hesitation or guilt, as if she no longer felt at home here in the family house.

'It seems ages since we met,' she said, giving Startsev her hand, and one could tell that her heart was beating apprehensively. 'How you *have* filled out,' she went on, staring inquisitively at his face. 'You're sunburnt, you're more mature, but you haven't changed much on the whole.'

She still attracted him, very much so, but now there was something missing . . . or added. Just what it was he couldn't have said, but something prevented him from feeling as before. He disliked her pallor, her

new expression, her faint smile and voice. Before long he was disliking
her dress and the arm-chair in which she sat—disliking, too, something
about the past when he had come near to marrying her. He remembered
his love, remembered the dreams and hopes which had disturbed him
four years ago. And felt uncomfortable.

They had tea and cake. Then Mrs. Turkin read them a Novel, all
about things which never happen in real life—while Startsev listened,
looked at her handsome, white head, and waited for her to finish.

'A mediocrity is not someone who can't write novels,' he reflected.
'It's someone who writes them and can't keep quiet about it.'

'Not so dusty,' said Mr. Turkin.

Then Catherine played long and noisily on the piano, and when she
stopped there were lengthy expressions of delighted appreciation.

'Lucky I didn't marry her,' thought Startsev.

She looked at him, evidently expecting him to suggest going into
the garden, but he did not speak.

'Well, let's talk,' she said, going up to him. 'How are you? What's
your news, eh?

'I've been thinking about you a lot lately,' she went on nervously.
'I wanted to write to you, wanted to go to Dyalizh myself and see
you. I did decide to go, actually, then changed my mind—heaven
knows how you feel about me now. I was so excited today, waiting
for you to come. For God's sake let's go into the garden.'

They went into the garden and sat down on the bench under the
old maple, as they had four years earlier. It was dark.

'How are you then?' Catherine said.

'Not so bad,' Startsev answered. 'I manage.'

That was all he could think of saying. There was a pause.

'I'm so excited,' Catherine said, covering her face with her hands.
'But don't let that worry you. I'm happy to be home, so glad to see
everyone. I just can't get used to it. What a lot of memories! I thought
we should go on talking and talking till morning.'

Now he could see her face, her shining eyes close to him. Out here in
the darkness she looked younger than indoors, and even her old childlike expression seemed to have returned. She was, indeed, gazing at him
with naïve curiosity, as if seeking a closer view and understanding of a
man who had once loved her so ardently, so tenderly, so unhappily.
Her eyes thanked him for that love. He remembered what had happened,
all the little details—how he had strolled round the cemetery and then
gone home exhausted in the small hours. Suddenly he felt sadness

and regret for the past, and a spark seemed to come alight inside him.

'Remember how I took you to the club dance?' he said. 'It was dark and rainy——'

The spark inside him was flaring up, and now he felt the urge to speak, to complain about life.

'Ah me,' he sighed. 'Here are you asking about my life. But how *do* we live here? The answer is, we don't. We grow old and stout, we run to seed. One day follows another, and life passes drearily without impressions or ideas. There's earning your living by day, there's the club of an evening in the company of card-players, alcoholics and loud-mouthed fellows I can't stand. What's good about that?'

'But you have your work, an honourable ambition. You used to like talking about your hospital so much. I was an odd girl in those days, thinking myself a great pianist. Young ladies all play the piano nowadays, and I was just one more of them—nothing remarkable about me. I'm about as much of a pianist as Mother is a writer. I didn't understand you at the time, of course. But in Moscow, later, I often thought of you—in fact I thought of nothing *but* you. What happiness to be a country doctor, to help the suffering, to serve ordinary people.

'What happiness!' Catherine repeated eagerly. 'When I thought of you in Moscow you seemed so admirable, so superior.'

Startsev remembered the bank-notes which he so much enjoyed taking out of his pockets in the evenings, and the spark died inside him.

He got up to go into the house, and she took him by the arm.

'You're the best person I've ever known,' she went on. 'We *shall* meet and talk, shan't we? Do promise. I'm no pianist. I've no illusions left, and I won't play music or talk about it when you're there.'

When they were in the house and Startsev saw her face in the lamplight and her sad, grateful, inquiring eyes fixed on him, he felt uneasy.

'Lucky I never married her,' he thought again.

He began to take his leave.

'You ain't got no statutory right to leave without supper,' Mr. Turkin said as he saw him off. 'Highly perpendicular of you in fact. Well, go on—perform!' he added, addressing Peacock in the hall.

Peacock—now no longer a boy, but a young man with a moustache —struck an attitude, threw up an arm.

'Unhappy woman, die!' he declaimed tragically.

All this irritated Startsev. Climbing into his carriage, he looked at the dark house and garden once so dear and precious to him. It all came back to him at once: Mrs. Turkin's 'novels', Pussy's noisy piano-playing, Mr. Turkin's wit, Peacock's tragic posturings. What, he asked himself, could be said of a town in which the most brilliant people were so dim?

Three days later Peacock brought a letter from Catherine.

Why don't you come and see us? I'm afraid your feelings for us have changed. I'm afraid—the very idea terrifies me. Do set my mind at rest. Do come and tell me that all is well.

I simply must talk to you.

Your
C. T.

He read the letter.

'Tell them I can't manage it today, my good fellow, I'm very busy,' he told Peacock after some thought. 'Tell them I'll come over—oh, in a couple of days.'

But three days passed, and then a week—and still he did not go. Once, when driving past the Turkins' house, he remembered that he should at least pay a brief call. But then he thought again. And did not.

Never again did he visit the Turkins.

V

A few more years have passed. Startsev has put on yet more weight—grown really fat. He breathes heavily and goes about with his head thrown back. Plump, red-faced, he drives in his troika with the bells, while Panteleymon—also plump, also red-faced, with a thick, fleshy neck—sits on the box holding his arms straight ahead as if they were wooden.

'Keep to the r-i-ight!' he bellows at oncoming traffic.

It is an impressive scene, suggesting that the passenger is not a man, but a pagan god.

He has a vast practice in the town and scarcely time to draw breath. Already he owns an estate and two town houses, and he is looking for a third—a better bargain. When, in the Mutual Credit Bank, he hears of a house for sale, he marches straight in without ceremony, goes through all the rooms—paying no attention to the half-dressed women and children who stare at him in fascinated horror—prods all the doors with his stick.

'This the study?' he asks. 'That a bedroom? What have we here?'
He breathes heavily all the time, wiping sweat from his brow.

He has a lot to do, but still does not give up his council post, being too greedy and wanting a finger in every pie. At Dyalizh and in town he is now known simply as 'the Doc'.

'Where's the Doc off to?' people ask. Or 'Shouldn't we call in the Doc?'

His voice has changed, probably because his throat is so congested with fat, and has become thin and harsh. His character has changed too —he has grown ill-humoured and irritable. When taking surgery he usually loses his temper and bangs his stick impatiently on the floor.

'Pray confine yourself to answering my questions!' he shouts unpleasantly. 'Less talk!'

He lives alone. It is a dreary life, he has no interests.

During his entire time at Dyalizh his love for Pussy has been his only joy, and will probably be his last. He plays bridge in the club of an evening, then dines alone at a large table. He is waited on by Ivan, the oldest and most venerable of the club servants, is served with Château Lafite No. 17, and everyone—the club officials, the cook, the waiter—knows his likes and dislikes, they all humour him in every way. Otherwise he's liable to fly into a rage and bang his stick on the floor.

While dining he occasionally turns round and breaks into a conversation.

'What are you on about? Eh? Who?'

When, occasionally, talk at a near-by table turns to the Turkins, he asks what Turkins. 'You mean those people whose daughter plays the piannyforty?'

There is no more to be said about him.

What of the Turkins? Mr. Turkin looks no older—hasn't changed a bit, but still keeps joking and telling his funny stories. Mrs. Turkin still enjoys reading those Novels to guests in a jolly, hearty sort of a way. And Pussy plays the piano for four hours a day. She looks much older, she is often unwell, and she goes to the Crimea with her mother every autumn. Mr. Turkin sees them off at the station, and when the train starts he wipes away his tears.

'Cheerio, chin chin!' he shouts.

And waves a handkerchief.

A CASE HISTORY

[Случай из практики]

(1898)

A CASE HISTORY

A TELEGRAM arrived for the Professor of Medicine from a textile mill—Lyalikov's—urgently requesting his presence. A girl was ill: daughter of some Mrs. Lyalikov, who seemed to be the mill-owner— that was all the long, ineptly framed message conveyed. The professor did not go himself, but sent one of his house-surgeons, Korolyov, instead.

Korolyov had to travel two stations down the line from Moscow, then drive three miles. He was fetched from the station in a three-horse carriage by a coachman sporting a peacock feather in his hat, whose answer to all questions was a loud regimental 'Yessir!' or 'No sir!'. It was Saturday evening, the sun was setting. Trooping from works to station, mill-hands bowed their heads to the horses pulling Korolyov's carriage. The evening, the country houses and cottages on each side, the birches . . . they all enchanted him. The whole atmosphere was so peaceful, as if fields, woodlands and sun were about to join the workers in their Saturday evening's rest and relaxation—in their prayers too, perhaps.

He had been born and grown up in Moscow, he knew nothing of country life, he had never taken an interest in factories, never visited them. But he had read about such things, he had been entertained by industrialists and had talked to them. Whenever he saw a factory— near by or afar—he always thought: how quiet and peaceful the façade, but how different the reality must be: the owners' crass boorishness and brute selfishness, the workers' unhealthy drudgery . . . the fights, the vodka, the vermin. Now, too, as the workers humbly and nervously made way for his carriage, he seemed to sense squalor, drunkenness, tension and bewilderment in faces, caps and gait.

They drove through the mill entrance. There was a glimpse of workers' cottages on both sides, of women's faces, of washing and blankets on the porches.

'Out of my way!' yelled the coachman, not slackening speed.

Now came a spacious area bare of grass. On it stood five vast chimneyed mill-sheds, some distance apart from each other. There were warehouses and barracks too, all covered with a film of grey dust. Here and there, like desert oases, were the wretched little gardens and the green or red roofs of the houses where the management lived.

The coachman pulled up his horses sharply, and the carriage halted at a house with a new coat of grey paint. Here was a small front garden with dusty lilac and a reek of paint on the yellow porch.

'Please come in, Doctor,' said female voices in the lobby and hall. There was some sighing and whispering. 'Come in, we've waited so long—oh, what a to-do! This way, please.'

Mrs. Lyalikov, a stout, elderly person in a black silk dress with modish sleeves—but homely and uneducated, from the look of her—gazed anxiously at the doctor, hesitating, not venturing to shake hands. Beside her stood a short-haired, emaciated, middle-aged, pince-nez-wearing creature in a brightly patterned blouse. The servants called her Miss Christine, and Korolyov put her down as the governess. It was as the most educated person in the house, probably, that she had been assigned to greet and receive the doctor—anyway, she was in a great hurry to rehearse the causes of the disease in niggling minor detail. Who the patient was, though, what this was all about . . . that she didn't say.

Doctor and governess sat talking while the mistress of the house stood motionless by the door, waiting. From what was said Korolyov learnt that it was a girl of twenty—Liza, Mrs. Lyalikov's only daughter and heiress—who was ill. She had been unwell for some time, she had been under various doctors, and during the entire previous night she had suffered heart palpitations so acute that no one in the house had slept—they had feared for her life.

'She's always been poorly since she was little, as you might say,' explained Miss Christine in a sing-song voice, now and then wiping her lips with her hand. 'The doctors call it nerves. But if you ask me it may be the scrofula she had as a child—drove it right inside her, them doctors did.'

They went to see the patient. Fully grown, large, well-built, but plain and like her mother—the same small eyes, the same wide, outsize lower jaw—hair uncombed, blankets up to her chin . . . she first struck Korolyov as a poor, miserable creature sheltered and cherished here out of pity. It was hard to see her as the future owner of five huge mills.

'Well, here we are,' began Korolyov. 'We've come to make you well. Good evening.'

He gave his name, took her hand: her large, cold, ungainly hand.

She sat up—long used to doctors, obviously, not caring that her shoulders and chest were uncovered—and let him examine her.

'It's palpitations,' she said. 'I felt terrible all night, nearly died of fright. Do give me something to take.'

'Yes, yes, don't worry.'

Korolyov examined her and shrugged his shoulders.

'There's nothing wrong with the heart,' he said. 'Everything's fine —no cause for worry. Your nerves must have been playing up a bit, but that's nothing. The attack must have ended, so you lie down and get some sleep.'

Then a lamp was brought into the bedroom. The sick girl squinted in the light, suddenly clutched her head in her hands—and burst out sobbing. The impression of a miserable, ungainly creature suddenly vanished, and Korolyov no longer noticed the small eyes and the out-size lower jaw. He saw a gentle, suffering look so wise, so moving that she seemed all feminine grace and charm—he wanted to soothe her, now, with a few simple, kind words: not with medicines or advice. The mother clasped her daughter's head and clutched her to herself. What grief, what despair was in the old lady's face! Mother had reared and nurtured daughter, no expense spared. She had sacrificed every-thing to have the girl taught French, dancing, music. She had engaged a dozen teachers and all the best doctors, she kept a governess. And now she couldn't understand: why all the tears, whence all the anguish? She couldn't understand, she was baffled, and she wore a guilty, anxious, desperate look. Was there something else—something crucial —that she had omitted? Had she left something undone? Was there someone or other, some unknown, whose services she had failed to enlist?

'You're crying again, Liza,' she said, clasping her daughter. 'My own dearest little darling, tell me what's the matter. Tell me, for pity's sake.'

Both wept bitterly.

Korolyov sat on the edge of the bed and took Liza's hand. 'There, there, don't cry,' he said kindly. 'There's nothing on earth worth all those tears, now, is there? So don't let's cry, then. No need to——'

The thought struck him that it was 'time she got married'.

'Our works doctor's been giving her potassium bromide,' said the governess. 'But it only makes her worse, I notice. If it's heart trouble, then it's my opinion she should have those drops—what are they called? Convallamarin, or something?'

Out came all the different details all over again. She interrupted

Korolyov, she wouldn't let him get a word in edgeways. And she wore a long-suffering expression which seemed to imply that she, as the most educated individual in the house, needs must keep up a non-stop, exclusively medical conversation with the doctor.

Korolyov found this a bore.

'I don't see anything to worry about,' said he, leaving the bedroom and addressing the mother. 'If the works doctor has been treating your daughter, let him carry on. The treatment's been all right so far, I see no need to change doctors. There's no point, anyway—it's quite a common ailment, nothing serious.'

He spoke slowly, putting on his gloves, while Mrs. Lyalikov stood motionless and looked at him with tear-filled eyes.

'I have half an hour to catch the ten o'clock train,' he said. 'I hope I shan't miss it.'

'Can't you stay with us?' she asked, and tears again flowed down her cheeks. 'I don't like troubling you, but do be so kind——. For God's sake,' she went on in a low voice, glancing round at the door, 'do stay the night here. She's all I have, my only daughter. She did scare me so last night, I can't get over it. For pity's sake don't leave us.'

He wanted to say that he had a lot to do in Moscow, that his family was expecting him home. To spend an entire evening and night in a strange house for no reason . . . it would be an ordeal. But he looked at her face, sighed—and silently removed his gloves.

All the lamps and candles had been lit for him in both drawing-rooms. He sat by the grand piano turning over the music, then scrutinized the portraits and other pictures on the walls. The paintings —in oils, gilt-framed—showed views of the Crimea, a small boat on a stormy sea and a Catholic monk with a wine-glass: dim, glib, uninspired stuff, all of it. As for the portraits, there wasn't a single handsome or attractive face among them—it was all broad cheek-bones, all startled eyes. Liza's father had a small forehead, a self-satisfied expression—and a baggy uniform which sat ill on his large, plebeian frame. He wore a medal and Red Cross badge on his chest. It was all in such poor taste: haphazard, mindless luxury as ill-fitting as that uniform. The gleaming floors irritated him, and so did the chandelier—they somehow suggested the merchant in the story, the one who always wore his medals in the bath.

There was a sound of whispering from the hall, and of someone softly snoring. Then, suddenly, certain noises—harsh, staccato, metallic —came from outdoors: noises such as Korolyov had never heard before and could not make out now. They aroused in him strange, unpleasant feelings.

'I don't think I'd live here for anything,' he thought, picking up the music again.

'Will you come and eat now, Doctor?' the governess called in a low voice.

He went in to the meal. There was a large table with quantities of food and wine—but only two for supper, himself and Miss Christine. She drank Madeira and ate greedily.

'We're very popular with the workers,' she said, eyeing him over her pince-nez. 'We have our own theatricals at the works every winter —with workers actually acting in them! They have their magic-lantern talks, such a lovely canteen, and all they could possibly want. They're devoted to us, and when they heard that Liza was worse they had prayers said for her. Ignorant folk, but they've got their feelings same as us.'

'You have no man about the house apparently,' said Korolyov.

'No. Mr. Lyalikov passed away eighteen months ago, and we were left on our own. That's how we live, us three. We spend summer here and winter in Moscow, in Polyanka Street. I've been with them over ten years—quite one of the family, I am.'

For supper sturgeon, chicken rissoles and stewed fruit were served. The wines were French . . . and expensive.

'Now, don't stand on ceremony, Doctor,' said Miss Christine, eating away, wiping her mouth with the back of her hand and obviously doing herself proud. 'Do help yourself.'

After supper the doctor was shown to the room where a bed had been made up for him. But he didn't feel like sleeping in this stuffy room smelling of paint. He put on his overcoat and went out.

It was cool outside, and there was already a glimmer in the sky. The five mills with their tall chimneys, the barracks, the warehouses . . . all showed up clearly in the damp air. All work had stopped because it was a Saturday night, and the windows were dark. In just one mill the furnace was still burning, two windows glowed blood-red and a flame occasionally issued from the chimney along with the smoke. Far from the works frogs croaked, a nightingale sang.

Looking at the mills, at the barracks where the workers slept, he again thought what he always thought when he saw factories. The workers had their theatricals, granted—their magic lanterns, their factory doctors, their various amenities. Yet those mill-hands he had seen on the road from the station this evening . . . they had looked exactly like the workers he had seen long ago as a boy, when there had been none of these theatricals and amenities. As a doctor accustomed to forming accurate diagnoses of incurable chronic ailments deriving from some unknown ultimate cause, he considered factories a mystery of comparably vague and intractable antecedents. As for improvements in the workers' lives, he didn't think them unnecessary, but compared them to the treatment of incurable diseases.

'It's all a misunderstanding, of course,' he thought, looking at the blood-red windows. 'Fifteen hundred or two thousand mill-hands work unceasingly in unhealthy conditions making cheap printed cotton. They live on the edge of starvation. Only occasionally do they sober up—and in the pub!—from this nightmare. A hundred people supervise the work. They devote their whole lives to recording fines, shouting abuse and mistreating people. Only two or three individuals —the "bosses"—reap the benefits, though they do no work at all and despise cheap cotton. What *are* the benefits, though, how *do* they enjoy them? The Lyalikov woman and her daughter are unhappy—they look pathetic—and the only one to enjoy life to the full is this Miss Christine: an elderly, rather silly old maid with a pince-nez. So what does it all come down to? What are these five mills working for? To what end is cheap cotton sold in eastern markets? Just so that Miss Christine can eat her sturgeon and drink her Madeira!'

Suddenly strange sounds rang out, just like those which Korolyov had heard before supper. Near one of the sheds someone was hitting a metal sheet, but then immediately muffling the sound—thus creating short, harsh, blurred thudding noises. Then, after thirty seconds' silence, from another shed rang out a sound similarly staccato and disagreeable—but on a lower, deeper, clanging note. Eleven times. Evidently the watchmen were striking eleven o'clock.

From the third shed came a similar repeated sound on yet another note. Such noises came from all the sheds, and then from behind the barracks and the gates. These sounds in the quiet of the night . . . they seemed to proceed from that monster with the blood-red eyes, that devil who ruled everyone around here—bosses and workers alike— deceiving one and all.

Korolyov went out of the grounds into the fields.

'Who goes there?' someone shouted roughly by the gate.

'Just like prison,' he thought, and made no answer.

Here nightingales and frogs were more audible, one sensed the May night. The sound of a train came from the station. Drowsy cocks were crowing somewhere, but still the night was quiet, still the world slept peacefully. In a field not far from the mills stood the framework of a building with material for its construction stacked near by. Korolyov sat on the planks.

'Only the governess enjoys life here,' he continued his reflections. 'The mill works for her pleasure. That's an illusion, though—she's only a figurehead. The principal, the main beneficiary, is the devil.'

Considering the devil, in whom he did not believe, he looked back at the two windows where the fire glowed. Those blood-red eyes watching him . . . they did belong, he felt, to the devil, to that mysterious force which has forged the relations between weak and strong—a gross blunder now wholly irreparable. The strong are bound to make life miserable for the weak, that is a law of nature. But only in a newspaper article or textbook is that law intelligible and psychologically acceptable, whereas in the chaos of everyday life—in the tangle of trifles which go to make up human relations—it ceases to be a law, and becomes a paradox rendering both weak and strong equal victims of their mutual relations as they unwillingly submit to some mysterious controlling force unconnected with life and alien to man. Such were Korolyov's thoughts as he sat on the planks, gradually overcome by the feeling that his mysterious unknown force really was close at hand, really was watching him. Meanwhile the east was growing ever paler, and time was passing quickly. Against the grey background of the gloaming, in the absence of any living soul, the world seemed dead, while the five mill-sheds and their chimneys had a special look—unlike that of daytime. Completely forgetting that they contained steam engines, electricity and telephones, he somehow kept thinking about ancient lake-dwellings and the Stone Age. He sensed the presence of that primitive, mindless force.

Once again those blurred thuds were heard: twelve strokes. Then there was quiet, thirty seconds' quiet, followed by the deeper clanging note at the other end of the works.

'How revolting!' thought Korolyov.

From a third place a harsh, staccato, seemingly exasperated sound rang out on yet another note.

It took four minutes to strike twelve o'clock. Then things grew quiet, and once again he had the impression that everything around him was dead.

Korolyov sat on for a while before going back to the house, but it was still a long time before he went to bed. There was whispering in the adjoining rooms. The shuffling of slippers and the padding of bare feet were heard.

'Has she had another attack?' wondered Korolyov.

He went out to look at his patient. It was already quite light indoors. Piercing the morning mist, a feeble sunbeam quivered on the drawing-room wall and floor.

Liza's door was open. She was sitting in an arm-chair by the bed wrapped in a house-coat and shawl, with her hair loose. The blinds were drawn.

Korolyov asked how she was.

'All right, thank you.'

He felt her pulse, pushed back the hair which had fallen on her forehead.

'You can't sleep,' he said. 'There's wonderful weather outside— spring, nightingale song—but you sit brooding in the darkness.'

She listened, gazed into his face. Her eyes looked sad and wise, she obviously wanted to tell him something.

'Does this happen to you often?' he asked.

She moved her lips. 'Yes, I feel depressed almost every night.'

Then the watchmen began striking two o'clock outside. Hearing those blurred thuds, she shuddered, and he asked whether the banging bothered her.

'I don't know. Everything bothers me here, everything,' she answered, gathering her thoughts. 'Your voice sounds sympathetic, and from the moment I saw you I've somehow felt I could talk to you about things.'

'Talk then. Do.'

'I want to tell you what I think. I don't think I'm ill at all. Why am I worried and scared? Because it *has* to be, because it can't be helped. Even the healthiest man can't help worrying if there's a burglar, say, prowling under his window. I'm always seeing doctors,' she went on with a shy smile, looking down at her lap. 'I'm most grateful, of course, I don't disbelieve in medicine. But I don't so much want to talk to a doctor as to someone close to me: a friend to understand me and show me whether I'm right or wrong.'

'Have you no friends, then?' asked Korolyov.

'I'm lonely. I do have a mother whom I love, but I'm still lonely. That's the way things are. Lonely people read a lot, but they don't talk or hear much, and they find life mysterious. They're mystics, and often

see the devil when he isn't there. Lermontov's Tamara was lonely, and
she saw the devil.'

'Do you read a lot?'

'Yes. After all, I am free all day from morning till evening. I read by
day, but at night my head's empty—only shadows instead of thoughts.'

'Do you see things at night?' Korolyov asked.

'No, but I feel them——'

She smiled again, raised her eyes to the doctor, and looked at him so
sadly and wisely that he felt she trusted him, shared his outlook, and
wanted to tell him what she really thought. But she said nothing,
perhaps waiting for him to speak.

He knew what to say to her now. Clearly she should run away from
her five mills and her million roubles, if she had that much money—
run away from this devil, this watcher of the night. Clearly, too, she
had the same ideas as he—and she was only waiting for someone she
trusted to confirm them.

But he didn't know how to put it. What could he say? It is awkward
asking a condemned man what he has been sentenced for, and it's the
same with very rich people: it's awkward asking them what they want
with all that money, why they manage it so badly, why they don't give
it up—even when they see it causing their unhappiness. Even if you do
get them talking about it, the talk is usually embarrassed, uncomfortable and tedious.

'What shall I say?' wondered Korolyov. 'Need I say anything,
actually?'

So he said what he had to say indirectly and obliquely.

'You, as mill-owner and rich heiress are dissatisfied, you don't
believe you have the right to such things. And now you can't sleep.
Well, that's better of course than if you were complacent, slept soundly
and thought all was for the best. Your insomnia is admirable—it's a
good sign, anyway. Indeed, the talk we're having now . . . it would
have been unthinkable for our parents. They didn't hold conversations
in the middle of the night; they slept soundly—whereas we, our
generation, sleep badly. We suffer, we talk a lot, and we keep worrying
whether we're right or wrong. Now, for our children or grandchildren this problem of being right or wrong will have been solved.
They'll see more clearly than we can. Life will be good in fifty years'
time—it's a shame we shan't live to see it, though. It would be interesting to have a peep.'

'What will our children and grandchildren do?' asked Liza.

'I don't know. Very likely drop everything and run away.'

'But where will they run to?'

'Where to? Why, anywhere!' laughed Korolyov. 'There's no lack of horizons for a decent, intelligent man.'

He looked at his watch. 'I say, the sun is up. It's time you went to sleep. You undress and have a really good sleep. I'm very glad to have met you,' he went on, pressing her hand. 'You're a fine, interesting woman. Good night.'

He went to his room and to bed.

When the carriage was brought round in the morning, everyone came out on the porch to see him off. Liza wore a white dress as it was Sunday, and a flower in her hair. She looked pale and languid. She gazed at him sadly and wisely, as on the previous night, smiling and speaking with the same air of wanting to say something special, something vital, something for his ears only. Larks sang, church bells pealed, mill windows glinted merrily. As he drove through the grounds along the station road, Korolyov had forgotten workers, lake-dwellings and devil—he was thinking of the time, which may already be near, when all life will be as bright and joyful as this quiet Sunday morning. How pleasant, thought he, to drive in a fine carriage pulled by three horses, sunning oneself on such a fine spring morning.

ANGEL

[Душечка]

(1898)

ANGEL

MISS OLGA PLEMYANNIKOV, daughter of a retired minor civil servant, sat brooding on the porch in her yard. She was hot, she was plagued by flies, she was glad it would soon be evening. Dark rain clouds were moving in from the east, and there were a few puffs of damp wind from the same quarter.

In the middle of her yard stood Vanya Kukin. He was in the entertainments business—he ran the Tivoli Pleasure Gardens—and he lived in a detached cottage in the grounds of Olga's house. He gazed up at the sky.

'Oh no, not *again*!' he said desperately. 'Not *more* rain! Why does it have to rain every single blessed day? This is the absolute limit! It'll be the ruin of me—such terrible losses every day!'

He threw up his arms.

'Such is our life, Miss,' he went on, addressing Olga. 'It's pathetic! You work, you do your best, you worry, you lie awake at night, you keep thinking how to improve things. But what happens? Take the audiences, to start with—ignorant savages! I give them the best operetta and pantomime, give them first-rate burlesque. But do they want it? Do they understand any of it? They want vulgar slapstick, that's what they want. And then, just look at this weather: rain nearly every evening. It started on May the tenth, and it's been at it the whole of May and June. It's an abomination! There are no audiences, but who has to pay the rent? Who pays the performers? Not me, I suppose, oh dear me no!'

Clouds gathered again late next afternoon.

'Oh, never mind, *let* it rain,' Kukin laughed hysterically. 'Let it swamp the whole Gardens, me included. May I enjoy no happiness in this world or the next! May the performers sue me! Better still, let them send me to Siberia: to hard labour! Even better, send me to the gallows, ha, ha, ha.'

It was just the same on the third day.

Olga listened to Kukin silently and seriously, with occasional tears in her eyes, until his troubles moved her in the end, and she fell in love. He was a short, skinny, yellow-faced fellow with his hair combed back over his temples. He had a reedy, high-pitched voice, he twisted his mouth when he spoke, he always had a look of desperation. Yet he aroused deep and true emotion in her. She was always in love with someone—couldn't help it. Before this she had loved her father: an invalid, now, wheezing in his arm-chair in a darkened room. She had loved her aunt who came over from Bryansk to see her about once every two years. Earlier still, at junior school, she had loved the French master. She was a quiet, good-hearted, sentimental, very healthy young lady with a tender, melting expression. Looking at her full, rosy cheeks, at her soft white neck with its dark birth-mark, at her kind, innocent smile whenever she heard good tidings—men thought she was 'a bit of all right'. They would smile too, while her lady guests couldn't resist suddenly clasping her hand when talking to her.

'You really are an *angel*!' they would gush.

The house where she had lived since birth, and which she was due to inherit, stood on the outskirts of town: in Gipsy Lane, near Tivoli Gardens. In the evenings and at night she could hear the band in the Gardens and the crash of bursting rockets, and it all sounded to her like Kukin battling with his doom and taking his main enemy—the indifferent public—by storm. She would feel deliciously faint—not at all sleepy—and when Kukin came back in the small hours she would tap her bedroom window, showing him only her face and one shoulder through the curtains . . . and smile tenderly.

He proposed, they were married, and when he had feasted his eyes on that neck and those plump, healthy shoulders, he clapped his hands.

'You *angel*!' he said.

He was happy, but it rained on his wedding day—*and* his wedding night—so that look of desperation remained.

They lived happily after the marriage. She would sit in the box-office, look after the Gardens, record expenses, hand out wages. Her rosy cheeks, her charming, innocent, radiant smile could be glimpsed, now through the box-office window, now in the wings, now in the bar. Already she was telling all her friends that there was nothing in this world so remarkable, so important, so vital as the stage. True pleasure, culture, civilization . . . only in the theatre were these things to be had.

'But does the public understand?' she would ask. 'They want slap-stick. We put on *Faust Inside Out* yesterday, and almost all the boxes were empty. But if we'd staged some vulgar rubbish, me and Vanya, we'd have had a full house, you take my word. We're presenting *Orpheus in the Underworld* tomorrow, me and Vanya. You must come.'

Whatever Kukin said about the theatre and actors, she echoed. Like him she scorned the public for its ignorance and indifference to art. She interfered in rehearsals, she corrected the actors, she kept an eye on the bandsmen. Whenever there was an unfavourable theatrical notice in the local newspaper she would weep—and then go and demand an explanation from the editor's office.

The actors liked her, they called her 'Me and Vanya' and 'Angel'. She was kind to them, she lent them small sums, and if any of them let her down she would go and cry secretly without complaining to her husband.

They did quite well in winter too. They had taken the town theatre for the whole season, and rented it out for short engagements to a Ukrainian troupe, a conjurer, some local amateurs. Olga grew buxom and radiated happiness, while Kukin became thinner and yellower, and complained of his appalling losses though business was pretty good all winter. He coughed at night, and she would give him raspberry or lime-flower tisane, rub him with eau-de-Cologne and wrap him up in her soft shawls.

'Oh, you are such a splendid little chap,' she would say, stroking his hair and meaning every word. 'You're such a handsome little fellow.'

When he was away in Moscow in Lent recruiting a new company she couldn't sleep, but just sat by the window looking at the stars. She compared herself to a hen—they too are restless and sleepless at night without a cock in the fowl-house. Kukin was held up in Moscow. But he'd be back by Easter, he wrote, and he was already making certain plans for the Tivoli in his letters. Then, late on Palm Sunday evening, there was a sudden ominous knocking at the gate as someone pummelled it till it boomed like a barrel. Shuffling barefoot through the puddles, the sleepy cook ran to answer.

'Open up, please,' said a deep, hollow voice outside. 'A telegram for you.'

Olga had had telegrams from her husband before, but this time she nearly fainted for some reason. She opened it with trembling fingers, and read as follows:

MR KUKIN PASSED AWAY SUDDENLY TODAY
NUBSCUTCH AWAIT INSTRUCTIONS FUFERAL
TUESDAY

That's what was printed in the telegram: FUFERAL. And there

was this meaningless NUBSCUTCH too. It was signed by the operetta producer.

'My darling!' Olga sobbed. 'My lovely, darling little Vanya, oh why did I ever meet you? Why did I have to know you, love you? For whom have you forsaken your poor, miserable little Olga?'

Kukin was buried in the Vagankov Cemetery in Moscow on the Tuesday. Olga returned home on Wednesday, flopped down on her bed as soon as she reached her room, and sobbed so loudly that she could be heard out in the street and in the next-door yards.

'Poor angel!' said the ladies of the neighbourhood, crossing themselves. 'Darling Olga—she *is* taking it hard, poor dear.'

One day three months later Olga was coming dolefully back from church, in full mourning. A neighbour, Vasya Pustovalov, manager of the Babakayev timber-yard—also on his way back from church—chanced to be walking by her side. He wore a boater and a white waistcoat with a gold chain across it. He looked more like a country squire than a tradesman.

'There's always a pattern in things, Mrs. Kukin,' said he in a grave, sympathetic voice. 'The death of a dear one must be God's will, in which case we must be sensible and endure it patiently.'

He saw Olga to her gate, he said good-bye, he went his way. Afterwards she seemed to hear that grave voice all day, and she need only close her eyes to see his dark beard in her imagination. She thought him very attractive. And she must have made an impression on him, too, because not long afterwards a certain elderly lady, whom she barely knew, came to take coffee with her . . . and had hardly sat down at table before she was on about Pustovalov. What a good steady man he was, said she—any young lady would be glad to marry him. Three days later Pustovalov called in person. He only stayed about ten minutes, he hadn't much to say for himself, but Olga fell so much in love with him that she lay awake all night in a hot, feverish state. In the morning she sent for the elderly lady, the match was soon made, a wedding followed.

After their marriage the Pustovalovs lived happily. He was usually at the timber-yard till lunch. Then he would do his business errands while Olga took his place—sitting in the office till evening, keeping accounts, dispatching orders.

'Timber prices rise twenty per cent a year these days,' she would tell customers and friends. 'We used to deal in local stuff, but now—just fancy!—Vasya has to go and fetch it from out Mogilyov way every year. And what a price!' she would say, putting both hands over her cheeks in horror. 'What a price!'

She felt as if she had been a timber dealer from time immemorial. The most vital and essential thing in life was wood, she felt. And she found something deeply moving in the words joist, logging, laths, slats, scantlings, purlins, frames, slabs. When she was asleep at nights, she would dream of mountains of boards and laths, and of long, never-ending wagon trains taking timber somewhere far out of town. She dreamt of a whole battalion of posts, thirty foot by one foot, marching upright as they moved to take the timber-yard by storm. Beams, baulks, slabs clashed with the resounding thud of seasoned wood, falling down and getting up again, jamming against each other, and Olga would cry out in her sleep.

'What's the matter, Olga dear?' Pustovalov would ask tenderly, and tell her to cross herself.

She shared all her husband's thoughts. If he thought the room too hot, if he thought business slack—then she thought so as well. Her husband disliked all forms of entertainment, and stayed at home on his days off. So she did too.

'You spend all your time at home or in the office,' her friends would say. 'You should go to the theatre or the circus, angel.'

'We haven't time for theatre-going, me and Vasya,' she would answer gravely. 'We're working people, we can't be bothered with trifles. What's so wonderful about your theatres, anyway?'

The Pustovalovs attended vespers on Saturday nights. On Sundays and saints'-days they went to early service, and walked back from church side by side—with rapt expressions, both smelling sweet, her silk dress rustling agreeably. At home they drank tea with fine white bread and various jams, and then ate pasties. At noon each day their yard, and the street outside their gate, were deliciously redolent of beetroot soup, roast lamb and duck—and of fish in Lent. You couldn't pass their gate without feeling hungry. They always kept the samovar boiling in the office, and they treated their customers to tea and buns. Once a week they both went to the public baths, and they would walk back side by side, red-faced.

'We're doing all right,' Olga told her friends. 'It's a good life, praise be. God grant everyone to live like me and Vasya.'

When Pustovalov went to fetch timber from the Mogilyov district she missed him terribly, she couldn't sleep at night, and she cried. She had an occasional evening visitor in young Smirnin, an army vet who was renting her cottage. He would tell her stories or play cards with her, and this cheered her up. She was fascinated by his accounts of his own family life—he was married and had a son, but he and his wife had separated because she had been unfaithful. Now he hated her and sent her forty roubles a month for the son's keep—hearing which, Olga would sigh, shake her head and pity Smirnin.

'God bless you,' she would say as she bade him good night and lighted his way to the stairs with a candle. 'Thank you for sharing your sorrows with me. May God and the Holy Mother keep you.' She always spoke in this grave, deliberate way, imitating her husband.

Just as the vet was vanishing through the door downstairs she would call him back. 'Mr. Smirnin, you should make it up with your wife, you know. Do forgive her, if only for your son's sake—that little lad understands everything, I'll be bound.'

On Pustovalov's return she would talk in low tones about the vet and his unhappy family history. Both would sigh, shake their heads—and discuss the little boy, who probably missed his father. Then, strange as it might seem, by association of ideas both would kneel before the icons, bow to the ground and pray to God to give them children.

Thus quietly and peacefully, in love and utter harmony, the Pustovalovs spent six years. But then, one winter's day, Vasya drank some hot tea in the office, went out to dispatch some timber without his cap on, caught cold and fell ill. He was attended by all the best doctors, but the illness took its course and he died after four months' suffering. Olga had been widowed again.

'Why did you forsake me, dearest?' she sobbed after burying her husband. 'How ever can I live without you? Oh, I'm so wretched and unhappy! Pity me, good people, I'm all alone now——'

She wore a black dress with weepers, she had renounced her hat and gloves for all time, she seldom went out of the house—and then only to church or her husband's grave—she lived at home like a nun. Not until six months had passed did she remove those weepers and open the shutters. She could sometimes be seen of a morning shopping for food in the market with her cook, but how did she live now, what went on in her house? It was a matter of guesswork . . . of guesswork based—shall we say?—on her being seen having tea in her garden with the vet while he read the newspaper to her, and also on what she said when she met a lady of her acquaintance at the post-office.

'There are no proper veterinary inspections in town, which is why we have so many diseases. You keep hearing of people infected by milk and catching things from horses and cows. We should really take as much care of domestic animals' health as of people's.'

She echoed the vet's thoughts, now holding the same views on all subjects as he. That she could not live a single year without an attachment, that she had found a new happiness in her own cottage . . . so much was clear. Any other woman would have incurred censure, but no one could think ill of Olga—everything about her was so aboveboard. She and the vet told no one of the change in their relations. They tried to hide it, but failed because Olga couldn't keep a secret. When his service colleagues came to visit she would pour their tea or give them their supper, while talking about cattle plague, pearl disease and municipal slaughter-houses . . . which embarrassed him terribly. He would seize her arm as the guests left.

'Haven't I asked you not to talk about things you don't understand?' he would hiss angrily. 'Kindly don't interfere when us vets are talking shop, it really is most tiresome.'

She looked at him in consternation and alarm. 'What can I talk about then, Volodya?'

She would embrace him with tears in her eyes, she would beg him not to be angry—and they would both be happy.

Their happiness proved short-lived, though. The vet left with his regiment. And since that regiment had been posted to far-away parts —Siberia practically—he left for good. Olga was alone.

She really was alone this time. Her father had died long ago, and his old arm-chair was lying around the attic minus one leg and covered with dust. She became thin, she lost her looks. People no longer noticed her, no longer smiled at her in the street. Her best years were over and done with, obviously. A new life was beginning, an unknown life—better not think about it. Sitting on the porch of an evening, Olga could hear the band playing and the rockets bursting in the Tivoli, but that did not stimulate her thoughts. She gazed blankly at her empty yard, she thought of nothing, she wanted nothing. When night came she went to bed and dreamt about that empty yard. She did not seem to want food and drink.

The main trouble was, though, that she no longer had views on anything. She saw objects around her, yes, she did grasp what was going on. But she could not form opinions. What was she to talk about? She did not know. It's a terrible thing, that, not having opinions. You see an upright bottle, say—or rain, or a peasant in a cart. But what are

they for: that bottle, that rain, that peasant? What sense do they make?
That you couldn't say . . . not even if someone gave you a thousand
roubles, you couldn't. In the Kukin and Pustovalov eras—and then in
the vet's day—Olga could give reasons for everything, she would have
offered a view on any subject you liked. But now her mind and heart
were as empty as her empty yard. It was an unnerving, bitter sensation:
like eating a lot of wormwood.

The town has been gradually expanding on all sides. Gipsy Lane is a
'road' now. Houses have mushroomed and a set of side-streets has
sprung up where once Tivoli and timber-yard stood. How time does
fly! Olga's house looks dingy, her roof has rusted, her shed is lop-sided,
her entire premises are deep in weeds and stinging nettles. Olga herself
looks older, uglier. In summer she sits on her porch with the same old
heartache and emptiness, there is the same old taste of wormwood. In
winter she sits by her window looking at the snow. If she scents the
spring air, or hears the peal of cathedral bells borne on the breeze,
memories suddenly overwhelm her, she feels a delicious swooning
sensation, tears well from her eyes. It lasts only a minute, though.
Then the old emptiness returns, and life loses all meaning. Her black
cat Bryska rubs up against his mistress, purring gently, but these feline
caresses leave Olga cold. She needs a bit more than that! She needs a
love to possess her whole being, all her mind and soul: a love to equip
her with ideas, with a sense of purpose, a love to warm her ageing
blood. She irritably shakes black Bryska off her lap. 'Away with you,
you're not wanted here.'

So day follows day, year follows year: a life without joy, without
opinions. Whatever her cook Mavra says goes.

Late one warm July afternoon, as the town cows are being driven
down the street, filling the whole yard with dust clouds, there is a
sudden knock at the gate. Olga opens it herself, looks out—and is
dumbfounded. At the gate stands veterinary surgeon Smirnin—now
grey-haired and wearing civilian clothes. It all comes back to her
at once and she breaks down and cries, laying her head on his
chest without a word. She is so shaken that they have both gone
into the house and sat down to tea before she has realized what is
happening.

'Dearest Volodya,' she mutters, trembling with joy. 'What brings
you here?'

'I want to settle down here for good,' he tells her. 'I've resigned and
I want to try my luck as a civilian—want to put down some roots.

Besides, it's time my son went to school, he's a big boy now. I've made it up with my wife, you know.'

Olga asked where she was.

'She's at a hotel with the boy while I look for somewhere to live.'

'Goodness me, then why not take *my* house, dear? It would be ideal for you! Oh, for heaven's sake, I wouldn't *charge* you anything.'

Overcome by emotion, Olga burst out crying again. 'You can live here and I'll manage in the cottage. Goodness, how marvellous!'

Next day they were already painting the roof and whitewashing the walls, while Olga strode up and down the yard, arms akimbo, seeing to everything. Her old smile shone on her face, but she was like a new woman—she seemed as fresh as if she had woken up after a long sleep. The vet's wife arrived—a thin, plain woman with short hair and a petulant expression—bringing little Sasha. He was small for his age (nine), he was chubby, he had bright blue eyes and dimpled cheeks. And no sooner had that boy set foot in the yard than he was off chasing the cat. His cheerful, merry laughter rang out.

'Is that your cat, Aunty?' he asked Olga. 'When it has babies, may we have one, please? Mummy's so scared of mice.'

Olga talked to him and gave him tea. She suddenly felt warm inside, and a delicious faintness came over her, just as if he was her own son. When he sat in the dining-room of an evening doing his homework she would gaze at him with loving pity.

'My darling, my little beauty, my child,' she would whisper. 'What a clever little, pale little fellow you are.'

'An island,' he read out, 'is a piece of land entirely surrounded by water.'

'An island is a piece of land—' she repeated. This, after so many years' silence and empty-headedness, was her first confidently expressed opinion.

Yes, she now had opinions of her own. At supper she would tell Sasha's parents how hard schoolchildren had to work these days. Better, even so, to have a classical than a modern education because the classical curriculum opens all doors. Doctor, engineer . . . you can take your pick.

After Sasha had started going to school his mother went to her sister's in Kharkov and did not return. His father was off every day inspecting cattle, and there were times when he was away from home for three days on end. They were completely neglecting Sasha, Olga felt—he wasn't wanted in the house, he was dying of starvation. So she moved him to her cottage and fixed him up with his own little room.

Now Sasha has been living in the cottage for six months. Every morning Olga goes to his room and finds him sound asleep with his hand beneath his cheek—not breathing, apparently. It seems a pity to wake him up.

'Get up, Sasha darling,' she says sadly. 'Time for school.'

He gets up, dresses, says his prayers, sits down to breakfast. He drinks three glasses of tea, he eats two large rolls, half a French loaf and butter. He is still not quite awake, and so is in rather a bad mood.

'That fable, Sasha—' says Olga. 'You didn't learn it properly.' She looks at him as though she is seeing him off on a long journey. 'Oh, you *are* such a handful! You *must* try and learn, dear, you must do what teacher says.'

'Oh, don't bother me, please!' replies Sasha.

Then he starts off down the street to school: a small boy in a large cap, satchel on back. Olga follows him silently.

'Sasha, dear,' she calls.

He looks round and she puts a date or caramel in his hand. When they turn off into the school road he feels ashamed of being followed by a tall, stout woman. He looks round.

'Go home, Aunty,' says he. 'I'll make my own way now.'

She stands and watches without taking her eyes off him until he disappears up the school drive. How she loves him! None of her earlier attachments has been so profound, never before has her innermost being surrendered as wholeheartedly, as unselfishly, as joyfully as it does now that her maternal feelings are increasingly welling up inside her. For this boy—no relative at all—for his dimpled cheeks, for his cap she would give her whole life, give it gladly, with tears of ecstasy. Why? Who knows?

After taking Sasha to school she goes home quietly—contented, at peace, overflowing with love. Her face glows—she has been looking younger these last six months—and she smiles. It is a pleasure to see her.

'Hallo, Olga, angel,' people say when they meet her. 'How are you, angel?'

'They do work schoolchildren so hard these days,' she says in the market. 'No, seriously—the First Form had to learn a whole fable by heart yesterday. *And* do a Latin translation. Sums too. It's too much for a little lad.'

What she says about teachers, lessons and textbooks . . . it's all pure
Sasha!

At about half past two they lunch together, and in the evening
they do Sasha's homework together, weeping. Putting him to bed, she
makes the sign of the cross over him at great length, whispering a
prayer. Then she goes to bed herself, and she dreams of that future—
vague, far distant—when Sasha will take his degree and become a
doctor or engineer . . . when he will own his own big house, his
horses and carriage, when he will marry and have children.

Still thinking these same thoughts, she falls asleep. From her closed
eyes tears course down her cheeks, and the black cat lies purring by
her side.

Then, suddenly, there is a loud knock on the garden gate and Olga
wakes up, too scared to breathe, her heart pounding. Half a minute
passes, there is a second knock.

'A telegram from Kharkov,' thinks she, trembling all over. 'Sasha's
mother wants him in Kharkov. Oh, goodness me!'

She is in despair. Her head, hands and feet are cold, and she feels as
if she's the most unhappy person in the world. But another minute
passes, voices are heard. It's the vet coming back from his club.

'Oh, thank God,' she thinks.

Her anxiety gradually subsides and she can relax again. She lies down
and thinks of Sasha: deep in slumber in the next room, and occasionally
talking in his sleep.

'You watch out!' he says. 'You go away! Don't you pick quarrels
with me!'

NEW VILLA

[Новая дача]

(1899)

NEW VILLA

I

A HUGE bridge was under construction two miles from Obruchanovo village. From the village, which stood high on a steep bank, the trellised skeleton could be seen: a picturesque—indeed, a fantastic—sight in misty weather and on quiet winter days, when the thin iron struts and all the surrounding scaffolding were frost-covered. Engineer Kucherov, who was building the bridge—a stout, broad-shouldered, bearded man with a crumpled soft cap—sometimes drove through the village in a fast droshky or carriage. Sometimes the navvies employed on the bridge came along on their days off—begged for money, jeered at the local women, occasionally absconded with something. That was exceptional, though. Usually the days passed as quietly and uneventfully as if no construction was in progress at all. Only in the evenings, when bonfires blazed near the bridge, was the navvies' singing borne faintly on the breeze. In daytime there was an occasional sad, metallic clanking.

Mrs. Kucherov, the engineer's wife, chanced to come over on a visit. Much taken with the river banks and the gorgeous view of the green valley with its hamlets, churches and cattle, she asked her husband to buy a small plot of land and build a villa. He did. They bought fifty acres, and on the high bank, in a meadow where once the village cows had strayed, they put up a handsome two-storey house with terrace, balconies, tower . . . and a spire which flew a flag on Sundays. After building it in about three months they planted large trees through the winter. Then, when spring came with all the fresh greenery, the new garden already had its paths. A gardener and his two white-aproned assistants dug near the house, a fountain played and a globe made of looking-glass gleamed so fiercely that it hurt the eyes. The estate already had its name: New Villa.

One fine warm morning at the end of May two horses were brought to Obruchanovo for shoeing by the local blacksmith, Rodion Petrov. They came from New Villa, they were snow-white, graceful, well-fed, and they bore a striking resemblance to each other.

'Like swans, they are,' said Rodion, awe-struck.

His wife Stepanida, his children, his grand-children . . . all came out of doors to see, and a crowd gradually collected. The Lychkovs, father and son—both naturally beardless, both puffy-faced and hatless—came along. So did Kozov: a tall, scraggy old boy with a long, narrow beard, carrying a walking-stick. He kept winking sly winks and smiling sardonic, knowing smiles.

'They're white, but they're no good,' said he. 'Put mine on oats, and they'd be just as sleek. I'd make 'em plough—whip 'em too.'

The coachman just gave him a look of scorn and said nothing. Then, as the smithy furnace was heated up, the coachman talked and smoked cigarettes. The villagers learnt many details. His master and mistress were rich. Before her marriage the mistress, Helen Kucherov, had been a poor governess in Moscow. She was kind, she was soft-hearted, she liked helping the poor. There was to be no ploughing or sowing on the new estate, said he. They were just going to enjoy themselves— breathing fresh air, that was their sole aim in life.

When he had finished and started leading the horses back home, a crowd of urchins followed him. Dogs barked. Kozov watched him go, winking sarcastically.

'Think they own everything!' he jeered. 'They build a house, they keep horses—but they're the lowest of the low, believe you me. Think they're the lords of creation, do they?'

Kozov had somehow conceived an immediate loathing for the new estate, for those white horses, for that sleek, handsome coachman. He was a lonely man, was Kozov, a widower. He led a dull life—couldn't work because of some illness: 'me rheumatics' he would call it, or 'the worms'. The money for his keep came from a son who worked at a Kharkov confectioner's. He would stroll idly along the river bank or village from dawn to dusk. If he saw someone carting a log, say —or fishing—he would tell him that his wood was 'dry, rotten stuff', or that he would 'never catch anything on a day like this'. During droughts he would say that there would be no rain before the frosts came, and when it did rain he would say that the crops would all rot, they were all ruined. And he would wink knowingly the while.

On the estate Bengal lights and rockets were set off in the evenings, and a boat with red lamps would sail past Obruchanovo. One morning the engineer's wife, Helen Kucherov, brought her little daughter to the village in a yellow-wheeled trap drawn by a pair of dark bay ponies. Mother and daughter both wore broad-brimmed straw hats turned down over their ears.

This happened at mucking-out time, and Blacksmith Rodion—a

tall, scraggy, bare-headed, barefoot old man with a pitchfork over his shoulder—stood near his nasty, dirty cart, staring flabbergasted at those ponies. He had never seen such small horses in his life . . . that was written on his face.

'Look at 'er in the trap!' the whisper was heard on all sides. 'It's that there Kucherov woman.'

Scanning the huts quizzically, Helen Kucherov halted her horses near the poorest of all, where there were masses of children's heads—fair, dark, red—in the windows. Out of the hut ran Rodion's wife, Stepanida, a stout old girl, her kerchief slipping off her grey hair. She peered at the trap against the sun, smiling and frowning like a blind person.

'This is for your children, my good woman,' said Helen Kucherov. And gave her three roubles.

Suddenly bursting into tears, Stepanida bowed to the ground, while Rodion too flopped down, showing his broad, brown pate and almost catching his wife in the side with his pitchfork. Helen Kucherov felt awkward and went home.

II

The Lychkovs, father and son, caught two cart-horses straying in their meadow, together with one pony and a broad-muzzled Aalhaus bull-calf. These they drove off to the village, helped by 'Ginger' Volodka—Blacksmith Rodion's son. They called the village elder, they collected witnesses, they went to assess the damage.

'Very well, let 'em try it on!' Kozov winked. 'Just let 'em try, that's all. Let's see them engineers wriggle out of this! Think themselves above the law, do they? Very well, we'll send for the sergeant, make out a charge.'

'Make out a charge,' echoed Volodka.

'I ain't a-going to overlook it,' shouted the younger Lychkov. His voice sounded louder and louder, seeming to make his beardless face bulge increasingly. 'A fine to-do, this is! Ruin all the pasture, they will, if we let 'em! They ain't got no right to harm the common man. We ain't living in the dark ages.'

'No, that we ain't,' echoed Volodka.

'We've got on without a bridge so far,' said Lychkov Senior gloomily. 'We never asked for one, we don't need one and we won't 'ave one!'

'They ain't getting away with this, mates!'

'Just let 'em try it on!' winked Kozov. 'Let 'em squirm! Who do they think they are?'

They turned back towards the village, and as they went Lychkov Junior pounded his chest with his fist, shouting, while Volodka also shouted, echoing his words. Meanwhile, in the village, a crowd had formed round the pedigree bull-calf and horses. The calf glowered in embarrassment, but suddenly dropped his head to the ground and ran, kicking up his back legs. Taking fright, Kozov swung his stick and everyone laughed. Then they locked the animals up and waited.

That evening the engineer sent five roubles in compensation, whereupon both horses, pony and bull-calf returned home: unfed, unwatered, hanging their heads in guilt as if on their way to execution.

Having received the five roubles, the Lychkovs Senior and Junior, the village elder and Volodka crossed the river by boat, set off for Kryakovo village on the other side, where there was a pub, and spent a long time whooping it up. Their singing and young Lychkov's shouting were heard. Back at the village the women couldn't sleep all night for worrying. Nor could Rodion.

'A bad business,' he sighed, tossing from side to side. 'He'll have the law on 'em, will Squire, if he be vexed. They done him wrong, oh, that they have. A bad business.'

One day the men, Rodion included, went into their wood to decide who should reap what plot of land. On their way home they met the engineer. He wore a red calico shirt and high boots, he was followed by a setter with its long tongue stuck out.

'Good day, my lads,' said he.

The peasants stopped, doffed their caps.

'I've been wanting to talk to you for some time, lads,' he went on. 'The thing is, your cattle have been in my garden and woods every day since early spring. It's all been trampled up. Your pigs have dug up the meadow, they're ruining the vegetable plot, and I've lost all the saplings in my wood. I can't get on with your shepherds, they bite your head off if you ask them anything. You trespass on my land every day, but I do nothing, I don't get you fined, I don't complain. Now you've taken my horses and bull—*and* my five roubles.

'Is it fair, is it neighbourly?' he went on, his voice soft and pleading, his glance anything but stern. 'Is this how decent men behave? One of you cut down two young oaks in my wood a week ago. You've dug up the Yeresnevo road, and now I have to go two miles out of my way. Why are you always injuring me? What harm have I done you?

For God's sake tell me. My wife and I have tried our level best to live in peace and harmony with you—we help the village as much as we can. My wife is a kind, warm-hearted woman, she doesn't refuse to help—she longs to be useful to you and your children. But you repay good with evil. You are unfair, my friends. Now, you just think it over, I beg you—think it over. We're treating you decently, so why can't you pay us back in the same coin?'

He turned and walked off. The peasants stood a little longer, put their hats on, and left. Rodion—who misinterpreted everything, always putting his own twist on things—gave a sigh.

'We'll have to pay, says he. Pay in coin, mates.'

They walked to the village in silence. At home Rodion said his prayers, took his boots off, and sat on the bench beside his wife. Stepanida and he always did sit side by side at home, and they always walked down the street side by side. They always ate, drank and slept together, and the more they aged the more they loved each other. It was hot and crowded in their hut, and there were children everywhere: on floor, window-ledges and stove.

Stepanida was still having babies despite her advanced years, and it was hard to tell which, in that huddle of children, were Rodion's and which Volodka's. Volodka's wife Lukerya—an ill-favoured young woman with bulging eyes and a beaky nose—was mixing dough in a tub. Her husband sat on the stove, feet dangling.

'On the road near Nikita's buckwheat, er . . . the engineer and his dog,' began Rodion after resting and scratching his sides and elbows. 'We must pay, says he. In coin, he says. I dunno about no coins, but ten copecks a hut—that we should collect. We're treating Squire right badly, we are. 'Tis a shame——'

'We've done without a bridge so far,' said Volodka, looking at no one. 'We don't want no bridge.'

'Oh, get away with you! 'Tis a government bridge.'

'We don't want none of it.'

'Who asked you? What's it got to do with you?'

' "Who asked you?" ' mimicked Volodka. 'We have nowhere to go, so what do we want with a bridge? We can cross by boat if we want.'

Someone outside banged the window so loudly that the whole hut seemed to shake.

'Volodka in?' said the voice of Lychkov Junior. 'Come out, Volodka. On our way!'

Volodka jumped down from the stove, looked for his cap.

'Don't go, Volodka,' Rodion said nervously. 'Don't go with them, son. You're such a silly boy, you're a proper baby, and they won't teach you no good. Don't go.'

'Don't go, son,' begged Stepanida, blinking on the brink of tears. 'They want to take you to the pub, I'll be bound.'

' "To the pub",' Volodka mimicked.

'You'll come back drunk again, you filthy hell-hound.' Lukerya gave him an angry look. 'You go! And may the vodka rot your guts, you blasted tailless wonder!'

'You hold your tongue!' Volodka shouted.

'I'm married to a half-wit, my life's been ruined—oh, I'm so alone and unhappy! You ginger-haired sot!' lamented Lukerya, wiping her face with a dough-covered hand. 'I wish I'd never set eyes on you.'

Volodka hit her on the ear and left.

III

Helen Kucherov and her little daughter went for a stroll and arrived in the village on foot. It happened to be a Sunday, and the women and girls were out and about in their bright dresses. Sitting side by side on their porch, Rodion and Stepanida gave Helen and her little girl a friendly bow and smile, while over a dozen children watched them from the windows, their faces expressing bafflement and curiosity. Whispering was heard.

'It's that there Kucherov woman.'

'Good morning,' said Helen and stopped.

'Well, how are you?' she asked after a pause.

'Can't complain, praise be,' answered Rodion rapidly. 'We manage, that's true enough.'

'Oh, it's no end of a life, lady, ours is,' Stepanida laughed. 'You can see how poor we are, love. We've fourteen in the family, and only two at work. It ain't much of a trade, a smith's ain't. People bring their horses for shoeing, but there's no coal—we can't afford it. It's a terrible life, lady,' she went on with a laugh. ''Tis a proper botheration!'

Helen sat on the porch and put her arms broodily round her little girl. The child too looked as if she was subject to gloomy musings, and pensively played with the smart lace parasol which she had taken from her mother.

'We're so poor,' said Rodion. 'We have lots of trouble and no end of work. And now God won't send us rain. It's a rotten life, that's plain enough.'

'You suffer in this life,' said Helen. 'But you'll be happy in the next.'

Not understanding, Rodion only coughed into his fist.

'The rich are well off, lady,' said Stepanida. 'Even in the next world they are, love. Your rich man pays for his church candles, he has his special services held. And he gives to the poor, does the rich man. But your peasant hasn't time to make the sign of the cross over his forehead, even. He's poor as a church mouse—so how *can* he save his soul? It makes for a mort of sinning, does poverty. Oh, it's a dog's life, ours —sheer howling misery, I call it! We've a good word for no one, missus. And the goings-on round here, love—well, all I say is, God 'elp us! There's no happiness for us in this world *or* the next. The rich have took it all.'

She spoke good-humouredly, obviously long accustomed to retailing her miseries. Rodion smiled too. He liked feeling that his old woman was so clever, that she had the gift of the gab.

'The rich aren't really so well off, appearances are deceptive,' said Helen. 'Everyone has some trouble or other. Now, we—my husband and I—don't live poorly, we do have means. But are we happy? I'm still young, but I have four children already. They're always ill. I'm ill too—I'm always seeing the doctor.'

'What's the matter with you then?' Rodion asked.

'It's a woman's complaint. I can't sleep, I'm plagued by headaches. Here I sit talking to you, but my head feels rotten, my body's weak all over, and I'd rather do the hardest labour than be in such a state. I'm worried too. You fear for your children and your husband all the time. Every family has some trouble or other, and we have ours. I'm not really a lady. My grandfather was an ordinary peasant, and my father a Moscow tradesman—so he was lower class too. But my husband has rich, well-connected parents. They didn't want him to marry me, but he disobeyed them, quarrelled with them. And they still haven't forgiven us. This bothers my husband—upsets him, makes him edgy all the time. He loves his mother, loves her very much. So I'm upset too, my feelings are hurt.'

Near Rodion's hut men and women now stood around listening. Up came Kozov. He halted, shook his long narrow beard. Up came the Lychkovs, father and son.

'And another thing—you can't be happy and contented if you feel out of place,' went on Helen. 'Each of you has his plot of land—you all

work, and you do know what you're working for. My husband
builds bridges. Everyone has his own job, in other words. But I just
drift, I have no bit of land, I don't work, I feel out of it. I'm telling you
all this so you shan't judge from appearances. If a person has expensive
clothes, and is well off, it doesn't follow that he's contented with his
lot.'

She got up to go away, taking her daughter's hand.

'I do like being with you here,' she smiled: a feeble, timid smile
which showed how unwell she really was—and how young and pretty.
She had a pale, thin face, dark brows and fair hair. The little girl was
just like her mother: thin, fair-haired, slender. They smelt of scent.

'I like the river, the woods, the village,' Helen went on. 'I could
spend all my life here. I feel as if I could get well here, and find a place
in life. I want, I do so much want, to help you: to be useful and close
to you. I know how poor you are, and what I don't know I can feel
and sense by instinct. I'm ill and weak myself—perhaps it's too late
for me, now, to change my life as I should like. But I do have children,
and I shall try to educate them to know you and like you. I shall always
impress on them that their lives belong to you, not to themselves. But
I beg most earnestly, I implore you—do trust us, do live in friendship
with us. My husband is a good, kind man. Don't upset and irritate him.
He's so sensitive to every trifle. Take yesterday—your cattle got into
our vegetable garden, and one of you broke the fence by our bee-
hives. It's your attitude to us . . . it drives my husband frantic.

'I beg you,' she pleaded, crossing her hands on her breast, 'do please
be good neighbours, do let us live in peace. A bad truce is better than a
good war, they say, and it's always neighbours you buy rather than a
house. My husband is, I repeat, a good, kind man. If all goes well we'll
do our utmost, I promise you: we'll mend roads, we'll build a school
for your children. You have my promise.'

'We thanks you kindly, lady—stands to reason,' said Lychkov
Senior, looking at the ground. 'You're educated, like, and you know
what's best. It's just that a rich villager—name of "Raven" Voronov—
once said he'd build a school in Yeresnevo, like. He too kept saying
he'd give this and he'd give that. But all he did was put up the framework and walk out. Them peasants had to build the roof and finish it
off—a thousand roubles, it cost 'em. Raven didn't care, just stroked his
beard—but it was kind of hard on the lads.'

'That was Master Raven's doing,' winked Kozov. 'Now it's Mrs.
Rook's turn!'

Laughter was heard.

'We don't need no school,' said Volodka gloomily. 'Our kids go to Petrovskoye. Let 'em! We don't want one.'

Helen suddenly felt nervous. She blenched, her face looked pinched, she flinched as at the touch of something coarse, and she went off without another word. She walked faster and faster without looking round.

'Lady,' called Rodion, going after her. 'Wait a moment, missus, I want to talk to you.'

He followed her, hatless. 'I've something to say, missus,' he told her quietly, as if begging for alms.

They left the village, and Helen stopped in the shadow of an old mountain-ash near somebody's cart.

'Don't you take offence, missus,' said Rodion. 'Don't you take no notice. Just have patience, put up with things for a couple of years. Stay on here and put up with it, it'll be all right. We're decent, quiet folk. The peasants are all right, I'll take my oath. Never mind Kozov and the Lychkovs, never mind my Volodka—that boy's an idiot, listens to the first that speaks. The rest are peaceable, quiet folk. One or two of them wouldn't mind putting in a good word and standing up for you, like, but they can't. They have feelings and consciences, but they ain't got no tongues. Don't you take offence, you just put up with it. What does it matter?'

Helen looked pensively at the broad, calm river, tears streaming down her cheeks. Embarrassed by her weeping, Rodion almost wept himself.

'Don't you take no notice,' he muttered. 'Put up with it for a couple of years. We can have the school and the roads—but not just yet. Suppose you wanted to sow crops on this hillock, say. You'd first have to grub up the roots and pick out all the stones. Then you'd plough it—for ever a-coming and a-going you'd be. Folk are the same, like, there's a lot of coming and going before you get things to rights.'

A crowd detached itself from Rodion's hut, and moved off up the road towards the mountain-ash. They began singing, an accordion struck up. They kept coming nearer and nearer.

'Do let's leave here, Mother,' said the little girl—pale, huddling up to her mother and trembling all over. 'Let's go away!'

'Where to?'

'Moscow. Let's go away, Mother.'

The child burst into tears. Rodion, his face sweating profusely, was utterly taken aback. He removed a cucumber from his pocket—a little, twisted, crescent-shaped cucumber covered with rye crumbs—and thrust it into the girl's hands.

'There there,' he muttered, frowning sternly. 'Take the cucumber and eat it, dear. Don't cry, now, or Mummy will smack you—she'll tell your father of you. There, there.'

They walked off. He followed, wanting to say something kind and persuasive. Then, seeing that both were too engrossed in their thoughts and grief to notice him, he stopped. Shielding his eyes from the sun, he watched them for a while until they vanished into their wood.

IV

The engineer had evidently grown irritable and niggling, now seeing in every trifle some act of robbery or other outrage. He kept his gates bolted even in daytime, and at night two watchmen patrolled his garden beating boards. He hired no more labour from Obruchanovo. And then, as ill luck would have it, someone—peasant or navvy, no one knew which—took the new wheels off his cart and replaced them with old ones. A little later two bridles and a pair of tongs were taken, and murmurs were heard even in the village. The Lychkovs' place and Volodka's ought to be searched, it was said. But then both tongs and bridles turned up under the engineer's garden hedge, where someone had thrown them.

Going from the wood one day, a crowd of peasants met the engineer on the road again. He stopped without saying good day.

'I have asked you not to pick mushrooms in my park and near my place, but to leave them for my wife and children,' said he, looking angrily from one to the other. 'But your girls come before dawn, and we're left without any. Whatever we ask or don't ask, it makes no difference. Pleading, kindness, persuasion . . . they're all useless, I see.'

He fixed his indignant gaze on Rodion.

'My wife and I have treated you as human beings, as equals,' he went on. 'But what about you? Oh—what's the use of talking? We shall end up looking *down* on you, very likely—what else can we do?'

Making an effort to keep his temper, in case he said too much, he turned on his heel and marched off.

Rodion went home, prayed, took his boots off, sat on his bench beside his wife.

'Aye,' said he when he was rested. 'We're walking along just now, and there's Squire Kucherov coming our way. Aye! He saw them girls at dawn. Why, says he, don't they pick some mushrooms for my wife and children? Then he looks at me. "Me and the wife, we're a-going to look *after* you," says he. I want to fall down at his feet, but I don't make so bold. God save him, Lord bless him——'

Stepanida crossed herself and sighed.

'Squire and his lady are so nice and kind, like,' Rodion went on. ' "We shall look after you"—he promises me that before them all. In our old age, er—. Not a bad thing, either—. I'd always remember them in my prayers. Holy Mother, bless him——'

The Fourteenth of September—the Feast of the Exaltation of the Cross—was the local church festival. After going over the river in the morning, Lychkov Senior and Lychkov Junior came back towards afternoon drunk. They lurched about the village for a while, singing and swapping obscenities, they had a fight, and they went up to the manor to complain. First Lychkov Senior entered the grounds carrying a long aspen stick. He halted indecisively, doffed his cap.

'What do you want?' shouted the engineer, who happened to be having tea on the terrace with his family.

'Begging your pardon, Squire,' began Lychkov, bursting into tears. 'Have mercy on me, sir—don't let me down. My son'll be the death of me. Ruined me, he has. He's always picking on me, sir——'

In came Lychkov Junior, hatless, also carrying a stick. He paused, he fixed a drunken, mindless stare on the terrace.

'It's not my job to deal with you,' said the engineer. 'Go and see the police, go to the magistrate.'

'I've been everywhere, I've made me applications,' said Lychkov Senior, sobbing. 'Where can I turn now? He can murder me now, I suppose. Do anything he likes, can he? And to his father? His own father?'

He raised his stick and hit his son on the head. Then Junior raised *his* stick and struck the old man straight on his bald pate so hard that the stick actually rebounded. Without so much as a wince, Lychkov *père* again hit Junior, again on the head. They just stood there clouting each other on the head—it looked more like some game than a fight. Massing beyond the gates, village men and women stared silently into the yard, all looking very serious. They had come to offer their holiday greetings, but when they saw the Lychkovs they were too ashamed to go in.

Next morning Helen left for Moscow with her children, and rumour had it that the engineer had put his house up for sale.

V

The bridge has long been a familiar sight—it is hard, now, to imagine this bit of river without its bridge. The heaps of building rubble have long been covered with grass, the navvies are a thing of the past, and instead of their shanties the noise of a passing train is heard almost hourly.

New Villa was sold long ago. It belongs, now, to a civil servant who brings his family over on his days off, has tea on his terrace and drives back to town. He wears a cockade on his cap, he talks and coughs like a bureaucrat of consequence, whereas in fact he's very much of a junior. When the villagers bow to him he makes no reply.

Everyone in Obruchanovo has aged. Kozov has died, Rodion has even more children in his hut, Volodka has grown a long ginger beard. They are just as poor as ever.

Early one spring the Obruchanovites are sawing wood near the station. See them going home after work: walking slowly, in single file. The wide saws sway on their shoulders, reflecting sunlight. Nightingales sing in the bushes on the river's bank, larks trill in the sky. At New Villa all is quiet, not a soul is to be seen—nothing but golden pigeons . . . golden because they are flying in the sunshine high above the house. Everyone—Rodion, both Lychkovs, Volodka—remembers white horses, little ponies, fireworks, lamp-lit boat. They remember the engineer's wife, so handsome and elegant, coming to the village, speaking to them so kindly. Yet none of it might ever have happened, it is all like a dream or legend.

They trudge along wearily, pensively.

We're decent, quiet, reasonable, god-fearing folk in the village, they reflect. Helen Kucherov had been a quiet, kind, gentle person too—you couldn't help liking her, poor thing. So why had they been on such bad terms, why had they parted as enemies? What was this mist which veiled everything of real importance, while disclosing only such trifles as trespass, bridles, tongs? Such nonsense it all seems when you remember it now! How is it that they can get on with the new owner when they were on such bad terms with the engineer?

Knowing no answer to these questions, they remain silent. Only Volodka mutters something.

'What's that?' asks Rodion.

'We've managed without a bridge,' says Volodka gloomily. 'We never asked for no bridge and we don't need none.'

No one answers. They trudge on silently, heads bowed.

ON OFFICIAL BUSINESS

[По делам службы]

(1899)

ON OFFICIAL BUSINESS

AN acting coroner and a country doctor were on their way to hold an inquest in the village of Syrnya when they were overtaken by a snowstorm. For a while they went round in circles, and instead of turning up (as intended) at noon they did not arrive until evening, when it was dark. They were to stay the night in a hut, the rural district council 'offices'. Now, it chanced that these same 'offices' housed the corpse: that of the council's insurance representative Lesnitsky, who had reached Syrnya three days earlier, settled down in the hut, ordered a samovar and shot himself much to everyone's surprise. The strange manner of his end—over that samovar, after he had spread his food out on the table—had given rise to widespread suspicions of murder. An inquest there must be.

Doctor and coroner shook the snow off in the passage, stamping their feet, while the elderly village constable, Eli Loshadin, stood near them holding a light: a tin lamp. There was a stink of paraffin.

'Who are you, my man?' asked the doctor.

'Conshtible,' answered the constable. That was how he signed his name in the post-office: conshtible.

'And where are the witnesses?'

'Gone for their tea, sir, I reckon.'

On the right was the parlour, or 'reception'—for persons of genteel rank—and on the left was the room for the vulgar, with its big stove and its shelf for sleeping on. Doctor and coroner, followed by the constable with the lamp above his head, went into 'reception'. Here, on the floor close to the table legs, a long, white-shrouded body lay stock still. Besides that white covering the dim lamp-light clearly showed some new rubber galoshes. It was all very eerie and nasty: the dark walls, the silence, those galoshes, the stillness of the corpse. On the table was the samovar, long cold, and around it were certain packets—the food, presumably.

'Shooting himself on council property—very tactless, that,' said the doctor. 'If he wanted to put a bullet through his brains he might have done it at home in some shed or other.'

Just as he was—in fur cap, fur coat, felt boots—he lowered himself on to the bench. His companion the coroner sat opposite.

'They're so selfish, these hysterical neurotics,' the doctor went on sadly. 'When a neurotic sleeps in the same room as you, he'll rustle a newspaper. When you dine together he'll start a row with his wife without minding you. And when he fancies shooting himself he does it like this: in a village, on official premises, just to create as much trouble as possible. No matter where they are they think only of Number One, these birds do—oh, they're a selfish lot. That's why old folk so dislike what they call this "nervous" age.'

'Old folk dislike so many things,' yawned the coroner. 'Why don't you tell the older generation about the difference between suicides as they used to be and as they are today? In the old days your gentleman, so-called, would shoot himself because he'd embezzled public money, but your present-day suicide does it because he's fed up with life and depressed. Which is better?'

'The fed-up-and-depressed brigade. Still, he didn't have to shoot himself on council property, now, did he?'

'Oh it's real vexing—more than flesh and blood can stand,' said the constable. 'The peasants are very upset, sir, they haven't slept these three nights. Their kids are crying. Their cows need milking, but the women are scared to go to the shed—afraid they'll see the gent's ghost in the dark. They're just silly women, I know, but there's some of the men scared too. They won't pass this hut on their own of an evening, they all troop by in a bunch. Them witnesses are the same.'

Middle-aged, dark-bearded, bespectacled Dr. Starchenko and Coroner Lyzhin—fair-haired, quite young, having taken his degree only two years previously and looking more like a student than an official—sat deep in silent thought. They were annoyed at arriving late. Now they had to wait till morning and spend the night here, but it wasn't even six o'clock yet, and they were faced with a long evening followed by a long, dark night, boredom, uncomfortable sleeping arrangements, cockroaches and the cold of early morning. Harking to the blizzard howling in chimney and loft, both thought how far this was from the life which they would have chosen, and of which they had once dreamed. How little they resembled their contemporaries who were now strolling down brightly-lit town streets not noticing the bad weather, who were getting ready for the theatre or sitting over books in their studies. What they would have given, now, just to stroll along the Nevsky Prospekt in St. Petersburg or down Moscow's Petrovka Street, to listen to decent singing, to spend an hour or so in a restaurant!

The blizzard whined and droned in the loft, there was a furious slamming outside: the office signboard, no doubt.

'I don't know about you, but I don't want to spend the night here.' Starchenko stood up. 'It's not six yet, it's too early for bed, so I'm off. There's a von Taunitz lives near by, only a couple of miles from Syrnya. I'll drive over for the evening. Constable, go and tell our driver not to take the horses out.'

'Now, what about you?' he asked Lyzhin.

'I don't know. I'll go to sleep, I suppose.'

The doctor wrapped his fur coat round him and went out. He was heard talking to the driver. Sleigh-bells jingled on cold horses. He drove off.

'It ain't right for you to sleep here, mister,' said the constable. 'You go in the other room. It ain't clean, but that won't matter for one night. I'll just get a samovar from the caretaker and put it on. Then I'll make a pile of this here hay for you, sir, and you can have a nice sleep.'

A little later the coroner was sitting in the other room drinking tea while Constable Loshadin stood by the door talking. He was an old man: turned sixty, short, very thin, hunched, pale, with a naïve smile and watery eyes. And he was for ever smacking his lips as if sucking sweets. He wore a short sheepskin coat and felt boots, he always held a stick. He was evidently touched by the coroner's youth, which must be why he spoke to him in this familiar way.

'Old Theodore, the gaffer on the parish council . . . he told me to report when the police inspector or the coroner arrived,' he said. 'Oh well, I suppose I must be on my way. It's nearly three miles to his place, there's a blizzard and there's drifts. Proper awful it is—I won't get there before midnight, belike. Hark at that howling!'

'I don't need your gaffer,' said Lyzhin. 'There's nothing for him to do here.'

He looked at the old man inquisitively. 'I say, old fellow, how long have you been constable round here?'

'How long? Why, thirty year, it must be. Five years after the serfs were freed I started the job, so you can reckon it yourself. Since then I've been at it every day. Others have their holidays, but I never have no day off. It may be Easter over there, with church bells ringing and Christ getting Himself resurrected, but I'm doing me rounds with me little bag. I go to the accounts department, the post-office, the police inspector's place. I visit the magistrate, the tax man, the town hall, the ladies and gentlemen, the peasants and all other god-fearing Russian folks. I carry parcels, notices, tax papers, letters, all sorts of forms, registers. These days, my dear good sir, there's all these form things—red, white, yellow—what you write figures on. Every squire, parson and rich villager must write down a dozen times a year what he's sown and reaped, how many bushels or hundredweight of rye he has, how much oats and hay—and also about the weather, different insects and that. They put down what they please, of course—it's only a form—but it's me as has to go round handing out them bits of paper and then go round again collecting them. Now, take this dead gentleman here. There ain't no call to cut his guts out—there's no point, as you know yourself, it's only dirtying your hands for nothing. But you've been put to this trouble—you've come out here—because of them forms, sir. It can't be helped. Thirty year I've been traipsing round with forms. Summer's all right, it's warm and dry—but in winter or autumn it's a nuisance. I've known times when I near drowned and froze, there's nothing as hasn't happened to me. There was that time when some villains stole me bag in a wood and beat me up. And I've been had up in court——'

'What ever for?'

'Fraud.'

'What do you mean, fraud?'

'Well, what happened is, our clerk—Khrisanf Grigoryev—sells a contractor some boards as weren't his . . . cheats him, like. I'm there when it's going on, and they send me out to the pub for some vodka. Well, the clerk doesn't cut me in—never even offers me a glass—but seeing as I'm poor and don't look reliable, seeing I'm kind of no good, like, they takes us both to court. He goes to prison, but I'm let off on all counts, thank God. They read out one of them bits of paper at the trial, and they're all wearing uniform—in court, that is. Now, you take it from me, sir, my kind of work . . . for someone as ain't used to it, it's hell on earth, God help me, but it ain't nothing to the likes of us. It's when you're *not* doing your rounds that your feet ache! And it's worse for us indoors. Back at the parish offices it's make up the clerk's stove, fetch the clerk's water, clean the clerk's boots.'

'What wages do you get?' Lyzhin asked.

'Eighty-four rouble a year.'

'But you must make a bit on the side, surely?'

'Bit on the side? No fear! Gentlefolk don't tip much these days. They're hard-hearted nowadays, are gentlefolk—proper touchy they are. Bring 'em a form and they take it amiss. Doff your hat to 'em, and they take that amiss. "You didn't use the proper entrance," they say. "You're a drunkard," they say. "You stink of onion, you oaf, you son of a bitch." There's some kind ones of course, but what good are they? They only laugh at you, call you names. Take that Mr. Altukhin, now. He's kind and he looks sober, like, he has his head screwed on. But when he sees you he starts shouting things he don't even understand himself. He gives me a nickname, er ——'

The constable pronounced a word, but so quietly that it made no sense.

'What?' asked Lyzhin. 'Say it again.'

'Mr. Administrator,' the constable repeated aloud. 'He's been calling me that for a long time, about six years. "Hallo there, Mr. Administrator." But it's all right, I don't mind—let 'im! And a lady will sometimes send you out a glass of vodka and a bit of pie—so you drink her health, like. The peasants give most. He's more warm-hearted, your peasant is, he fears God. He'll give you a bit of bread, a sup of cabbage stew, or a glass of something. Or the gaffers give you tea in the pub. Like now, say—them witnesses have gone for their tea. "You stay and keep watch, Loshadin," they tell me. And they give me a copeck each. They're scared because they ain't used to these things. And yesterday they gave me fifteen copecks and a glass of tea.'

'And you—aren't *you* afraid?'

'I am that, mister, but it's all part of the job, ain't it? That's service life for you. Last year I was taking a prisoner to town, when he suddenly starts beating me up—he doesn't half lam into me! There's open country and forests all around, no refuge anywhere. Now, take this business here. I remember Mr. Lesnitsky when he was only so high, I knew his father and his mum. I come from Nedoshchotovo village, and they—the Lesnitsky family—live half a mile away . . . less, in fact, their land joins ours. Now, old Mr. Lesnitsky had an unmarried sister, a god-fearing, kind-hearted soul—Lord, remember Thy servant Julia, may her name live for ever! She never married, and when she was dying she split her property, leaving the monastery two hundred and fifty acres, and giving us—Nedoshchotovo village— five hundred to remember her by. But they do say as how the old squire her brother hid that paper—burnt it in his stove, he did, and took all the land himself. He's doing himself a good turn, thinks he. But that ain't so, mate. You can't live by injustice, brother, not on this earth you can't. And the old squire didn't go to confession for twenty year, he turned against the church, like, and he died unrepentant. Burst himself he did—he wasn't half fat. Right along his whole length he burst. Then they take everything away from the young master here—name of Seryozha—to pay them debts. They take the lot. Well, seeing he hasn't much book-learning—or sense, either—his uncle, who's Council Chairman, thinks he'll take him on as insurance man. "Let Seryozha try it," says he. "It's easy enough, is the insurance." But the young master's proud, he is. He wants something with a bit more scope too, a bit more stylish, a bit more free and easy. Traipsing round the county in some broken-down cart talking to peasants . . . it's rather a come-down. When he's on his rounds he always has his eyes fixed on the ground. He don't say nothing. "Mr. Seryozha!" you can shout right into his ear, and he'll just look round with an "Eh?" And he'll fix his eyes on the ground again. And now he's done himself in, see? It's awkward, sir—it ain't right. The things that happen . . . you can't make head nor tail of them, God help us. Say your father was rich, but you're poor—well, it's real hard on you, true enough, but you must put up with it. I once lived well myself, sir, I've kept my two horses, my three cows, my twenty head of sheep. But a time came when I was left with only me little bag—even that wasn't mine but the government's. And now I've got what you might call the rottenest house in our village. Fell off me perch, I did—came down with a bump: it was king of the castle one day and dirty rascal the next!'

'What made you so poor?' the coroner asked.

'My sons don't half knock back the vodka. The amount they shift . . . if I told you, you'd never believe it.'

Lyzhin realized as he listened that he himself would be back in Moscow sooner or later, whereas this old boy would be stuck here doing his rounds for ever. How many more of them would he meet in life . . . these bedraggled, unkempt, 'no good' old men in whose consciousness the concept of the fifteen-copeck piece was somehow indissolubly fused with that of their glass of tea and a profound faith that honesty is the only possible policy in life? Then he grew tired of listening and told the old man to bring hay for his bedding. Though there was an iron bedstead, with pillow and blanket, in 'reception', and though it could have been brought in, the corpse—the man who had perhaps sat on that bed before he died—had lain alongside for nearly three days. To sleep in it now would be unpleasant.

'Only half-past seven, how awful!' thought Lyzhin, looking at his watch.'

He was not sleepy, but having nothing else to do he lay down and pulled a rug over himself—just to pass the time. Loshadin cleared away the tea things, popping in and out several times, smacking his lips, sighing, fidgeting near the table. He took his lamp and went out in the end. Looking at that long grey hair and bent body from behind, Lyzhin thought that the old man was just like a wizard in an opera.

It was dark. There must have been a moon behind the clouds because the windows and the snow on their frames could be so clearly seen. The blizzard howled and howled.

'Oh lord, lord, lord—' moaned a woman in the loft. Or so it seemed.

Then something struck the outside wall with a great thudding crash.

The coroner pricked up his ears. That was no woman but the howling wind. Feeling chilly, he put his fur coat over the rug, reflecting as he warmed up on all this stuff: blizzard, hut, old man, corpse next door. What a far cry, all this, from the life of his dreams—how alien, how petty, how dull! If the man had killed himself in Moscow or those parts, if the coroner had had to hold *that* inquest, how interesting and important it would all have been. He might even have been scared to sleep in the next room to a corpse. Here, though, more than six hundred miles from Moscow, all these things appeared in different guise. This wasn't life, these weren't people—they were just 'things on forms' (as Loshadin would put it). None of this would leave the faintest trace in the memory, it would be forgotten as soon as Lyzhin left Syrnya. His country—real Russia—was Moscow and St. Petersburg. This place was just a provincial outpost. When you dream of making a stir, becoming popular—being an ace investigator, say, prosecuting at the assizes, making a splash socially—you're bound to think of Moscow. Moscow . . . that's where the action is! Whereas here you want nothing, you easily come to terms with your own insignificance, and you expect only one thing of life: just let it hurry up and go away. Borne in imagination along Moscow streets, Lyzhin called at friends' houses, met relatives and colleagues. His heart leapt for joy to think that he was only twenty-six—and if he escaped from here and reached Moscow in five or ten years it still wouldn't be too late, there would still be a whole life ahead of him. Sinking into unconsciousness, his thoughts now more and more confused, he imagined the long corridors of the Moscow court-house, himself giving a speech, his sisters, and an orchestra which was droning away for some reason.

And again he heard the same howling, again the same thudding crashes.

Then he suddenly remembered talking to a cashier once at the council offices, when a certain thin, pale, dark-eyed, black-haired individual had approached the counter. He had that unpleasant look about the eyes which you see in people who have slept too long after lunch—it spoilt his subtle, intelligent profile. He wore jack-boots which didn't suit him: they looked too rough. The cashier had introduced him as 'our insurance man'.

So that was who Lesnitsky had been—the very same, Lyzhin now reckoned. He remembered Lesnitsky's quiet voice, pictured his walk ... and seemed to hear someone walking near him now: someone who walked just like Lesnitsky.

Suddenly he panicked, his head went cold.

'Who's there?' he asked in alarm.

'The conshtible.'

'What do you want?'

'It's just a question, sir. You said just now you didn't need the gaffer here, but I'm afraid he might get vexed, like. He told me to fetch him, so hadn't I better?'

'Oh, bother you,' said Lyzhin, testily, covering himself up again. 'I'm fed up with you.'

'He might get vexed, like. I'll be on my way, sir, and you make yourself at home here.'

Loshadin left. There was coughing and murmuring in the passage— the witnesses must be back.

'We'll let those poor fellows off early tomorrow,' thought the coroner. 'We'll start the inquest at daybreak.'

Then, just as he was losing consciousness, more footsteps—not timid, these, but swift and noisy—were heard. A door slammed, there were voices, a match was struck.

'Asleep, eh?' rapped Dr. Starchenko crossly, lighting match after match. He was completely covered with snow and brought a chill air in with him. 'Asleep, eh? Get up, we're going to von Taunitz's, he's sent his own horses for you. Come on, you'll at least get your supper and a decent sleep. I've come for you myself, you see. The horses are splendid, and we'll make it in twenty minutes.'

'What time is it?'

'A quarter past ten.'

Sleepy and disgruntled, Lyzhin donned boots, coat, cap and hood, and went out with the doctor. Though the cold was not intense, a piercing gale blew, driving clouds of snow down the road before it—seemingly in panic-stricken rout. There were already deep snowdrifts by fences and doorways. Doctor and coroner got into the sledge, and a white driver bent over them to button up the cover. They were both hot.

'We're off!'

Off they drove through the village. The coroner idly watched the trace-horse's legs working, and thought of Pushkin's 'He clove the snow in powdered furrows'. There were lights in all the huts, as on the eve of a major festival: the villagers were too scared of the corpse to go to bed. Bored, no doubt, by his wait outside the hut—brooding, too, on the dead body—their driver preserved a sullen silence.

'When Taunitz's people realized you were staying overnight in that hut,' said Starchenko, 'they all went on at me for not bringing you along.'

On a bend at the end of the village the driver suddenly yelled at the top of his voice that someone should 'get out of the way!' They glimpsed a figure knee-deep in snow: someone who had stepped off the road and was watching the sledge with its three horses. The coroner saw a crook, a beard, a slung satchel. It was Loshadin, it struck him, a Loshadin who was actually smiling! It was just a glimpse and then he vanished.

The road first skirted a wood, then ran down a broad forest ride. They glimpsed old pines, young birches and tall, gnarled young oaks standing alone in clearings where timber had recently been felled, but soon the air was all a-blur with snow flurries. The driver claimed to see trees, but the coroner saw only the trace-horse. The wind blew against their backs.

Suddenly the horses halted.

'What is it this time?' asked Starchenko crossly.

The driver silently climbed off his box and ran round the sledge, digging in his heels. He described ever wider circles further and further from the sledge, and seemed to be dancing. At last he came back and turned right.

'Missed the road, did you, my man?' asked Starchenko.

'We're all right——'

Here was some village without a single light. Then came more woods, more fields, they lost the road again, the driver climbed off the box and danced again. The sledge careered down a dark avenue, flying rapidly on while the heated trace-horse kicked into the front of the bodywork. Here the trees gave a hollow roar. It was terrifying, pitch black—as if they were hurtling into an abyss. Then, suddenly, the bright light of a drive and windows struck their eyes, a welcoming bark rang out, there were voices.

They had arrived.

As they took off their coats and boots in the hall, someone was playing the waltz 'Un petit verre de Cliquot' on a piano upstairs, and the stamp of children's feet was heard. Warm air suddenly breathed on the travellers the scent of rooms in an old manor where life is always so snug, clean and comfortable, never mind the weather outside.

'Capital, capital!' said von Taunitz, a fat man with side-whiskers and an unbelievably broad neck, as he shook the coroner's hand. 'Now do come in—delighted to meet you. After all, we're colleagues in a way, you and I. I was deputy prosecutor once, but not for long—only two years. I came here to run this place, and I've grown old here. I'm an old fogy, in fact.

'Do come in,' he went on, obviously trying not to speak too loud, and took the guests upstairs. 'I have no wife. She died, but here are my daughters. May I introduce you?'

He turned round. 'Tell Ignatius to bring the sledge round for eight o'clock tomorrow,' he shouted downstairs in a voice of thunder.

His four daughters were in the drawing-room: pretty young girls, all in grey dresses, all with the same hair style. There was an attractive young cousin too, with her children. Having met them already, Starchenko at once asked them to sing something, and two of the young ladies assured him at length that they couldn't sing and had no music. Then the cousin sat down at the piano and they rendered a quavering duet from *The Queen of Spades*. 'Un petit verre de Cliquot' was played again, while the children skipped and beat time with their feet. Starchenko pranced a bit too, and everyone laughed.

Then the children said good night and went to bed. The coroner laughed, danced a quadrille, flirted, and wondered if he was dreaming. The peasants' quarters in the council hut, the hay pile in the corner, the rustle of cockroaches, the revoltingly mean appointments, the witnesses' voices, the wind, the snowstorm, the danger of losing one's way—then, suddenly, these superb, brightly-lit rooms, piano-playing, lovely girls, curly-haired children and gay, happy laughter! The transformation seemed magical. And for it to be accomplished within a couple of miles or so, a single hour . . . that seemed incredible. Dismal thoughts marred his enjoyment. This wasn't life around him, he mused, it was only scraps of life—mere fragments. You could draw no conclusions, things were all so arbitrary. He even felt sorry for these girls who lived, who would end their lives, out here in this provincial dump, far from the sort of cultured setting where nothing is arbitrary, where everything makes sense and conforms with its own laws—and where, for instance, every suicide is intelligible, where one can explain why it happened, and what part it plays in the general scheme of things. If he couldn't make sense of the life around him in this backwater, if he couldn't even see it—then there couldn't *be* any life round here, he supposed.

Conversation at supper turned to Lesnitsky.

'He left a wife and child,' said Starchenko. 'These neurotics and other mentally unstable persons . . . I wouldn't let them marry, I'd deny them the right and opportunity to reproduce their kind. It's a crime to bring mentally disturbed children into the world.'

'Poor young fellow,' von Taunitz sighed quietly, shaking his head. 'What brooding, what agony one must suffer before finally venturing to take one's life—a young life. It can happen in any family, such a disaster. It's terrible, it's hard to endure, it's unbearable——'

The girls all listened silently, with grave faces, looking at their father. Lyzhin felt that he was expected to comment too, but all he could think of was that, yes, suicides were an 'undesirable phenomenon'.

He slept in a warm room on a soft bed with a quilt above him and a finely woven fresh sheet beneath, but somehow failed to appreciate these amenities—perhaps because the doctor and von Taunitz kept up a long conversation next door while the storm was making just as big a racket above the ceiling and in the stove as it had back in the hut. It was that same old droning, piteous whine.

Taunitz's wife had died two years before. He still hadn't resigned himself to the fact, and kept mentioning her no matter what he was talking about. There was nothing of the lawyer about him any longer.

'Could *I* ever be reduced to such a state?' wondered Lyzhin as he fell asleep, hearing the other's subdued and bereaved-sounding voice through the wall.

The coroner slept badly. He was hot and uncomfortable. In his sleep he seemed not to be in Taunitz's house, or in a soft clean bed—but still back in the hut on the hay, listening to the witnesses' muffled voices. He felt as if Lesnitsky was near: about fifteen paces away. In his dreams he once more remembered the insurance man—black-haired, pale, in dusty boots—approaching the cashier's counter. ('This is our insurance man.') Then he imagined Lesnitsky and Constable Loshadin walking side by side through the snow-fields, supporting each other. The blizzard whirled above them, the wind blew at their backs, while they went on their way quietly singing that they were 'marching along, marching along'.

The old man looked like an operatic wizard, and both were singing as though on stage.

'We're marching, marching along. You're warm, you have light and comfort, but we are marching into the freezing cold and blizzard through the deep snow. We know no peace, no joy. We bear all the burdens of this life, our own and yours.

'We are marching, marching along,' they droned.

Lyzhin woke and sat up in bed. What a confused, evil dream! Why had he dreamt of the insurance man and the constable together? What nonsense! But while Lyzhin's heart throbbed, while he sat up in bed clutching his head in his hands, it occurred to him that the insurance man and the constable really did have something in common. Had they not indeed been marching along through life side by side, clinging to each other? There was some link—invisible, but significant and essential—between the two, between them and Taunitz, even . . . between all men. Nothing in this life, even in the remotest backwater, is arbitrary, everything is imbued by a single common idea, everything has but one spirit, one purpose. Thinking and reasoning are not enough to furnish insights into these things. Very likely one also needs the gift of penetrating life's essence—a gift which has obviously not been granted to everyone. The miserable, broken-down, suicidal 'neurotic' (the doctor's word for him), the old peasant who had spent every day of his life wandering from one person to another . . . only to someone who also finds his own existence arbitrary are these arbitrary fragments of life. To him who sees and understands his own life as part of the common whole these things are all part of a single miraculous and rational organism. Thus did Lyzhin brood, such was his own long-cherished secret idea. But only now had it unfurled itself so broadly and clearly in his mind.

He lay down, began dozing off. Then, suddenly, they were walking along together again.

'We're marching, marching along,' they sang. 'We take upon ourselves all the hardest and bitterest elements in life. We leave you the easy, enjoyable things, and so you can sit at your supper table coldly and sensibly discussing why we suffer and perish, why we are less healthy and happy than you.'

The burden of their song had occurred to him before, but as an idea somehow masked by other ideas. It had flickered timidly like a distant light in foggy weather. This suicide, this village tragedy . . . they lay heavy on his conscience, he felt. To resign oneself to the fact that these people, so submissive to their fate, have taken on the burden of everything most grim and black in life . . . how horrible! To resign oneself to that while yet desiring a bright, lively life for oneself amid happy, contented people, and while yearning constantly for such a life . . . this was to desire yet more suicides among those crushed by toils and tribulations, among the weak and the outcast: among those very people who may be the subject of the occasional annoyed or sardonic mention over the supper-table . . . yet without anyone ever going to their help.

Once again he heard their 'marching, marching along', and he felt as if someone was banging his temples with a hammer.

Next morning he woke early with a headache, roused by a noise.

'You can't leave now,' von Taunitz was shouting at the doctor in the next room. 'Just look out of doors! Don't argue, you ask the driver—he won't take you in this weather for a million roubles.'

'But it is only two miles, isn't it?' the doctor pleaded.

'I don't care if it's two hundred yards. What can't be done can't be done. The moment you're through those gates all hell will break loose, you'll be off that road inside a minute. Say what you like, but nothing would induce me to let you go.'

'It'll quieten down by evening, I reckon,' said the peasant who was tending the stove.

The doctor next door was talking about Russia's rugged climate influencing her national character, about the long winters impeding freedom of movement and thus retarding the people's intellectual growth. Meanwhile Lyzhin listened with vexation to these disquisitions, gazing through the windows at the snowdrifts against the fence, at the white dust filling all visible space, at the trees bending desperately to right and left. He listened to the howling and banging.

'Well, what moral can we draw?' he wondered gloomily. 'That this is a blizzard, that's all.'

They lunched at noon, then wandered aimlessly about the house and went to the windows.

'Lesnitsky lies there,' thought Lyzhin, looking at the snow flurries whirling furiously above the drifts. 'There he lies, while the witnesses wait.'

They talked about the weather, saying that a snowstorm usually lasts forty-eight hours, rarely longer. They dined at six, then played cards, sang, danced and finally had supper. The day was over, they went to bed.

The storm dropped just before dawn. When they got up and looked out of the windows, bare willows with their feebly drooping branches stood completely still. It was overcast and quiet, as if nature was now ashamed of her orgy, of her mad nights, of giving vent to her passions. Harnessed in tandem, the horses had been waiting at the front door since five o'clock that morning. When it was fully daylight, doctor and coroner put on their coats and boots, said good-bye to their host, and went out.

By the porch, near the driver, stood the familiar figure of the 'conshtible'. Hatless, with his old leather bag across his shoulder, Eli Loshadin was covered with snow. His face was red and wet with sweat.

A footman—he had come out to help the guests into the sledge and wrap up their feet—looked at the old man sternly. 'Why are you hanging around, you old devil? Clear out!'

'The village people are upset, sir,' said Loshadin, smiling innocently all over his face—and obviously glad to see, at last, those whom he had so long awaited. 'Very restive, them peasants are, and the kids are crying. They thought you'd gone back to town, sir. Have pity on them, good, kind sirs——'

Doctor and coroner said nothing, got in the sledge and drove to Syrnya.

A LADY WITH A DOG

[Дама с собачкой]

(1899)

A LADY WITH A DOG

I

THERE was said to be a new arrival on the Esplanade: a lady with a dog.

After spending a fortnight at Yalta, Dmitry Gurov had quite settled in and was now beginning to take an interest in new faces. As he sat outside Vernet's café he saw a fair-haired young woman, not tall, walking on the promenade—wearing a beret, with a white Pomeranian dog trotting after her.

Then he encountered her several times a day in the municipal park and square. She walked alone, always with that beret, always with the white Pomeranian. Who she was no one knew, everyone just called her 'the dog lady'.

'If she has no husband or friends here she might be worth picking up,' calculated Gurov.

He was still in his thirties, but had a twelve-year-old daughter and two schoolboy sons. His marriage had been arranged early—during his second college year—and now his wife seemed half as old again as he. She was a tall, dark-browed woman: outspoken, earnest, stolid and—she maintained—an 'intellectual'. She was a great reader, she favoured spelling reform, she called her husband 'Demetrius' instead of plain 'Dmitry', while he privately thought her narrow-minded, inelegant and slow on the uptake. He was afraid of her, and disliked being at home. He had begun deceiving her long ago, and his infidelities were frequent—which is probably why he nearly always spoke so disparagingly of women, calling them an 'inferior species' when the subject cropped up.

He was, he felt, sufficiently schooled by bitter experience to call them any name he liked, yet he still couldn't live two days on end without his 'inferior species'. Men's company bored him, making him ill at ease, tongue-tied and apathetic, whereas with women he felt free. He knew what to talk about, how to behave—he even found it easy to be with them without talking at all. In his appearance and character, in his whole nature, there was an alluring, elusive element which charmed and fascinated women. He knew it, and he was himself strongly attracted in return.

Kc

As experience multiple and—in the full sense of the word—bitter had long since taught him, every intimacy which so pleasantly diversifies one's life, which seems so easy, so delightfully adventurous at the outset ... such an intimacy does, when reasonable people are involved (not least Muscovites—so hesitant and slow off the mark), develop willy-nilly into some vast, extraordinarily complex problem until the whole business finally becomes quite an ordeal. Somehow, though, on every new encounter with an attractive woman all this experience went for nothing—he wanted a bit of excitement and it all seemed so easy and amusing.

Well, he was eating in an open-air restaurant late one afternoon when the lady in the beret sauntered along and took the next table. Her expression, walk, clothes, hair-style ... all told him that she was socially presentable, married, in Yalta for the first time, alone—and bored.

Much nonsense is talked about the looseness of morals in these parts, and he despised such stories, knowing that they were largely fabricated by people who would have been glad to misbehave themselves, given the aptitude! But when the young woman sat down at the next table, three paces away, he recalled those tales of trips into the mountains and easy conquests. The seductive thought of a swift, fleeting *affaire*—the romance with the stranger whose very name you don't know—suddenly possessed him. He made a friendly gesture to the dog. It came up. He wagged his finger. The dog growled and Gurov shook his finger again.

The lady glanced at him, lowered her eyes at once.

'He doesn't bite.' She blushed.

'May I give him a bone?'

She nodded.

'Have you been in Yalta long, madam?' he asked courteously.

'Five days.'

'Oh, I've nearly survived my first fortnight.'

There was a short pause.

'Time goes quickly, but it *is* so boring,' she said, not looking at him.

'That's what they all say, what a bore this place is. Your average tripper from Belyov, Zhizdra or somewhere ... he doesn't know what boredom means till he comes here. Then it's "Oh, what a bore! Oh, what dust!" You might think he'd just blown in from sunny Spain!'

She laughed. Then both continued their meal in silence, as strangers.

After dinner, though, they left together and embarked on the bantering chat of people who feel free and easy, who don't mind where they go or what they talk about. As they strolled they discussed the strange light on the sea: the water was of a soft, warm, mauve hue, crossed by a stripe of golden moonlight. How sultry it was after the day's heat, they said. Gurov described himself as a Muscovite who had studied literature but worked in a bank. He had once trained as an opera singer but had given that up and owned two houses in Moscow.

From her he learnt that she had grown up in St. Petersburg, but had married in the provincial town where she had now been living for two years, that she was staying in Yalta for another month, that her husband (who also wanted a holiday) might come and fetch her. She was quite unable to explain her husband's job—was it with the County Council or the Rural District?—and even she saw the funny side of this. Gurov also learnt that she was called Anne.

In his hotel room afterwards he thought about her. He was very likely to meet her tomorrow, bound to. As he went to bed he remembered that she had not long left boarding-school, that she had been a schoolgirl like his own daughter—remembered, too, how much shyness and stiffness she still showed when laughing and talking to a stranger. This must be her first time ever alone in such a place, with men following her around, watching her, talking to her: all with a certain privy aim which she could not fail to divine. He remembered her slender, frail neck, her lovely grey eyes.

'You can't help feeling sorry for her, though,' he thought. And dozed off.

II

A week had passed since their first meeting. It was a Sunday or some other holiday. Indoors was stifling, and outside flurries of dust swept the streets, whipping off hats. It was a thirsty day, and Gurov kept calling in at the café to fetch Anne a soft drink or an ice-cream. There was no escaping the heat.

In the evening things were a little easier, and they went on the pier to watch a steamer come in. There were a lot of people hanging around on the landing-stage: they were here to meet someone, and held bunches of flowers. Two features of the Yalta smart set were now thrown into sharp relief. The older women dressed like young ones. There were lots of generals.

As the sea was rough the steamer arrived late, after sunset, and manœuvred for some time before putting in at the jetty. Anne watched boat and passengers through her lorgnette as if seeking someone she knew. Whenever she turned to Gurov her eyes shone. She spoke a lot, asking quick-fire questions and immediately forgetting what they were. Then she lost her lorgnette: dropped it in the crowd.

The gaily-dressed gathering dispersed, no more faces could be seen, and the wind dropped completely while Gurov and Anne stood as if waiting for someone else to disembark. Anne had stopped talking, and sniffed her flowers without looking at Gurov.

'The weather's better now that it's evening,' said he. 'So where shall we go? How about driving somewhere?'

She did not answer.

Then he stared at her hard, embraced her suddenly and kissed her lips. The scent of her flowers, their dampness, enveloped him, and he immediately glanced around fearfully: had they been observed?

'Let's go to your room,' he said softly.

They set off quickly together.

Her room was stuffy and smelt of the scent which she had bought in the Japanese shop.

'What encounters one does have in life,' thought Gurov as he looked at her now.

He still retained memories of the easy-going, light-hearted women in his past: women happy in their love and grateful to him for that happiness, however brief. He also recalled those who, like his wife, made love insincerely, with idle chatter, affectations and hysteria, their expressions conveying that this was neither love nor passion but something more significant. He thought of two or three very beautiful frigid women whose faces would suddenly flash a rapacious, stubborn look of lust to seize, to snatch more from life than it can give . . . women no longer young, these: fractious, unreasonable, overbearing and obtuse. When Gurov had cooled towards them their beauty had aroused his hatred, and the lace on their underclothes had looked like a lizard's scales.

In this case, though, all was hesitancy, the awkwardness of inexperienced youth. There was the impression of her being taken aback, too, as by a sudden knock on the door. Anne, this 'lady with a dog', had her own special view—a very serious one—of what had happened. She thought of it as her 'downfall', it seemed, which was all very strange and inappropriate. Her features had sunk and faded, her long hair drooped sadly down each side of her face. She had struck a pensive, despondent pose, like the Woman Taken in Adultery in an old-fashioned picture.

'This is all wrong,' she said. 'Now you'll completely despise me.'

There was a water-melon on the table. Gurov cut a slice and slowly ate. Half an hour, at least, passed in silence.

He found Anne touching. She had that air of naïve innocence of a thoroughly nice unworldly woman. A solitary candle, burning on the table, barely lit her face, but it was obvious that she was ill at ease.

'Why should I lose respect for you?' asked Gurov. 'You don't know what you're saying.'

'God forgive me,' she said, her eyes brimming with tears. 'This is terrible.'

'You seem very much on the defensive, Anne.'

'How *can* I defend what I've done? I'm a bad, wicked woman, I despise myself and I'm not trying to make excuses. It's not my husband, it is *myself* I've deceived. I don't just mean what happened here, I've been deceiving myself for a long time. My husband may be a good, honourable man, but he *is* such a worm. What he does at that job of his I don't know—all I know is, he's a worm. I was twenty when I married him—I longed to know more of life. Then I wanted something better. There must *be* a different life, mustn't there? Or so I told myself. I wanted a little—well, rather *more* than a little—excitement. I was avid for experience. You won't understand me, I'm sure, but I could control myself no longer, I swear, something had happened to me, there was no holding me. So I told my husband I was ill and I came here. And I've been going round here in a daze as if I was off my head. But now I'm just another vulgar, worthless woman whom everyone is free to despise.'

Gurov was bored with all this. He was irritated by the naïve air, the unexpected, uncalled-for remorse. But for the tears in her eyes he might have thought her to be joking or play-acting.

'I don't understand,' said he softly. 'What is it you want?'

She hid her face on his breast and clung to him.

'Please, please believe me,' she implored. 'I long for a decent, moral life. Sin disgusts me, I don't know what I'm doing myself. The common people say the "Evil One" tempted them, and now I can say the same: I was tempted by the Evil One.'

'There there, that's enough,' he muttered.

He looked into her staring, frightened eyes, kissed her, spoke softly and gently. She gradually relaxed and cheered up again. Both laughed.

Then they went out. The promenade was deserted, the town with its cypresses looked quite dead, but the sea still roared, breaking on the beach. A single launch with a sleepily glinting lamp tossed on the waves.

They found a cab and drove to Oreanda.

'I've only just discovered your surname, downstairs in your hotel,' Gurov told her. '"Von Diederitz", it says on the board. Is your husband German?'

'No, his grandfather was, I think, but he's Russian.'

They sat on a bench near the church at Oreanda, gazing silently down at the sea. Yalta was barely visible through the dawn mist, white clouds hung motionless on the mountain peaks. Not a leaf stirred on the trees, cicadas chirped. Borne up from below, the sea's monotonous, muffled boom spoke of peace, of the everlasting sleep awaiting us. Before Yalta or Oreanda yet existed that surf had been thundering down there, it was roaring away now, and it will continue its dull booming with the same unconcern when we are no more. This persistence, this utter aloofness from all our lives and deaths . . . do they perhaps hold the secret pledge of our eternal salvation, of life's perpetual motion on earth, of its uninterrupted progress? As he sat there, lulled and entranced by the magic panorama—sea, mountains, clouds, broad sky—beside a young woman who looked so beautiful in the dawn, Gurov reflected that everything on earth is beautiful, really, when you consider it—everything except what we think and do ourselves when we forget the lofty goals of being and our human dignity.

Someone—a watchman, no doubt—came up, looked at them, went away. Even this incident seemed mysterious—beautiful, too. In the dawn they saw a steamer arrive from Feodosiya, its lights already extinguished.

'There's dew on the grass,' Anne said, after a pause.

'Yes, time to go home.'

They went back to town.

After this they met on the promenade each noon, lunched, dined, strolled, enthused about the sea together. She complained of sleeping badly, of palpitations. Disturbed by jealousy, and by the fear that he did not respect her enough, she kept repeating the same old questions. And often in the Square or Gardens, when there was nobody near them, he would suddenly draw her to him and kiss her ardently. This utter idleness, these kisses in broad daylight, these glances over the shoulder, this fear of being seen, the heat, the sea's smell, the repeated glimpses of idle, elegant, sleek persons . . . it all seemed to revitalize him. He told Anne how pretty she was, how provocative. He was impetuous, he was passionate, he never left her side, while she was for ever brooding and begging him to admit that he did not respect her, that he loved her not at all, that he could see in her no more than a very ordinary woman. Late almost every evening they would drive out of town: to Oreanda or the waterfall. These trips were invariably a great success, leaving an impression of majesty and beauty.

They had been expecting the husband to arrive, but he sent a letter to say that he had eye trouble, and begged his wife to come home soon. Anne bestirred herself.

'It's just as well I *am* leaving,' she told Gurov. 'This is fate.'

She left by carriage and he drove with her. This part of her journey took all day. When she took her seat in the express train, which was due to leave in five minutes, she asked to look at him once more.

'One last look—that's right.'

She did not cry, but was so sad that she seemed ill. Her face quivered.

'I'll think of you, I'll remember you,' she said. 'God bless and keep you. Don't think ill of me. We're parting for ever. We must, because we should never have met at all. God bless you.'

The train departed swiftly, its lights soon vanishing and its noise dying away within a minute, as though everything had conspired to make a quick end of that sweet trance, that madness. Alone on the platform, gazing into the dark distance, Gurov heard the chirp of grasshoppers and the hum of telegraph wires, feeling as if he had just awoken. Well, there went another adventure or episode in his life, he reflected. It too had ended, now only the memory was left.

He was troubled, sad, somewhat penitent. This young woman whom he would never see again . . . she hadn't been happy with him, now, had she? He had treated her kindly and affectionately. And yet his attitude to her, his tone, his caresses had betrayed a faint irony: the rather crude condescension of your conquering male—of a man nearly twice her age into the bargain. She had kept calling him kind, exceptional, noble—so she hadn't seen him as he really was, obviously, and he must have been deceiving her without meaning to.

Here at the station there was already a whiff of autumn in the air, and the evening was cool.

'It's time I went north too,' thought Gurov, leaving the platform. 'High time.'

III

Back home in Moscow it was already like winter. The stoves were
alight. It was dark when his children breakfasted and got ready for
school in the mornings, so their nanny lit the light for a short time.
The frosts had begun. It is always such a joy to see the white ground
and white roofs when the snow first falls, on that first day of sleigh-
riding. The air is so fresh and good to breathe, and you remember the
years of your youth. White with frost, the old limes and birches have
a kindly look, they are dearer to your heart than any cypresses or
palm-trees, and near them you no longer hanker after mountains
and sea.

A Moscow man himself, Gurov had come home on a fine frosty
day. He put on his fur coat and warm gloves and strolled down the
Petrovka, he heard church bells pealing on Saturday evening . . . and
his recent trip, all the places he had visited, lost all charm for him. He
gradually plunged into Moscow life. He was zealously reading his
three newspapers a day, now—while claiming to read no Moscow
newspapers on principle! He felt the lure of restaurants, clubs, dinner
parties, anniversary celebrations; he was flattered to be visited by
famous lawyers and actors, flattered to play cards with a professor at
the Doctors' Club. He could tackle a large helping of 'Moscow hot-
pot' straight from the pan.

In a month or two's time the memory of Anne would become
blurred, thought he—he would just dream of her, of her adorable
smile, occasionally as he used to dream of those other ones. But more
than a month passed, real winter set in, and yet everything was still as
clear in his mind as if they had parted only yesterday. His memories
flared up ever more brightly. When, in the quiet of evening, his children's voices reached his study as they did their homework, when he
heard a sentimental song or a barrel organ in a restaurant, when a
blizzard howled in his chimney . . . it would all suddenly come back
to him: that business on the pier, the early morning with the mist on
the mountains, the Feodosiya steamer, the kisses. He would pace the
room for hours, remembering and smiling until these recollections
merged into fantasies: until, in his imagination, past fused with future.
Though he did not dream of Anne, she pursued him everywhere like
his shadow, watching him. If he closed his eyes he could see her
vividly—younger, gentler, more beautiful than she really was. He
even saw himself as a better man than he had been back in Yalta.

She gazed at him from the book-case in the evenings, from the hearth, from a corner of the room. He heard her breathing, heard the delightful rustle of her dress. In the street he followed women with his eyes, seeking one like her.

He was plagued, now, by the urge to share his memories. But he could not talk about his love at home, and outside his home there was no one to tell—he couldn't very well discuss it with his tenants or at the bank! What was there to say, anyway? Had he really been in love? Had there really been anything beautiful or idyllic, anything edifying—anything merely interesting, even—in his relations with Anne? He was reduced to vague remarks about love and women, and no one guessed what he had in mind. His wife just twitched those dark eyebrows and told him that 'the role of lady-killer doesn't suit you at all, Demetrius'.

As he was leaving the Doctors' Club one night with his partner, a civil servant, he could not help saying that he had 'met such an enchanting woman in Yalta—did you but know!'

The civil servant climbed into his sledge and drove off, but suddenly turned round and shouted Gurov's name.

'What is it?'

'You were quite right just now, the sturgeon *was* a bit off.'

For some reason these words, humdrum though they were, suddenly infuriated Gurov, striking him as indelicate and gross. What barbarous manners, what faces, what meaningless nights, what dull, featureless days! Frantic card-playing, guzzling, drunkenness, endless chatter always on one and the same topic. Futile activities, repetitious talk, talk, talk . . . they engross most of your time, your best efforts, and you end up with a sort of botched, pedestrian life: a form of imbecility from which there's no way out, no escape. You might as well be in jail or in a madhouse!

Gurov lay awake all night, fuming—then had a headache all next day. He slept badly on the following nights, too, sitting up in bed thinking, or pacing the room. He was fed up with his children, fed up with his bank, there was nowhere he wanted to go, nothing he wanted to talk about.

Towards Christmas he prepared for a journey. He told his wife that he was going to St. Petersburg on a certain young man's business—but he actually went to the town where Anne lived. Why? He didn't really know himself. He wanted to see her, speak to her—make an assignation if he could.

He reached the town one morning and put up at a hotel, in the 'best' room with wall-to-wall carpeting in coarse field-grey material. On the table stood an inkstand, grey with dust and shaped as a horseman holding his hat up in one hand and minus a head. The porter told him what he needed to know: von Diederitz lived in Old Pottery Street in his own house near the hotel. He did things in style, kept his own horses, was known to everyone in town. The porter pronounced the name as 'Drearydits'. Gurov sauntered off to Old Pottery Street, found the house. Immediately facing it was a long, grey fence crowned with nails: 'a fence to run away from', thought Gurov, looking from windows to fence and back.

Local government offices were closed today, so the husband was probably at home, Gurov reckoned. In any case it would be tactless to go into the house and create a disturbance. If he sent a note, though, it might fall into the husband's hands and ruin everything. Better trust to chance. He paced the street near the fence, awaiting this chance. He saw a beggar go through the gate, saw him set upon by dogs. An hour later he heard the faint, muffled sound of a piano—that must be Anne playing. Suddenly the front door opened, and out came an old woman with the familiar white Pomeranian running after her. Gurov wanted to call the dog, but his heart suddenly raced and he was too excited to remember its name.

He paced about, loathing that grey fence more and more. In his irritation, he fancied that Anne had forgotten him and might be amusing herself with another man—what else could be expected of a young woman compelled to contemplate this confounded fence morning, noon and night? He went back to his room, sat on the sofa for hours not knowing what to do, then lunched and dozed for hours.

'It's all so stupid and distressing,' he thought, waking up and seeing the dark windows—it was already evening. 'Now I've had a good sleep for some reason, but what shall I do tonight?'

He sat on the bed—it was covered with a cheap, grey hospital blanket.

'So much for your ladies with dogs!' said he in petulant self-mockery. 'So much for your holiday romances—now you're stuck in this dump.'

In the station that morning his eye had been caught by a poster in bold lettering advertising the opening of *The Geisha*. Recalling this, he drove to the theatre, reflecting that she very probably attended first nights.

The theatre was full. As usual in provincial theatres a mist hung above the chandelier, while the gallery was restive and rowdy. In the first row before the performance began stood the local gallants, hands clasped behind their backs. In the Governor's box, in front, sat that worthy's daughter complete with feather boa, while the Governor himself lurked modestly behind a *portière*, only his hands showing. The curtain shook, the orchestra tuned up protractedly. As the audience came in and took its seats, Gurov peered frantically around.

In came Anne. She sat down in the third row, and when Gurov glimpsed her his heart seemed to miss a beat. He saw clearly, now, that she was nearer, dearer, more important to him than anyone in the whole world. Lost in the provincial crowd, this very ordinary little woman carrying her vulgar lorgnette now absorbed his whole being. She was his grief, his joy—the only happiness he wanted, now. To the strains of that abominable orchestra with its atrocious, tasteless fiddling he thought how lovely she was . . . thought and brooded.

A young man with short dundrearies, very tall, round-shouldered, had come in with Anne and sat down beside her. He kept bobbing his head as if making obeisance with every step he took. It must be the husband whom, in that bitter outburst back in Yalta, she had dubbed a 'worm'. His lanky figure, his side-whiskers, his small bald patch . . . there actually *was* something menial and flunkey-like about them. He gave an ingratiating smile, the emblem of some learned society glinting in his buttonhole like a hotel servant's number.

The husband went for a smoke in the first interval, while she remained seated. Gurov—his seat was also in the stalls—approached her. His voice trembling, forcing a smile, he wished her good evening.

She glanced at him, she blenched. Then she looked again—aghast, not believing her eyes, crushing fan and lorgnette together in her hands in an obvious effort to prevent herself from fainting. Neither spoke. She sat, he remained standing—alarmed by her discomfiture, not venturing to sit down beside her. Fiddles and flute started tuning up, and he suddenly panicked: from all the boxes eyes seemed to be staring at them. Then she stood up and quickly made for the exit, while he followed, both walking at random along corridors, up and down stairways, glimpsing men in the uniforms of the courts, the schools and the administration of crown lands, all wearing their decorations. There were glimpses of ladies and fur coats on pegs. A draught enveloped them with the smell of cigarette ends.

'Oh God—why all these people, this orchestra?' wondered Gurov, his heart pounding.

Suddenly he recalled the evening when he had seen Anne off at the station, when he had told himself that it was all over and that they would never meet again. How far they were now, though, from any ending!

On a narrow, gloomy staircase labelled ENTRANCE TO CIRCLE she stopped.

'How you did scare me,' she panted, still pale and dazed. 'I nearly died, you scared me so. Why, why, why are you here?'

'Try and understand, Anne,' he said in a rapid undertone. 'Understand, I implore you——'

She looked at him—fearfully, pleadingly, lovingly. She stared, trying to fix his features in her memory.

'I'm so miserable,' she went on, not hearing him. 'I've thought only of you all this time, my thoughts of you have kept me alive. Oh, I did so want to forget you—why, why, why are you here?'

On a landing higher up two schoolboys were smoking and looking down, but Gurov did not care. He pulled Anne to him, kissed her face, cheek, hands.

'Whatever are you doing?' she asked—horrified, pushing him from her. 'We must be out of our minds. You must go away today—leave this very instant, I implore you, I beg you in the name of all that is holy. Someone's coming.'

Someone indeed was coming upstairs.

'You *must* leave,' Anne went on in a whisper. 'Do you hear me, Gurov? I'll visit you in Moscow. I've never been happy, I'm unhappy now, and I shall never, never, never be happy. So don't add to my sufferings. I'll come to Moscow, I swear it, but we must part now. We must say good-bye, my good, kind darling.'

She pressed his hand and went quickly downstairs, looking back at him, and he could see from her eyes that she really was unhappy. Gurov waited a little, cocked an ear and, when all was quiet, found the peg with his coat and left the theatre.

IV

Anne took to visiting him in Moscow. Once every two or three months she would leave her home town, telling her husband that she was going to consult a professor about a female complaint. The husband neither believed nor disbelieved her. In Moscow she would put up at the Slav Fair Hotel, and at once send a red-capped messenger to Gurov. Gurov would visit her hotel, and no one in Moscow knew anything about it.

It thus chanced that he was on his way to see her one winter morning —her messenger had called on the previous evening, but had not found him at home. He was walking with his daughter, wanting to take her to her school, which was on his way. There was a heavy downpour of sleet.

'It's three degrees above zero, yet look at the sleet,' said Gurov to his daughter. 'But it's only the ground which is warm, you see—the temperature in the upper strata of the atmosphere is quite different.'

'Why doesn't it thunder in winter, Daddy?'

He explained this too, reflecting as he spoke that he was on his way to an assignation. Not a soul knew about it—or ever would know, probably. He was living two lives. One of them was open to view by— and known to—the people concerned. It was full of stereotyped truths and stereotyped untruths, it was identical with the life of his friends and acquaintances. The other life proceeded in secret. Through some strange and possibly arbitrary chain of coincidences everything vital, interesting and crucial to him, everything which called his sincerity and integrity into play, everything which made up the core of his life . . . all that took place in complete secrecy, whereas everything false about him, the façade behind which he hid to conceal the truth— his work at the bank, say, his arguments at the club, that 'inferior species' stuff, attending anniversary celebrations with his wife—all that was in the open. He judged others by himself, disbelieving the evidence of his eyes, and attributing to everyone a real, fascinating life lived under the cloak of secrecy as in the darkness of the night. Each indivi- dual existence is based on mystery, which is perhaps why civilized man makes such a neurotic fuss about having his privacy respected.

After taking his daughter to school, Gurov made for the Slav Fair. He removed his coat downstairs, went up, tapped on the door. Anne was wearing his favourite grey dress, she was tired by the journey— and by the wait, after expecting him since the previous evening. She was pale, she looked at him without smiling, and no sooner was he in the room than she flung herself against his chest. Their kiss was as protracted and lingering as if they had not met for two years.

'Well, how are things with you?' he asked. 'What's the news?'

'Wait, I'll tell you in a moment—I can't now.'

Unable to speak for crying, she turned away and pressed a handker- chief to her eyes.

'Let her cry, I'll sit down for a bit,' thought he, and sat in the arm-chair.

Then he rang and ordered tea. Then he drank it while she still stood with her back to him, facing the window.

She wept as one distressed and woefully aware of the melancholy turn which their lives had taken. They met only in secret, they hid from other people like thieves. Their lives were in ruins, were they not?

'Now, do stop it,' he said.

He could see that this was no fleeting affair—there was no telling when it would end. Anne was growing more and more attached to him. She adored him, and there was no question of telling her that all this must finish one day. Besides, she would never believe him.

He went up to her, laid his hands on her shoulders, meaning to soothe her with a little banter—and then caught sight of himself in the mirror.

His hair was turning grey. He wondered why he had aged so much in the last few years and lost his looks. The shoulders on which his hands rested were warm and trembling. He pitied this life—still so warm and beautiful, but probably just about to fade and wither like his own. Why did she love him so? Women had never seen him as he really was. What they loved in him was not his real self but a figment of their own imaginations—someone whom they had dreamed of meeting all their lives. Then, when they realized their mistake, they had loved him all the same. Yet none of them had been happy with him. Time had passed, he had met new ones, been intimate with them, parted from them. Not once had he been in love, though. He had known everything conceivable—except love, that is.

Only now that his head was grey had he well and truly fallen in love: for the first time in his life.

Anne and he loved each other very, very dearly, like man and wife or bosom friends. They felt themselves predestined for each other. That he should have a wife, and she a husband . . . it seemed to make no sense. They were like two migratory birds, a male and a female, caught and put in separate cages. They had forgiven each other the shameful episodes of their past, they forgave each other for the present too, and they felt that their love had transformed them both.

Once, in moments of depression, he had tried to console himself with any argument which came into his head—but now he had no use for arguments. His deepest sympathies were stirred, he only wanted to be sincere and tender.

'Stop, darling,' he said. 'You've had your cry—that's enough. Now let's talk, let's think of something.'

Then they consulted at length about avoiding the need for concealment and deception, for living in different towns, for meeting only at rare intervals. How could they break these intolerable bonds? How, how, how?

He clutched his head and asked the question again and again.

Soon, it seemed, the solution would be found and a wonderful new life would begin. But both could see that they still had a long, long way to travel—and that the most complicated and difficult part was only just beginning.

AT CHRISTMAS

[*На святках*]

(1900)

AT CHRISTMAS

I

'TELL me what to write,' said Yegor as he dipped his pen in the ink.

Not for four years had Vasilisa seen her daughter. The daughter, Yefimya, had gone to St. Petersburg with her husband after their wedding, and she had written home twice. But not a word had been heard of her after that, she might have vanished into thin air. Milking the cow at dawn, making up the stove, dreaming at night, the old woman had only one thing on her mind: how was Yefimya getting on, was she alive? Vasilisa ought to send a letter, but her old man couldn't write—and there was no one else to ask.

Well, when Christmas came round Vasilisa could bear it no longer, and went to see Yegor at the inn. This Yegor was the landlady's brother who had been hanging round that pub doing nothing ever since he had come home from the army. He was said to turn out a good letter if he was properly paid. Vasilisa first had a word with the pub cook, and then with the landlady, and finally with Yegor himself. A fifteen-copeck fee was agreed.

And now, in the pub kitchen on Boxing Day, Yegor sat at the table holding a pen. Vasilisa stood before him brooding. She had a care-worn, grief-stricken air. Her old husband, Peter—very thin, tall, brown-pated—had come in with her and stood staring straight before him like a blind man. On the stove a pan of pork was frying. It hissed, it spurted, it even seemed to be saying 'flue', 'flu', 'flew' or some such word. The room was hot and stuffy.

'What shall I write?' Yegor repeated.

'None of that, now!' said Vasilisa with an angry and suspicious look. 'Don't you rush me. You ain't doing us no favour. You're being paid, ain't you? So you write "to our dear son-in-law Andrew and our only beloved daughter Yefimya our love, a low bow and our parental blessing which shall abide for ever and ever."'

'O.K. Carry on shooting!'

'We also wish you a Happy Christmas. We are alive and well, and we wish the same to you from Our Lord, er, and Heavenly King.'

Vasilisa pondered, exchanged glances with the old man.

'We wish the same to you from Our Lord, er, and Heavenly King,' she repeated—and burst into tears.

That was all she could say. And yet, when she had lain awake at night thinking, a dozen letters hadn't seemed enough to say it all. Since the daughter and her husband had left, a great deal of water had flowed under the bridge, and the old people had lived a life of utter loneliness, sighing deeply of a night as if they had buried their daughter. So many things had happened in the village since then, what with all the weddings and funerals. How long the winters had seemed, how long the nights!

'It's hot in here,' said Yegor, unbuttoning his waistcoat. 'About seventy degrees, I reckon.

'All right then—what else?' he asked.

The old people said nothing.

'What's your son-in-law's job?' asked Yegor.

'He was a soldier, sir, as you know,' answered the old man in a frail voice. 'He left the service same time as you. He was a soldier, but now he works in St. Petersburg, like—in the hydropathetics. There's a doctor cures the sick with the waters, and he's a doorman at that doctor's institution.'

'It's all written here,' said the old woman, taking a letter out of her kerchief. 'This came from Yefimya, God knows when. Perhaps they ain't alive no more.'

Yegor reflected and wrote rapidly.

'At the present juncture,' he wrote, 'seeing as how destinny has been determined in the Soldiering Feild we advises you to look in the Regulations of Disciplinnary Penalties and the Criminal Law of the War Department and you will see in them said Laws the civilization of the Higher Ranks of the War Deppartment.'

After writing this, he read it out aloud while Vasilisa was thinking that he ought to write how miserable they had been last year, when their grain hadn't even lasted till Christmas and they'd had to sell the cow. She ought to ask for money, she ought to write that the old man was often poorly—and was bound, soon, to be called to his Maker.

But how could she put it in words? What did you say first and what next?

'Pay attenshon,' Yegor went on writing. 'In Volume Five of Milittary Regulations. Soldier is a genneral Term as is well known your most important Genneral and the least importtant Private is both called Soldiers.'

The old man moved his lips.

'It would be nice to see our grandchildren,' he said softly.

'What grandchildren?' the old woman asked, looking at him angrily. 'Perhaps there ain't none.'

'Ain't none? But perhaps there is. Who can tell?'

'By which you can judge,' Yegor hurried on, 'which enemy is Foreign and which Internnal the most important Internnal Enemy is Bacchus.'

The pen squeaked, making flourishes like fish-hooks on the paper. Yegor was in a hurry and read out each line several times. He sat on a stool, legs sprawling under the table: a smug, hulking, fat-faced, red-necked creature. He was the very soul of vulgarity—of vulgarity brash, overbearing, exultant, and proud of having been born and bred in a pub. That this indeed was vulgarity Vasilisa fully realized, though she could not put it into words, but only looked at Yegor angrily and suspiciously. His voice, his meaningless words, the heat, the stuffiness ... they made her head ache and muddled her thoughts, so she said nothing, thought nothing, and only waited for that pen to stop squeaking. But the old man was looking at Yegor with absolute faith. He trusted them both: his old woman who had brought him here, and Yegor. And when he had mentioned the 'hydropathetics' institution just now, his faith—alike in that institution and in the curative power of 'the waters'—had been written all over his face.

Yegor finished, stood up and read out the whole letter from the beginning. Not understanding, the old man nodded trustingly.

'Pretty good, a smooth job,' said he. 'God bless you. Pretty good.'

They put three five-copeck pieces on the table and left the pub. The old man stared straight before him as if he was blind, absolute faith written on his face, but as they came out of the pub Vasilisa swung her fist at the dog.

'Ugly brute!' she said angrily.

The old woman got no sleep that night for worrying. At dawn she rose, said her prayers and set off for the station to post the letter—a distance of between eight and nine miles.

II

Dr. B. O. Moselweiser's Hydro was open on New Year's Day, as on any ordinary day, the only difference being that Andrew the doorman wore a uniform with new galloons. His boots had an extra special shine and he wished everyone who came in a Happy New Year.

It was morning. Andrew stood by the door reading a newspaper. At exactly ten o'clock in came a general whom he knew—one of the regulars—followed by the postman.

'Happy New Year, sir,' said Andrew, helping the general off with his cloak.

'Thank you, my good fellow. Same to you.'

On his way upstairs the general nodded towards a door and asked a question which he asked every day, always forgetting the answer.

'What goes on in there?'

'Massage room, sir!'

When the general's steps had died away, Andrew examined the postal delivery and found one letter addressed to himself. He opened it, read several lines. Glancing at the newspaper, he sauntered to his room which was down here on the ground floor at the end of the passage. His wife Yefimya sat on the bed feeding a baby. Another child, the eldest, stood near her with his curly head on her lap while a third slept on the bed.

Entering his room, Andrew gave his wife the letter.

'This must be from the village.'

Then he went out, not taking his eyes off the newspaper, and paused in the corridor near his door. He could hear Yefimya read out the first lines in a quavering voice. After reading them she couldn't carry on—those few lines were quite enough for her, she was bathed in tears. Hugging and kissing her eldest child, she began to speak—crying or laughing, it was hard to say which.

'This is from Granny and Grandpa,' she said. 'From the village. May the Holy Mother and the Blessed Saints be with them. They have snow drifts right up to the roofs now, and the trees are white as white. The children are sliding on their tiny toboggans. And there's dear old bald Grandpa on the stove. And there's a little yellow dog. My lovely darlings.'

As he listened, Andrew remembered that his wife had given him letters three or four times, asking him to post them to the village, but some important business had always prevented him. He had not posted those letters, and they had been left lying around somewhere.

'There's little hares running about them fields,' Yefimya chanted, bathed in tears and kissing her boy. 'Grandpa is quiet and gentle, and Granny is also kind and loving. In the village they live a godly life and fear the Lord. There's a little church, with such nice peasants singing in the choir. Holy Mother, our protector, take us away from this place!'

Andrew came back to his room for a smoke before anyone else arrived, and Yefimya suddenly stopped talking, quietened down and wiped her eyes. Only her lips quivered. She was so afraid of him, oh dear she was! His footsteps, his glance . . . they made her tremble with fright. She dared not utter a word in his presence.

No sooner had Andrew lit a cigarette than there was a ring from upstairs. He put out his cigarette, adopted an expression of great solemnity, and ran to his front door.

The general was descending from aloft, pink and fresh from his bath.

'What goes on in there?' he asked, pointing at a door.

Andrew drew himself up to attention, and announced in a loud voice that it was the 'Charcot showers, sir!'

IN THE HOLLOW

[В овраге]

(1900)

IN THE HOLLOW

I

UKLEYEVO village was at the bottom of a hollow. Only its belfry and the chimneys of its calico-printing factories could be seen from the main road and railway station. When travellers asked what village it was, they would be told 'where the sexton ate all the caviare at the funeral'.

Once, after a funeral at factory-owner Kostyukov's place, an elderly sexton had spotted some unpressed caviare among the eatables and begun gulping it down. People jostled him, tugged his sleeve, but he was in a sort of ecstatic trance: felt nothing, just went on eating. He wolfed the lot, and the jar had held about four pounds! This had been some time ago and the sexton had long since died, yet they still remembered that caviare. Was life there really so miserable? Or were people just incapable of noticing anything but this trivial episode, now ten years old? Anyway, it was all one ever heard about Ukleyevo village.

Malaria was endemic in the place. There was gluey mud, even in summer: especially beneath the fences broadly overshadowed by ancient stooping willows. It always smelt of factory waste, and o acetic acid as used in processing cotton. The factories—three calico print-works, one tannery—were not in the actual village, but on the outskirts or some distance away. They were small concerns, employing no more than four hundred workers all told. The tannery often made the stream stink, its waste polluted the meadow, the villagers' cattle suffered from anthrax. There had been an order to close it down, and it did indeed rate as closed. But it functioned clandestinely—the police inspector and the county health officer were in the know, and each was paid his ten roubles a month by the owner. There were only two decent stone-built, iron-roofed houses in the whole village. One contained the local council offices, while the other—two-storeyed, right opposite the church—was the home of Gregory Tsybukin, a shopkeeper from Yepifan.

Gregory kept a grocery store, but only as a cover for dealing in vodka, cattle, skins, grain, pigs and whatever else was going. For instance, when there was a demand to export peasant bonnets as ladies' headgear, he made thirty copecks a pair on the deal. He bought standing timber, lent money at interest. He was, by and large, a resourceful old boy.

He had two sons. The elder, Anisim, was in the police detective branch, and was seldom at home. The younger, Stephen, had gone into the business, and assisted his father, but they didn't expect real help from him as he was deaf and ailing. His wife Aksinya was a beautiful, well-built woman. She sported her hat and sunshade of a Sunday, rose early, went to bed late, and was on the go all day in barn, cellar and shop—skirts hitched up, keys jingling. It made old man Tsybukin happy to look at her, and his eyes would light up—yet he was sorry that she was not married to his elder son, but to the younger: deaf and clearly no connoisseur of feminine beauty!

The old boy had always been domestically inclined, and loved his family more than anything on earth: especially his elder, detective son and his other son's wife. No sooner had Aksinya married her deaf husband than she was already showing an unusual head for business. She knew who could and could not be given credit, she kept her keys on her, not trusting even her husband with them, she clicked away at her counting-frame. She looked horses in the mouth like a peasant, and she was always laughing or shouting. Whatever she did or said, the old man just doted on her.

'Good for you, daughter!' he would mutter. 'Well done, my lovely darling——'

He had been a widower, but one year after his son's marriage had again succumbed to wedlock. They found him a girl of good family, called Barbara, twenty miles from Ukleyevo. Though not in her first youth, she was a fine figure of a woman. And no sooner had she settled into her little first-floor room than everything in the house was sparkling like a new pin. Lamps burned before icons, tables were covered with snow-white table-cloths, red-eyed flowers appeared on window-sills and in the front garden, meals were no longer eaten from a common bowl—everyone had his own little dish. Barbara's warm, friendly smile seemed to make the whole house smile. Also—and this was new—beggars and various pilgrims began to call. The piteous whining of the Ukleyevo women was heard outside the windows, as also was the apologetic coughing of their frail, haggard menfolk dismissed from the works for drunkenness. Barbara gave them money, food, old clothes. When she was a bit more sure of herself she also took to fetching them odd things from the shop. The deaf man once saw her taking two two-ounce packets of tea, which disconcerted him.

'Mum just took two packets of tea,' he informed his father later. 'Who shall I charge it to?'

The old man made no answer—just stood and thought, twitching his eyebrows—then went upstairs to his wife.

'Barbara, dear,' said he affectionately, 'if you want something in the shop you take it. Take as much as you like, don't you hesitate.'

Next day the deaf man ran across the yard shouting 'if you want something, Mum, you take it.'

There was something fresh, cheerful and light-hearted about her alms-giving, just as there was in those icon-lamps and little red flowers. Just before fasts, or on the village saint's-day (it actually lasted three days), they used to palm off putrid salt beef on the villagers: stuff with so vile a stench that you could hardly go near the barrel. And they let drunks pawn their scythes, their caps and their women's kerchiefs, while mill-hands—befuddled by foul vodka—sprawled in the mud, the very air seeming clogged by a dense miasma of sin . . . at which times it rather helped to remember that over there in the house was a neat, quiet woman who had nothing to do with that beef or vodka. On such oppressive, hazy occasions her charity operated as a safety valve.

These were busy days at the Tsybukins'. Aksinya would be spluttering as she washed herself in the passage before sun-up, while the kitchen samovar hissed and droned like a prophet of doom. Gregory— a nice, clean little old fellow in his long black frock-coat, nankeen trousers and sparkling jack-boots—paced the rooms, tapping his heels like 'My Husband's Dear Old Dad' in the popular song. They would open the shop. When it was light the fast droshky would be brought to the porch, and in the old man would jump, jauntily, pulling his large peaked cap down over his ears. No one looking at him would have thought him fifty-six years old. His wife and daughter-in-law would see him off. Now, at such times, when he wore his nice, clean frock-coat and the great black three-hundred-rouble stallion was hitched to the droshky, the old man disliked the yokels coming up to complain and beg favours. He hated peasants, they riled him.

'Why are you hanging round? You clear off,' he would yell wrathfully if he saw one waiting by the gate. Or, if it was a beggar, he would shout that God would 'pervide'.

When he was away on business his wife, in her dark clothes and black apron, would tidy the house or help in the kitchen. Aksinya

served in the shop, and you could hear the jingle of bottles and coins
out in the yard while she laughed or shouted and her offended customers raged. That the clandestine vodka trade was in full swing in the
shop was also evident.

The deaf husband would also sit in the shop, or pace the street bare-
headed, hands in pockets, looking absently at huts and sky. They drank
tea half a dozen times a day in the house and sat down to about four
meals. In the evening they counted the takings and entered them,
after which they slept soundly.

All three Ukleyevo print-works were connected by telephone, as
were the homes of the owners: Khrymins, Khrymin Sons and Kostyukov. The parish offices had been connected up too, but that instrument
soon stopped working, having become infested with bugs and cockroaches. The parish chairman could hardly read, and he began every
word in his documents with a capital letter, but when the telephone
stopped working he said, yes, it was going to be 'a bit difficult, like,
without that there telephone'.

Khrymins were always suing Khrymin Sons, while Khrymin Sons
sometimes quarrelled among themselves and went to law, whereupon
their works would stand idle for a month or two until they made it up
again—which amused the Ukleyevites, seeing that each squabble
provoked much discussion and tittle-tattle. On Sundays Kostyukov
and Khrymin Sons would go out driving and career through Ukleyevo
running down the calves. Rustling her starched skirts and dressed up to
the nines, Aksinya would parade in the street near her shop until
Khrymin Sons swooped down and whisked her off as if abducting her
by force. Then old Tsybukin would drive out too, to show off his new
horse, taking Barbara with him.

In the evening, when the driving was over and folk were going to
bed, an expensive-sounding accordion would be played in Khrymin
Sons' grounds, and if there was a moon these sounds thrilled and
gladdened the heart. No longer did Ukleyevo seem quite such a dump.

II

The elder son Anisim came back very seldom, only on the major
saints' days, but he often got people from the village to take home
presents and letters beautifully written in someone else's hand. They
were always on a good-quality paper, they had an official look about
them, and they abounded in expressions never used by Anisim in

conversation, such as 'dearest Mum and Dad, I send you a pound of herbal tea for the gratification of your physical requirements.'

At the foot of each letter was scratched ANISIM TSYBUKIN, as if with a cross-nibbed pen, and beneath this, in the same ornate hand as before, the word AGENT.

The letters were read aloud several times.

'Ah well, he wouldn't stay at home, he would be a scholar,' said the old man, much moved and crimson with excitement. 'So be it then. Everyone should go his own way.'

Once, just before Shrovetide, there was heavy rain and sleet. The old man and Barbara went to the window for a look—and behold Anisim sleighing in from the station. Completely unexpected, he entered anxiously as if he had something on his mind, and kept this up during the rest of his time there. He seemed a bit off-hand too, and was in no hurry to leave. Could he have lost his job? That's what it looked like. Barbara was glad to see him and kept giving him rather arch looks, sighing and shaking her head.

'Now, goodness me, this won't do at all,' she clucked. 'Here's a lad turned twenty-seven—and he's still the gay bachelor! Goodness gracious me!'

From another room her quiet, level speech sounded like a continuous susurration. She took to whispering to the old man and Aksinya, and their faces also adopted that arch, mysteriously conspiratorial look.

They decided to marry Anisim off.

'Your younger brother's been wed long since,' clucked Barbara. 'But you're unspliced still, like a cockerel at market—it ain't right, that. You can marry, God willing, and then do as you please: go back to work, and your wife can stay at home and help. You've got into bad ways, my lad, I can see that. Forgotten what's what, you have. Proper shockers you town folks are, goodness gracious me!'

When Tsybukins married they had the pick of the best-looking girls, seeing that they were rich. For Anisim too a beautiful bride was found. His own looks were drab and unprepossessing. His build was frail and sickly, he was short of stature, he had plump, bulging cheeks which looked as if he was puffing them out. He had a sharp, unwinking stare and a sparse, gingery beard which, in pensive mood, he was always chewing at. He liked his dram, too—that showed in his face and walk. But when informed that a very beautiful bride had been found for him, he said that he was, 'well, not exactly misshapen' himself.

'We Tsybukins are a good-looking breed, and that's a fact.'

Adjoining the local town was the village of Torguyevo, half of which had recently been amalgamated with the town, the other half remaining a village. In the town part lived a certain widow in a cottage which she owned. She had a sister who was very poor and went out to work by the day. This sister had a daughter, Lipa, who was a hired drudge like her mother. Lipa's beauty was the talk of Torguyevo. The trouble was, though, she was so terribly poor. The view was that some elderly man or widower would marry her, overlooking her poverty—or else, 'you know, just live with her'—and then the mother would be provided for as well. Hearing of Lipa from local marriage-brokers, Barbara went over to Torguyevo.

Then a bride-showing was laid on at the aunt's house—it was all done properly with the usual snacks and drinks. Lipa wore a new pink dress specially made for the occasion, and a crimson ribbon flamed in her hair. She was a frail, slim, pale little thing with fine, delicate, features, sunburnt from work in the open air. A sad, nervous smile played on her face. And there was a childlike look, trustful and inquisitive, about her eyes.

She was young—no more than a little girl, her bosom barely developed—but already of marriageable age. She really was beautiful, having only one feature which might seem unattractive: large arms, like a man's, now dangling idly like two great claws.

'There's no dowry, but that don't bother us,' the old man told the aunt. 'We took a girl from a poor family for our son Stephen too, and we're as pleased as could be. About the house, in the shop . . . oh, she's a real treasure.'

Lipa stood by the door, and seemed to be trying to tell them to 'do what you like with me, I trust you.'

Her mother Praskovya, the hired hand, skulked in the kitchen almost too shy to breathe. In her youth a merchant whose floors she was scrubbing once flew into a rage and stamped his feet at her. She had been terribly frightened, it had given her rather a turn, and that terror had remained with her all her life: a terror which kept her arms and legs for ever trembling—her cheeks too. From her seat in the kitchen she tried to hear what the guests were saying, and she kept crossing herself, pressing her fingers to her forehead and glancing at the icon. Slightly drunk, Anisim kept opening the kitchen door.

'Why sit out here, dearest Mum?' he would ask jauntily. 'We've been missing you.'

Praskovya timidly pressed her hands to her gaunt, emaciated bosom. 'Oh, you shouldn't, sir, really,' she answered. 'It's far too good of you, sir.'

They inspected the bride, they named the wedding day—after which Anisim kept pacing the rooms at home and whistling. Or he would suddenly remember something, start brooding and fix a piercing stare on the floor as if his eyes sought to penetrate deep into the earth. He evinced neither pleasure at the prospect of marrying soon (the week after Easter) nor any wish to see his bride either, he only whistled. He was only marrying because his father and step-mother wanted him to, that was obvious—and because it's a village custom: the son takes a wife to help in the house. When he left for town again he did so without haste. This time his whole conduct had differed from that of his previous visits: he had been particularly off-hand and said all the wrong things.

III

In Shikalovo village lived two dressmakers—sisters, belonging to the Flagellant sect. They were given the order for the wedding clothes, they often came over for fittings, and they drank tea for hours. For Barbara they made a brown dress trimmed with black lace and bugles, and for Aksinya a light green one with a train and a yellow bodice. When the dressmakers had finished, Tsybukin paid them: not in cash, but in goods from his shop. They went away sadly, holding bundles of tallow candles and sardines for which they had no use at all, and when they came out of the village into open country they sat on a tussock and wept.

Three days before the wedding Anisim turned up in a completely new outfit: shiny rubber galoshes, a red cord with bobbles instead of a tie. A greatcoat, also new, was slung loosely over his shoulders.

He prayed solemnly before the icon, greeted his father—and gave him ten silver roubles and ten fifty-copeck pieces. He gave the same to Barbara, and he gave Aksinya twenty quarter-roubles. The main charm of these gifts was this: the coins were all brand new, in mint condition, and glinted in the sunlight. Trying to look solemn and earnest, Anisim pulled a long face, puffed out his cheeks and gave off a whiff of spirits. He'd popped into the bar at every station, very likely. Once again there was something off-hand, something rather otiose, about the fellow. Then Anisim and the old man had tea while Barbara fingered the bright new roubles and asked about folk from their village who had gone to live in town.

'They're all right, praise the Lord—doing well, they are,' said Anisim. 'Oh, there has been an incident, though, in Ivan Yegorov's domestic life. His old woman Sophia passed on. The consumption, it was. The caterers handled the wake at two-and-a-half roubles a head. There was wine too. There was peasants there—some of our lot—and they charged two-and-a-half roubles for them too, though they never ate nothing. What do them bumpkins know about sauce?'

'Two-and-a-half roubles each!' The old man shook his head.

'What else do you expect? It ain't like a village. You go into a restaurant for a bite, you order a few things, a few of your pals look in, you have a drink—and then, lo and behold, it's already dawn, and it's fork out your three or four roubles a head if you please. And when Samorodov's there, he wants his coffee and brandy after everything—and with brandy at "sixty copecks the glass, sir"!'

The old man was ecstatic. 'What nonsense he does talk!'

'I spend all my time with Samorodov these days. He's the one who writes my letters to you—oh, he's a great writer, is Samorodov.'

Anisim turned to Barbara. 'You'd never believe me, Mum,' he went on cheerfully, 'if I told you what Samorodov's like. We call him Mukhtar because he looks like an Armenian: black all over. Read him like a book, I do—I know all his business like the palm of my hand, Mum. And don't he feel it! He's always making up to me, won't leave me alone, we're thick as thieves now, we are. He's a bit scared of me, but he can't do without me. Where I go he goes. I've got a real good eye, Mum, that I have. Like when I see a peasant selling a shirt in the flea-market. "Hey there," says I, "that's stolen property!" And I'm always right, the shirt *is* stolen, it turns out——'

'But how can you tell?' asked Barbara.

'I *can't* tell, I've just got the eye for it. I don't know nothing about that shirt, I somehow just feel it's stolen, and that's that. That's what they say in the office. "Anisim's gone sniping," say they: looking for stolen goods, that is. True enough, anyone can steal things—it's keeping them that counts. Big as the world is, there ain't nowhere to hide the swag.'

'Last week a ram and two ewes were stolen from the Guntorevs here in the village,' sighed Barbara. 'Goodness gracious me! There was no one to look for them.'

'Very well, I might take it on—I wouldn't mind.'

The wedding day arrived. It was a cool April day, but bright and brisk. Troikas and two-horse carriages—harness-bells jingling, with gaudy ribbons on yokes and manes—had been driving round Ukleyevo since early morning. Disturbed by all the coming and going, rooks chattered in the willows and starlings nearly burst their lungs, seeming to celebrate the Tsybukin wedding with their non-stop singing.

Indoors the tables were already groaning with long fishes, hams, stuffed birds, boxes of sprats, various salted and pickled items, and an array of vodka and wine bottles. There was a smell of salami and stale lobster. Near those tables, clattering his heels and sharpening knife on knife, paraded the old man. They kept calling Barbara and asking for something, and she—panting, looking distracted—would run into the kitchen where Kostyukov's chef and Khrymin Sons' cook had been hard at work since dawn. Hair curled, in corsets but no dress, new boots squeaking, Aksinya whirled round the yard with flashes of bare knee and breast. It was noisy, there was cursing and swearing. Passers-by paused at the wide open gate, and could sense that something most unusual was afoot.

'They've gone for the bride.'

Harness-bells jingled, then died away far beyond the village.

At about half-past two a crowd ran up, and the bells were heard again. They were bringing the bride!

The church was full, the candelabra blazed, the choristers sang from sheet music—old Tsybukin's wish, this. The glittering lights, the bright dresses blinded Lipa, the choir's loud voices rang like hammers in her head. Her corset—the first she had ever worn—and her shoes were pinching her: she looked as if she had just come out of a faint, gazing about her but not understanding. Anisim, in his black frock-coat with his bit of red cord for a tie, was plunged in thought, staring fixedly and hastily crossing himself whenever a great shout came from the choir. He was deeply moved, to the point of tears. He had known this church since he was a little boy. His mother of blessed memory had brought him here for the sacraments, he had once sung in the boys' choir. Each little nook, each icon . . . he remembered them all so well. Now he was being married here because that was the done thing, but his mind was elsewhere, he no longer thought of his wedding, some-how—had forgotten it entirely. He could not see the icons for tears, there was a lump in his throat. He was praying, he was begging God that those fell disasters about to burst on him any day now . . . that they might somehow pass him by as clouds pass over a village in time of drought without shedding one drop of rain. And what of the weight of accumulated sin in his past—the many sins which had ensnared him beyond redemption, sins past praying forgiveness for, even? Pray forgiveness, though, he did—he even sobbed aloud, but no one heeded.

They just thought he'd had a drop too much.

A child's tearful cry rang out. 'Mummy, darling! Take me away from here!'

'Silence there!' the priest shouted.

On their way back from church the peasants thronged after them, and there were more crowds near shop and gate, and beneath the windows facing the yard. Village women had come to sing the bridal songs. No sooner had the young couple crossed the threshold than the choristers, waiting ready in the hall with that sheet music, shrieked for all they were worth. The band, specially hired from town, struck up. Tall goblets of Cossack 'bubbly' were offered round, and the jobbing carpenter Yelizarov—a tall, lean old man with brows so bushy that they nearly masked his eyes—addressed the newly-weds.

'Anisim and you, child, love each other and lead godly lives, my children, and the Holy Mother will not forsake you.' He leant on the old man's shoulder and sobbed.

'Gregory Tsybukin, let us weep aloud, let us weep tears of joy!' he said in a reedy little voice followed by a sudden loud guffaw.

'And this new daughter-in-law of yours is a real good-looker too,' he went on in a loud, deep voice. 'She has everything in the right place, like: all smooth stuff, it won't rattle, the whole mechanics is in tip-top order—plenty of screws.'

He came from out Yegoryevsk way, but had worked in the Ukleyevo mills and near-by parts since youth—he'd settled down. He had looked just as old, lean and lanky as he was now for as long as folk remembered. For years he had had the nickname 'Lofty'. For over forty years he had done nothing but maintenance work at the mills, which is perhaps why he judged everyone and everything solely in terms of their durability: did they need repair? Before sitting down at table he had tested a few chairs for soundness, also prodding the cold salmon.

After the 'bubbly' they all took their places at table. The guests spoke and moved their chairs, the choir sang in the hall, the band played, while the women in the yard simultaneously sang their folk songs in unison: a ghastly, grotesque medley of noise which made your head spin.

Now crying, now laughing aloud, Lofty fidgeted in his chair, elbowed his neighbours, wouldn't let them get a word in edgeways.

'Children, children, children,' he muttered rapidly. 'Aksinya, my dear, and Barbara, let us all live in peace and harmony, my darling little hatchets——'

No great drinker, he was quite merry, now, on one glass of 'English bitters'. This revolting brew, made of God knows what, stunned all who drank it as if they had been slugged. Tongues became entwined.

There were clergy here, there were clerks from the mills with their wives, there were traders and pub-keepers from other villages. The parish chairman and his clerk—they'd been working together for fourteen years now, and never during all that time had they signed a single document, nor let a soul leave their office, without cheating and insulting somebody—sat side by side: fat and smug, both of them . . . and seemingly so steeped in skulduggery that the very skin of their faces had a curiously depraved texture. The clerk's scrawny, cross-eyed wife had brought all her children along. She was squinting vulture-like at the bowls, grabbing whatever came her way and putting it in her own and the children's pockets.

Lipa sat there like a statue with the same look on her face as in church. Not having exchanged a single word with her since their first meeting, Anisim still didn't know what her voice sounded like. Now, as they sat side by side, he still wasn't speaking, but drank those 'English bitters'. Then, when he was tipsy, he addressed Lipa's aunt—sitting opposite.

'I have a friend, name of Samorodov. He's rather special, like. He's a cut above the rank and file, and he has something to say for himself. But I read him like a book, Aunty—and don't he feel it! May we now drink Samorodov's health together, Aunty dear?'

Barbara hovered round the table pressing the guests to eat—puffed, flustered, obviously glad that there were so many dishes. It was all on so lavish a scale that no one could sneer at them now. The sun went down, but the meal went on. No longer did they know what they were eating or drinking, nor could they hear what was said, but now and then when the band was quiet some village woman's shout carried clearly from the yard.

'Rotten swine, grinding the faces of the poor! May you rot in hell!'

In the evening they danced to the band. Khrymin Sons had

brought their own drink, and during the quadrille one of them held a bottle in each hand and a glass in his mouth, which was all great fun. In mid-quadrille they suddenly launched into a squatting dance. Green Aksinya kept flashing past with a breath of wind from her train. Someone had trodden on one of her flounces.

'Hey, her skirting board's come loose, children!' shouted Lofty.

Aksinya had naïve grey eyes which rarely blinked and a naïve smile for ever playing on her face. In those unblinking eyes, in the small head on the long neck, in her litheness, there was something of the snake. Dressed in green, yellow-bodiced, smiling, she looked like a viper: coiled, head uplifted in the young rye, as it watches someone go past in spring time. The Khrymins took liberties with her, and it was only too obvious that she had long been on the closest terms with the eldest. The deaf husband sensed nothing, though—he wasn't looking at her, but sat with his legs crossed, eating nuts and cracking them loudly with his teeth. It sounded like pistol shots.

Out came old Tsybukin himself into the middle and flipped a handkerchief to show that he too wanted to do the squat-dance. A roar of approval ran through the crowded house and yard.

''Tis the old gaffer himself going to dance!'

Barbara danced, while the old man only waved his handkerchief and shuffled his heels, but the folk out in the yard—clinging to each other as they peered through the windows—were in ecstasy and straightway forgave him everything: his money, his insults. Voices were heard in the crowd.

'Good old Gregory!' they laughed. 'That's it, you have a go! So you ain't past it, eh? Ha, Ha.'

It all ended late, after one in the morning. Anisim staggered round choir and band, giving everyone a new half-rouble as a parting gift, while the old man—steady on his feet, but vaguely limping—saw his guests off, telling everyone that the wedding had 'cost me a cool two thousand'.

As they were dispersing it turned out that someone had taken the Shikalovo pub-keeper's new jacket, leaving an old one behind in its place. Anisim flared up.

'Stop, everyone! I'm going to make a search,' he shouted. 'I know who took that. Hold it!'

He ran out into the street, started chasing someone.

They caught Anisim, they dragged him back by the arms. They thrust him—drunk, crimson with rage, wet with sweat—into the room where Aunty had been undressing Lipa. And locked him in.

IV

Five days passed. Anisim was ready to leave, and went upstairs to say good-bye to Barbara. Her icon-lamps were all lit, there was a smell of incense and she sat by the window knitting a red woollen stocking.

'You didn't stay long,' said she. 'Got bored, eh? Goodness gracious me. We do ourselves well, we don't want for anything. And your wedding was done right and proper—two thousand it cost, the old man said. We live off the fat of the land in fact, but it's a dull life, this is. Too hard on them peasants, we are. It grieves me so, dear, to think how we wrong them. Bartering horses, buying things, hiring workmen . . . it's all fraud, fraud, fraud, Lord help us. The olive oil in the shop's sour and rancid—no better than tar, it isn't. How come we can't sell proper oil, eh? You tell me that.'

'None of my business, Mum.'

'But we all die in the end, don't we? You really should talk to your father, dear me you should.'

'Talk to him yourself.'

'Not me. If I do he only answers same as you: it ain't none of my business. Whose business it is . . . that'll be settled in the next world. God's judgement is righteous.'

'Of course it won't be settled,' sighed Anisim. 'There ain't no such thing as God anyway, is there, Mum? So much for your next world!'

Barbara looked at him in amazement, laughed and threw up her arms. That she so genuinely marvelled at his words, that she really did think him a freak . . . it quite disconcerted him.

'Perhaps there is a God, and it's just me that can't believe,' he said. 'I felt a bit funny at the wedding—like when you take an egg from the hen, and there's a chick squeaking in it. It was that way with my conscience—it suddenly started squeaking, and during the service I kept thinking that God does exist. Then I come out of church and the feeling's gone. Anyway, how can *I* tell if there's a God or not? That's not what they taught us as kids. From when we was babes in arms we was taught only one thing: you keep your place. Now, Dad don't believe in God either, do he? You once mentioned some sheep being stolen from Guntorevs'. It was a Shikalovo peasant stole 'em, I discovered. He stole them, but it's Dad who's got the skins. There's your religion for you!'

Anisim winked and shook his head.

'The parish chairman don't believe in God either,' he went on. 'Nor does the clerk, nor does the sexton. If they go to church, if they keep the fasts, they only do it so folks won't speak badly of them, and to be on the safe side—what if there should really be a Judgment Day? Folk are so feeble nowadays, don't respect their parents and all that—so people think it's the end of the world. Nonsense! The way I see it is this, Mum: all this grief, it comes from folk not having enough conscience. I read 'em like a book, Mum, I know what's what. If a man has a stolen shirt, I can tell. Or take someone sitting in a pub—all you can see is him drinking his tea, no more than that. But *I* see that, tea or no tea, he ain't got no conscience. You can search all day and still not see one man with a conscience. And for why? Because they don't know if there's a God or not. Well, good-bye, Mum. Long life and good health to you, don't think too badly of me.'

Anisim bowed low to Barbara.

'We thanks you for everything, Mum,' he added. 'You've been real good to our family, you have. You're a very proper sort of a woman, and I'm real pleased with you.'

Deeply touched, Anisim went out, but came back again.

'Samorodov's got me involved in some deal,' said he. 'It's riches or ruination for me. If it don't go right, do comfort the old man, won't you, Mum?'

'Oh dear, whatever next! Goodness gracious me! God have mercy on us!' she clucked. 'Now, you be nice to your wife, Anisim. You look as if you'd taken agin each other. You might at least laugh a bit, really!'

'Yes, she's a strange one,' sighed Anisim. 'Doesn't understand nothing, never says nothing. She's very young, though—wait till she grows up.'

Near the porch stood a tall, sleek, white stallion harnessed to a dog-cart. Old Tsybukin took a run up, jumped jauntily aboard, seized the reins. Anisim kissed Barbara, Aksinya and his brother. Lipa too stood in the porch—stock still, eyes averted, looking as if she hadn't come out to see him off but had just somehow happened to be there. Anisim went up, lightly brushed her cheek with his lips, and said good-bye.

Not looking at him, she gave a somewhat strange smile. Her face trembled, and everyone felt rather sorry for her. Anisim too leapt aboard, and sat with arms akimbo, thinking himself handsome.

As they drove up out of the hollow Anisim kept looking back at the village. It was a warm, bright day. The cattle had been driven out for the first time, girls and women were walking about near the herd

wearing holiday dresses. A brown bull bellowed, enjoying his freedom and pawing the ground with his front hooves. Larks sang everywhere, both above and below. Anisim looked round at the church so
neat and white—it had just been whitewashed—and remembered
worshipping there five days ago. He looked round at the school with
its green roof, at the stream where he had once bathed and fished—and
joy stirred within his breast. If only the earth would suddenly throw
up a wall to bar his way and leave him alone with his memories.

They went into the station buffet for a glass of sherry. Wanting to
pay, the old man felt in his pocket for his purse.

'This one's on me,' said Anisim.

Delighted, the old man clapped him on the shoulder, and winked at
the barman to show what a fine son he had.

'Why don't you stay at home and join the business, Anisim,' he
asked. 'You'd be a real asset. I'd make you a mint of money, son.'

'It's quite out of the question, Dad.'

The sherry was rather bitter and smelt of sealing-wax, but they had
another glass.

When the old man arrived home from the station he at first failed
to recognize his younger daughter-in-law. No sooner had her husband
left the premises than Lipa became transformed, suddenly cheering up.
Barefoot, in a worn old skirt, sleeves rolled up to her shoulders, she
was washing the staircase in the hall and singing in a thin, silvery little
voice. And when she carried out the great pail of dirty water, looking
into the sun with her childlike smile, she might have been another lark
herself.

Walking past the porch, an old labourer shook his head and cleared
his throat. 'Fine women, Mr. Gregory, your son's wives. God has
blessed you with real treasures, sir.'

V

On Friday the eighth of July 'Lofty' Yelizarov and Lipa were on
their way back from making a pilgrimage to Kazanskoye village
in honour of Our Lady of Kazan, whose festival this was. Far behind
walked Lipa's mother Praskovya—being ailing and short of breath,
she always did lag behind. It was late afternoon. Listening admiringly
to Lipa, Lofty kept sighing and mumbling.

'I'm very fond of jam, I am, Mr. Yelizarov,' said Lipa. 'I sit in my
own little corner drinking my tea and jam. Or Barbara and I have it

together, and she tells some sad story, like. They have lots of jam—
four jars at a time. "You have some, Lipa," they tell me. "You help
yourself." '

'Aha! Four jars, eh?'

'They do themselves proud. They have white rolls with their tea,
and there's as much beef as you like. They live well, but it's so frightening there, Mr. Yelizarov—it don't half scare me.'

'What have you to fear, child?' asked Lofty, looking round to see if
Praskovya was very far behind.

'At first, after the wedding, I was scared of Mr. Anisim. He never
done nothing, he weren't nasty to me—it's just that when he comes
near me a shudder goes through every bone in me body. And I don't
sleep a wink at nights, just keep shivering and praying. Now I'm a-
feared of Aksinya, Mr. Yelizarov. She seems all right, she's always
laughing—it's just that you see her look out of the window sometimes
with them angry green eyes afire, like a sheep's in the shed. Them
Khrymin Sons are always on at her. Your old man has a bit of land at
Butyokino—over a hundred acres, they tell her. There's sand, they tell
her, and water too. So you build a brickyard on it in your own name,
say they, and we'll go shares with you. Bricks fetch twenty roubles a
thousand now—it's good business, that is. Well, at dinner yesterday
Aksinya tells the old man she wants to start this brickyard at Butyokino—wants to go into business for herself. She's laughing as she says
it, but Mr. Gregory gives her a black look—he don't like it, that's clear
enough. "So long as I'm alive," says he, "we ain't going to split up,
we must stick together." Well, she flashes them eyes and kind of
grinds her teeth. We had pancakes, but she wouldn't eat none.'

'Oh, so she wouldn't eat none?' Lofty was surprised.

'And another thing—when does she sleep if you please?' Lipa went
on. 'She'll sleep half an hour, then up she'll jump, rummage round
everywhere to see if the peasants have set anything on fire or stolen
anything. She scares me, Mr. Yelizarov. And after the wedding them
Khrymin Sons never went to bed. They went to town to have the law
on each other, and it was all Aksinya's doing—or so folks say. Two of
them brothers promised to build her the works, but that annoyed the
third one and their mill was shut for a month—my uncle Prokhor
was out of work and had to go round begging for scraps. "Why don't
you go a-ploughing for a bit, Uncle," I ask him. "Or saw some wood.
Why bring shame on yourself?" "I've lost the habit of farm work,"
says he. "There ain't nothing I can do, Lipa dear." '

They paused near a grove of young aspens to rest and wait for Praskovya. Yelizarov had been doing contract work for years, but he didn't keep a horse. He travelled the whole county on foot with a little bag of bread and onions—walked with long strides, swinging his arms, so that he was hard to keep up with.

At the entrance to the copse was a boundary post, and Yelizarov touched it to see if it was sound. Up came Praskovya, panting. Her wrinkled face, with its perpetual look of fear, beamed happiness. She had been to church today like a real person, then she had visited the fair and drunk pear kvass. It was such a rare treat, she even felt as if she had enjoyed herself today for the first time in her life. After a rest the three of them went on together. The sun was setting, its rays piercing the copse and shining on tree trunks. There was a murmur of voices ahead of them. The Ukleyevo girls had gone a long way in front, but had tarried in this copse—to pick mushrooms, probably.

'Hey there, lasses!' shouted Yelizarov. 'Hallo my beauties.'

'That's old Lofty, that is,' they laughed in reply. 'Silly old geezer!' The laughter echoed after them.

The copse was behind them, now, the tops of the mill chimneys had come into view, the belfry cross glittered. Here was the village 'where the sexton ate all the caviare at the funeral'. They were nearly home, they only had to go down into that great ravine. Lipa and Praskovya, who had been walking barefoot, sat on the grass to put their shoes on, and the carpenter sat down beside them. From up here Ukleyevo—with its willows, white church and stream—seemed pretty and peaceful. The only eyesores were the mill roofs, painted a gloomy greyish colour for economy reasons. On the far slope they could see rye: stooks and sheaves of it here and there, as if scattered by a storm, and newly reaped swathes. The oats were ripe and gleamed like mother-of-pearl in the sun. It was harvest time, but today was a day off. Tomorrow, Saturday, they would get in the rye and cart hay. Then it would be Sunday, another holiday. There was a rumbling of distant thunder every day, it was steamy and looked like rain. Gazing at the fields, now, they all hoped to harvest their crops in time, God willing. It was a cheerful, joyous—yet uneasy—feeling.

'Reapers come dear nowadays,' said Praskovya. 'One rouble forty a day.'

More and more folk were rolling in from Kazanskoye fair: peasant women, mill-hands in new caps, beggars, children.

A cart would drive past, raising the dust, with an unsold horse trotting behind it and seeming glad not to have been bought. Someone would drag a reluctant cow by the horns. Or another cart would come along with drunken peasants dangling their legs. An old woman led a little boy in a large hat and large boots. Exhausted by the heat and his heavy boots, which stopped him bending his knees, he was yet blowing non-stop for all he was worth at a toy trumpet. Even when they had reached the bottom and turned into the village street that trumpet could still be heard.

'There's something wrong with our mill-owners,' said Yelizarov. 'Real vexing, it is. Kostyukov's annoyed with me. "You used too many laths on them cornices," says he. "What do you mean, too many?" says I. "I used what I needed, Mr. Kostyukov," I tells him. "I don't eat 'em with me porridge, them laths." "How dare you talk to me like that?" he asks. "You oaf, you so-and-so! You forget your place. It was me as first set you up in business," he shouts. "You think you're very clever," says I. "But I still drank tea every day even when I didn't have me own business." "You're all swindlers," says he. I says nothing. "Oho!" I thinks. "We may be swindlers in this world, but you'll be swindlers in the next!" On the day after that he caves in. "Don't you be vexed, my good man," says he. "Don't you mind what I said. If," says he, "I said a bit too much—well, I'm a member of the chamber of commerce, so I'm a better man than you are, and you'd better not answer me back." "You," says I, "may well be a member of the chamber of commerce, while I'm just a carpenter. True enough. But Saint Joseph was a carpenter too," says I. "It's righteous, our work is, and pleasing to God. And if," says I, "you think you're a better man than me, Mr. Kostyukov, then the best of good luck to you, sir." After this—after this here talk, I mean—I get to thinking: what *is* better: big businessman or carpenter? I reckon it's the carpenter, children.

'That's the way of it,' Lofty added after a moment's thought. 'It's the one as labours and puts up with things as is better.'

The sun had gone down, and a dense, milk-white mist was rising over the river, in the churchyard and in the clearings near the mills. Now, with darkness so quickly descending, with the lights flashing down there, with the mist seeming to cloak a bottomless abyss, Lipa and her mother, who had been born beggars and were ready to live as such to the end—sacrificing to others everything but their frightened, gentle souls—briefly fancied perhaps that in the unnumbered, never-ending catalogue of lives in this vast, mysterious universe, they too

amounted to something. Perhaps even they were 'better' than someone? It was good to be sitting up here, and they smiled merrily,
forgetting that they did, after all, have to go back down to the bottom.

They reached home at last. By the gate, near the shop, reapers sat
around on the ground. Tsybukin's fellow-Ukleyevites usually refused
to work for him, so he had to hire strangers—now, in the darkness,
they all seemed to have long black beards. The shop was open, and
through the door the deaf man could be seen playing draughts with a
boy. The reapers sang softly, barely audibly, or loudly demanded
yesterday's pay, but that had been kept back to stop them leaving
before the morning. Old Tsybukin—minus his frock-coat, in waistcoat
and shirt sleeves—was having tea with Aksinya beneath the birch-tree
by the porch. There was a lighted lamp on the table.

'Hey there, Gaffer!' drawled a teasing voice behind the gate—one of
the reapers. 'At least pay us the half, Gaffer!'

There was laughter, after which they again sang, barely audibly.
Lofty sat down to tea as well, and began a yarn.

'Well, there we are at the fair. We're having a good time, children—
a real good time, praise be—when a rather nasty thing happens.
Blacksmith Sashka buys some tobacco, and he gives the shopkeeper a
half-rouble piece, like. But it was a bad one.'

Lofty glanced round. He was trying to whisper, but spoke in a
hoarse, strangled voice which everyone could hear.

'It was a bad half-rouble, that. "Where did you get it?" they ask.
"Anisim Tsybukin give it me when I was a guest at his wedding," says
he. They call the sergeant, they take him off. You'd better watch out,
old Gregory—there might be talk or summat——'

'Gaffer,' drawled the same teasing voice behind the gate. 'Hey there,
Gaffer!'

Silence followed.

'Ah, children, children, children,' muttered Lofty rapidly, and stood
up. He was practically dozing off. 'Well, thanks for the tea and sugar,
children. Time for bed. I'm a-mouldering away, I am—me joists are
all a-rotting, ho, ho, ho!

'Time I was in me grave,' he said as he left. And sobbed.

Old Tsybukin did not finish his tea, but sat brooding and looking as
if he was listening to Lofty's footsteps, though he was now far down the
street.

'He was lying, was Blacksmith Sashka, I reckon,' said Aksinya,
guessing his thoughts.

Gregory went indoors and came back a bit later with a bundle which he untied. The brand-new roubles glinted, and he took one, bit it, threw it down on the tray. Then he threw down another.

'Them roubles really are forged,' said he, looking at Aksinya as if in a quandry. 'It's the same ones—them as Anisim brought from town that time, the ones he gave us. Now, you take them, my girl,' he whispered, thrusting the bundle in her hands. 'Take them and throw them down the well, confound them. And mind there ain't no talk! I hope it's going to be all right. Now clear away the samovar and put that light out.'

Sitting in the shed, Lipa and Praskovya saw the lights going out one after the other. Only from Barbara's upstairs room did the blue and red icon-lamps still shed a glow of peace and blissful ignorance. Praskovya just couldn't accept her daughter's marriage to a rich man. She would cringe timidly in the passage during her visits, and smile pleadingly— and they would send tea and sugar out. Lipa couldn't resign herself to it either. After her husband had left she stopped using her bed, and would just lie down any old where in kitchen or shed. Every day she scrubbed floors or laundered, feeling like a charwoman. Now, after having returned from their pious mission, they had had tea in the kitchen with the cook, and had then gone into the shed and lain down on the straw between sledge and wall. It was dark and smelt of horse-collars. The lights round the house went out. Then they heard the deaf man locking up the shop and the reapers dossing down in the yard. Far away, at Khrymin Sons', someone was playing that expensive-sounding accordion.

Praskovya and Lipa began to doze off.

The moon was already bright when they were woken by footsteps. By the entrance to the shed stood Aksinya carrying her bedding.

'Perhaps it's cooler out here,' she said, coming in and lying down almost on the threshold, all bathed in moonlight.

Unable to sleep, she breathed heavily, tossing and turning about in the heat and throwing almost all the clothes off her. What a fine, proud beast she looked in the magical moonlight! A little later more steps were heard, and the old man showed up in the doorway, entirely white.

'You in here, Aksinya?' he called.

'Yes,' she responded angrily.

'Remember me telling you to throw them coins down the well just now? Did you do it?'

'Throw good money down a well—no fear! I gave it to them reapers.'

'God, oh God!' exclaimed the old man, horror-struck. 'You *are* a wild woman, God you are!'

With a gesture of annoyance he went muttering on his way. Not long afterwards Aksinya sat up with a deep, exasperated sigh, got to her feet and went out with an armful of bedding.

'Oh, Mother dear, why did you make me marry into this house?' Lipa asked.

'Folks must get wed, child. It ain't us decides these things.'

Grief and despair seemed about to overwhelm them. But they could sense someone looking down on them from heaven's height, from that starry dark-blue vault: someone who saw all that went on in Ukleyevo, and kept watch. However great the evil, the night was still calm and splendid. God's truth—no less calm, no less splendid—still stood, and would remain, in his creation. All things on earth were only waiting to mingle with that truth, as the moonlight mingles with the night.

Comforted, they fell asleep in each other's arms.

VI

News of Anisim's arrest for coining and uttering counterfeit money had arrived long ago. Months—more than half a year—went by, the long winter ended, spring came on, and Anisim's imprisonment became an accepted fact in his house and village. Anyone passing the house or shop at night would remember that he was in jail. The tolling of the bells in the parish church was also a reminder, somehow, that he was in prison awaiting trial.

A shadow seemed to lie over the premises. The house looked dirtier, the roof was rusty, the heavy, iron-bound, green-painted shop door had shrivelled until it was 'proper mortified', according to the deaf man. Old Tsybukin seemed a bit dingy himself. He had long stopped trimming his hair and beard, he looked shaggy, he was no longer leaping jauntily aboard that four-wheeler, nor did he shout at beggars that God would 'pervide'. His powers were waning, that was abundantly clear. Folk feared him less, now, and the local police sergeant sent in a report on the shop—even though he was still getting his usual cut. Three times the old man was summoned to town to stand trial for illicit vodka-dealing, but the case was repeatedly adjourned because of the witnesses' non-appearance. He was worn to a shadow.

He was for ever visiting his son, hiring lawyers, making submissions, presenting churches with banners. On the chief warder of Anisim's prison he bestowed a silver glass-holder with an enamelled inscription—MODERATION IN ALL THINGS—and a long spoon.

'There's no one, no one to put in a proper word for us,' clucked Barbara. 'Gracious me, you should get one of the nobs to write to the powers that be. They might at least give him bail—why torment the lad?'

She too was grieved, but she had put on weight, her complexion was whiter, and she still lit the icon-lamps, still kept the house clean, still regaled her guests with jam and apple-cheese.

The deaf man and Aksinya served in the shop. That new business—the Butyokino brickyard—had been started up, and Aksinya went over almost daily in the four-wheeler. She always drove herself, and when she met anyone she knew she would stretch up her neck like a snake in the young rye, smiling her naïve, enigmatic smile.

Lipa was always playing with her baby, born just before Lent. He was a tiny, emaciated, pathetic little thing. How strange that he could cry and see, that he rated as a human being and was even called Nikifor! As he lay in his cradle Lipa would go towards the door, bow and wish 'a very good day to you, Master Nikifor Tsybukin!' Then she would rush headlong to him and kiss him, before going back to the door, bowing and again wishing a very good day to 'Master Nikifor Tsybukin'. He would kick up his little red legs—crying and chuckling at the same time, like Yelizarov the carpenter.

A date had been fixed for the trial at last, and the old man left five days early. Then they heard that some peasants from the village had been called as witnesses. Their old labourer went too, having also had a summons.

The trial was on a Thursday. But Sunday passed and the old man still wasn't back, there was still no news. Late on the Tuesday afternoon Barbara sat by an open window listening for his return. Lipa was playing with her baby in the next room.

'You're going to be a big, big man,' she gleefully exclaimed, throwing him up in her arms. 'You'll be a peasant and we'll go and work in the fields together, that we shall.'

'Well, really!' Barbara was offended. '"Work in the fields!" What do you mean, you silly girl? We'll make a merchant of him.'

Lipa started singing softly, but forgot herself a little later and repeated that he would grow up to be a big, big man and a peasant, and that they would go and work in the fields together.

'Oh, really! You're at it again!'

Carrying Nikifor in her arms, Lipa paused in the doorway.

'Why do I love him so much, Mother?' she asked. 'Why do I feel so sorry for him?' she went on in a quavering voice, her eyes shining with tears. 'Who is he? What's he really like? He's light as a feather or a crumb, but I love him—I love him as a real person. He can't do anything, see, he can't speak, but I always know what he wants by the look in his dear little eyes.'

Barbara pricked up her ears, and a distant sound was heard: the evening train coming into the station. Might the old man be on it? She no longer heard what Lipa was saying, she couldn't take it in, she was not conscious of the passage of time, she just shook all over: not from fear, from overwhelming curiosity. She saw a cartful of peasants clatter swiftly by: the witnesses on their way home from the station. As the cart sped past the shop their old labourer jumped off it and came into the yard. Folk were heard greeting him out there, asking questions.

'Deprived of rights and property,' he said loudly. 'And six years' hard labour in Siberia.'

Aksinya was heard coming out of the shop by the back door. She had been serving paraffin, she had a bottle in one hand and a can in the other, and there were silver coins in her mouth.

'Where's Father?' she mumbled.

'At the station,' answered the labourer. 'Says he'll come on later when it's dark.'

When the news of Anisim's hard-labour sentence spread through the household, the cook suddenly started keening out in the kitchen— supposing this to be what propriety dictated.

'Why, oh why, have you forsaken us, Anisim, son of Gregory, light of our lives——'

The dogs, disturbed, started barking. Barbara ran to the window.

'Stop it, Stepanida, do!' she shouted to the cook in an anguished paroxysm, straining her voice to the limit. 'For Christ's sake stop tormenting us!'

They forgot to put on the samovar, they couldn't keep their minds on anything any more. Lipa alone had no idea what it was all about, but went on nursing her baby.

When the old man arrived from the station they asked him no questions. He greeted them, then paced the house in silence. He ate no supper.

Nc

'There ain't no one to put in a word for us,' clucked Barbara when they were alone together. 'I told you to see some of the nobs, but you wouldn't listen. We should make an application——'

'I *have* been putting in a word for us!' said the old man with an impatient gesture. 'When Anisim was sentenced I went to the gent as was defending him. "There's nothing to be done now," says he. "It's too late." Anisim himself says it's too late. Still, I did speak to one lawyer when I came out of court, gave him something in advance. I'll wait another week and then go back again. It's all God's will.'

Again the old man paced about the house in silence, then returned to Barbara.

'I must be unwell,' said he. 'In my head there's an—er, a sort of a fog. I can't think straight.'

He closed the door so that Lipa should not hear.

'It's money that's troubling me,' he went on quietly. 'Remember Anisim bringing me some new rouble and half-rouble coins? Before his wedding it was, the week after Easter. I hid one packet of 'em, but I got the others all mixed up with me own. Now, me Uncle Dmitry, God rest his soul . . . used to fetch merchandise from Moscow and the Crimea in his time. He had a wife, did Uncle. And while he was a-fetching of his goods, this wife of his would be having fun with other men. Six children she bore. How dear old Uncle used to laugh when he'd had a drop to drink! "I can't make out them kids," says he. "Which of 'em is true coin and which is the counterfeit?" A bit of a light-weight was Uncle. Now it's the same with me: I can't make out which of me money's true coin and which is the counterfeit. It all seems counterfeit.'

'Oh, really, get away with you!'

'I buy a ticket at the station in town, I pay me three roubles—and then I feel they must be bad ones. It don't half scare me. Unwell, I must be.'

'None of us will last for ever, goodness me, it stands to reason,' declared Barbara with a shake of her head. 'That's what you should be thinking of, Gregory. Something might happen to you—you never know, you're not young any more. You watch they don't harm your grandson when you're dead and gone—oh, they'll do that child an injury, I fear, that they will. He ain't got no father, properly speaking, and his mother's young and silly. You might put the little lad down for something, Gregory, if only some land: that Butyokino, say. You think about it,' Barbara pressed him. 'He's a pretty little lad, it's such a shame. You go and write the paper tomorrow. No sense in waiting.'

'Now, I'd quite forgotten my little grandson,' said Tsybukin. 'I must say hallo to him. The boy's all right, you tell me? Well well, so may he grow up, God willing!'

He opened the door and beckoned Lipa, who came up with the baby in her arms.

'Lipa dear, you ask for anything you need,' said he. 'And you must eat whatever you like—we don't grudge you nothing so long as you keep well.' He made the sign of the cross over the child. 'And you look after my little grandson. My son's gone, so there's only my grandson left.'

Tears coursed down his cheeks. He sobbed and moved away. Soon afterwards he went to bed and slept soundly after seven sleepless nights.

VII

The old man had made a short visit to town. Someone told Aksinya that he had gone to a lawyer's to make a will—and that he was leaving Butyokino, that same Butyokino where she was firing bricks, to his grandson Nikifor. She learnt this one morning when the old man and Barbara were sitting under the birch-tree drinking tea. She locked the shop doors, front and back, collected all the keys, and flung them at the old man's feet.

'I ain't a-going to work for you no longer!' she shouted, and suddenly burst out sobbing. 'I ain't no daughter of yours, it seems, I'm your servant. Everyone's laughing at me: "See what a good maid them Tsybukins have found!" I never asked you for no job. I ain't no beggar—I ain't common, like, I do have a father and mother.'

Not wiping her tears, she glared at the old man—eyes swimming, vicious, squinting with rage. Her face and neck were red with strain.

'I ain't going to be your servant no longer,' she went on, yelling for all she was worth. 'Worn to a shred, I am! Oh yes, when it comes to work, minding the shop day in day out, and sneaking out to fetch the vodka of a night—then *I* can do it! But when there's land going begging you give it to that jail-bird's woman and her brat! She's the mistress, she's the fine lady round here, and I'm her drudge. Give her the lot, the convict's woman! May it choke her! I'm going home. And you can find yourself some other ninny, you rotten swine!'

Never in his life had the old man used bad language or punished children. That any member of his family could be rude to him, or treat him disrespectfully . . . the very idea was inconceivable. Absolutely terrified, he rushed into the house and hid behind a cupboard, while Barbara was so flabbergasted that she couldn't get up from her chair, but just waved both arms about as if trying to ward off a bee.

'Dear, oh dear, what can this be?' she muttered in horror. 'Why does she shout like this? Goodness gracious me! Folks may hear. Not so loud, oh dear, less noise, please!'

'They've given Butyokino to the jail-bird's moll!' Aksinya shouted. 'Well, you can give her the lot now, I don't want nothing from you! You can go to hell! A lot of gangsters, you are. I've seen enough, I don't care. Rich and poor, old and young . . . they've robbed all who came their way, the crooks! Who sold vodka without a licence? And what of them forgeries? They stuff their coffers with false coin, and now they don't need me no more!'

By now a crowd had gathered at the open gates, and folk were staring into the yard.

'Let 'em stare!' shouted Aksinya. 'I'll disgrace you yet, I'll make you burn with shame, you'll crawl to me, you will!'

'Hey, Stephen,' she called the deaf man. 'Come on—we're going home this instant: home to me father and me mother. I ain't living with no jail-birds! You get your things together.'

Washing was hanging on the clothes lines in the yard. Snatching down her skirts and blouses, she threw them, still damp, into the deaf man's arms. Then she charged round the washing in the yard in a towering fury, tearing off everything—other people's clothes too— hurling it to the ground and trampling on it.

'Gracious, can't someone stop her?' groaned Barbara. 'What on earth is she at? Let her have Butyokino—give it her, for Christ's sake!'

'Well, well, well!' said people by the gate. 'What a woman! Gone berserk she has, and no mistake!'

Aksinya ran into the kitchen where the washing was being done. Lipa was working on her own, the cook having gone down to the stream to do some rinsing.

The tub and the copper near the stove gave off steam, misting and darkening the stuffy kitchen. On the floor was a heap of clothes still unwashed, and Nikifor had been put near it on a bench so that he wouldn't hurt himself if he fell. He was kicking up his little red legs. When Aksinya came in Lipa had just taken a shift of hers out of the pile, put it in the tub, and was reaching for the large can of boiling water on the table.

'You give that here!' said Aksinya, glaring her hatred, and snatched the shift from the tub. 'You take your dirty hands off of my under-clothes! You're a jail-bird's woman, that's what you are, and you should know your place.'

Lipa looked at her, utterly taken aback, not understanding. But she suddenly caught the look which Aksinya gave the baby . . . and then she *did* understand and turned pale as death.

'You stole my land, now take that!'

Thus speaking, Aksinya seized the can and splashed the boiling water on Nikifor.

There followed a yell like none ever heard in Ukleyevo—that a small, weak creature like Lipa could make such a noise was incredible. A sudden silence fell on the premises. Aksinya went wordlessly into the house with her usual naïve smile.

The deaf man was still out in the yard holding an armful of washing. Then he started hanging it up again—silently, without haste. Not until the cook came back from the stream did anyone dare go in the kitchen and see what was there.

VIII

Nikifor was taken to the local hospital, but was dead by evening. Not waiting to be fetched, Lipa wrapped the body in a little blanket and started to carry him home.

The hospital—newly built, with large windows—stood high on a hill and shone in the setting sun, seeming to be on fire inside. At the foot of the hill was a small village. Lipa walked down the road and sat by a little pond before reaching the village. A woman led a horse to the pond, but it would not drink.

'What more do you want?' asked the woman softly, quite bewil-dered. 'Ain't that good enough for you?'

A red-shirted boy sat at the water's edge washing his father's boots. Neither in the village nor on the hill was another soul to be seen.

'Won't drink,' said Lipa, looking at the horse.

Then the woman and the boy with the boots left, and there was no one to be seen at all. The sun went to his rest under a coverlet of purple and gold brocade, while long red and mauve clouds watched over his sleep, straddling the sky. From some unknown far-away spot came the doleful, muffled boom of a bittern—it sounded like a cow shut in a shed. Each spring the cry of this mysterious bird was heard, but no one knew what it was or where it lived. Up the hill near the hospital, in the bushes right here by the pond, beyond the village, in the fields all round, nightingales were trilling. A cuckoo was counting someone's age, but kept losing count and going back to the beginning. In the pond frogs bandied enraged croaks, straining their lungs, and you could even hear what they said: 'Hark at *her*! Hark at *her*!' What a racket! All these creatures seemed to be crying and singing with the express aim of making sleep impossible on this spring evening, and of ensuring that all—even those angry frogs—might relish and savour each passing minute. We do only live once, after all.

A silver crescent moon shone in the sky, and there were many stars. Lipa could not remember how long she had been sitting by the pond, but when she got up to go everyone in the little village was asleep, and there was not a light anywhere. It must be eight miles to her home, but she was worn out and had no idea of the way. The moon shone—now in front, now on the right—while that cuckoo, hoarse by now, still teased her with its mocking laughter and a 'Yoo-hoo—you fool— you'll lose—your route!'

Lipa walked quickly, and the kerchief had fallen from her head.

She looked at the sky and wondered: where might her little boy's soul now be—following her, or floating up there with the stars, unmindful of his mother? How lonely it was in the open country at night amid all the singing when you couldn't sing yourself, amid those non-stop cries of joy when you couldn't rejoice yourself . . . with the moon—also solitary—looking down from the sky and not caring whether it was spring or winter, whether people were alive or dead.

It is hard to have no one near you when your heart is broken. If only her mother Praskovya had been there! Or Lofty, or the cook, or one of the peasants.

The bittern gave a slow, protracted boom.

Then, suddenly, a man's voice was distinctly heard. 'Put them horses in, Vavila.'

Ahead of her a bonfire was burning on the roadside. The flames had died down, and there was only a glow of red embers. She heard horses munching. Two carts loomed up in the darkness—one containing a barrel, and another, lower one, with sacks—and two men. One was taking a horse to put it in the shafts, the other stood stock-still near the fire with his hands behind his back. A dog growled near the cart.

The man leading the horse stopped. 'Seems to be someone on the road.'

'Sharik, quiet!' the other shouted to the dog in what sounded like an old man's voice.

Lipa stood still and said 'God be with you.'

The old man came up to her, paused briefly, and wished her good evening.

'Your dog won't bite, will he, Grandpa?'

It's all right, come on—he won't hurt you.'

'I've been to hospital,' said Lipa after a short silence. 'My little son died there. Now I'm taking him home.'

The old man must have disliked hearing this because he stepped back. 'Never mind, dear, it's God's will,' he said rapidly.

He turned to his companion. 'Don't waste time, lad—get a move on.'

'Your yoke ain't here—can't see it,' said the lad.

'You're a proper so-and-so, Vavila.'

Picking up an ember, the old man blew on it, but lit up only his eyes and nose. Then, when the yoke had been found, he took the light over to Lipa and gazed at her. His look expressed sympathy and tenderness.

'You're a mother,' he sighed, shaking his head. 'Every mother loves her child.'

Vavila threw something on the fire, trod it down—and it suddenly grew very dark. The scene disappeared, and they were left with the same old fields, the starlit sky and the racket of the birds preventing each other from sleeping. A corncrake's cry came: from the very spot, seemingly, where the fire had been.

A minute later, though, carts, old man and tall Vavila were seen again. The carts creaked as they came out on to the road.

'Are you holy men?' Lipa asked the old fellow.

'No. We're from Firsanovo.'

'When you looked at me just now my heart melted. And the lad's so quiet—so I thought these must be holy men.'

'Have you far to go?'

'Ukleyevo.'

'Get in, then, we'll take you to Kuzmyonki. You go straight on there, we turn left.'

Vavila got into the cart with the barrel, the old man and Lipa into the other. They set off at a walk, Vavila in front.

'My little boy was in agony all day,' said Lipa. 'He looks at me with them little eyes and says nothing. He wants to tell me, but he can't. Lord God above us! Holy Mother! I keep falling on the floor, I'm so grieved. I stand near his bed and just can't keep me feet. Tell me, Grandpa, why should a little baby suffer so before he dies? When a grown person is in pain, man or woman, their sins are forgiven, but why, oh why should it happen to a baby which ain't never sinned at all?'

'Who knows?' the old man answered.

They drove for half an hour in silence.

'You can't know the rights and wrongs of everything,' the old man said. 'Birds are made with two wings, not four. And for why? Because two's enough to fly with. Man's the same—he ain't made to know everything—only the half or the quarter. What he needs to live . . . that's what he knows.'

'I'd rather walk, now, Grandpa. Me heart's trembling, like.'

'Never mind, you sit tight.'

The old man yawned and made the sign of the cross over his mouth.

'Never mind,' he repeated. 'Your grief ain't so bad. Life is long. There's good and bad, there's all kind of things to come.

'Great is Mother Russia,' said he, looking about him. 'I've been all over Russia, my dear—I've seen it all, I have, believe you me. There's good to come, and there's bad too. I been on village business to Siberia, I been on the Amur, in the Altay. I settled in Siberia—farmed land there—but then I got homesick for Mother Russia and I came back to me native village. We came back home on foot. We're on a ferry once, as I recall, and I'm thin as a rake. All tattered, barefoot and frozen, I am, and I'm sucking a crust, when a gentleman as was going through on the same ferry—if he's passed on since, may he rest in peace—looks at me in pity and his tears start flowing. "Ah me!" says he. "Your bread is black—and so's your prospects." And when I get back home I've nothing to bless meself with, as they say. I did have a wife once, but I left her behind in Siberia—she was buried there. So I worked as a farm-hand. And then what? I'll tell you. There was bad times and good times both, my dear. And now I don't want to die, see—I'd like to live another twenty year. So there must have been more good than bad.

'Great is Mother Russia!' he said, again looking around and glancing back.

'Grandpa, when someone dies . . . how long does his soul wander the earth? How many days?'

'Who can tell? Let's ask Vavila—he's been to school. They teach them everything nowadays.

'Vavila!' called the old man.

'What?'

'When someone dies, Vavila, how many days does his soul walk the earth?'

Vavila stopped the horse before answering. 'Nine days, I reckon. When me Uncle Cyril died, his soul lived on in our hut for thirteen days.'

'How do you know?'

'There were a banging in the stove for thirteen days.'

'Oh well. Drive on,' said the old man, obviously not believing a word.

Near Kuzmyonki the carts turned on to the metalled road and Lipa walked straight on. It was growing light. As she descended into the canyon the huts and church of Ukleyevo were hidden in mist. It was cold, and she still seemed to hear that same cuckoo calling.

Lipa reached home before they had driven the cattle out. Everyone was asleep. She sat on the steps and waited. First to appear was the old man, who took in what had happened at a glance but could not utter a word for a long time: only smacked his lips.

'Ah, Lipa,' said he. 'You didn't save him then, my little grandson.'

They woke Barbara. She threw up her arms, burst out sobbing, and at once started laying out the baby.

'Such a pretty little boy he was,' said she. 'Goodness me, she couldn't even keep the one baby she had—silly little thing!'

They held a requiem in the morning and again in the evening, and buried him next day. At the wake the guests and clergy stuffed themselves—you'd have thought they were starving, they were so greedy! Lipa helped to serve at table.

'Grieve not for the babe, for of such,' said the priest picking up a fork with a pickled mushroom on it, 'is the Kingdom of Heaven.'

Only when they had all left did it really come home to Lipa that Nikifor was—and would be—no more, and she burst out sobbing. But she didn't know what room to go and sob in, for she felt out of place in this house after the child's death—she counted for nothing here, she felt, she was only in the way. And others felt so too.

'Hey, what's all this hullabaloo?' shouted Aksinya, suddenly appearing in the doorway. She was wearing an entirely new outfit for the funeral, and had powdered her face. 'Shut up, you!'

Lipa tried to stop crying, but could not—only sobbed louder than ever.

'Do you hear me?' shouted Aksinya, stamping her foot in a mighty rage. 'Who do you think *you* are? You clear out of here! Don't you never show your face again, you convict scum! Away with you!'

'There, there,' fussed the old man. 'Calm down, Aksinya dear. It's only natural for her to cry—her baby died.'

'"*Only natural*"!' sneered Aksinya. 'She can spend tonight here, but tomorrow she can clear out lock stock and barrel!

'"Only natural"!' she sneered again, and went off to the shop with a laugh.

Early next morning Lipa went to her mother's at Torguyevo.

IX

Today the shop roof and door have been painted and shine like new. The usual cheerful geraniums bloom in the windows, and what happened at the Tsybukins' three years ago is almost forgotten.

Old Gregory Tsybukin still rates as head of the house, but in fact everything has passed into Aksinya's hands. She does the buying and selling, and nothing goes without her say-so. The brickyard is doing well. Bricks are needed for the railway, so the price has gone up to twenty-four roubles a thousand. The local women and girls cart bricks to the station, and load the wagons—all for a quarter of a rouble a day.

Aksinya has gone into partnership with Khrymins, and their works is now called 'Khrymin Sons & Co.'. They have opened a pub near the station, and it's here—not at the works—that the expensive-sounding accordion is played nowadays. The regulars include the postmaster—who has also started up some business of his own—and the station-master. Khrymin Sons have given deaf Stephen a gold watch, and he keeps taking it out of his pocket and holding it to his ear.

In the village Aksinya is said to have 'come on mighty powerful'. And it's true enough that when she drives to the works of a morning—naïvely smiling, handsome and happy—and when she is running that works, she indeed does convey a great air of power. At home, in the village, at the works . . . they're all scared of her. When she goes to the post-office the postmaster jumps to his feet with an 'I humbly beg you to be seated, Mrs. Tsybukin, ma'am.'

A certain dandified squire in his jerkin of fine cloth and patent-leather jack-boots—a middle-aged man—was once selling her a horse, and was so taken with her as they spoke that he let her have it on her own terms. He held her hand for some time, looking into her merry, artful, naïve eyes.

'For a woman like you, madam, there's no pleasure I wouldn't provide,' said he. 'Only tell me when we can meet without interruption.'

'Why, whenever you like.'

Ever since that the middle-aged dandy has driven to the shop almost daily for his glass of beer. The beer is atrocious—bitter as wormwood—but the squire shakes his head and drinks it.

Old Tsybukin takes no more part in business. He keeps no cash on him, for he simply can't tell true coin from false. But he holds his peace, never mentioning this infirmity. He has become rather absent-minded and if they don't give him his meals he never asks for them. They are used to eating without him by now, and Barbara often remarks that her 'old man went to bed without his supper again last night'. She speaks as if it didn't matter because she takes it for granted.

For some reason he goes about in his fur coat, summer and winter alike—it is only on the very hottest days that he doesn't go out at all, but stays at home. After donning that coat, raising the collar and wrapping up well, he usually potters round the village and the road to the station. Or sits on the bench near the church gate from morn till eve. There he sits, not moving. Folk bow as they pass, but he makes no reply: he still dislikes peasants as much as ever. If anyone asks him a question he answers quite rationally and politely—but briefly.

Village gossip says that his son's wife has driven him out of house and home, that she won't feed him, that he lives on what people give him. Some are glad, others are sorry for him.

Barbara is even plumper and paler, and she still goes about doing good—unhampered by Aksinya. They make so much jam nowadays that there's no time to eat it all before the new season's berries are ripe. It candies, and Barbara almost weeps for not knowing what to do with it.

They are beginning to forget Anisim. A letter did once arrive from him—written in verse on a large sheet of paper resembling an official document, and in the same imposing handwriting as before. Obviously he and his friend Samorodov were doing time in the same place. Beneath the verses a single line had been added in an ugly, barely legible hand: 'I'm always ill here, I'm miserable, for Christ's sake help me.'

Late one fine autumn afternoon old Tsybukin was sitting by the church gate with his coat collar up and only his nose and cap peak showing. At the other end of the long bench sat the carpenter Yelizarov, and beside him the school caretaker Jacob: a toothless old fellow of about seventy. Lofty and the caretaker were talking.

'Children should give old folks their food and drink—honour thy father and thy mother,' said Jacob testily. 'But that young woman has thrown her husband's old dad out of his own house, like. Nothing to eat nor drink, the old fellow has—where's he to go now? Three days he ain't had no food.'

Lofty was surprised. 'Three days!'

'Aye, there he sits, never says a word. Proper weak, he is. Why keep quiet about it? They ought to take her to court—she wouldn't get off lightly!'

'Who got off lightly?' asked Lofty, not hearing.

'Eh?'

'The woman's all right. A hard worker, she is. In their line of business you can't manage without it—not without cutting corners, I mean.'

'Out of his own home!' Jacob went on testily. 'Let her build a house herself before she starts throwing folks out of it. What a woman, though! A proper plague, she is.'

Tsybukin listened, but made no move.

'His own house or someone else's . . . what's the difference so long as it's warm and the womenfolk don't quarrel?' laughed Lofty. 'Very fond of my Nastasya, I was as a young fellow. She was a quiet little woman. "You buy a house, Eli," says she—kept on at me all the time, she did with this "you buy a house, Eli" stuff. And when she was a-dying she was on about "you buy yourself a good fast droshky, Eli, so you don't need to walk". But all I ever buys her is gingerbread, that's all.'

'That deaf husband of hers is a fool,' went on Jacob, not hearing. 'A proper dunce he is, a real old goose. Can the likes of him understand? Hit a goose on the head with a stick—it still won't understand.'

Lofty stood up to go home to the works. Jacob got up too, and they set off together, still talking. When they had gone about fifty yards old Tsybukin also stood up and doddered after them, treading gingerly as if walking on ice.

Now the village was plunged in twilight. The sun sparkled only on the top part of the road snaking up the hillside from below. Old women were on their way back from the woods bringing the children and carrying baskets of pink and yellow-white mushrooms. From the station, where they had been loading wagons with bricks, came a group of women and girls, their noses and their cheeks under the eyes red with brick dust. They were singing. In front of all walked Lipa singing in a reedy voice—carolling away as she looked up at the sky and seeming to exult and rejoice that the day, thank God, was over and that she could rest. In the group was her mother Praskovya, the hired drudge, carrying a bundle in her hand and panting as usual.

'Good day, Eli, my dear,' said Lipa, seeing Lofty.

'Good day, Lipa darling.' Lofty was delighted. 'Hey, you women and girls, be nice to the rich carpenter.

'My children, my dear children,' he sobbed. 'Oho, my darling little hatchets!'

Lofty and Jacob were heard talking to each other as they moved off. Then old Tsybukin came up with the crowd, and silence suddenly fell. Lipa and Praskovya had lagged behind a little.

'Good day, Mr. Tsybukin,' said Lipa with a low bow as the old man drew level.

Her mother bowed too. The old man stopped, looked at them both wordlessly, lips shaking, eyes full of tears. Lipa got a piece of buckwheat pasty from her mother's bundle and gave it to him. He took it and started eating.

Now the sun had completely set—even from the top part of the road the fire had faded. It was growing dark and chilly. Lipa and Praskovya went on their way, crossing themselves for a long time afterwards.

THE BISHOP

[Архиерей]

(1902)

THE BISHOP

I

It was the eve of Palm Sunday service at the Old Convent of St. Peter. When they started handing out the palm leaves it was nearly ten o'clock, lights had dimmed, wicks needed snuffing, everything was blurred and the congregation swayed like a sea in the gloomy church. To Bishop Peter, who had been unwell for three days, all these faces—old and young, male and female—appeared alike: coming up for their palms, they all had that same look about the eyes. He could not see the doors for haze, and the congregation kept moving— never-ending, it seemed. A women's choir sang, a nun was reading the lesson.

It was so hot, so stuffy. The service seemed interminable, and his lordship was tired. He was breathing heavily—panting—his throat was parched, his shoulders ached with fatigue, his legs trembled. He was upset, too, by the occasional shrieks of some religious maniac in the gallery. Then, suddenly, as if dreaming or delirious, he thought he saw his mother whom he had not set eyes on for nine years—or an old lady resembling his mother—approach him in the congregation, take her palm and move away, gazing at him with a bright, radiant, kindly smile until lost in the crowd. Tears began trickling down his face, he knew not why. He felt serene and all was well, but he stared at the choir on his left where the lesson was being read and where he could no longer see who was who in the gloaming—and wept. Tears glittered on his face and beard. Then someone near him also started crying, followed by someone else a little further off, and then by more and more people until the whole church was gradually filled with this quiet weeping. But about five minutes later the nuns' choir was singing, the crying had stopped, everything was back to normal.

The service ended soon afterwards. As the Bishop climbed into his carriage to go home a melodious, rich, merry clang of heavy bells flooded the moonlit convent garden. White walls, white crosses on graves, white birches, black shadows, the moon far away in the sky directly over the convent . . . all seemed to be living a life of their own —a life incomprehensible yet close to man's. It was early April with the seasonal chill which follows a warm day, there was a touch of frost and a breath of spring in the soft, cold air. The road from convent to city was sandy, and they had to keep their horses to a walk. In the moonlight, bright and serene, churchgoers were trudging through the sand on both sides of the carriage. All were silent, plunged in thought. So congenial, fresh and intimate was this ambience—trees, sky and moon too—that one found oneself hoping it would never change.

The carriage reached town at last and rumbled down the main street. The shops were shut, except that at Yerakin's—the millionaire merchant's—the electric lighting was being tested, and flickered violently while a crowd stood around. Then came a series of wide, dark, deserted streets followed on the far side of town by a metalled road (built by the local authority), open fields, fragrant pines. Suddenly a white castellated wall arose before his eyes and behind it a tall bell-tower bathed in moonlight with a cluster of five large, glittering onion-domes. It was the Monastery of the Almighty, where Bishop Peter lived. Here too, high above the monastery, rode that same calm, dreaming moon. The carriage drove in at the gate, crunching on sand. Here and there black monkish figures flitted through the moonlight, footsteps echoed on flagstones.

'Your mother called while you were out, my lord,' said the lay brother as the Bishop was entering his quarters.

'My mother? When did she arrive?'

'Before the service—she asked where you were, then went to the convent.'

'So it *was* her I saw in church just now—good heavens!' The Bishop laughed happily.

'She asked me to tell your lordship that she'll be here tomorrow,' the lay brother continued. 'She has a little girl with her—her grand-daughter, I suppose. They're staying at Ovsyannikov's inn.'

'What time is it now?'

'Just after eleven.'

'Oh, what a pity.'

The Bishop sat for a while in his parlour, meditating and somehow not believing that the hour was so late. His arms and legs ached, the back of his neck hurt, he felt hot and uncomfortable. After resting he went to his bedroom, where he also sat for a while, still thinking of his mother. He heard the lay brother going away, and a monk—Father Sisoy—coughing in the next room. The monastery clock struck the quarter.

The Bishop changed and began saying his bed-time prayers. While carefully reciting the old familiar words he thought about his mother. She had had nine children and about forty grandchildren. She had once lived with her husband, a deacon, in a poor village: lived there for most of her life, between the ages of seventeen and sixty. The Bishop remembered her from early childhood—from the age of three, almost—and how he had loved her! Dear, precious, unforgettable childhood, that time now vanished and gone beyond recall . . . why does it always seem brighter, richer, more carefree than it actually was? When he had been ill in childhood or youth . . . how tender, how solicitous his mother had been! By now his prayers were mingled with memories which blazed up like flames, ever more radiantly, and his prayers did not stop him thinking about his mother.

His prayers finished, he undressed and lay down. No sooner had darkness closed around him than he had a vision of his father—now dead—his mother, his native village of Lesopolye.

Wheels creaking, sheep bleating, church bells pealing on bright summer mornings, gipsies at the window . . . how delightful to think of these things. He remembered the Lesopolye priest, Father Simeon: that meek, mild, good-natured man—short and lean, but with an enormously tall theological student son who had a thundering bass voice. Losing his temper with a cook, once, the son had called her 'thou ass of Jehudiel', hearing which Father Simeon had gone very quiet—ashamed that he could remember no such ass in the Bible. His successor at Lesopolye had been Father Demyan: a heavy drinker who sometimes reached the point of seeing green serpents and was even nicknamed Old Snake-Eye. The Lesopolye schoolmaster had been a Matthew Nikolayevich: a former divinity student—kind, rather intelligent, also a drunkard. He never beat his pupils, but for some reason always had a birch hanging on the wall with a notice under it in 'Latin' gibberish: BETULA KINDERBALSAMICA SECUTA. He had a shaggy black dog called Syntax.

The bishop laughed. Five miles from Lesopolye was another village, Obnino, with a miracle-working icon which was carried in procession round the neighbouring villages every summer while bells rang all day —first in one village, then in another. To the Bishop ('Young Paul' at the time) the very air had seemed vibrant with rapture, and he had followed that icon—bare-headed and barefoot, blissfully happy with his innocent faith and his innocent smile. At Obnino, he now recalled, there had always been a large congregation, and Father Alexis—the local priest—had saved time in church by getting his deaf nephew Ilarion to recite the notices and the inscriptions attached to communion loaves: all about prayers 'for the health of' and 'for the soul of' various people. Ilarion did it, receiving the occasional five or ten copecks for these services, and only when he was grey and balding—only when life had passed him by—did he suddenly notice one day a paper with the words ILARION IS A FOOL written on it. Young Paul had been backward until the age of fifteen or more, and had done so badly at his church school that they had even thought of taking him away and placing him in a shop. When fetching letters once from Obnino post-office, he had directed a prolonged stare at the clerks, and had then asked them to 'permit me to enquire' how they received their salary: was it monthly or daily?

The Bishop crossed himself, turning over so that he could stop thinking and go to sleep. Remembering that his mother had come to see him, he gave a laugh.

The moon shone in at the window, the floor gleamed and shadows lay across it. A cricket chirped. On the other side of the wall, in the next room, Father Sisoy was snoring. There was a forlorn, bereaved note—something of the homeless wanderer, even—in the old boy's snores. Sisoy had once looked after a diocesan bishop, and was now known as the 'Father Ex-Housekeeper'. He was seventy years old and lived in a monastery ten miles from the city—but stayed in town too when convenient. Three days ago he had called at the Monastery of the Almighty, and the Bishop had put him up in his own quarters so that they could discuss business and certain local arrangements at their leisure.

The bell rang for a service at half past one. Father Sisoy was heard to cough and mumble discontentedly, after which he got up and paced the rooms barefoot. The Bishop called him by name, whereupon Sisoy went to his own room, but appeared a little later in his boots, carrying a candle. He wore cassock over his underclothes and a faded old skull-cap.

'I can't sleep,' said the Bishop, sitting up. 'I must be unwell. But just what the matter is I don't know. I feel so hot.'

'You must have caught cold, my lord. You need rubbing down with candle grease.'

Sisoy stood there for a moment. 'Lord, forgive me, miserable sinner.' He yawned and added that 'they had the electricity on at Yerakin's just now—I don't hold with it, I don't.'

Father Sisoy was old, wizened, bent, always discontented. He had angry, bulging eyes like a crab's.

'I don't hold with it, confound it, that I don't,' he repeated as he went out.

II

On the next day, Palm Sunday, the Bishop took morning service in the cathedral, then visited the diocesan bishop and an old lady—wife of some general—who was very ill, and finally returned home. At about half past one he was entertaining some very special guests to lunch: his old mother and his little eight-year-old niece Katya. Throughout lunch the spring sun shone through the windows which looked on the yard, sparkling merrily on the white tablecloth and in Katya's red hair. Through the double frames rooks were heard cawing in the garden, starlings chattered.

'Nine years it is since we met,' said the old lady. 'But then I saw you in the convent yesterday, and—goodness me, you haven't changed a bit except that you're thinner and your beard's longer, Blessed Virgin, Mother of God! Yesterday at the service no one could help crying, and when I looked at you I suddenly started crying myself, I don't know why. It's the Lord's will.'

Fondly though she spoke she was clearly ill at ease, apparently wondering how intimately she should address him, and whether she might laugh or not. She seemed to feel herself more the deacon's widow than the bishop's mother, while Katya stared unblinking at her right reverend uncle as if trying to guess what manner of a man this was. Her hair sprouted up like a halo from her comb and velvet ribbon, she had a turned-up nose and an artful look. She had broken a glass before lunch, and her grandmother was now moving the tumblers and wineglasses away from her as she spoke. Listening to his mother, the Bishop remembered her long, long ago taking him with his brothers and sisters to see some supposedly rich relatives. She had been busy with her children then. Now it was her grandchildren, and so she had brought this Katya.

'Your sister Barbara has four children,' she explained. 'And Katya here's the eldest. Now, Father Ivan—your brother-in-law—fell ill, Lord knows why, and died three days before Assumption. And now she's real hard up, is poor Barbara.'

The Bishop asked after Nikanor, his eldest brother.

'He's all right, thank God. He hasn't much, but it's enough to live on, praise be. The thing is, though, his son Nicholas—my grandson—decided against a church career. He's at college, studying to be a doctor. That's better, thinks he, and who knows? 'Tis the Lord's will.'

'Nicholas cuts up dead bodies,' put in Katya, spilling water on her lap.

'Sit still, child,' the grandmother remarked serenely, taking the glass from her hands. 'Say a prayer as you eat.'

'It's so long since we met,' said the Bishop, fondly stroking his mother's arm and shoulder. 'I missed you when I was abroad, Mother, I really did.'

His mother said that she 'thanked him kindly'.

'Some evenings you'd be sitting on your own by an open window when a band would strike up—and you'd suddenly want to be back in Russia. You'd feel you'd give anything to go home and see your mother——'

His mother beamed, but at once pulled a serious face and repeated that she 'thanked him kindly'.

Then his mood changed rather abruptly. Looking at his mother, he was baffled—why this nervous, deferential expression and tone of voice? What was the point? It didn't seem like her. He felt depressed and annoyed. Besides, he also had a headache like yesterday's and a gnawing pain in his legs. The fish seemed tasteless and unappetizing, he felt thirsty all the time.

After the meal two rich ladies, estate-owners, arrived and sat for an hour and a half in silence with long faces. The Father Superior—taciturn and a trifle deaf—came on some errand. Then the bell rang for evensong, the sun sank behind the woods, and the day was done. The Bishop came back from church, hastily prayed, went to bed and covered himself up warmly.

That lunch-time fish had left a disagreeable aftertaste, the moonlight disturbed him, and then he heard voices. Father Sisoy was discussing politics in a near-by room, probably the parlour.

'The Japanese are at war now. Fighting, they are. The Japanese are like the Montenegrins, missus. Belong to the same tribe, they do, they were under Turkish rule together.'

Then the Bishop's mother was heard to speak. 'So, having said our prayers, like, er, and had a cup of tea, we went to see Father Yegor at Novokhatnoye er——'

From all this 'having had a cup' and 'having drunk a pot' stuff you'd have thought she'd never done anything in life but drink tea. Slowly and apathetically the Bishop recalled his theological school and college. He had taught Greek at that school—by then he could no longer read without glasses. Then he had become a monk and second master, then he had taken his doctor's degree. He had been made headmaster and Father Superior at the age of thirty-two, and life had been so easy and pleasant: looked as if it would go on and on like that for ever and ever. But then he had fallen ill, he had lost a lot of weight, he had nearly gone blind—and had had to drop everything and go abroad on doctors' orders.

'Then what?' asked Sisoy in the next room.

'Then we had tea,' answered the Bishop's mother.

'Father, you have a green beard,' Katya suddenly said with a surprised laugh.

Remembering that grey-haired Father Sisoy's beard really did have a greenish tinge, the Bishop laughed.

'The girl's a thorough pest, Lord help us,' said Sisoy loudly and angrily. 'She's so spoilt! You sit still!'

The Bishop remembered the completely new white church where he had held services when living abroad, remembered the roar of that warm sea. He had had an apartment of five high, airy rooms with a new desk in the study and a library. He had read and written a great deal. He remembered being homesick for Russia, remembered the blind beggar-woman singing of love and playing a guitar under his window every day—listening to her had always reminded him of the past, somehow. Then eight years had passed, he had been recalled to Russia. Now he was a suffragan bishop, and his entire previous life had vanished into some distant mist, as if it had all been a dream.

Entering the bedroom with a candle, Father Sisoy gave a surprised exclamation. 'Asleep, already, my lord?'

'What is it?'

'Why it's still early—ten or even earlier. I've just bought a candle, I wanted to rub you over with grease.'

'I have a temperature.' The Bishop sat up. 'We really should do something, my head's bad——'

Sisoy took the Bishop's shirt off and began rubbing his chest and back with candle grease.

'There, there,' he said. 'Lord bless us! There, there. I went into town today and visited that Father what's-his-name—Sidonsky—had tea with him. I don't hold with him, Lord love us, that I don't.'

III

The diocesan bishop—old, very stout and rheumaticky or gouty—had been bedridden for the last month. Bishop Peter visited him almost daily, and saw the people who came to ask the other's help. But now that he was unwell himself he was struck by the triviality and futility of all their tearful applications. Their ignorance and nervousness riled him. All this pettiness and pointlessness . . . the sheer weight of it got him down. He felt that he could understand the diocesan bishop: author of a *Studies in Free Will* in youth, but now apparently submerged in trifles, having forgotten everything and never thinking about God. Bishop Peter must have lost touch with Russian life while he was abroad. It wasn't easy for him now, what with the peasants seeming so rough and the ladies who sought his help so tiresomely stupid—while theological students and their teachers were ill-educated and at times barbarous. As for the documents coming and going, they were reckoned by their tens of thousands! And what documents! The higher clergy of the entire diocese were accustomed to award conduct marks to their juniors of whatever age—to wives and children, even—just as if they were school-children, all of which had to be discussed, perused and solemnly reported in documentary form. Never, never was there a single free minute: it was nervous tension all day long for Bishop Peter, who could relax only when he was in church.

Nor could he inure himself to the terror which, through no wish of his own, he inspired in others despite his meek and modest demeanour. Everyone in the county seemed small, frightened and guilty when he looked at them. Everyone—even older, senior clerics—wilted in his presence, they all prostrated themselves before him. So scared had one of his recent petitioners been (an old woman, wife of a country priest) that she had gone away empty-handed without uttering a single word. Meanwhile the Bishop—who could never bring himself to disparage anyone in his sermons, who felt too sorry for people to reproach them —was raging and losing his temper with those who consulted him, and throwing their applications on the floor. Not once since he had come to this place had anyone spoken to him sincerely and simply, as one human being to another. Even his old mother seemed to have changed, indeed she did. Why, he wondered, did she chatter away non-stop and laugh so much when she was with Sisoy, whereas with her own son she was so solemn, so tongue-tied, so embarrassed—which didn't suit her at all? The only person to behave freely and speak his mind in the Bishop's presence *was* old Sisoy, whose whole life had been spent attending bishops, and who had outlasted eleven of them—which was why his lordship felt at ease with him, difficult and cantankerous though the old boy assuredly was.

After Tuesday morning's service the Bishop went to the palace to deal with his appointments, which was all very upsetting and annoying, after which he went home. Again he felt unwell, again he wanted to go to bed. But hardly had he reached his room before he was informed that Yerakin—a young businessman and contributor to charities—had arrived on a most urgent errand. There was no question of not seeing him. Yerakin stayed for about an hour talking very loudly, practically shouting, so that it was hard to make out what he said.

'God grant something-or-other,' he said as he left. 'Oh, most emphatically! Depending on the circumstances, my lord. Wishing you something-or-other.'

Then came the Mother Superior of a distant convent. After she had left the bells rang for evensong, and he had to go to church.

That evening the monks' singing was tuneful and inspired. A black-bearded young priest was officiating. Hearing about the bridegroom who cometh at midnight and the mansion richly adorned, the Bishop felt neither grief nor repentance but spiritual calm and serenity as his thoughts floated back to the distant past, to his childhood and youth when that same bridegroom and mansion had also been hymned. That past now seemed vivid, wonderful and joyful. Not that it had really been anything of the sort, probably. In the next world, in the life to come, we shall perhaps recall the distant past and our present life with just such a feeling. Who knows? Tears coursed down the Bishop's face as he sat in the darkness of the chancel. He had achieved everything possible for a man in his position, he reflected. He had kept his faith. And yet not all was clear to him—something was missing. He didn't want to die. He still felt the lack of some crucial element which he had once vaguely imagined, and he was still disturbed at this very moment by that same hope for the future which had been his in boyhood, at college and abroad. Listening to the singing, he thought how good it was today: very good indeed.

IV

On Maundy Thursday he took morning service in the cathedral. As the congregation dispersed afterwards the weather was sunny, warm and cheerful, with water gurgling in ditches and ceaseless lark-song, sweet and restful, wafting over from the fields beyond the city. Newly burgeoning trees smiled their welcome, and above them a fathomless expanse of blue sky soared off into the unknown.

Arriving home, Bishop Peter had tea, changed, went to bed and told the lay brother to close the shutters. The bedroom grew dim. How tired he was, though, how his legs and back did ache with that dull, cold pain, and what a ringing there was in his ears! He felt as if he hadn't slept for a long time, felt himself prevented from sleeping by some trifle which glimmered in his brain as soon as his eyes were shut. Through the walls of adjoining rooms he heard voices, and the chink of glasses and tea-spoons—just like yesterday.

His mother was telling Father Sisoy some jolly tale with lots of little jokes while he responded sullenly and discontentedly with a 'confound them!', a 'not likely!' or a 'no fear!' Again the Bishop was annoyed, and then hurt, that the old lady could behave so normally and naturally with strangers—yet remained so nervous and tongue-tied with her own son, always saying the wrong thing, and even seeking a pretext all this time (or so he felt) to stand up in his presence because she was too shy to sit down. And what of his father? Had the old man still been alive he would probably have been unable to utter one word in his son's presence.

In the next room something fell on the floor and broke. Katya must have dropped a cup or saucer because Father Sisoy suddenly spat, announcing angrily that the girl was a thorough pest. 'Lord forgive me, miserable sinner, we'll soon have nothing left!'

Then all was quiet except for noises outside. When the Bishop opened his eyes he saw Katya in his room. She stood stock still, looking at him with that red hair sprouting as usual out of her comb like a halo.

'Is it you, Katya?' he asked. 'Who keeps opening and closing that door downstairs?'

'I can't hear it,' answered Katya, listening.

'There—someone just went through.'

'But it was your stomach rumbling, Uncle.'

He laughed and stroked her hair.

'So Cousin Nicholas cuts up dead bodies, does he?' he asked after a pause.

'Yes. He's a medical student.'

'Is he nice?'

'Yes, he's all right. But he doesn't half drink vodka!'

'What did your father die of?'

'Daddy was weak and ever so thin, and then suddenly he had a bad throat. I fell ill too, and so did my brother Theo—we all had bad throats. Then Daddy died, but we got better, Uncle.'

Her chin quivered. Tears filled her eyes and crawled down her cheeks.

'My lord,' said she in a thin little voice, now weeping bitterly. 'Mummy and I are so miserable, Uncle. Do give us a bit of money— please, Uncle darling.'

He wept as well. For some time he was too upset to say a word. Then he stroked her head, touched her shoulder.

'All right, all right, little girl. Soon it will be Easter Sunday and we'll have a talk. I will help you, certainly——'

His mother came in quietly and nervously, faced the icon and said a prayer. Noticing that he was still awake, she asked if he would 'like a drop of soup'.

'No thank you. I'm not hungry.'

'You seem unwell now I look at you. I'm not surprised, though. On the go all day long—goodness me, a sorry sight you are! Well, Easter isn't far off and then you can have a rest, God willing, and we'll talk. I won't bother you with my chatter now. Come on, Katya, let the Bishop sleep.'

He remembered her addressing some church dignitary just like this— long, long ago during his boyhood—with that same mixture of jocularity and respect.

The unusually kind look in her eyes and the nervous, anxious glance which she flashed as she left the room . . . these were the only indications that this *was* his mother. He closed his eyes and seemed to be sleeping, but twice heard the striking of the hours, heard Father Sisoy coughing behind the wall. His mother came in again and watched him nervously for a minute. He heard some coach or carriage drive up to the porch. Suddenly there was a knock, the door banged, and the lay brother came into the bedroom shouting 'your lordship'.

'What is it?'

'Your carriage is waiting. Time for evening service.'

'What time *is* it then?'

'A quarter past seven.'

He dressed and drove to the cathedral where he had to stand motion-less in the centre during all twelve lessons from the gospels. The first of these—the longest and most beautiful—he read himself. A buoyant, vigorous mood came over him. That first reading ('Now is the Son of Man glorified') he knew by heart. Reciting it, he occasionally raised his eyes, he saw a sea of lights around him and he heard the sputter of candles, but the congregation remained invisible as before. It was, he felt, that self-same congregation which he had seen as a boy and youth, and it would remain unchanged year after year—for how long God alone knew.

His father had been a deacon, his grandfather a priest, his great-grandfather a deacon. His entire family had quite possibly belonged to the clergy since Christianity had first come to Russia. His love of church services, of the priesthood, of ringing bells was innate, deep, ineradicable. In church—especially when he himself was officiating—he always felt active, cheerful and happy, which was just how he felt now. But after the reading of the eighth lesson he felt that his voice was failing, he could not even hear himself cough, a splitting headache came on. He began to worry—feared he might be about to fall down. Yes, his legs had grown completely numb, gradually losing all sensation. How he stayed upright and kept his feet—why he didn't just fall down—he could not tell.

The service finished at a quarter to twelve. Arriving home, the Bishop undressed and went to bed at once without even saying his prayers. He could not speak, he felt that he had lost the use of his legs. As he was pulling the blanket over him he suddenly felt an urge—an absolute craving—to go abroad. He was ready to sacrifice life itself just to be spared the sight of those wretched cheap shutters and low ceilings, to escape this oppressive monastic smell. If only there was one single person that he could talk to, open his heart to!

For some time he heard footsteps in the next room, but whose they might be he simply could not recall. Then the door opened at last, and in came Sisoy with a candle and tea-cup.

'Already in bed, my lord? It's me—come to rub you down with vodka and vinegar. Very good for you it is if you rub it in well, Lord love us. There, there. I've just been in our monastery, but I don't hold with it, like. I'm leaving tomorrow, Bishop. I want no more of it, Lord love us! There, there.'

Sisoy could never stay long in one place, and he felt as if he'd already spent a whole year at the Monastery of the Almighty. It was hard, indeed, to figure him out from the way he talked. Where was his home? Did he love anyone or anything? Did he believe in God?

He had no idea himself why he was a monk, he gave it no thought—
and as for the time when he had taken his vows, his mind was a blank.
It was as if he had simply been born a monk.

'I'm going tomorrow, confound it all!' said Sisoy.

'I'd like to talk to you, but I never seem to manage it.' The Bishop
spoke softly, with great effort. 'I don't know anyone or anything here,
you see.'

'I'll stay till Sunday if you like. So be it. I want no more of it,
confound them!'

'Why am I a bishop?' the Bishop went on quietly. 'I should have been
a village priest, a sexton or an ordinary monk. It all seems to—to
crush me.'

'Eh? Lord love us! There, there! Now, you have a good sleep, my
lord. Goodness gracious, whatever next? Good night to you.'

The Bishop did not sleep all that night. In the morning, at about
eight o'clock, he had an intestinal haemorrhage. The lay brother was
terrified. He rushed off: first to the Father Superior, and then to the
monastery doctor, Ivan Andreyevich, who lived in town. The doctor—
a stout old man with a long white beard—examined the Bishop at
length, shaking his head and frowning. Did his lordship realize that
this was 'typhoid fever, you know'?

Within about an hour the effect of the haemorrhage had been to
make the Bishop thin, pale and hunched. His face was wizened, his
eyes enormous. He seemed aged and shrunk. He felt thinner, feebler
and more insignificant, now, than everyone else—felt that all his past
had escaped him to some infinitely remote place beyond all chance of
repetition or continuation.

'And a very good thing too,' he thought.

His old mother arrived. Seeing his wizened face and big eyes she
took fright, fell on her knees beside the bed and began kissing his
face, shoulders and hands. She too rather felt that he was thinner,
feebler and more insignificant than everyone else, she forgot that he
was a bishop and she kissed him like a dearly loved child.

'Paul darling,' she said. 'My darling little son. What's happened to
you? Answer me, Paul.'

Katya stood near by—pale, stern, not understanding. What was the
matter with Uncle? Why did Grandmother look so unhappy, why
was she saying such moving, sad words? But the Bishop was past
speech, he could take nothing in. He just felt as if he was an ordinary
simple man walking quickly and cheerfully through a field and

thumping his walking-stick under a broad, sun-drenched sky. Now he was free as a bird, now he could go where he liked.

'Paul, answer me, son,' said the old lady. 'What's the matter, darling?'

'Don't bother the Bishop.' Sisoy went angrily through the room. 'Let him sleep. There's nothing to be done, no point——'

Three doctors arrived, consulted, went away. The day seemed to go on and on and on, and was followed by a night no less interminable. Just before dawn on Saturday the lay brother went to the old lady as she lay on a sofa in the parlour, and invited her to step into the bedroom because the Bishop had gone to his fathers.

The next day was Easter Sunday. There were forty-two churches in the city, and six religious houses. The clangorous, joyful, ceaseless pealing of bells haunted and stirred the spring air above the buildings from morn to eve. Birds sang. The sun was bright. The large market square was all a-bustle. Swings swung, hurdy-gurdies played, an accordion squealed, drunken shouts echoed. In the afternoon there was buggy-riding up and down the main street. It was all great fun, in other words, everything was all right—just as it had been all right last year and would probably go on being all right in years to come.

A month later a new suffragan bishop was appointed. No one remembered Bishop Peter any more. They forgot him altogether except for the old lady—the deceased's mother—who went to live with her deacon son-in-law in a remote provincial town. Going out of an evening to fetch her cow from the meadow, and meeting other women there, she would talk about her children and grandchildren, and about her son who had been a bishop. She spoke nervously, afraid of being disbelieved.

Nor did everyone believe her, actually.

A MARRIAGEABLE GIRL

[Невеста]

(1903)

A MARRIAGEABLE GIRL

I

It was ten o'clock in the evening and a full moon shone above the garden. At the Shumins' home a prayer meeting—arranged by the grandmother—had just ended. Nadya had gone into the garden for a minute. She could see them laying the dining-room table for supper while Grandmother bustled about, resplendent in her silk dress. Father Andrew, a canon from the cathedral, was talking to Nadya's mother Nina, who somehow looked very young when seen through the window in the evening light. Father Andrew's son—himself an Andrew—stood by listening attentively.

All was quiet and cool in the garden. Tranquil black shadows lay across the ground, while far, far away—out of town, no doubt—frogs croaked. May, lovely May, was in the air. Nadya could breathe freely, and liked to fancy that there was another place—beneath the sky, above the trees, far beyond town, in fields and woods—where springtime had generated a secret life of its own: a life wonderful, rich and hallowed . . . a life beyond the understanding of weak, sinful man. She felt rather like crying.

Nadya was twenty-three, had longed to be married since she was sixteen, and was engaged at last to this Andrew who could be seen through the window: Father Andrew's son. Though she liked him, and though their wedding was to be on the seventh of July, yet there was no joy in her heart, she was sleeping badly and her spirits were low.

Through the open window came the sound of people scurrying and clattering knives in the kitchen, which was in the basement. A door banged on its block and pulley. There was a smell of roast turkey and pickled cherries. Such, it rather looked, was to be the pattern of her life from now on for ever and ever without end.

Then someone came out of the house and stood on the steps. This was Alexander Timofeyevich—Sasha for short. He was staying with them, having arrived from Moscow about ten days earlier. At one time long ago a distant relative of Grandmother's—an impoverished widowed gentlewoman, small, thin and ailing—had been in the habit of visiting her and receiving assistance. Sasha was her son. He was said to be an excellent artist, goodness knows why, and on his mother's death Nadya's grandmother had tried to improve her chances in the next world by sending him to the Komissarov School in Moscow. A couple of years later he had moved on to the Fine Arts Institute, where he spent practically fifteen years before barely scraping through with a diploma in architecture. He hadn't practised architecture, though, but had taken a job with a Moscow lithographic firm. He would come and stay with Grandmother almost every summer—to rest and recuperate, for he was more or less an invalid.

At the moment he wore a buttoned-up frock-coat and shabby canvas trousers frayed at the bottoms. His shirt was unironed. He looked rather frowsty, by and large. Very lean, with big eyes and long, thin fingers, he was bearded and swarthy—yet handsome. He was practically one of the family, feeling completely at home with the Shumins. For years the room in which he stayed had been called Sasha's.

While standing in the porch he spotted Nadya and went up to her. 'Isn't it nice here?'

'Of course it is. You should stay on till autumn.'

'Yes, I expect it will come to that. I dare say I'll stay till September.' He laughed for no reason and sat down by her.

'I've been sitting looking at Mother,' said Nadya. 'She seems so young from here. Mother does have her foibles, of course,' she added after a pause. 'Still, she is rather special.'

'Yes, she's a good sort,' Sasha agreed. 'In her own way your mother's a very kind and charming woman, of course, but—how can I put it—I happened to go into the kitchen early this morning and four of your servants were asleep on the bare floor. They have no beds or bedding: only rags, stink, bugs, cockroaches. Nothing's changed in twenty years, nothing at all. Never mind your grandmother, now—she can't help it. But your mother does speak French, you know, doesn't she? She acts in private theatricals. You'd think she'd understand.'

While speaking Sasha would point two long, wasted fingers at whoever he was addressing.

'This place seems rather outlandish when you're not used to it,' he went on. 'Nobody ever does anything, damn it! Your mother spends all day gadding about like some duchess, your grandmother doesn't do anything either. Nor do you. Nor does your future husband, Andrew.'

Nadya had heard all this last year and also—she thought—the year before. That Sasha was incapable of thinking in any other way she knew. Once that had amused her, now it rather annoyed her.

'That stuff's all out of date and boring.' She stood up. 'Can't you think of something new?'

Laughing, he stood up too, and they went to the house together. Tall, good-looking, well-built, she looked so healthy and presentable compared with him—sensing which, she felt sorry for him and rather embarrassed.

'You're always putting your foot in it,' she told him. 'You just said something about my Andrew, for instance. But you don't know him, do you?'

'*My* Andrew! To hell with *your* Andrew! Your wasted youth ... that's what I deplore.'

As they went into the dining-room everyone was just sitting down to supper. Grandmother—'Gran' to the family, a very stout, ugly, bushy-browed, bewhiskered old woman—spoke loudly, unmistakably the head of the household in her voice and manner. She owned rows of stalls in the market and this period house with its columns and garden, but every morning she prayed to be preserved from bankruptcy, weeping as she did so. Then there was her daughter-in-law Nina—Nadya's mother: a fair-haired, tightly corseted woman sporting a pince-nez and diamonds on every finger. There was old Father Andrew—thin, toothless, looking poised to tell a very funny story. And there was his son: Andrew Junior, Nadya's fiancé—stout, handsome, curly-haired, looking like a musician or artist. All three were discussing hypnotism.

Gran addressed Sasha. 'One week in my house and you'll be well again. But you must eat more—just look at you!' She sighed. 'Dreadful, you look. A regular Prodigal Son, I call you.'

'He wasted his substance with riotous living,' said Father Andrew slowly, with laughter in his eyes. 'He filled his belly with the husks that the swine did eat.'

'I'm so fond of my old man,' said Andrew, touching his father's shoulder. 'A wonderful old chap, he is—such a dear old boy.'

No one spoke. Then Sasha suddenly laughed and pressed a napkin to his mouth.

'So you believe in hypnotism, do you?' Father Andrew asked Nina.

'That I believe in it I naturally cannot asseverate,' Nina answered, assuming an earnest—not to say severe—expression. 'But that many things in nature are mysterious and incomprehensible I must own.'

'I quite agree—while adding, however, that religion materially curtails the realm of the Unknown.'

A large, exceedingly plump turkey was served. Father Andrew and Nina went on talking. Diamonds sparkled on Nina's fingers, after which tears sparkled in her eyes. She was excited.

'I don't dare argue with you,' she said. 'But there are plenty of insoluble puzzles in life, grant me that.'

'Not one, I venture to assure you.'

After supper Andrew played the violin, accompanied by Nina on the piano. Ten years ago he had taken an arts degree, but he had never done a job and had no fixed occupation apart from an occasional appearance at charity concerts. They called him a 'musician' in town.

Andrew played while everyone listened in silence. The samovar quietly bubbled on the table, but only Sasha drank tea. Then, after twelve o'clock had struck, a violin string suddenly snapped. They all laughed, bestirred themselves and began to say good night.

After seeing her fiancé out, Nadya went upstairs, where she and her mother had their rooms—Gran occupied the lower floor. Down in the dining-room they had started putting out the lights, but Sasha sat on drinking his tea. He always spent a long time over his tea, Moscow fashion, drinking seven glasses at a sitting. Long after Nadya had undressed and gone to bed she could hear the servants clearing away downstairs and Gran's angry voice. In the end all was quiet except for the occasional deep cough proceeding from Sasha's room.

II

It must have been about two o'clock when Nadya woke. Dawn was breaking, and a watchman was making his banging noises somewhere far away. She wasn't sleepy. It was uncomfortable lying there—too soft. As always on past May nights, she sat up in bed and reflected, her thoughts being the same as those of the night before. Monotonous, futile and obsessive thoughts they were: about Andrew paying his addresses and proposing, about her accepting him and then gradually growing to appreciate so kind, so intelligent a man. But now that the wedding was less than a month away she felt vaguely scared and troubled as if faced by some prospect imprecise but disagreeable.

A desultory clicking thud was heard: that watchman again.

Through the large old-fashioned window she could see the garden with burgeoning lilac beyond it—drowsy and lifeless in the cold. A thick white mist slowly bore down on that lilac, wanting to submerge it. On far-away trees tired rooks cawed.

'God, why am I so depressed?'

Perhaps—who knows?—every young girl felt like this before her wedding. Or was it Sasha's influence? But Sasha had been on and on about all this for several years now, hadn't he? He sounded like a copybook: so unsophisticated and strange. Why, why, why couldn't she get him out of her head, though?

The watchman had long stopped his din. Birds started singing beneath the window and in the garden, the mist vanished, everything was radiant in smiling spring sunlight. Soon the whole garden, warmed and caressed by the sun, came to life with dew-drops glittering on the leaves like diamonds. Though old and long neglected, the garden seemed young and brightly decked that morning.

Gran was awake already, Sasha was coughing his deep, rough cough. Nadya heard the servants putting on the samovar downstairs and moving chairs.

The hours passed slowly. Nadya had been up and about the garden long ago, but still the morning dragged on.

Out came Nina, tears in her eyes, carrying a glass of mineral water. She practised spiritualism and homoeopathy, she read a lot, and she liked discussing the doubts which assailed her—all of which, thought Nadya, had some deep, mysterious significance. She kissed her mother and fell in by her side.

'Why were you crying, Mother?'

'I was reading a story last night about this old man and his daughter. The old fellow has a job somewhere, you see, and the man he works for falls in love with the daughter. I haven't finished it, but there was one bit . . . you couldn't help crying.' Nina sipped from her glass. 'I remembered it this morning and cried again.'

'I've been so depressed these last few days,' said Nadya a bit later. 'Why can't I sleep?'

'I don't know, darling. When I can't sleep I close my eyes ever so tight, like this, and imagine Anna Karenin walking about and talking. Or I think of something historical, from the ancient world.'

Her mother neither did nor could understand her, Nadya felt, felt it for the first time in her life—which positively terrified her. Wanting to hide, she went to her room.

They lunched at two. As it was a Wednesday—a Church fast—Grandmother was served with beetroot soup followed by steamed bream and buckwheat.

To tease Grandmother, Sasha took two kinds of soup: the beetroot variety *and* some meat broth of his own. He joked all through lunch, but his jokes all had some laboured moral and fell flat. When he introduced a witticism by uplifting his long, wasted, corpse-like fingers, and when you noticed how ill he was—that he wasn't long for this world—the effect was anything but funny, and you felt so sorry for him that you could cry.

After lunch Grandmother went to lie down in her room. Nina played the piano for a while, and then she went out too.

Sasha started his usual after-lunch discourse. 'My dear, good Nadya —if you would only, only listen to me——'

She was ensconced in an antique arm-chair, eyes closed, while he slowly paced the room.

'If you would only go away and study,' said he. 'Educated, dedicated people . . . they're the interesting ones, we don't need any other kind. The more such people there are, the more quickly the Kingdom of Heaven will come on earth, won't it? Bit by bit, you'll find, there won't be one stone left on another in your town. The place will turn topsy-turvy, change as if by magic. There will be splendid great mansions, marvellous gardens, wonderful fountains, outstanding people. But that's not what matters. The great thing is that the rabble as we know it, as it exists today . . . that evil will be no more because each man will have faith. Each will know the purpose of his life, and none will seek support in public opinion. Do leave this place, Nadya darling. Do show them all how bored you are by this stagnant, drab, reprehensible existence—or at least show your own self!'

'I can't, Sasha, I'm getting married.'

'Oh, really! What nonsense!'

They went out in the garden and walked a little.

Sasha continued. 'Say what you like, my dear, but this idleness of yours is sordid and immoral. Don't you realize, can't you see? Look— isn't it obvious that if you, say, and your mother and the wretched Gran never do anything, it means you're living on others, you're ruining the lives of people you don't even know. Pretty sordid, that! Pretty squalid, eh?'

Nadya wanted to say that, yes, he was quite right—wanted to tell him that she understood. But tears came to her eyes, she suddenly grew quiet, hunched her shoulders and went off to her room.

Andrew arrived in the late afternoon and as usual played his violin for a long time. Never a talkative man, he perhaps liked fiddling because it gave him an excuse to say nothing.

He started leaving for home at about half past ten, and already had his overcoat on when he embraced Nadya, greedily kissing her face, shoulders, hands.

'My dear, my darling, my beautiful one!' he muttered. 'Oh, how happy I am, I'm in a sort of mad ecstasy.'

But it sounded like something she had heard long ago in the distant past, or had read about in some antiquated, dog-eared, long-abandoned novel.

Sasha sat at the dining-room table drinking tea and balancing the saucer on his five long fingers. Gran played patience, Nina read. The icon-lamp sputtered, all was quiet and—it seemed—well. Nadya said good night, went up to her room, lay in bed and fell asleep at once—but woke up, as on the previous night, with the first glimmer of dawn. She wasn't sleepy, she felt troubled and depressed, she sat with her head on her knees—thinking of her fiancé and her wedding.

She happened to recall that her mother had never loved her husband, now deceased, and that she now had nothing, being entirely dependent on Gran—her mother-in-law. Why had Nadya always regarded her mother as someone special and out of the ordinary? Why had she never noticed that this was a commonplace, average, unhappy woman? Why? However much Nadya racked her brains she just couldn't say.

Sasha couldn't sleep either—she heard him coughing down below. What an oddity, what an innocent he was, thought Nadya. His dreams, all those 'marvellous gardens' and 'wonderful fountains' . . . there was something rather absurd about them, she felt. But his innocence, his very absurdity even . . . they had something so fine about them that the very thought of going away and studying at once sent a cold thrill through her, body and soul, flooding her with joy and rapture.

'But it's far, far better not to think about it, I mustn't,' she whispered.

The watchman's clicking thuds echoed from somewhere far away.

III

In mid-June Sasha suddenly felt bored and prepared to leave for Moscow.

'I can't stand this town,' said he gloomily. 'No water supply! No drains! It's not a very nice place to eat your meals—that kitchen's filthy beyond description.'

'Not so fast, Prodigal Son,' Grandmother urged him, in a whisper for some reason. 'The wedding's on the seventh.'

'I don't care.'

'But weren't you going to stay till September?'

'Well, I don't want to now, I have work to do.'

The summer had turned out damp and cold, the trees were sodden, everything in the garden looked dejected and uninviting—it really did make you feel like working. All over the house, upstairs and down-stairs, strange women's voices sounded, and the sewing-machine rattled away in Grandmother's room as Nadya's trousseau was hurriedly made up: there were no less than six fur coats—to mention nothing else—and the cheapest of them was costing three hundred roubles, Gran said. All this fuss irritated Sasha, who sat fuming in his own room. Still, they did persuade him to stay on—he promised not to leave before the first of July.

Time passed quickly. After lunch on St. Peter's Day Andrew took Nadya to Moscow Street for another look at the house which had been rented and made ready for the young couple some time ago. It was of two storeys, but so far only the upper floor had been decorated. The drawing-room had a gleaming floor painted to look like parquet, Viennese chairs, a grand piano and a violin-stand. There was a smell of paint. On the wall hung a large, gilt-framed painting of a naked lady with a broken-handled mauve vase by her side.

'Exquisite!' signed Andrew respectfully. 'A Shishmachevsky!'

Then came a parlour with a round table, a sofa and arm-chairs upholstered in bright blue. Above the sofa hung a large photograph of Father Andrew complete with purple hat and decorations. They entered a dining-room with a sideboard, and then the bedroom. Two beds stood side by side in the murk, looking as if that room had been furnished with the idea that nothing either would, or possibly could, ever go wrong in the place. Andrew led Nadya through the house, clutching her waist all the time. But she felt weak and guilty, she hated all these rooms, these beds, these arm-chairs. And that naked lady made her feel sick. She was no longer in love with Andrew, that was obvious —perhaps she never had loved him. But how she could say it, who she could say it to, what the point would be . . . that she neither did nor could understand, though she thought about it all day and night.

Andrew held her by the waist, he spoke so affectionately and modestly, he was so happy striding about these rooms of his, whereas she could see nothing in all this but sheer complacency—sheer stupid, mindless, intolerable smugness. That arm encircling her waist . . . it seemed hard and cold as an iron hoop. Every minute she was on the point of running away, sobbing, or throwing herself out of a window. Andrew took her to the bathroom, reached for a tap fixed in the wall —and suddenly water flowed.

'How about that!' he laughed. 'I had a two-hundred-gallon tank put in the loft, so we shall have water now, you and I.'

They walked round the yard, then into the street and took a cab. There were thick clouds of dust blowing. It looked like rain.

'Aren't you cold? asked Andrew, squinting in the dust.

She said nothing.

'Remember yesterday—Sasha criticizing me for never doing anything?' he asked after a brief pause. 'Well, he's right, absolutely right! I don't do anything, I can't. Now, why is that, my dear? The mere thought of ever sticking a cockade on my cap and going into government service . . . why does it so repel me? Why am I so put off when I see a lawyer, a Latin master, a county councillor? Oh Russia, Russia, Russia—what a lot of useless loafers you do support! My poor long-suffering motherland, fancy having to put up with so many people like me!'

He even built a theory round his own idleness, seeing it as a sign of the times.

Then he went on to say that 'when we're married, dear girl, we'll live in the country together. We're going to work! We'll buy a small plot of land by a river with a garden. We shall toil, we shall watch the world go by. Now, won't that be nice?'

He took off his hat and his hair streamed in the wind.

'God, God, I want to go home!' she thought as she listened.

They had nearly reached the house when they overtook Father Andrew.

'Ah, there's Father,' rejoiced Andrew Junior with a wave of the hat. 'I'm so fond of my old man, honestly,' he said, paying the cabby. 'A wonderful chap he is, such a dear old boy.'

As Nadya went into the house she felt cross and unwell. There would be guests to entertain all evening, she reflected. She must smile, listen to that fiddle and all sorts of rubbish, talk of nothing but her wedding. Grandmother, magnificently dignified in her silk dress, and haughty— as she always seemed with visitors—sat by the samovar. Father Andrew came in, smiling his crafty smile.

'I have the pleasure and blissful gratification of seeing you in good health,' he told Grandmother—seriously or in jest, it was hard to tell which.

IV

The wind beat on windows and roof, there was whistling, and a phantom in the chimney set up a grim, piteous drone. It was past midnight and everyone in the house had gone to bed, but no one could sleep, and Nadya had an impression of someone playing a violin downstairs. There was a sharp bang—a shutter must have been ripped off. A minute later in came Nina in her nightgown, with a candle, and asked Nadya what 'that bang' was.

With her hair in a single plait, with her nervous smile, Nadya's mother looked older, uglier, shorter, on this stormy night. Nadya remembered how recently she had thought of her mother as someone rather special. How proudly she had listened to her mother's words, whereas now she simply couldn't recall those words—all that came to mind was so feeble and futile.

Suddenly, it seemed, several bass voices seemed to start intoning in the stove—even the words could be distinguished: 'Oh good God, good God.' Nadya sat up in bed, suddenly clutched her hair.

'Darling Mother,' she sobbed. 'Oh, if only you knew what is happening to me! Please, I beseech you, let me leave this place.'

'What's that?' Nina asked, not understanding, and sat down on the bed. 'Where is it you want to go?'

Nadya cried for a long time, couldn't utter one word. 'Let me leave this town,' she said at last. 'There can't be any wedding—there shan't be, I tell you. I don't love that man, I can't even talk about him.'

'No, no, no, darling,' said Nina quickly. She was utterly horrified. 'Do calm yourself. You're just upset—it will pass. These things happen. I suppose you've been quarrelling with Andrew, but lovers' tiffs always end in kisses.'

'Oh, go away, Mother, do!' sobbed Nadya.

'Yes,' said Nina after a pause. 'You were a child, just a little girl not so long ago—and now you're engaged to be married. It's a law of Nature, this is: the transmutation of matter. You'll be a mother yourself before you know where you are—you'll be just another old lady with a naughty little daughter like mine.'

'My good, kind darling, you're so clever, really, and you're un-happy,' said Nadya. 'You're so unhappy—but why, for God's sake why, must you make these cheap remarks?'

Nina wanted to speak, but couldn't utter one word—just gulped and went to her room. Those bass voices seemed to be booming in the stove again and Nadya suddenly took fright, jumped out of bed and rushed to her mother's room. Nina, her eyes full of tears, lay in bed under a pale blue quilt with a book in her hand.

'Do listen, Mother,' said Nadya. 'Do please concentrate, do try and see—just try and see how petty and degrading our lives are. My eyes have been opened now, I see everything. Just what does the wretched Andrew add up to? He's not at all bright, you know, Mother. God, he's so stupid—can't you see that, Mother?'

Nina sat up abruptly.

'You and your grandmother are torturing me,' she sobbed. 'I want a bit of life—yes, life!' she repeated, twice striking her chest with her fist. 'So give me my freedom. I'm still young, I want a bit of fun—and you two have made an old woman out of me!'

She wept bitterly, lay down and curled up under the quilt, seeming oh so small, pathetic and foolish, while Nadya went to her room, dressed, sat by the window and settled down to wait for morning. She sat there all night musing, while someone seemed to be banging a shutter from outside and whistling.

In the morning Grandmother complained that the wind had blown all the apples off in the orchard during the night, and had broken an old plum-tree. It was so grey, so dim, so cheerless—dark enough for the lamps. Everyone complained of the cold, rain drummed on the windows. After breakfast Nadya went to see Sasha and knelt down in the corner by his arm-chair without a word, hiding her face in her hands.

Sasha asked what the matter was.

'It's too much!' she said. 'How I could ever stand this life . . . I don't, I simply don't understand. I despise the man I'm engaged to. I despise myself, I despise this idle, pointless existence.'

'Now, now,' said Sasha, not yet realizing what the trouble was. 'It's nothing, it'll be all right.'

'I'm sick of this life,' Nadya went on. 'I can't face another day of it, I shall leave this place tomorrow. For God's sake take me with you.'

Sasha looked at her for a minute in surprise. Then, at last, he understood and was childishly pleased, throwing up his hands and gleefully doing a sort of tap-dance in his slippers.

'Splendid!' He rubbed his hands. 'God, this is wonderful!'

She stared at him—her eyes unblinking and enormous, like a girl in love, like one spellbound—expecting him to come straight out with some saying of vital and transcendental significance. He hadn't told her anything yet, but she felt broad, new, hitherto unsuspected horizons opening out before her and gazed at him in rapt expectation, ready for anything: death, even.

'I'll leave tomorrow,' he said after reflection. 'You can pretend to see me off at the station. I'll put your things in my trunk and get you your ticket. Then, when the bell rings for the train to leave, you can jump on board and off we'll go. You can come with me as far as Moscow, and then go on to St. Petersburg on your own. Have you your identity documents?'

'Yes.'

'You'll have no regrets, I swear it, no second thoughts,' said Sasha eagerly. 'You go and do your studying—then let your destiny take over. Only transform your way of life and everything else will change too. The great thing is to revolutionize your whole life. Nothing else matters. Do we leave tomorrow then?'

'Yes, yes, for God's sake yes!'

Nadya was greatly agitated, she had never been so depressed in her life, she was faced with misery and agony of mind from now till the moment of her departure. Or so she felt. But no sooner had she gone up to her room and lain down than she immediately dropped off and slept soundly—with tears in her eyes and a smile on her face—right up to evening.

V

A cab had been sent for. Nadya went upstairs in hat and coat for one more look at her mother and everything that had been home. She stood in her own room near the still warm bed, looked about her, then went softly to her mother's room. Nina was asleep, it was quiet in there. Nadya kissed her mother, patted her hair, stood for a couple of minutes.

Then she walked slowly downstairs.

It was raining hard. The cabby had put the top up and stood by the porch, wet through.

'There's no room for you, Nadya,' said Grandmother as the servants began loading the luggage. 'Fancy seeing someone off in this weather! You should stay at home—goodness me, what rain!'

Nadya wanted to speak, but couldn't. Then Sasha helped her in, covered her legs with a rug and settled down by her side.

'Good luck and God bless you,' Grandmother shouted from the porch. 'Now, do write to us from Moscow, Sasha.'

'Certainly. Bye bye, Gran.'

'May heaven protect you.'

'Confound this weather,' said Sasha.

Only now did Nadya start weeping. She actually was leaving home, only now did she realize it—she still hadn't believed it when saying good-bye to Grandmother and looking at Mother. Farewell, old town! Everything suddenly came back to her: Andrew, his father, the new house, that naked lady with vase—but none of it scared or depressed her any longer, it was all so inoffensively trivial and seemed to be receding further and further into the past. They got into their carriage, the train started, and all her past life—which had once loomed so large and serious—now shrank into a small compass, and a vast, broad future unfurled before her . . . a future hitherto barely conceivable. The rain drummed on the carriage windows and nothing was seen but green fields with glimpses of telegraph-posts and birds sitting on the wires. She suddenly caught her breath out of sheer joy: remembered that she was on her way to freedom, that she was going to study—it was just like running away to join the Cossacks in the old days. She laughed, wept, prayed.

'Everything's all right, it really is,' Sasha grinned.

VI

Autumn passed, winter followed. Nadya was very homesick. She thought about Mother and Grandmother every day—about Sasha too. The letters which came from home were calm and friendly—all had been forgotten and forgiven, it seemed. Healthy and cheerful, she set off for home after her May examinations, stopping on the way to see Sasha in Moscow. He hadn't changed since last summer. He still had that same beard and dishevelled hair, still wore the same frock-coat and canvas trousers, still had those fine big eyes. Yet he looked ill and worn out—he had aged, he was thinner, he kept coughing. To Nadya he seemed rather grey and provincial.

'Good God, if it isn't Nadya!' He laughed merrily. 'My own dearest little darling!'

They sat for a while in the printing room with its smoke and overpowering, stifling smell of indian ink and paint. Then they went into his room—also smoke-impregnated, with traces of sputum. On the table near a cold samovar lay a broken bowl and a piece of dark paper. There were masses of dead flies on table and floor. All this showed how slovenly Sasha's way of life was. He lived any old how, utterly scorning all comforts. Had anyone raised the question of his personal happiness, of his private life—or of anyone loving him—it would have meant nothing. He'd just have laughed.

'Everything's fine, it's all been for the best,' Nadya said quickly. 'Mother came to see me in St. Petersburg in the autumn. She says Grandmother isn't angry, but keeps going into my room and making the sign of the cross over the walls.'

Sasha looked cheerful, but kept coughing and spoke in a cracked voice. Nadya kept watching him. Was he really seriously ill? Or was it just her fancy? She couldn't tell.

'You *are* ill really, aren't you, Sasha dear?' she asked.

'No, I'm all right. I am ill, but not very——'

This upset Nadya. 'Good God, why don't you see a doctor, why don't you look after your health? My dear, good, darling Sasha——'

Tears spurted from her eyes. And why did Andrew loom up in her imagination, together with that nude lady with vase and all that past life which seemed as distant from her, now, as her childhood? She cried because she found Sasha less modern, intellectual and attractive than last year.

'Sasha dear, you are very, very ill. I'd do anything to stop you being so pale and thin. I owe you so much. You've done such a lot for me, my good, kind Sasha—more than you can ever imagine. You're nearer and dearer to me than anyone, now, you really are.'

They sat and talked for a while. But Nadya found, after spending a winter in St. Petersburg, that Sasha—his words, his smile, his entire person—had the outmoded, antiquated, obsolete air of something long dead and buried.

'I'm off to the Volga the day after tomorrow,' said Sasha. 'And then, well, I'm taking a koumiss cure: going on a fermented mare's milk diet. A friend and his wife are coming with me. The wife's a wonderful person. I've been working on her, trying to persuade her to go away and study. I want her to turn her life upside down.'

After this chat they went to the station, where Sasha treated her to tea and apples. When the train started he smiled and waved his handkerchief, the very shape of his legs indicating that he was extremely ill and not long for this world.

Nadya reached her native town at noon. As she was driven home from the station the streets seemed very wide, the houses small and squat. There was no one about except for the German piano-tuner in his brown overcoat. The houses all seemed covered with dust. Grandmother—a really old woman now, as stout and ugly as ever—flung her arms round Nadya and cried for some time, pressing her face against the girl's shoulder and unable to break away. Nina also looked much older and worse for wear. She had a rather haggard air, but was as tightly laced as ever, with those diamonds still flashing on her fingers.

'Darling, darling, darling!' She trembled all over.

They sat silently weeping. That the past was utterly lost and gone for ever Grandmother and Mother both sensed, obviously. Their social position, their former prestige, their right to entertain guests . . . they were all gone. It was like living without a care in the world until, suddenly, there is a police raid, the house is searched, and the head of the family turns out to be an embezzler or forger . . . which puts paid to all that living without a care in the world.

Nadya went upstairs and saw the same old bed, the same old windows with their unpretentious white curtains, and through those windows the same old garden: cheerful, noisy, drenched with sunlight. She touched her table, she sat, she brooded. Then she had a good lunch and drank tea with delicious thick cream. There was something missing, though, the house felt empty inside and the ceilings seemed so low. When she went to bed that night and pulled the blankets over her it seemed rather funny to be back in that same snug, very soft bed.

Nina came in for a moment and sat down guiltily, looking nervously about her.

'Well, how are things, Nadya?' she asked after a pause. 'Happy, are you? Very happy?'

'Yes, Mother.'

Nina stood up and made the sign of the cross over Nadya and the windows. 'I've taken up religion, you see. I study philosophy now, you know, I do a lot of thinking. Many things are crystal clear to me these days. The great thing, I think, is to filter your whole life through a prism.'

'Tell me, Mother, how is Grandmother keeping?'

'She seems all right. When you went off with Sasha and we got your telegram, Grandmother just collapsed when she read it. Three days she lay—never moved. Then she kept praying and crying, but she's all right now.'

Nadya's mother stood up and paced the room.

Clicking thuds were heard: that watchman again.

'The great thing is to filter your whole life through a prism,' said Nina. 'In other words, that is, one's apprehension of life must be split down into its simplest components like the seven colours of the rainbow, and each component must be studied in isolation.'

What else Nina said Nadya did not hear. Nor did she hear her mother leave because she soon fell asleep.

May passed, June began, Nadya had grown used to being at home. Grandmother fussed over the samovar, sighing deeply, and Nina spoke of her philosophy in the evenings. She was still very much the poor relation and had to ask Grandmother for every twenty-copeck piece. The house was full of flies and the ceilings seemed to get lower and lower. Gran and Nina never went out in the streets, fearing to meet one of the Andrews, father or son. Nadya walked in the garden, walked down the street, looked at the houses, looked at the grey fences. The whole town was so outmoded and antiquated, she felt. Was it awaiting its own end? Or expecting something fresh and original to begin? It was never quite clear which. Oh, if it would only hurry up and begin . . . that brave new world where you can face your own destiny boldly, where you can be cheerful and free, knowing you're in the right! Now, such a life *will* come about sooner or later. The time will surely come when Grandmother's house, so arranged, now, that four servants are forced to share a single filthy basement room . . . the time will come when that house will vanish without trace, be forgotten, pass from memory. Meanwhile Nadya's only diversion came from the little boys next door who would bang on the fence when she was walking in the garden, laughing and jeering at her.

'Who thought she was going to get married?'

A letter came from Sasha in Saratov. In his sprightly, dancing hand he wrote that his Volga trip had been a complete success, but that he had contracted some minor ailment in Saratov, had lost his voice and had been in hospital for a fortnight. Realizing what this meant, Nadya felt a foreboding akin to certainty. It was disagreeable, though, to find that neither this premonition nor her thoughts of Sasha distressed her so much as before. She craved excitement, she wanted to be back in St. Petersburg, while her friendship with Sasha—delightful as it was —now seemed a thing of the far, far distant past. After lying awake all night she sat by the window next morning, listening. Yes, there really were voices down there: the agitated Gran was firing off questions about something, and then someone burst into tears.

Going downstairs, Nadya found Grandmother praying in a corner, her face tear-stained. There was a telegram on the table.

After walking about the room listening to Grandmother crying for some time, Nadya took the telegram and read it. Its burden was that Alexander Timofeyevich or Sasha for short had perished of tuberculosis in Saratov.

Grandmother and Nina went to church to arrange a memorial service while Nadya went on pacing about the house, musing. That her life had been transformed to Sasha's recipe, that she was a lonely stranger—unwanted in a place from which *she* wanted nothing—that her entire past life had been ripped away, had disappeared as if burnt to ashes scattered in the breeze . . . all these things she keenly realized.

She went and stood in Sasha's room. 'Farewell, Sasha darling.'

Thus brooding, she pictured her new life opening before her, with its broad horizons. Still obscure, still mysterious, that life lured and beckoned her.

She went up to her room to pack. Next morning she said good-bye to the family. Vigorous, high-spirited, she left town: for ever, presumably.

Qc

STORY NOT INCLUDED BY CHEKHOV
IN HIS *COLLECTED WORKS*

ALL FRIENDS TOGETHER

(A Story)

**[*У знакомых
(Рассказ)*]**

(1898)

ALL FRIENDS TOGETHER

(*A Story*)

ONE morning a letter arrived.

> Kuzminki, 7 June
>
> Dear Misha,
>
> You've quite forgotten us. Do come and visit us soon, we miss you. Come out today—we beg you, sir, on bended knee! Prince Charming, show yourself!
>
> Dying to see you,   TA and BA

The letter was from Tatyana Losev: 'Ta', as she had been called when Podgorin was staying at Kuzminki ten or twelve years ago.

But who might Ba be?

Podgorin remembered long conversations, gay laughter, flirtations, evening walks and a whole bevy of girls and young women who had once lived at Kuzminki and near by. Then he remembered that frank, lively, intelligent face with the freckles which so well set off the dark auburn hair of ... Barbara, Tatyana's friend. Barbara had taken a medical degree and had a job at a factory somewhere out beyond Tula. Now she was obviously staying at Kuzminki.

'Dear old Ba!' thought Podgorin, letting memories engulf him. 'Splendid girl!'

Tatyana, Barbara and he were of an age. But he had only been a student then, and they marriageable girls who regarded him as a mere boy. Now that he was a lawyer with greying hair they still treated him as not quite grown up, still stressed how young he was, still said he knew nothing of life.

He was very fond of them—but rather as figures of the past, he felt, than as anything else. Of their present situation he knew very little: it sounded all very mysterious and alien to him. Alien too was this short, jocular letter, no doubt composed with much time and effort. When Tatyana was writing it her husband Sergey must have been standing behind her.

The estate of Kuzminki had come to her as part of her dowry only six years ago, but had already been run into debt by this same Sergey. Whenever a bank or mortgage payment fell due these days they would ask Podgorin for legal advice. They had, moreover, twice asked him for a loan. Now too it was either advice or money they wanted from him, obviously.

Kuzminki had lost its old hold over him. It was so sad out there. The laughter, the bustle, the jolly, carefree faces, the trysts on quiet moonlit nights . . . these things were no more. Above all, they weren't as young as they had been. And it was only in retrospect, probably, that it all seemed so magical.

Besides Ta and Ba there had also been a Na: Tatyana's sister Nadya whom—half in jest, half seriously—they used to call his fiancée. He had watched her grow up, and they had reckoned on his marrying her. He had indeed been in love with her at one time, he had been going to propose. But she was twenty-three now and he still hadn't married her.

'Odd, how it has all turned out,' he thought as he re-read the letter with embarrassment. 'And I can't *not* go because they'd be offended.'

His failure to visit the Losevs recently . . . it weighed heavily on his conscience, and so, after pacing his room and brooding, he overcame his reluctance and decided to go and stay for a couple of days. His duty thus discharged, he could relax and feel free until next summer at least. As he made ready to leave for the Brest Station after lunch he told his servants that he would be back in three days.

From Moscow to Kuzminki was a two-hour train ride followed by a twenty-minute coach drive from the station. When he got out of the train Tatyana's wood came into view together with three tall, narrow summer cottages which Losev—who had taken up various business enterprises during the first years of his marriage—had started building but hadn't finished. He had been ruined by these cottages, by other money-making schemes and by his frequent trips to Moscow—what with lunching at the Slav Fair, dining at the Hermitage and ending up on Little Bronny Road or at the gipsy dive called Knacker's Yard.

He called this 'pushing the boat out'.

Podgorin drank a certain amount himself, quite a lot at times, and consorted with women indiscriminately—but coldly and sluggishly, without enjoyment, and he was quite disgusted when his associates went in for that sort of thing wholeheartedly. As for those who felt more relaxed at Knacker's Yard than in their own homes with respectable women . . . such men he neither understood nor liked. Anything the least bit smutty . . . it seemed to stick to them like burrs. He disliked Losev—he thought him a dull dog, utterly incompetent and lazy. Many were the times he'd found his company rather off-putting.

Sergey and Nadya met him just beyond the woods.

'Why have you been neglecting us, my dear chap?' asked Losev, kissing him thrice and then putting both arms round his waist. 'You don't love us any more, old pal.'

He had gross features, a fleshy nose, a thin, light brown beard. He combed his hair to one side, merchant fashion, to give himself that simple, oh-so-Russian look. He breathed straight in your face when he spoke and when he wasn't speaking he breathed heavily through his nose. His beefy frame, his air of excessive self-indulgence . . . they embarrassed him, and he kept puffing out his chest to ease his breathing —which gave him a haughty look. His sister-in-law Nadya seemed ethereal by comparison. She was very fair, pale and graceful with friendly eyes which seemed to caress one. Was she or was she not beautiful? Podgorin couldn't tell, having known her since childhood and taking her looks for granted. She wore a white, open-necked dress, and the view of that long, white, bare neck was new to him and not altogether nice.

'Tatyana and I have been expecting you since morning,' she said. 'Barbara's staying with us, and she's looking forward to seeing you too.'

She took his arm and abruptly laughed for no reason, giving a spontaneous cry of joy as if enchanted by some sudden thought. The fields of blooming rye so still in the quiet air, the sun-drenched woods . . . how lovely they were! But only now that she was walking beside Podgorin did Nadya seem to notice these things.

He told her that he would be staying for three days. 'I'm sorry, I couldn't get away from Moscow any sooner.'

'You've quite neglected us—very, very naughty of you!' was Sergey's good-humoured reproach. '*Jamais de ma vie!*' he suddenly added, clicking his fingers.

He had this trick of unexpectedly bringing out some utterly irrele-vant exclamation with a snap of the fingers. He was for ever mimicking someone: if he rolled his eyes, nonchalantly tossed back his hair or struck a pathetic pose, the reason was that he had been to the theatre on the previous night, or had attended a banquet with speeches. Now he was walking like a gouty old man—taking short steps, not bending his knees: aping someone or other, no doubt.

'Tatyana couldn't believe you'd come, you know,' Nadya said.

'But Barbara and I felt sure you would—I somehow knew you'd come by this train.'

'*Jamais de ma vie!*' repeated Sergey.

The ladies awaited them on the garden terrace. Ten years ago Podgorin—then a poor student—had coached Nadya in mathematics and history in exchange for his board and lodging, while Barbara (a medical student at the time) had incidentally had some Latin lessons from him. As for Tatyana, that strapping, good-looking girl had thought only of love. Love and happiness . . . she was obsessed with them, she craved them, she was for ever expecting to meet that future husband who filled her dreams morning noon and night. Now turned thirty, she was just as beautiful and striking as ever, in her loose peignoir, with her plump white arms. Her thoughts were only of her husband and her two little girls. She might be talking and smiling now, her expression said, but her mind was really on other things: she was still mounting guard over her love and over her rights to that love, she still stood poised to pounce on any enemy who might want to remove her husband and children. Hers was a strong love and she felt that it was reciprocated, but jealousy and fear for her children tormented her unceasingly and prevented her from being happy.

After a noisy reunion on the terrace everyone except Sergey went to Tatyana's room. Lowered blinds kept out the sun, and the light was so dim that all the roses in a large vase seemed of the same colour. They sat Podgorin down in an old arm-chair by the window while Nadya sat on a low stool at his feet. Besides the friendly reproaches, the jokes and the laughter which he now heard, and which reminded him so vividly of the past, there would—he knew—also be a disagreeable conversation about promissory notes and mortgages. There was no escape, so he thought it might be best to have their business talk now, without more ado, and get it over with—then go out into the garden and the fresh air.

'Might we talk business first?' he asked. 'What's new here in Kuzminki? Anything rotten in the state of Denmark?'

'Kuzminki *is* in a rotten way,' Tatyana sadly sighed. 'Things are in such a mess, dear me, they really are—they could hardly be worse.' She paced the room in agitation. 'The estate's up for sale, the auction's on the seventh of August, there are advertisements everywhere, and prospective buyers come here and walk round the house staring. Anyone has the right to come and look round my room these days. Oh, it may be perfectly legal, but I find it deeply humiliating and insulting. We're out of funds—*and* out of places to borrow them from. It's simply awful.'

She paused in the middle of the room, her voice trembling, tears starting from her eyes. 'I swear, I swear by everything most sacred, by my children's happiness, I can't live without Kuzminki. I was born here, it's my home, and if it's taken away from me I can't carry on, I shall die of despair.'

'I think you take too gloomy a view,' said Podgorin. 'It will be all right. Your husband will get a job, you'll find a new niche: live a new life.'

'How can you say such a thing!' shouted Tatyana, looking very beautiful and fierce. She was poised to pounce on that enemy who might try to remove her husband, children and home—as her face, her whole figure, expressed with particular force. 'New life, indeed! How can you say such a thing? Sergey has been making inquiries, and he's been promised a tax inspectorship somewhere out Ufa or Perm way. And I don't mind where I go. Let it be Siberia, even, I'm prepared to stay there ten, twenty years. But I must be sure of coming back to Kuzminki sooner or later. I can't live without Kuzminki, I can't, I shan't, I won't!'

She shouted, stamped her foot.

'You're a lawyer, Misha,' said Barbara. 'You know all the tricks, and it's your job to tell us what to do.'

There was only one fair and rational reply: that the situation was hopeless. But Podgorin could not bring himself to blurt it out.

'I must think about it,' he mumbled indecisively. 'I'll give it some thought.'

He was two different men. As a lawyer he'd had to handle some pretty nasty cases. In court, with clients, he behaved arrogantly and always expressed his opinion directly and harshly. He was used to somewhat crude jollifications with his cronies. But in the intimacy of his personal life, with people very close to him or old friends, he showed extraordinary delicacy, he was shy and sensitive, and he could never put things bluntly. A single tear, one sidelong glance, a lie—an ugly gesture, even . . . they were enough to make him flinch and cave in. And now that Nadezhda was sitting at his feet he disliked her bare neck. It put him off and even made him want to leave for home. A year ago he had chanced to run across Sergey at a certain Madame's premises in Bronny Road, and he was as embarrassed by Tatyana's presence, now, as if it was he who had been unfaithful to her. Besides

this talk about Kuzminki put him in a very difficult position. He was
used to having judges, juries—or simply some legal provision—settling
all ticklish and unpleasant questions, and when faced with a problem
for his personal decision he was lost.

'You're our friend, Misha, we all love you, you're like one of the
family,' Tatyana went on. 'Now, I'll be perfectly frank with you:
you're our only hope. Tell us what to do, for God's sake. Perhaps
there's somewhere we could apply for help? Perhaps it's not too late to
put the estate in Nadya's name, or Barbara's? What shall we do?'

'Save us, Misha, save us,' said Barbara, lighting a cigarette. 'You
were always such a clever boy. You haven't really lived, you're not
very experienced, but you do have your head screwed on. You'll help
Tatyana, I know you will.'

'I must think—perhaps I'll come up with something.'

They went for a walk in the garden and then in the fields. Sergey
came along too and took Podgorin's arm—kept leading him ahead,
obviously intending to discuss something: probably the mess he was
in. This walking and talking with Sergey were quite an ordeal too.
Sergey kept embracing his guest—always the regulation three kisses—
took Podgorin's arm, put his own arm round Podgorin's waist,
breathed in his face. It was as if he had been smeared with a sweet glue
which was liable to stick fast to you whenever he touched you. And
that look about the eyes which showed that he wanted something out
of Podgorin, that he was just going to ask Podgorin for it . . . it was
downright depressing, as if the man was pointing a revolver at you.

The sun set, it was getting dark. Along the railway line green and
red lights came on here and there.

Barbara paused, looked at the lights and recited.

> 'Through narrow cuttings, over bridges
>   Past posts the line runs true and brave.
> Behold that splendid railway's verges:
>   The Russian workers' common grave!

How does it go on? Good Lord, I've forgotten!

> 'In sultry heat, in freezing winter
>   We strained our sinews, bent our backs.'

She declaimed with gusto in a magnificent contralto voice, her face
flushing vividly, tears in her eyes. This was the old Barbara, the college
girl. Hearing her reminded Podgorin of his own old student days

when he had known a lot of good poetry by heart and had enjoyed reciting it.

> 'His back still hunched and never straightened,
> The navvy grimly holds his peace——'

But Barbara remembered no more.

She fell silent, smiling weakly and feebly. The green and red signal lights seemed sad now that her recitation was over.

'Oh, I've forgotten it.'

But Podgorin did suddenly remember—it had somehow stuck in his memory from his student days—and he recited softly, under his breath.

> 'Enough our Russian worker suffered
> To build another railway line.
> Next will he build a mighty future:
> His own new highway broad and fine!
> The pity is——'

'The pity is,' Barbara broke in, now remembering the words.

> 'The pity is that neither you nor I
> Will see that brave new world before we die.'

She laughed and clapped him on the back.

They went home and sat down to supper. Sergey nonchalantly tucked a corner of his napkin into his collar in imitation of someone or other.

'Let's have a drink,' he said, pouring vodka for himself and Podgorin. 'At college in the old days we could hold our liquor, we had the gift of the gab, and we got things done. I drink your health, old pal. Now, why don't you drink to a silly old idealist, coupled with the wish that he may die an idealist. Can the leopard change his spots?'

All through supper Tatyana was casting tender, jealous glances at her husband, afraid of his eating or drinking something which might disagree with him. He had been spoilt by women, exhausted by them, she felt—which attracted her, but also caused her pain. Barbara and Nadya had a soft spot for him too, their worried looks betraying the fear that he might suddenly make off and leave them. When he made to pour himself a second glass of vodka Barbara's expression grew peeved.

'You're poisoning yourself, Sergey,' she said. 'You're a highly-strung, sensitive person, and you might easily become an alcoholic. Tell them to remove the vodka, Tatyana.'

Sergey was a great ladies' man on the whole. They liked his height, his build, his strong features, his idleness, his misfortunes. His extravagances were only due to kindness, said they—he was impractical because he was an idealist, he was honest, he had integrity. If he owned nothing and couldn't find a proper job, that was because he couldn't truckle to people and circumstances. Such great faith did they have in him, idolizing him, spoiling him with their adoration . . . he even began thinking that he *was* idealistic, impractical and the soul of decency and integrity: head and shoulders above these very women, in fact.

'Now, why don't you say something nice about the children?' asked Tatyana, looking lovingly at her two little girls—healthy, sleek and resembling cream buns—as she piled their bowls with rice. 'Just look at them, now! All mothers dote on their children, it's said. But I'm quite unbiased, believe me, and my little girls are outstanding. Especially the elder.'

Podgorin smiled at her and the little girls while wondering how a healthy and rather intelligent young woman—so essentially large and complex an organism—could lavish her entire energy and vital forces on a labour as trivial and devoid of complexity as managing a home which was perfectly well managed already.

'There may be some reason for it,' thought he. 'But how dull and dreary it all is!'

> *'Before he'd time to turn a hair*
> *He'd been knocked over by a bear,'*

said Sergey, snapping his fingers.

They finished supper. Tatyana and Barbara sat Podgorin down on the drawing-room sofa and began a low-voiced discussion: business again.

'We must rescue Sergey, it's our moral duty,' said Barbara. 'He has his weaknesses, he's not provident—doesn't put by for a rainy day—but that's because he's so kind and generous. He's just a child at heart. Present him with a million roubles, and none of it would be left in a month, he'd give it all away.'

'It's true, it really is,' said Tatyana, tears streaming down her cheeks. 'I've had an awful lot to put up with from him, but he is a wonderful person, there's no denying it.'

Then Tatyana and Barbara were both sufficiently cruel, in a small way, to reproach Podgorin by saying that his generation was 'quite different, Misha'.

Why this generation stuff, wondered Podgorin—after all, Losev was only six years older than he, no more.

'Life isn't easy,' sighed Barbara. 'One's always threatened with losing something. Either they want to take your estate, or someone dear to you falls ill and you fear for their life. So it goes on, day in day out. But what can we do, my dears? We must submit to a Higher Will without complaining, we must remember that nothing in this world is accidental, but that everything has its own ultimate purpose. You haven't really lived, Misha, you haven't suffered much, and you'll laugh at me. All right—laugh, but I'll say it all the same. During my acutest periods of anxiety I have had several experiences of second sight. This has quite transformed my consciousness, and I now know that nothing is contingent—that everything in life is necessary.'

How different she was, this Barbara . . . grey-haired now, corseted, in her modish dress with its puffed sleeves . . . Barbara twisting her cigarette in her long, thin, nervously twitching fingers . . . Barbara so prone to mysticism . . . Barbara of the flat, monotonous voice—how different she was from Barbara the medical student, that jolly, merry, hearty, venturesome red-head!

'What ever became of all that?' wondered Podgorin, bored with her chatter.

'Sing us something, Ba,' he asked, to cut short this talk of second sight. 'You used to sing so beautifully.'

'That's all ancient history, Misha.'

'Then recite some more Nekrasov.'

'I've forgotten all that. Those quotations just now . . . I just remembered them by accident.'

Despite that corset and those puffed sleeves she was obviously not well off, and had a pretty thin time of it out at that factory beyond Tula. Obviously, too, she had been overworking. Hard, grinding toil, perpetual worry about other people and interfering in their affairs . . . it had exhausted her, aged her. Looking at that sad face, which had already lost its bloom, Podgorin reflected that *she* was the one who really needed help: not Kuzminki and this Sergey whom she was making such a fuss about.

Her college education, her career as a doctor . . . they did not seem to have affected the woman in her. Like Tatyana she adored weddings, births, christenings, endless chat about children. She liked reading thrillers with happy endings and in newspapers she only read the bits about fires, floods and public ceremonies. She was very keen for

Podgorin to propose to Nadya—were it to happen she would burst into tears of ecstasy.

Whether accidentally or through Barbara's contrivance, Podgorin now found himself alone with Nadya. But the mere suspicion that he was under observation, that something was expected of him . . . it constrained him, cramped his style. In Nadya's presence he felt as if the two of them were shut up in a cage together.

'Let's go into the garden,' said she.

They went off to the garden: he disgruntled and annoyed, not knowing what to talk about, and she delighted, proud to be with him, obviously pleased that he was staying on another three days—possessed too, perhaps, by delicious fancies and hopes. Was she in love with him? That he didn't know. But that she was fond of him he did know—that she had long been attached to him, that she still looked on him as her teacher, and that she was now passing through the same emotional phase as her sister Tatyana before her: she was obsessed, that is, with love, with marrying as soon as possible, with having a husband, children, her own little place. She still retained that capacity for friendship which is so intense in children. Could it be that her feelings for Podgorin were only those of respect and friendliness—that she was not in love with him so much as with those dreams of a husband and children?

'It's getting dark,' he said.

'Yes, the moon rises late now.'

As they walked they kept to one path near the house. Podgorin didn't want to go far into the garden where it was dark, and where he would have to take her by the arm and be very close to her. Shadows moved on the terrace: Tatyana and Barbara watching him, he felt.

'I must ask your advice.' Nadya halted. 'If Kuzminki's sold Sergey will go away and get a job, and our lives are bound to change completely. I shan't stay on with Tatyana—we shall separate because I don't want to be a burden on the family. I must work. I'll get a job in Moscow and earn some money to help Tatyana and her husband. You will advise me, won't you?'

Knowing nothing at all about it, she was yet inspired by the idea of an independent working life, she was making plans for the future—it was written all over her face. Working, helping others . . . she thought it all so wonderfully romantic. Seeing her pale face and dark brows close to him, he remembered what a keen, intelligent, promising pupil she had been—remembered how he had enjoyed coaching her. She was no longer just a young lady looking for a husband, probably, but a decent, intelligent, exceptionally kind, tender, soft-hearted girl who could be moulded, like wax, to one's wishes. Given a proper environment, what an admirable woman she might become!

'Now, why *don't* I marry her, actually?' wondered Podgorin, but at once rather took fright at the idea and made for the house. Tatyana was sitting at the grand piano in the drawing-room. Her playing brought back vivid memories of the time when playing, singing and dancing had gone on until late at night in this same drawing-room with the windows open and the birds also singing away in the garden and by the river. Podgorin cheered up, became exuberant, danced with Nadya and Barbara, and then sang. Hampered by a corn on his foot, he asked if he could wear Sergey's slippers. And, oddly enough, he felt at home—quite one of the family—in those slippers: 'a typical brother-in-law' flashed through his mind. He became even cheerier. Looking at him, everyone else came to life and brightened up as if rejuvenated. Their faces glowed with hope: Kuzminki was saved! It was all so simple, wasn't it? They only needed to devise some scheme, rummage around in law books, or have Nadya marry Podgorin.

That affair was obviously prospering. Nadya—pink, happy, eyes filled with tears in anticipation of excitement—twirled as she danced. Her white dress billowed, showing her pretty little legs in flesh-coloured stockings.

Barbara was delighted and took Podgorin's arm. 'Don't run away from your happiness, Misha,' she said quietly, with a meaningful expression. 'Just take it when it's offered—otherwise you'll be chasing after it when it's too late to catch it.'

Podgorin wanted to give an undertaking, confirm her hopes. By now he himself believed that Kuzminki was saved: there was nothing to it!

'Thou sha-alt be the quee-een of all the world,' he sang, striking a pose. But then he suddenly realized that there was nothing, absolutely nothing, that he could do for these people—so he stopped singing, looking guilty.

Then he sat silently in a corner, tucking under him those feet shod in someone else's slippers.

The others realized from the way he looked that nothing could be done. They too fell silent. The piano was closed. Everyone noticed that it was late—time for bed—and Tatyana extinguished the big lamp in the drawing-room.

They had made up a bed for Podgorin in the same little hut in the grounds where he used to sleep in the old days. Sergey went along to say good night, holding a candle high above his head, though the moon had risen and it was already bright. They went down a path flanked by lilac bushes, gravel crunching underfoot.

> *'Before he'd time to turn a hair*
> *He'd been knocked over by a bear,'*

said Sergey.

Podgorin felt as if he'd heard these lines a thousand times. He was sick of them!

When they reached the hut Sergey produced a bottle and two glasses from his loose-fitting jacket and put them on the table.

'Cognac,' said he. 'Double Zero brand. One can't drink in the house with Barbara around because she only starts nagging about alcoholism. But here we're free. A fine cognac, this!'

They sat down, and the cognac was indeed good.

'Let's have a proper drink tonight,' went on Sergey, chewing on a lemon. 'I've always been rather one of the boys, myself, and I do like pushing the boat out now and then. Matter of necessity!'

But there was still that look about his eyes which said that he needed something from Podgorin and was just about to ask for it.

'Drink up, old boy,' he sighed. 'Things are pretty tough, I can tell you. It's all up with chaps like me—us individualists. We're finished. Idealism's out of fashion these days. It's money that talks nowadays, and if you don't want to be kicked aside you must fall down and worship Mammon. But that I can't do—I'm a sight too squeamish!'

'When's the auction?' Podgorin asked, to change the subject.

'Seventh of August. But I have no hope of saving Kuzminki, old boy. Those arrears are colossal, and the estate brings in nothing: it's losses, losses, losses every year. The game's not worth the candle. Tatyana's upset of course—it *is* her family home—but I'm not all that sorry, quite frankly. I'm not cut out for the country. Give me a large, bustling city! Conflict . . . there's my element!'

He went on, still dodging the issue, while watching Podgorin keenly as if waiting his chance. Then, suddenly, Podgorin saw those eyes near to him and felt the man's breath on his face.

'Come to my rescue, dear old boy!' gasped Sergey. 'Lend me two hundred roubles, I beg you.'

Podgorin wanted to say that he was short of money himself. It seemed better to give those two hundred roubles to some poor man, or just lose them at cards, even. But he was terribly embarrassed. Feeling trapped in this small room with the one candle, desiring a swift escape from that breath, from those soft arms round his waist—which already seemed glued to his person—he hastily rummaged in his pockets for his note-case.

'There you are,' he mumbled, taking out a hundred roubles. 'You can have the rest later, I have no more on me. As you see, I can't refuse.' He was annoyed and beginning to lose his temper. 'I'm an insufferably feeble character. But please let me have it back sometime because I'm hard up myself.'

'Grateful, grateful indeed, old chap.'

'And for God's sake stop fancying yourself an idealist. You're as much an idealist as I am a turkey-cock. You're just a frivolous, idle person, that's all.'

Sergey sighed deeply and sat on the sofa.

'You're angry, dear old boy,' he said. 'Oh, if you did but know what I have to put up with! I'm having a hellish time. Now, it's not myself I'm sorry for, dear old boy—it's the wife and kids, believe you me. If it wasn't for the wife and kids I'd have ended it all long ago.'

His shoulders and head suddenly shook and he burst out sobbing.

'This is the last straw,' said Podgorin, agitatedly pacing the room and feeling exasperated.

'Look here, what am I to do about someone who first behaves like a scoundrel and then bursts into tears? Your tears disarm me, I can say nothing to you. You sob, therefore you are right.'

'*Me* behave like a scoundrel!' said Sergey, standing up and staring at Podgorin with amazement. 'How can you say such a thing, dear old boy? Me behave like a scoundrel! Oh, how little you know me, how little you understand me!'

'All right then, I don't understand you, but please stop blubbering. It's revolting.'

'Oh, how little you know me!' repeated Sergey in all sincerity. 'How little indeed!'

'Just look at yourself in the mirror,' Podgorin went on. 'You're getting on in life, you'll soon be old, and it's high time to pull yourself together and take stock of who you are and what you are. Your whole life has been one long round of idleness, affectations, posturings and futile, childish chit-chat. I wonder it doesn't nauseate you. Aren't you sick of it all? Oh, you *do* depress one so! And you *are* such a stupefying bore!'

Rc

This said, Podgorin left the hut and slammed the door. It was just about the first time in his life that he had ever been sincere and said what he meant.

Soon afterwards he was regretting his brusqueness. What was the good of talking seriously or arguing with a congenital liar, guzzler and toper who spent large quantities of other people's money while remaining convinced that he was an idealist and a martyr? The problem here was either sheer stupidity or ingrained bad habits corroding his organism like an incurable disease. Indignation, severe reprimands . . . they were useless here, anyway. It would have been better to laugh at him. One good sneer would do more than ten sermons!

'Better still, pay no attention,' thought Podgorin. 'And above all don't lend him money.'

Soon afterwards he had forgotten both Sergey and his hundred roubles. It was a quiet, melancholy night, very bright. When Podgorin gazed at the sky on moonlit nights he always felt as if only he and the moon were awake, and that everything else was asleep or dozing. He forgot all about people and money. A calm, peaceful mood gradually came over him. He felt alone in the world and his footsteps had a melancholy sound in the silence of the night.

The garden was enclosed by a white stone wall. On the right-hand corner of the side facing open country was a tower built long ago in the days of serfdom. The lower part was of stone, while the top was wooden—consisting of a platform, a conical roof and a tall spire with a black weathercock on it. Below were two gates giving access from garden to fields. A staircase led up to the platform and creaked underfoot. Some broken old arm-chairs dumped under the stairs were now bathed in moonlight filtering through the gate. With their crooked legs sticking up, those chairs seemed to have become alive at nightfall and to be lying in wait for someone here in the silence.

Podgorin climbed the stairs to the platform and sat down. Just beyond the fence were a ditch and bank marking the boundary of the estate, and beyond that were broad moonlit fields. Podgorin knew that there was a wood directly opposite, about two miles from the grounds, and thought he could descry a dark strip in the distance. Quails and landrails were calling. Now and then the cry of a cuckoo, also suffering from insomnia, was borne from the direction of the wood.

There was a sound of footsteps: someone walking in the garden and coming towards the tower.

A dog barked.

'Beetle! Come back, Beetle,' a woman's voice softly called.

Someone was heard entering the tower below, after which a black dog—an old friend of Podgorin's—appeared on the bank. It paused and looked up towards where Podgorin was sitting, wagging its tail affectionately. A little later a ghostly white figure arose from the black ditch and also paused on the bank. It was Nadya.

'What can you see there?' she asked the dog, and looked up.

She couldn't see Podgorin but evidently sensed his presence because she smiled, and her pale, moonlit face looked happy. The tower's black shadow running along the ground far into the field, the still, white figure with the beatific smile on the pale face, the black dog and the shadows of them both . . . it was all so dream-like.

'There *is* somebody there,' said Nadya softly.

She stood and waited for him to come down or call her: to declare his love at last and make them both happy on this calm, lovely night. White, pale, slim, lovely indeed in the moonlight, she awaited his caress. Her perennial dreams of happiness and love . . . they had wearied her. No longer could she hide her feelings. Her whole figure, her brilliant eyes, her fixed and blissful smile . . . all betrayed her secret thoughts. He felt awkward huddled there in the silence. Should he speak? Should he turn it all into the usual joke? Hold his peace? He didn't know, and he felt aggrieved. All he could think of was that here, in this garden, on this moonlit night, close to this beautiful, love-lorn, wistful girl, his emotions were as uninvolved as on Little Bronny Road. Just as dead for him—evidently—was this poetic vision, as that prosaic squalor. They meant nothing to him now, did these assignations on moonlit nights, these slim-waisted white figures, these mysterious shadows, towers, country houses, these types like Sergey and other types like himself—this Podgorin with his apathy, his boredom, his perpetual bad temper, his inability to adapt to real life, his incapacity for making the most of it, his tiresome, obsessive craving for what did not, what never could, exist on earth. Now that he was up here in the tower he would have preferred a good firework display, a moonlight procession, or Barbara reciting Nekrasov's 'Railway' again. He would rather have seen another woman on that bank instead of Nadya standing there: one who might tell him of something fresh and original unconnected with love and happiness, or who—had she indeed spoken of love—would have summoned him to those new, lofty, rational modes of existence such as we shall perhaps live to see one day and already sometimes anticipate.

'There's no one there,' said Nadya.

After waiting a little longer she set off slowly towards the wood, bowing her head. The dog ran ahead. For some time Podgorin saw her as a white shape.

'Odd, how it has all turned out,' he reflected again as he returned to the hut. What he would say to Sergey and Tatyana tomorrow he had no idea. How would he behave towards Nadya? And what about the day after that? The prospect was embarrassing, frightening, boring. How was he to fill the three interminable days which he had promised to spend here? He remembered the talk about second sight and Sergey's 'before he'd time to turn a hair he'd been knocked over by a bear'. He remembered that he would have to humour Tatyana by smiling at those sleek, tubby little girls on the morrow. So he decided to leave.

At half past five in the morning Sergey appeared on the terrace of the big house wearing a Bokhara dressing-gown and a tasselled fez. Losing no time, Podgorin went up to him and started saying good-bye.

'I must be in Moscow by ten,' he said, averting his eyes. 'I have an appointment with some solicitors—it had entirely slipped my mind. Please don't detain me. When the others get up tell them I apologize, I'm most frightfully sorry——'

He did not hear Sergey's reply as he hurried away, casting glances at the manor windows and fearful of the ladies waking up and trying to stop him leaving. He was ashamed of being so neurotic. This was, he felt, his last visit to Kuzminki—never would he go there again. As he drove off he cast several backward glances at the hut in which he had spent so many happy days. But he merely felt indifferent: not sad.

When he reached home the first thing he saw on the table was yesterday's letter.

Dear Misha,
    You've quite forgotten us. Do come and visit us soon——

For some reason he remembered Nadya twirling in the dance, with her dress billowing and showing her legs in those flesh-coloured stockings.

Ten minutes later he was working at his desk. Kuzminki had been forgotten.

MANUSCRIPT FRAGMENTS

(1900–3)

THE CRIPPLE

[*Калека*]

(1900)

THE CRIPPLE

I

REMEMBERING that there was to be a christening at his sister's, Alexander Ivanovich drove out to her country villa. Anyuta was not his real sister. His parents had adopted her as a little orphan girl, having had no children during their first five years of marriage, and he himself had been born two years later. Though she wasn't his real sister he loved her as dearly as if she had been. He loved her children too.

He should have caught the six o'clock evening train. But that had already left, and so he had to take a cab. He arrived at the house late: long after the christening, when the guests had gone back to town. The white-aproned old nanny was going round the house collecting the children to put them to bed.

'Gleb, Gleb, where are you?' she shouted. 'Come and eat your yoghurt, sir!'

The lights were extinguished in the two drawing-rooms. Anyuta was relaxing in an arm-chair in her own room—glad that all the fuss about the birth and the christening had ended, and that ordinary life could resume its normal course. Near her was her four-year-old daughter Lelya who had light brown hair and big bright eyes.

'So it's you, Alexander.' Anyuta was delighted to see him. 'You're late! We waited for you till seven, and then decided you weren't coming.'

He explained why he was so late, he asked about her health and the baby's. They conversed while Lelya listened, looking her uncle straight in the eye very solemnly, unmoving, unblinking—like an expensive doll.

'Baby was christened today,' she said loudly.

He kissed her head and asked his sister who the guests had been.

Anyuta disregarded his question. 'Quite frankly, I thought you'd stayed away out of pique.' She laughed. 'Do excuse my not inviting you to be godfather—for goodness' sake don't take it as a slight or anything like that. I was meaning to write, but my Sergey suddenly asked me if I realized just what I was doing! Well, I could see what he meant. The fact is, we'd asked Sasha Kolosov to be godmother, you see?

Now, you're fond of Sasha—you might even lead her to the altar one day, she's a very nice girl. But it's said you can't marry someone after you've both become godparents of the same child.'

He had known as he drove out that there would be some discussion of this girl that he was fond of, and about his being likely to marry her quite soon. It was the talk of the town.

POOR COMPENSATION
[*Расстройство компенсации*]
(1902–3)

POOR COMPENSATION

I

An evening service was held at the home of Michael Bondaryov, a gentleman of some note in the county. The officiating priest was a plump, broad-nosed young man with fair curls like a lion's mane. The only singers were a sexton and a clerk. A very sick man, Bondaryov sat in his arm-chair—still, pale, corpse-like, eyes closed. His wife Vera stood by him leaning her head to one side in the lazy, submissive posture of a person indifferent to religion but obliged to stand there and make the sign of the cross from time to time. Alexander Yanshin—Vera's brother—and his wife Lenochka stood next to each other behind the arm-chair. It was Whit Sunday eve. Trees softly rustled in the garden and a superb sunset flamed uninhibitedly, engulfing half the sky.

The ringing of the city and monastery bells borne through the open windows, a peacock screaming in the grounds, a cough in the hall . . . these sounds automatically evoked the thought that Michael Bondaryov was seriously ill, that he was to go abroad on doctors' orders as soon as he felt better, but that he felt better one day and worse the next. It was all very confusing, and as time went on the uncertainty had begun to pall. Back at Easter Yanshin had arrived to help his sister take her husband abroad, but now he and his wife had been here nearly two months. Meanwhile this must be the third service to be held since then, the future was still as obscure as ever and nothing seemed to make sense. Nor was there any guarantee that this nightmare might not drag on till autumn.

Yanshin was bored and fed up. He was tired of getting ready to go abroad every day, and wanted to return home to his own place at Novosyolki. Not that it was much fun at home either, but at least they had no vast drawing-room like this one with the four columns in the corners. There were none of these white arm-chairs with their gold upholstery, no yellow curtains, no chandeliers, there was none of this vulgar display of bad taste parading as magnificence. Nor was there an echo which repeated your steps every night. Above all, there was no sickly, yellow, bloated face with closed eyes.

At home you could laugh, talk nonsense, quarrel openly with your

wife or mother—live as you pleased, in fact—whereas here it was just
like boarding school. You had to pad around on tiptoe, speak only
in whispers, talk sensibly or not at all. Or else, as now, you had
to stand listening to a service which was not held out of religious
sentiment but—as Bondaryov himself said—because it was the done
thing.

Is there anything more exhausting and degrading than having to
defer to someone whom, at heart, you think a nonentity—than having
to coddle an invalid whom you don't feel sorry for?

There was something else too, Yanshin reflected. Last night his wife
had told him that she was pregnant. The news was interesting only in
further complicating the problem of the journey abroad. What was to
happen now? Should he take Lenochka abroad with them? Or send
her to his mother's at Novosyolki? But it was inadvisable for her to
travel in her condition. And going home was out of the question
because she didn't get on with her mother-in-law and would never
consent to stay in the country on her own without her husband.

'Or shall I make this an excuse to go home with her?' wondered
Yanshin, trying not to listen to the sexton. 'No, it would be awkward
to leave Vera here alone,' he decided, looking at his sister's slim figure.
'So what shall I do?'

He thought and wondered what to do, seeing his life as something
highly complex and tangled. All these problems—the trip, his sister,
his wife, his brother-in-law and so on—perhaps each of them could
have been settled very easily and conveniently in isolation, but they
were all mixed up together. It was like being stuck in a bog and unable
to get out. Solve one or other of them, and it only made an even
greater muddle out of all the rest.

When the priest, who was just about to read the lesson, turned
round and said 'peace be with you', the ailing Bondaryov suddenly
opened his eyes and fidgeted in his arm-chair.

'Alexander,' he called.

Yanshin darted over and leant down.

'I don't like his way of conducting the service,' said Bondaryov
under his breath, but in a voice which carried clearly through the
room. He was breathing heavily, wheezing and whistling. 'I'm going.
Will you help me, Alexander?'

Yanshin helped him to his feet and took his arm.

'You stay here, dear,' Bondaryov pleaded with his wife in a weak
voice as she made to take his other arm. 'Stay here!' he repeated

irritably, looking at her expressionless face. 'I can manage without you.'

The priest stood waiting, his gospel open. Then, in the ensuing silence, the harmonious singing of a male voice choir was clearly heard: the singing came from somewhere beyond the garden—from the river no doubt. And what a delightful effect was produced when bells suddenly pealed out in the neighbouring monastery, their soft, melodious chimes mingled with the singing! Yanshin's heart seemed to miss a beat in delicious anticipation of something splendid, and he almost forgot that he was supposed to be helping the invalid. These irrelevant noises drifting into the drawing-room . . . they somehow reminded him how little pleasure and freedom he enjoyed nowadays. How trivial, contemptible and dreary they were . . . those problems with which he wrestled so frantically all day, every day. As he helped Bondaryov out, while servants stepped aside and made way for them— watching with that lugubrious curiosity with which village people normally regard a corpse—he suddenly felt a hatred, an acute loathing, for the sick man's plump, clean-shaven actor's face, for his waxen hands, for his plush dressing-gown, for his wheezing, for the tapping of his black cane. This feeling, which he was now experiencing for the first time in his life, and which had come over him so suddenly . . . it chilled his head and hands, it made his heart pound. He felt a violent longing for Bondaryov to drop dead there and then—to give one last cry and collapse on the floor—but then he immediately visualized such a death and recoiled from it in horror.

After they had left the drawing-room he no longer wanted the sick man to die—rather did he want to live himself. Oh, to snatch his hand away from that warm arm-pit and run away—run on and on without looking back.

Bondaryov's bed had been made up on an ottoman in the study—he felt hot and uncomfortable in his bedroom.

'The man should make up his mind whether he's a priest or a cavalry officer,' said Bondaryov, lowering himself heavily on to the ottoman. 'What airs and graces! Good God, I'd reduce that ordained popinjay to sexton if I had my way!'

Noting the sick man's captious, unhappy expression, Yanshin wanted to object, say something impudent, confess his hatred, but he remembered that the other was not to be upset on doctors' orders, so held his peace. This was no medical issue, anyway. If only the fate of his sister Vera had not been so permanently and irretrievably bound up with this odious creature, he'd have shouted at him—he'd have told him a few home truths all right! Bondaryov had a trick of pursing his lips, puffing them out and moving them from side to side as if sucking a lozenge. This mumbling of those plump lips set in that clean-shaven face . . . it irritated Yanshin.

'You'd better go back, Alexander,' said Bondaryov. 'You're in good health—and quite indifferent to the church, I understand. You don't care who officiates, so go.'

'But you don't care about the church either,' said Yanshin quietly, trying to control himself.

'Yes, I do. I believe in Providence, and I recognize the Church.'

'Precisely. What you want from religion, it seems to me, is neither God nor the truth, but just words like "providence" and "exalted".'

'Otherwise,' Yanshin wanted to add, 'you wouldn't have been so rude to the priest tonight.' But he said nothing—having already let himself say too much anyway, he felt.

'Please go!' said Bondaryov impatiently—he disliked being contradicted or talked about. 'I don't want to be in anyone's way. I know how depressing it is to be with an invalid. I know, old man. There's no harder or more saintly job than a nurse's, if I've said it once I've said it a thousand times. Now, do please go!'

Yanshin left the study. He went down to his own room, donned his coat and hat, and passed through the front door into the garden. It was already turned eight o'clock. Upstairs they were singing the Consecration. Making his way between flower beds, rose-bushes and ciphers of the initials V and M—for Vera and Michael—in blue heliotropes, he passed quantities of splendid flowers, which gave no one on this estate any pleasure . . . they too grew and bloomed, probably, because it was the 'done thing'. Yanshin hurried on, fearing that his wife might call him back from upstairs—she could easily have seen him. But after cutting across the park he emerged in a long, dark avenue of firs through which the sunset was visible of an evening. Even on windless days these decrepit old trees always rustled gently and forbiddingly. They smelt of resin, and one's feet slipped on the dry needles.

The loathing which Yanshin had so suddenly conceived during tonight's service . . . it would be with him for ever and he would just have to come to terms with it, he reflected as he strolled along. It had yet further complicated his life, and it boded little good. But the firs, the calm, distant sky, the festive sunset . . . all breathed peace and serenity. He enjoyed listening to his footsteps' lonely, muffled echo in that dark avenue. No longer did he wonder what he was to do.

Almost every evening he walked to the station to pick up newspapers and letters: his sole diversion since he had been staying at his brother-in-law's. The mail train came in at a quarter to ten—the very hour of most intolerable evening boredom in the house. There was no one to play cards with, they never served supper, you didn't want to sleep, so you were reduced to sitting with the invalid or reading to Lenochka those translated novels which she was so keen on. It was a large station with a buffet and book-stall. One could have a snack or a glass of beer, and browse among the books. Most of all Yanshin liked seeing the train arrive. He envied the passengers, who all had some destination and seemed happier than himself.

When he reached the station there were already people strolling on the platform, waiting for the train to come in: the same crowd that he saw here every evening. There were summer visitors who lived near the station, a couple of officers from town, some landowner wearing a spur on his right leg and followed by a great dane with a sadly drooping head. Holidaymakers of both sexes, obviously good friends, were talking and laughing loudly. The most animated, as usual—the one with the loudest laugh—was a visiting engineer: a very stout, broad-beamed fellow of about forty-five with side-whiskers in an open-necked cotton shirt and baggy velveteen trousers. When he thrust his large paunch out, stroked his whiskers and walked past Yanshin, gazing at him affectionately with those poached eyes, Yanshin always felt that the man had a great zest for life. The engineer even had a special facial expression as if to say that everything was 'oh so delicious!' He had a cumbrous, triple-barrelled surname which Yanshin only remembered because the engineer—he liked a bit of rumbustious chat about politics, liked a bit of an argument—was in the habit of driving home a point with the assertion 'Or my name's not Bitny-Kushle-Suvremovich!'

He was said to be a gay dog, a cordial host, a keen bridge player. Yanshin had long wished to meet him, but had never ventured on an approach, though sensing that the other was not averse to an acquaintanceship. Strolling down the platform on his own, listening to the holidaymakers ... somehow it always reminded Yanshin that he was thirty-one years old, and that he hadn't enjoyed a single day of his life since graduating at the age of twenty-four. A boundary dispute with a neighbour, his wife miscarrying, his sister Vera seeming unhappy or this Bondaryov falling ill and having to be taken abroad—if it wasn't one thing it was another. These things would, he reckoned, continue to repeat themselves indefinitely in various guises. His worries and concerns would be just the same when he was forty or fifty as they were when he was thirty-one. Not till his dying day, in fact, would he ever shuffle off this hard shell—any other view would be sheer illusion. But he would have preferred to escape his oyster-like existence, if only for an hour. He wanted to glimpse a different world, to be caught up in something unconnected with himself, to talk to strangers: if only to this fat engineer or the lady visitors who all seemed so lovely, high-spirited—and above all young—in the evening twilight.

The train drew in and the landowner with one spur greeted a stout elderly lady who embraced him, repeating the name Alexis several times in an agitated voice: his mother, probably. With great ceremony, like the junior lead in a ballet, he clicked his one spur and offered her his arm. 'Pray fetch our luggage,' he told the porter in a velvety, sugary baritone.

The train soon left. Taking their newspapers and letters, the holiday-makers went their several ways. Silence ensued.

Yanshin walked up and down the platform a bit longer, then went into the first-class waiting-room. He didn't feel hungry, but ate a slice of veal and drank some beer. The exquisite, courtly manners of that bespurred squire, his mawkish baritone, his politeness so devoid of spontaneity . . . they had made an indelibly painful impression on Yanshin. He remembered the man's long moustaches, his kind, rather unintelligent but oddly inscrutable face, his way of rubbing his hands as if it was cold. If that stout elderly lady really was his mother, thought Yanshin, she was probably very unhappy. She had pronounced only the one word Alexis in that agitated voice, but her nervously dis-traught expression, her loving eyes told all the rest.

II

Vera watched through the window as her brother left. Knowing that he was bound for the station, she pictured the avenue of firs from beginning to end, followed by the drop to the river, the broad vista and that mood of peace and simplicity which rivers and water-meadows always evoked in her. Beyond all that lay the station and the birch-wood with its holiday cottages, while far away to the right was the little country town and the monastery with its golden onion-domes.

Again she pictured the avenue, the darkness, her fear and shame, the familiar footsteps and everything else which was liable to happen all over again—today, even.

Leaving the drawing-room for a minute to see about the priest's tea, she went into the dining-room and took out of her pocket a stiff envelope folded in two and bearing a foreign stamp. The letter had been handed to her five minutes before the service and she had already read it twice.

'My dear one, my darling, my torment, my anguish,' she read, holding the letter in both hands, letting each hand exult in the touch of these lines so precious and so ardent.

Then she started reading it again from the beginning.

My dear one, my darling, my torment, my anguish,
          What you write is very convincing, but I still don't know what to do. You say you're *definitely* going to Italy, and I rush ahead like a maniac so as to be here to meet you and love my darling one, my joy. Here, think I, you will no longer be scared of your husband or brother seeing my shadow through the window on moonlit nights. Here we could walk the streets together, and you would not be scared of Rome or Venice finding out that we love each other. I'm sorry to say this, precious, but there are two Veras. One is nervous, faint-hearted, indecisive. The other is cold, proud and unconcerned. She addresses me formally in the presence of strangers, pretending that she hardly notices me. It is this second—this proud, beautiful Vera—that I want to love me.

I don't want to be an owl which can enjoy itself only at night-time. Give me light! Darkness oppresses me, darling. Loving stealthily like this, by fits and starts, I feel half starved, I fret, I suffer, I rage.

Briefly, then, I thought that here abroad where it's easier not to attract attention than in Russia, *my* Vera—Number Two, that is—would give me a single hour, at least, of love true and unalloyed without all this looking over one's shoulder, so that I might for once in my life feel like a real lover, not a smuggler, and not have the woman in my arms keep saying that it's 'time for me to go'. So I thought, but I've been in Florence for a whole month now, you haven't turned up, and I'm completely in the dark. You write that you 'doubt if we'll get away this month'. Now, what am I to make of that? My despair, what are you doing to me? I can't live without

Sc

you, don't you see, I can't, I can't, I can't!!! Italy's said to be very beautiful. But I am as bored as if I was in exile, my great love pines like some deported criminal. My way of putting it may not be very funny, but I'm certainly a figure of fun myself. I rush about—to Bologna, to Venice, to Rome—and everywhere I go I watch for a woman in the crowd who looks like you. I've toured all the galleries and museums half a dozen times out of sheer boredom, but on all those canvases I've seen only you. In Rome I pant up the Pincio, whence I survey the Eternal City, but eternity, beauty, the sky . . . all blends into a single image which has your face and wears your dress. Here in Florence I visit the shops where they sell sculptures, and if the place is empty I embrace the statues, feeling as if I'm embracing you. I need you now, this minute.

Vera, I may be out of my mind, but forgive me—I can't stand this any longer. Tomorrow I'll be on my way to see you.

I shouldn't have written this letter, but never mind. It's all settled, darling. I leave tomorrow.

A LETTER

[Письмо]

(1902–3)

A LETTER

Dear Mary,

I enclose the book I wrote about on Wednesday. Do read it. May I draw your attention to pages 17–42, 92, 93 and 112, especially the passages underlined by me in pencil? What force! The form is obviously clumsy, but what range, what freedom, what formidable, unbridled artistry one does sense in that very clumsiness! The word 'which' occurs three times in one sentence, and 'evidently' comes in twice. The sentence is badly constructed—it *is* rather laid on with a trowel. But what a torrent does gush out of these 'whiches', what flexible, elegant, profound thinking lurks beneath them, what a clarion call of Truth! As you read between the lines you picture an eagle soaring in the firmament and recking little for the beauty of his feathers. Ideas, beauty . . . they should be like the hurricane and the waves, they should know nothing of conventionally prescribed forms. *Their* form is freedom unconstrained by any considerations about 'whiches' and 'evidentlys'. Now, I always feel constrained when I write to you—annoyed by my own stylistic peccadilloes. But that only means I'm no artist: that it's only words, not images and moods, which engross my mind.

Please do read the book. I read it all day yesterday and it quite took my breath away—I could sense new, hitherto unknown vital elements penetrating the very fibre of my being. With each new page I grew richer, stronger, taller. Dumbfounded, weeping in ecstasy, exulting, I conceived a faith, profound and mystical, in the divine origin of true talent. Not for nothing, I felt, had even one of these mighty, elemental pages been created. By the virtue of their very genesis and being they were bound to provoke in Nature some manifestation of comparable force such as a subterranean rumbling, a change of climate, a storm at sea. I reject the thesis, reject it a thousand times over, that Nature—in which everything is functional —can be indifferent to her own most beautiful, rational, dynamic, invincible constituent element, viz.: the element created by Man independently of her Will. I feel I must seem to be writing non-sense. Laugh then, but don't try and stop me from rhapsodizing, romanticizing and building castles in the air. You just can't imagine how delightful and enjoyable it is to write even this delirious nonsense when one knows that your kind eyes will see these lines.

Yesterday I was so carried away by the book that I didn't even welcome Travnikov's arrival, fond of him as I am. He arrived with a headache, in a bad mood. He always does have a headache after major operations, being poisoned by carbolic acid fumes. He started asking about my leg, and I replied by reading him the twenty lines underlined on page 92. A literary argument began.

'The time I've spent reading philosophy, poetry and fiction I consider entirely wasted,' said Travnikov. 'Though riddled with pretensions, that stuff has never explained nor illuminated a single phenomenon, which is why I don't like it. It's purely subjective, and so one half of it is entirely false, while the other half is a jumble of lies and truth, being neither one thing nor the other. The claim that such books are indispensable . . . it's sheer superstition. Like theatres and circuses, they serve only for entertainment, and so it's purely for entertainment that I read them nowadays. I favour the authors with least pretensions, in which respect the most suitable books are French novels.'

'But who, pray, teaches us to think,' I asked.

'Anyone who speaks the truth, which is just what poetry and novels don't do.'

Etcetera, etcetera. What a way to argue! And what an obstinate, prejudiced man! The conversation turned to beauty.

'Beauty is agreeable,' said he. 'Its sole function is to purvey enjoyment: an element which cannot easily be dispensed with. To seek from beauty either truth or knowledge rather than entertainment is to be seduced, betrayed, bemused with will-o'-the-wisps. In the days when I so casually studied beauty—as a means of training my mind— it dazzled me, intoxicated me. For instance, I read *Faust* without noticing that Gretchen murdered her baby, and in Byron's *Cain* I found Cain himself and the Devil wholly sympathetic. And that was by no means all!'

He clutched his aching head in his hands, leant it on the table.

'Beauty, talent, all that is highest, finest, most artistic . . . these things are all very charming,' he intoned. 'But they do have their limitations. Neither are they bound by the dictates of logic nor can one single incontrovertible law be derived from them. Since before the flood people have been calling the nightingale the "lover of the rose"—speaking of the "mighty oak" and "the gentle wild convolvulus". And we believe them! But, why?'

I got rather hot under the collar as usual and said all the wrong things.

'I don't know why you're so angry,' he observed, raising his head. 'What's so insulting about the arts being a mere form of entertainment? I'd even consent to being a bad writer, old boy, provided that my books amused the sick and those confined in institutions. To have made you happy all today ... is that so contemptible an achievement for a writer? Anyway, I have a splitting headache, old man. Perhaps you're right—I don't really claim to know anything.'

Poetry and fiction have never explained one single phenomenon. Does a flash of lightning explain anything? Nor should it—it's we who should explain *it*! A fine thing it would be if we stopped investigating electricity and began denying its validity on the sole grounds that there are so many things which it fails to make clear to us! Now, it's the same with poetry and all the so-called fine arts— they too are natural phenomena, hazardous and spectacular, which we must learn to explain without waiting for *them* to explain things to us! How regrettable, how painful that even good and clever men approach every phenomenon from so specialized, so prejudiced, so excessively subjective an angle! Travnikov, for instance, is particularly exercised by the problem of God and the purpose of existence. Now, the arts don't tackle this problem—they offer no guidance to life beyond the grave—and so Travnikov rates them as sheer superstition, degrading them to the level of mere entertainment: something easily expendable. They're a form of 'original sin', he once joked in your mother's presence. Doesn't this rather remind you of a certain lady known to us both, who denies the validity of medicine, and of science in general, on the sole grounds that doctors are so bad at dancing the mazurka? A wine may have a delicious flavour, it may warm the cockles of your heart, but that's not enough because you can no doubt find some tailor who'll abjure it as being no substitute for turpentine: it doesn't remove stains, you see!

But enough of generalizations! My leg is in its former condition. Travnikov insists on an operation, but I don't agree. Nature is a great healer: a propensity of hers on which I'm banking heavily. With luck I can dispense with an operation. It's appallingly dull here. But for my books I think I'd be in tears for days on end out of sheer boredom. To live five miles from you without the right to visit you ... I might as well be put on the rack!

Your mother looked us up yesterday while visiting the Zelenins'.

She gave me and Father a wigging because I left theological college. Everyone tells me I behaved stupidly—they're unanimous about it, and they may be right. Just why I left I don't myself know, but neither do I know any reason for staying on. I pine, I crave for a bit of real life and I avoid places where it isn't to be found or isn't rigged to my liking. You are my life—all you whom I love devotedly. I can't bear not seeing your beautiful, gentle face—so radiant, so kind. I must hear your voice, if only once a month. I can't bear not seeing your generous-hearted mother and your entire high-spirited, philanthropically minded family, which God has so richly blessed, and which is as dear to me as my own brothers and father. I need to see my poor old suffering father near me every day—need to hear him as he lies awake every night, thinking aloud about my brother in prison. I need my other brother, the mad monk, to come and visit us from his monastery once every two or three months—just to see him flash his eyes and curse civilization before he goes back again. My life is incomplete if I don't see Travnikov at least once a week—Travnikov whom I increasingly love the more deeply he is engulfed in the swamp of his own ardent, inflexible, agonizing ideas. He craves faith at all costs, he wants God and seeks Him—seeks Him day and night—but finds only an abyss which becomes deeper and darker the longer you stare into it. And what a refined pleasure I derive from walking round the village, calling on people in their huts and talking to them! What a range of faces, voices, minds, tastes, beliefs! Old Paul, our deacon . . . now, isn't he a dear? He's had one foot in the grave for two years now, but he can't quite pull it off and laughs at his own vitality. 'I'm dying, I'm dying . . . but I'm still alive!' Life is good, Mary. It is hard to bear, it is fleeting—true—but it is also rich, intelligent, interesting. It is astounding! Travnikov's poisoning himself with his craving for immortality and eternal bliss. I'm less greedy, though. I'm completely satisfied with this so brief, so small—but so beautiful—span.

As soon as I'm on my feet again I shall start work. I'll run the farm and lay down my life for art. I shall write—but write what? My story isn't taking shape properly. I handle the technique badly and I tend to polish too much. My head's bursting with images and pictures—I'm rich in such goods—but somehow my heroes aren't cast as characters, they're all as alike as two peas. They have little movement and they're always arguing—whereas it should be the other way round. Now I've taken up criticism. I shall study and do my

best to explain the things which I so adore, and which I see as the
only true bulwark against superstition, ignorance and slavery.

Father stumbled and fell in the street yesterday. He put it down to
being tired—he's holding services almost all day owing to Holy
Week. Thank God it was nothing serious.

My heartfelt greetings to all your family. Give my regards to one
and all. My ears tell me that spring has arrived on the other side of
my window, but I see nothing. How nice it would be to visit you
now. I'd like just one little stroll up the hill with you, and that would
be all. Are the cherries in bloom? No—it's too early, actually.
Farewell. Be happy, healthy, cheerful. Don't forget a cripple who
loves you from the bottom of his heart, and is devoted to you.

Sincerely,

IGNATIUS BASHTANOV

His letter finished, Ignatius put it in an envelope and addressed it to
MRS. M. S. VOLCHANINOV.

At that moment Father Alexis came into the room with a glass of
tea on a tray, and the embarrassed Ignatius thrust the letter under his
pillow.

APPENDIX I

THE 'TRILOGY'

The three works *A Hard Case*, *Gooseberries* and *Concerning Love* are linked by theme and characters in a manner which makes them unique among Chekhov's short stories. Each takes the form of a tale told by one of three narrators (Burkin, Ivan Ivanovich and Alyokhin) to one or both of the others. And all are essays on freedom: moral homilies, in effect, hinging in each instance on a single central figure (Belikov; Nicholas Chimsha-Gimalaysky; Alyokhin himself) implicitly condemned by Chekhov for allowing his life to be unnecessarily circumscribed by self-imposed restrictions. For these reasons critics have sometimes referred to the three stories as a 'trilogy', a term which Chekhov is not himself recorded as having applied to them.

All three stories of the Trilogy appeared, as was appropriate, in the same publication: the magazine *Russkaya mysl* [*The Russian Idea*], but not in the same issue. The first to be published was *A Hard Case*: in the July 1898 number. In the following, August, issue *Gooseberries* and *Concerning Love* both appeared: on consecutive pages. The three stories had originally been submitted to *Russkaya mysl* in corresponding sequence: *A Hard Case* (independently) on 15 June 1898; the other two stories (together) on 28 July.

Writing to V. A. Goltsev, editor of *Russkaya mysl*, on the latter date, Chekhov expressed the intention of adding another story (he called it a 'third') when he had read the proofs of the other two. Had he done so, his projected 'third' story would in fact have been a *fourth* so far as the Trilogy is concerned; but in any case no such third (or fourth) story has come to light.

For at least twelve months after first publication of the Trilogy the idea of further extending the sequence persisted in Chekhov's mind. On 28 September 1899 he wrote to A. F. Marks (the first publisher of his *Collected Works*) of *A Hard Case*, *Gooseberries* and *Concerning Love* as 'belonging to a series which is still far from complete. It can't appear until Volume XI or XII [of the *Collected Works* then being prepared for publication by Marks] after the entire series has been concluded.'

A trilogy, however, the Trilogy remained, though the form was indeed such as to have permitted Chekhov to extend it indefinitely had he so wished.

APPENDIX II

A HARD CASE

1. Composition
2. Text
3. Variants

1. COMPOSITION

According to no less than three memoirists—Chekhov's brother Michael, 'Tan' (V. G. Bogoraz) and P. Surozhsky—the real life prototype of the 'Hard Case' in the story (the schoolmaster Belikov) was a certain A. F. Dyakonov, the 'inspector'—more or less Second Master, in effect—of the Taganrog High School during the period when Chekhov was a pupil there (W., ix, 589-90). That at least one other model contributed to the make-up of Belikov is, however, shown by a passage from Chekhov's diary for the year 1896 in which he describes the journalist M. O. Menshikov—his guest in August of that year—as someone who 'wears galoshes in dry weather, carries an umbrella to prevent himself from dying of sun-stroke, is afraid to wash in cold water, and complains of a weak heart' (W., xii, 333).

In January 1898, while planning to visit Algiers, Chekhov stated that the obligation to write a story for the magazines *Russkaya mysl* [*The Russian Idea*] and *Cosmopolis* was hanging over him like a sword of Damocles and bringing him out in a cold sweat (letter to Ye. Z. Konovitser, 2 Jan. 1898). The first reference to work in progress on *A Hard Case* occurs in a letter of 6 June 1898 from Chekhov to V. A. Goltsev, editor of *Russkaya mysl*. Here Chekhov requests the return of another (unnamed) story, previously submitted to Goltsev—probably *Doctor Startsev*—and says that he is preparing a new, longer, also unnamed story [presumably *A Hard Case*] to take its place. 'My machine has started working again.' On 12 June Chekhov informs A. S. Suvorin that he has 'finished two stories' (*A Hard Case* and *Doctor Startsev*). On 15 June he sends *A Hard Case* to Goltsev, writing that he intends to 'polish it in proof'. He receives and reads the proofs towards the end of the month.

Chekhov's *Notebooks* include the following entry bearing on *A Hard Case*:

'A man in a capsule, wearing galoshes, his umbrella in a cover, his watch in a case, his knife in a holder. Lying in his coffin, he seemed to smile—having attained his ideal.' (N. I, 86/2)

2. TEXT

The present translation is made from the text in *Works*, 1944–51, vol. ix, itself based on that of Chekhov's *Collected Works* (1906), vol. xi.

There is one previous recension: that published in the magazine *Russkaya mysl*, no. vii, July 1898.

3. VARIANTS

When preparing the *Russkaya mysl* text for his *Collected Works*, Chekhov revised the punctuation and made eleven minor changes.

APPENDIX III

GOOSEBERRIES

1. Composition
2. Text
3. Variants

1. COMPOSITION

According to Chekhov's brother Michael, one scene in *Gooseberries*—the bathe in the river—was inspired by Bakumovka, the Ukrainian estate of the brothers A. I. and S. I. Smagin, of whom the former had been a suitor for the hand of Chekhov's sister (W., ix, 593 and xiv, 501).

What is probably the first mention of *Gooseberries* occurs in a letter from Chekhov of 6 July 1898 to the dramatist A. I. Sumbatov (Yuzhin), where he states that, in addition to one story written for *Niva* (*Doctor Startsev*) and another written for *Russkaya mysl* (*A Hard Case*), he is now writing 'a third'.

Gooseberries and *Concerning Love* were written at Melikhovo in July 1898. Late in the month (between the 23rd and the 27th) Chekhov reports from that country seat that. 'I have something to write for *Russkaya mysl*—I've already done some of it and must finish' (W., xvii, 288). When sending the two stories to the magazine *Russkaya mysl*, Chekhov wrote (to the editor, V. A. Goltsev, on 28 July) that if he found the stories acceptable he should 'have the type set up quickly so that I can pick up the proofs on my way through to Tver on 1–2 August. When I read them I may perhaps add a third story.' This 'third' story— by inference a continuation of the series *A Hard Case*, *Gooseberries*, *Concerning Love*—was never written; nor was the 'Trilogy' ever further extended, as Chekhov seems to have planned at one time (see Appendix I, above).

Chekhov's *Notebooks* include the following entries bearing on *Gooseberries*:

'Title: *Gooseberries*. X works in a government office, is frightfully stingy, hoards money. His ambition: marry, buy an estate, sleep in sun, drink on green grass, eat stew made from own cabbages. Twenty-five, forty, forty-five years pass. He's given up the idea of marriage, but is still dreaming of that estate. Reaches sixty. Reads evocative, seductive advertisements about so many hundreds of acres, about woods, rivers, ponds and mills. Retires. Buys a little estate on a pond through an agent. Tours his garden, but feels there's something missing. Concludes it's gooseberries, sends to nursery. A couple of years later has cancer of the stomach, is about to die, is served with bowl of own gooseberries. Looks at them with complete indifference.

'Meanwhile, his niece—big-breasted, noisy creature—is throwing her weight about in the next room. (He planted his gooseb. in autumn, took to his bed that winter and has never left it. Looking at the bowl of gooseberries: "that's all I ever got out of life in the last resort".) Is son of impoverished landowners, often remembers boyhood spent in the country.' (N. I, 56/5)

'The gooseberries were sour. "How stupid," said the retired civil servant. And died.' (N. I, 62/4)

'Behind the happy man's door there ought to be someone standing with a little hammer to keep banging and reminding him that unhappy people do exist, and that a brief period of happiness is bound to be followed by unhappiness.' (N. I, 71/4)

'A certain rich old man, sensing the approach of death, ordered a bowl of honey and ate his money with it.' (N. I, 74/4)

'"Man needs six feet of earth."
'"Not man—corpse. Man needs the earth's whole globe."' (N. I, 87/9)

'Why should I wait for the ditch to become overgrown or fill with water? I'd do better to jump it or build a bridge.' (N. I, 88/4)

'Having enough to eat is the beginning of liberal moderation.' (N. III, 35/2)

'Gentlemen, even human happiness has something sad about it.
'We must train people in conscientiousness and clarity of mind.
'His conceit developed, our surname Ch.-G. now seemed melodious and magnificent to him.
'Moderate liberalism: "A dog needs freedom, but it must be kept on a chain all the same."
'Yet the only protests come from statistics.' (N. III, 36/2–6)

2. TEXT

The present translation is made from the text in *Works*, 1944–51, vol. ix, itself based on that of Chekhov's *Collected Works* (1906), vol. xi.

There is one previous recension: that published in the magazine *Russkaya mysl*, no. viii, August 1898.

3. VARIANTS

When revising the *Russkaya mysl* text for his *Collected Works*, Chekhov made a few minor corrections. These included the removal of the figure 'II', which had appeared before the title of the story: an indication of its links with *A Hard Case*, as published in the previous issue of the same magazine. Similarly, the figure III (which precedes the title of *Concerning Love*, as printed consecutively after *Gooseberries* in the August issue of *Russkaya mysl*) was also removed: an indication that Chekhov, when revising the three stories for his *Collected Works*, wished to play down the links between them.

Among four minor changes in wording (also made during the revision of the *Russkaya mysl* text for the *Collected Works*) was the removal of a sentence which originally followed '. . . *something higher and more rational*' (p. 37):

'There is Life, there is a moral law: that Higher Law by which we are bound.'

APPENDIX IV

CONCERNING LOVE

1. Composition
2. Text
3. Variants

1. COMPOSITION

According to the memoirs of the authoress Lydia Avilov, the relations between 'Alyokhin' and 'Anne' were modelled on the real-life relations between herself and Chekhov: 'I did not doubt that *Concerning Love* concerned me' (see further *Chekhov v vospominaniyakh sovremennikov*, pp. 242-4). This claim cannot be proved or disproved, but probably reflects a considerable retrospective exaggeration—not to say jactitation—of the degree of Chekhov's emotional involvement with Avilov.

The story was written, presumably after *Gooseberries*, at Melikhovo in July 1898; see Appendix III, above.

The following entry in Chekhov's *Notebooks* contains the basic idea of *Concerning Love*, and in part coincides verbally with certain passages in the story's dénouement.

'We did not declare our love for each other, but concealed it fearfully and jealously. It seemed incredible that a love so quiet, so sad as mine could disrupt the life of a husband and children, and of a whole household where they were so fond of me. And where could I persuade her to go to? Things would have been different if my life had been interesting: if I'd been fighting for my country's freedom, say, if I'd been someone out of the ordinary. As it was I should be conveying her from one humdrum, colourless milieu to another equally humdrum. And she obviously took the same view herself, fearing to make me miserable. She wanted me to marry some decent, worthy girl and often said as much. Only later, as I embraced her in the train, did I realize with a burning pain in my heart how inessential and insignificant all our arguments were. Theorize one must, granted, but one must proceed from a premiss loftier and more significant than someone or other's happiness.' (N. I, 84/2)

Other items in the *Notebooks* bearing on *Concerning Love* are as follows:

'Lonely people go to restaurants and the bath-house for the sake of conversation.' (N. I, 62/7)

'A lady of thirty-five, a suburban mediocrity. When he had seduced her and was holding her in his arms she was wondering what monthly allowance he would make her.' (N. I, 82/3)

'Landowner: "At first I too lived like a professional man, I had coffee and liqueurs served after lunch. But the priest drank my liqueurs at two sittings, so I gave up living like that and started having my meals in the kitchen."' (N. I, 86/4)

'When you love you discover such a treasure inside you—so much tenderness and affection—that you really can't believe yourself capable of so much love.' (N. I, 88/3)

2. TEXT

The present translation is made from the text in *Works*, 1944-51, vol. ix, itself based on that of Chekhov's *Collected Works* (1906), vol. xi.

There is one previous recension: that published in the magazine *Russkaya mysl*, no. viii, August 1898.

3. VARIANTS

When revising the *Russkaya mysl* text for his *Collected Works*, Chekhov made three cuts, the last of which involved ending the story at an earlier point:

... *just like a little boy* (p. 45). When you're in love you discover such treasures, such an infinitude of tenderness and affection in yourself that you can't actually believe you're capable of a love so profound.

... *but not one word of truth was there in all their gossip* (p. 47). My conduct in Luganovich's house had, indeed, been wholly irreproachable, and this role of integrity incarnate occasionally depressed me to the point of tears.

... *and had thought her very good-looking* (p. 48).
'I have to be in town by this evening,' said Ivan Ivanovich, stepping back into the room. 'I'll go straight to the railway halt from here.'
'I'll go with you,' said Alyokhin. 'But it's too muddy to walk. Some women from our village will be fetching a load of lime from Fedotovo at about half past four—they can give you a lift while they're about it. I must just see to it that we don't get our lunch too late.'

APPENDIX V

DOCTOR STARTSEV

1. Composition
2. Text
3. Variants

1. COMPOSITION

The cemetery in *Doctor Starstev* was modelled on that of Chekhov's home town, Taganrog, according to his brother Michael (W., ix, 600).

After returning from abroad in early May 1898, Chekhov sent the manuscript of a story, probably *Doctor Startsev*, to the magazine *Russkaya mysl* [*The Russian Idea*], but requested its return in the following terms in a letter of 6 June to the editor, V. A. Goltsev: 'Give me that story back—it's not suitable for *Russkaya mysl*. If it has already been set up in type, then I shall be most obliged if you will send me it in proof form. I am preparing another, longer story [presumably *A Hard Case*] for *Russkaya mysl*.' Chekhov received the returned *Doctor Startsev* on 10 June and sent it to the magazine *Niva* [*The Meadow*] a few days later. He returned corrected proofs to *Niva* on 29 July.

The entries in Chekhov's *Notebooks* bearing on *Doctor Startsev* go back to February or March 1897 (Gitovich, pp. 45–7). They include the following items:

'His banknotes smell of fish oil.' (N. I, 76/10)

'Boy footman: "Unhappy woman, die!"' (N. I, 83/1)

'Pleased to meet you, I'm sure. What statutory right have you?' (N. I, 84/1)

'The Filimonovs [= the Turkins] are a talented family, or so it's said everywhere in town. He is a civil servant, acts on the stage, sings, does tricks, makes funny remarks. ("Pleased to meet you, I'm sure.") She writes liberal stories, she does imitations. In her husband's presence she tells everyone that "Oh, I'm so in love with you! Oh, my husband will notice!" Boy in hall: "Unhappy woman, die!" In the drab, dreary town all this really did seem amusing and brilliant when you heard it for the first time. So it did when you heard it for the second time. Three years later I paid my third visit, the boy had grown a moustache and there was more of this "Oh, I'm so in love with you, oh, my husband will notice" stuff. There was that same burlesqued "Unhappy woman, die!" I left the Filimonovs with the feeling that there were no greater bores and mediocrities on this earth.' (N. I, 85/5)

'Grown fat. Dines at a large table in the club of an evening, and when conversation turns to the Turkins, asks: "What Turkins are you on about? You mean those people whose daughter plays the piannyforty?" Has a large practice in town but doesn't give up his council post—being too greedy.' (N. III, 31)

2. TEXT

The present translation is made from the text in *Works*, 1944–51, vol. ix, itself based on that of Chekhov's *Collected Works* (1901), vol. ix.

There are two previous recensions:

(*a*) a corrected manuscript in the author's hand preserved in the Central State Literary Archives in Moscow;

(*b*) the text as published in the *Monthly Literary Supplements* to the magazine *Niva*, no. 9, September 1898.

3. VARIANTS

One or two minor alterations are to be traced in the fair copy (legible erasures). But neither these, nor the two minor changes made by Chekhov when revising the *Niva* text for his *Collected Works*, are recorded here (see further W., ix, 595–6, 600).

A somewhat more extensive revision was made when Chekhov read the proofs of the story for publication in *Niva*. This involved expanding the ending to include new details about Mr. and Mrs. Turkin: from *What of the Turkins . . .* to . . . *hearty sort of a way* (see p. 66).

Otherwise this revision consisted largely in making cuts, among which were the following:

Mr. Turkin welcomed him in the porch (p. 52). His face was sleepy and somewhat puffy as the result of his after-lunch nap.

'*A thing of beauty is a joy for ever* (p. 53).' He kissed her on both cheeks, forehead and shoulder, then wiped his wet eyes with a handkerchief.

'*There might be bad influences in a high school or a boarding school, you know* (p. 54).' Other girls may not always set a good example, so I adhere to the following principle in bringing up children:

. . . stamping her foot (p. 54).

Again they surrounded her, admiring, congratulating and assuring her that no one in the entire town played as well as she.

'Fine! Excellent!'

'She's going to be a star performer,' said her father proudly.

The mother, Vera Turkin, also looked at her daughter with tender pride. But then she suddenly felt the pangs of envy, of jealousy for another's success, felt the selfishness of a talent unrecognized, and she could endure these praises no longer, but sent her daughter out of the room.

'Go and look for my pencil, Puss,' she said. 'It's in the bedroom.'

'. . . *Alexis Feofilaktovich* (p. 56).'

Footsteps were heard as Mr. Turkin led his guests under the spreading maple-tree.

Startsev was annoyed. 'They won't leave us alone, you see. It really is awful!'

'. . . *how little they know* (p. 60)*!*' The time when I wasn't in love myself, but indulged in long harangues about love . . . it's a painful memory to me now.

. . . *and put them in his current account* (p. 62). And what cheerful thoughts, what attractive plans that money sometimes did put into his head!

And felt uncomfortable (p. 63). Catherine's stare, her affectionate attitude . . . they worried him and he would have been glad to go away.

. . . *and waited for her to finish* (p. 63).

'That,' thought he with bored irritation, 'is the most mediocre female in the whole town.'

. . . *lengthy expressions of delighted appreciation* (p. 63). Yet she no longer listened with dignity, as of old—but diffidently, with an apathetic smile.

. . . *and the spark died inside him* (p. 64).

'But I must be on my way,' he said, feeling a strong urge to go to the club. 'Permit me to leave.'

. . . *Peacock's tragic posturings* (p. 65). And the house impressed him as gloomy—it might have been a workhouse or a prison.

APPENDIX VI

A CASE HISTORY

1. Composition
2. Text
3. Variants

1. COMPOSITION

The first reference to *A Case History* in Chekhov's correspondence occurs in a letter from Yalta of 11 November 1898 to I. I. Orlov: 'Owing to the rain and bad weather I have settled down to work and have already written an entire story.' The work was finished by 14 November, on which date Chekhov writes to V. M. Lavrov and V. A. Goltsev, editors of the magazine *Russkaya mysl* [*The Russian Idea*], informing them of its dispatch, asking to see proofs, and promising to return them by 4–5 December. On 29 November Chekhov writes to Goltsev complaining that he has received neither the proofs for which he asked nor any other form of acknowledgement. The proofs are eventually read by Chekhov between 30 November and 3 December (Gitovich, p. 531).

The entries in Chekhov's *Notebooks* bearing on *A Case History* go back to the period between 13 November and 13 December 1897 (Gitovich, p. 487). They include the following items:

'Just as it is awkward to ask a convict what he has been sentenced for, similarly it's awkward to ask a very rich man why he has so much money, and why he makes such poor use of his wealth. This usually leads to an embarrassed, awkward conversation after which mutual coldness sets in.' (N. I, 75/7)

'You look at a factory in some provincial dump. Quiet, peaceful. But if you look inside, how crass is the owners' boorishness! How crudely selfish they are! How hopeless the workers' conditions: fights, vodka, lice!' (N. I, 81/4)

'A factory. A thousand workers. Night. Watchman banging board. Lots of work, lots of suffering—all on behalf of the nonentity who owns the factory. Stupid mother, governess, daughter.
'Daughter falls ill, professor is summoned from Moscow but doesn't go—sends house-surgeon. House-surgeon hears watchman banging at night and

thinks. Lake dwellings come to mind. "Must I really work all my life, like this factory: just for these smug, fat, idle, stupid nonentities?"

'"Who goes there?" just like prison.' (N. I, 83/2)

2. TEXT

The present translation is made from the text in *Works*, 1944–51, vol. ix, itself based on that of Chekhov's *Collected Works* (1901), vol. ix.

There is one previous recension: that published in the magazine *Russkaya mysl*, no. xii, December 1898.

3. VARIANTS

In revising the *Russkaya mysl* text for his *Collected Works*, Chekhov made two minor changes of wording.

APPENDIX VII

ANGEL

1. Composition
2. Text
3. Variants

1. COMPOSITION

In mid-1898 N. Ye. Efros, editor of the magazine *Semya* [*Family*], wrote to Chekhov soliciting contributions, in answer to which Chekhov sent Efros *Angel*—but not until early December of the same year. In a telegram of 9 December Efros asked permission to publish the story twice: in *Semya*, and also in the Christmas number of the newspaper *Novosti dnya* [*News of the Day*]. That Chekhov did not consent is evident from a passage in Efros's letter to him of 13 December: 'I shall, of course, punctiliously carry out all your wishes. I shall publish the story as a whole in *Semya*, and not in the Christmas number, since you don't want that' (W., ix, 602).

Chekhov's *Notebooks* include one entry bearing on *Angel*, dating from between 1892 and 1895 (Gitovich, p. 334):

'She was an actor's wife—liked the theatre, writers, seemed totally absorbed in her husband's job. Everyone was surprised at his making so successful a marriage. But then he dies. She marries a confectioner, and it now turns out that her favourite occupation is making jam. She despises the theatre, now, having become religious in emulation of her second husband.' (N. I, 48/1)

2. TEXT

The present translation is made from the text in *Works*, 1944–51, vol. ix, itself based on that of Chekhov's *Collected Works* (1901), vol. ix.

There is one previous recension: that published in the magazine *Semya*, no. 1, 3 January 1899.

3. VARIANTS

When revising the story for his *Collected Works* Chekhov made six minor alterations.

APPENDIX VIII

NEW VILLA

1. Composition
2. Text
3. Variants

1. COMPOSITION

The story was completed by 24 December 1898, on which date Chekhov sent it to the newspaper *Russkiye vedomosti* [*The Russian Gazette*]. In a letter to Chekhov of 1 January 1899, the editor, V. M. Sobolevsky, wrote of his intention to publish the story in the next Sunday issue (on 3 January), adding: 'I hope it won't be interfered with by the censor, though I can't vouch for one passage (about the rich and well-fed): that's the *bête noire* of the censor we've so far been dealing with' (W., ix, 604). Reference was, presumably, to the conversation (about rich and poor people) between Helen Kucherov and the black-smith Rodion in Chapter III. But it is not known whether or not the censor in fact imposed any changes.

Chekhov's *Notebooks* include the following items bearing on *New Villa*:

'While they were building the bridge the engineer rented a country property and stayed there with his family as if they were summer visitors. He and his wife helped the peasants, whereas they robbed—and trespassed on his land.

'He turns up at a parish meeting.

'"I've done this that and the other for you," says he. "But you repay good with evil. If you were fair men you would repay good with good."

'He turned round and left. The peasants scratched themselves.

'"He wants paying," said they. "Aye! But how much we're to pay we don't know."

'"Let's ask the magistrate."'

'Upshot: rumour that the engineer's on the fiddle.' (N. I, 52/8)

'Squire to peasant: "If you don't give up drinking I shall look down on you."

'Peasants' wives at home: "What did Squire say?"

'"Says he'll look after us."

'Wives are glad.' (N. I, 87/1)

2. TEXT

The present translation is made from the text in *Works*, 1944-51, vol. ix, itself based on that of Chekhov's *Collected Works* (1901), vol. ix.

There is one previous recension: that published in the newspaper *Russkiye vedomosti*, no. 3, 3 January 1899.

3. VARIANTS

When revising the *Russkiye vedomosti* version for his *Collected Works*, Chekhov made four minor changes in the wording.

APPENDIX IX

ON OFFICIAL BUSINESS

1. Composition
2. Text
3. Variants

1. COMPOSITION

Chekhov's brother Michael reveals that 'Loshadin' in the story is modelled on the local *sotsky* (village constable) in the Melikhovo area, who used to bring official papers to Chekhov (W., ix, 605), also occasionally delivering his private mail.

The story was written in November 1898. It had been dispatched to the magazine *Knizhki nedeli* [*Books of the Week*] by the 26th of that month, on which day Chekhov wrote to M. O. Menshikov: 'I am sending a story to *The Week*. Please send me proofs. The story is unfinished in its details and I'll polish it in proof. At the moment I haven't felt like sitting for a long time over the rough draft—I'm somewhat unwell and in a hurry to get it off.'

The entries in Chekhov's *Notebooks* bearing on *On Official Business* go back to autumn 1891 (Gitovich, p. 300). They include the following items:

'Nowadays they shoot themselves because they're fed up with life, but it used to be because they'd embezzled government money.' (N. I, 10/1)

'A council employee—an embezzler—has shot himself. The police inspector and I go along to the post-mortem. We arrive. He lies on a table. It is late. We postpone the autopsy till tomorrow. The Inspector goes off to play cards at a neighbour's. I go to bed. The door keeps opening and shutting. The dead man's ghost seems to be abroad.' (N. I, 41/5)

2. TEXT

The present translation is based on the text in *Works*, 1944–51, vol. ix, itself based on that of Chekhov's *Collected Works* (1901), vol. ix.

There is one previous recension: that published in the magazine *Knizhki nedeli*, January 1899.

3. VARIANTS

When revising the *Knizhki nedeli* text for his *Collected Works*, Chekhov made two minor changes in the wording.

APPENDIX X

A LADY WITH A DOG

1. Composition
2. Text
3. Variants

1. COMPOSITION

Few details survive of the composition of *A Lady with a Dog*: possibly Chekhov's best-known short story. The first reference to it in his correspondence occurs on 15 September 1899, when he writes to V. A. Goltsev, editor of *Russkaya mysl* [*The Russian Idea*] that 'you will receive the story in time for your December issue.' On 30 October Chekhov sends the story to Goltsev, asking for proofs to be sent quickly so that he can 'polish it a little'. By 13 November he has corrected the proofs and returns them to Goltsev on that day with the request to receive a second set.

The entries in Chekhov's *Notebooks* bearing on *A Lady with a Dog* go back to October or November 1897 (Gitovich, p. 482). They include the following items:

'The provinces: in a box in the theatre Governor's daughter must wear a feather boa.' (N. I, 68/2)

'The lace on their panties is like a lizard's scales.' (N. I, 90/4)

2. TEXT

The present translation is based on the text in *Works*, 1944–51, vol ix, itself based on that of Chekhov's *Collected Works* (1906), vol. xi.

There is one earlier recension: that published in the magazine *Russkaya mysl*, no. xii, December 1899.

A single page of the rough draft of the story, in Chekhov's hand—the last page of Chapter IV—also survives, and is preserved in the State Literary Museum in Moscow; see further *Literaturnoye nasledstvo: Chekhov*, pp. 133 ff.

3. VARIANTS

When revising the story for publication in his *Collected Works*, Chekhov considerably shortened it. The following passages cover the most significant of these cuts:

'You seem very much on the defensive, Anne' (p. 131).
'You must listen to me, I'll tell you why it happened.'
'There's nothing, absolutely nothing, I need to know about it.'
'But do let me tell you, it will relieve my mind——'
'Later, darling!' he said, patting her hair. 'Why look so earnest and clever about it all? Which isn't, actually, very clever of you, I'm sorry to say—because it doesn't fit the circumstances.'
'No, you must hear me out, I implore you. As I've told you before, I married and went to S—— with my husband. Other people live in the provinces, so why shouldn't I? But I found S—— disgusting after my first week in the place. I look out of the window and I see a grey fence—a long, grey fence, for heaven's sake! I'd go to bed at nine o'clock. Lunch at three, bed at nine . . . such were my only recreations.'

She hid her face on his breast and clung to him (p. 131).
'You're a good, kind man, I can feel it,' she said. 'I don't know you very well, but you seem so kind, so decent, so intelligent, somehow—you're not like all the others, and you'll understand me. *Please, please believe me . . .'*

. . . leaving an impression of majesty and beauty (p. 133). Gurov was enjoying himself, though he knew that these impressions were ill suited to him, that they were quite superfluous—since his life was neither beautiful nor majestic, and he had no wish for it to become any such thing.

'This is fate (p. 133). I nearly became infatuated with you. You're so good, so charming. You're a wonderful, a rare person—it's so easy to fall in love with you. But what do I need with love? It would wreck my life. To love you in secret, to hide from everyone . . . that would be awful, wouldn't it?'

. . . lost all charm for him (p. 134). He cursed the Crimea, Yalta, Tatars, women. He insisted that Switzerland was superior. He gradually plunged into Moscow life, he was now quarrelling with tenants, doorkeepers and the police, he was zealously reading his three newspapers a day, and then claiming to read no Moscow newspapers on principle! He felt the lure of restaurants, clubs, dinner parties, anniversary celebrations. Gone were his easy, carefree mood and that sense of personal freedom.

. . . a large helping of 'Moscow hot-pot' straight from the pan (p. 134). Had Anne seen him emerging—red-faced, gloomy, disgruntled—from a restaurant, she might have realized that there was nothing exalted or extraordinary about him.

'. . . *in Yalta—did you but know* (p. 135)*!*'

'When?'

'This autumn. She couldn't be called particularly beautiful, but she made an indelible impression on me. I still haven't quite recovered.'

APPENDIX XI

AT CHRISTMAS

1. Composition
2. Text
3. Variants

1. COMPOSITION

The story was published in the newspaper *Peterburgskaya gazeta* [*The Petersburg Gazette*] (to which Chekhov had not contributed since 1888) after the editor, S. N. Khudekov, had—in a letter dated 27 December 1899—asked permission to reprint one of Chekhov's early stories, *Khudozhestvo* [*Artistry*; 1886] in the paper, adding that: 'you would of course oblige us infinitely by sending a nice new little yarn for our Christmas number' (W., xviii, 533-4).

2. TEXT

The present translation is made from the text in *Works*, 1944-51, vol. ix, itself based on that of Chekhov's *Collected Works* (1906), vol. xi.

There is one previous recension: that published in the newspaper *Peterburgskaya gazeta*, no. 1, 1 January 1900.

3. VARIANTS

When revising the material for his *Collected Works*, Chekhov made a number of cuts, the following being the most significant:

'. . . *the most important Internnal Enemy is Bacchus* (p. 147). If so be the Soldier is in the embraces of Bacchus all day long that ain't right, like. And there is a reason of a different type. You are a Porter now and must respect your employer, the one as is your present Boss.'

. . . *while a third slept on the bed* (p. 148). Andrew had only three children, but Dr. B. O. Moselweiser always displayed indignation when walking along the downstairs corridor, shouting: 'What's the meaning of this? You've got sixteen children here, Andrew! I won't have it, indeed I will not!'

APPENDIX XII

IN THE HOLLOW

1. Composition
2. Text
3. Variants

1. COMPOSITION

According to Chekhov's brother Michael, *In the Hollow* describes 'a Sakhalin episode': that is, the kind of story which Chekhov heard from or about the convicts in the penal colony of Sakhalin during his visit to that Russian Devil's Island in 1890. But, Michael Chekhov adds, 'the scene is set near Melikhovo', Chekhov's country residence south of Moscow in 1892-9 (W., ix, 612).

The writer Ivan Bunin claims to have told Chekhov of a village deacon eating about two pounds of caviare at his father's name-day party: hence the episode which begins *In the Hollow*, where Chekhov has converted the deacon into a sexton and doubled the amount of caviare consumed (ibid.).

S. N. Shchukin quotes Chekhov as making the following comment on *In the Hollow:* 'I describe the life of the Russian midlands, the life I know best. Businessmen like my Khrymins do exist in real life—except that they're even worse. Their children take to vodka-drinking at the age of eight. These are debauched children who have infected the whole area with syphilis. I don't bring that into the story because I think it inartistic to discuss the matter' (ibid.).

In the Hollow was written for the legally published Marxist magazine *Zhizn* [*Life*] after urgent repeated requests (dating from December 1898) to Chekhov for a contribution from the editor, V. A. Posse, and from Maxim Gorky (who was also closely associated with the publication). The first mention of *In the Hollow* occurs in a letter of 14 November 1899 from Chekhov to his sister Masha: 'I am writing a long story, I shall soon finish it and start another.' On 19 November Chekhov informs Posse that he is writing a story for *Zhizn* which 'will be ready soon: by the second half of December for sure. It is only three printers' sheets [about forty-eight pages] long, but there are masses of characters jostling each other and there's hardly room to move—so a great deal of contrivance is necessary to prevent this cramped atmosphere becoming unduly obtrusive. Anyway, it will have taken shape sufficiently by 10 December, and you'll be able to set it. But the snag is, I'm terrified of the censor mucking it about. I can't stand any censor's blue-pencilling, or I don't think I can. The fact that the story was, in part, turning out a somewhat dubious prospect from the censorship point of view . . . this was why I didn't venture to write to you in explicit terms and give you a definite answer. Now, of course, I *am* giving you a definite answer, but on condition that you return the story to me if you too think passages of it liable to create censorship difficulties: that is, if you too foresee a danger of the censor messing it about.' On 25 November Chekhov informs Gorky that he is 'writing a story for *Zhizn*, for the January issue'. On 3 December Chekhov reports to Vl. I. Nemirovich-Danchenko that he is at work on a story for *Zhizn* and offers to send an offprint.

By 6 December Chekhov has 'finished' *In the Hollow* (W., xviii, 278): presumably its rough draft. Not until 20 December does he dispatch the manuscript to *Zhizn*, writing to Posse as follows: 'You must forgive me— firstly for being a little late, and secondly for dispatching so untidy a manu- script. I haven't done a fair copy, fearing to hold things up even longer and make further alterations in the process of copying. Please have the type set up and send me proofs. I shall do in proof what is usually part of the copying process: render the indecorous decorous. I shall keep the proofs two days. So if you could postpone publication till your February issue that would be fine. I may change the title *In the Hollow* if I think of something more impressive and eye-catching.'

On 26 December 1899 Chekhov informs M. O. Menshikov that he has sent the story to *Zhizn*, adding that he describes factory life, dealing with its melancholy aspects. 'Then, only yesterday, I chanced to discover that *Zhizn* is a Marxist—a factory—organ. What *am* I to do now?' The comment reveals extreme naïveté about or (according to point of view) a healthy ignorance of Russian revolutionary politics.

On 2 January 1900 Chekhov writes to his wife: 'My story—a very horrifying one—will appear in the February issue of *Zhizn*. There are many characters, there's a landscape. There's a half moon, there's a bittern booming away somewhere in the distance and mooing like a cow shut in a shed. The story has everything.' In a letter of 21 January 1900 to G. I. Rossolimo, Chekhov refers to *In the Hollow* as his 'last story of peasant life'.

In a letter to Posse, of 5 February 1900, Chekhov complains of the misprints in the published story. 'There was no point in my reading the proofs as the printers didn't make my corrections. . . . All these misprints . . . have so shocked me that I can't stand the sight of the story. I've never known such a profusion of misprints: a very orgy of typographical slovenliness, it seems to me.'

The entries in Chekhov's *Notebooks* bearing on *In the Hollow* go back to 1898 (Gitovich, 538). They include the following items.

'Little girl washes father's boots in pond.' (N. I, 74/2)

Uc

'A sexton eats all the unpressed caviare at a factory-owner's funeral. The priest nudges him, but he's in an ecstatic trance, notices nothing, just goes on eating. As they return home later the angry priest won't answer the sexton's questions. That night the sexton prostrates himself before the priest: "For Christ's sake, forgive me!" Now, that caviare was never forgotten. "What sexton's that?" people would ask. "Why, the one who ate all the caviare at Khrymin's funeral." "Which village is that?" "Oh, the one with the sexton who ate all the caviare." "Who's that?" "The sexton who ate all the caviare."' (N. I, 86/11)

'They put a telephone in the parish offices, but it soon stopped working, being infested with cockroaches and bugs. Girl keeps saying "How divine!"' (N. I, 95/3)

'X, former odd-job man, sees everything from the maintenance angle and seeks a wife who's in a good state of repair. N. attracts him because, despite her bulk, she walks quietly and smoothly, doesn't rattle. "So everything's in its proper place, the whole mechanism's in good working order."' (N. I, 98/2)

'An employee of the detective branch goes home to his village. Wears galoshes, doesn't tuck his trousers inside his boots. His folks are glad he's made his way in the world. Looks at a certain peasant and keeps worrying that "he's wearing a stolen shirt". He's right, as it turns out.' (N. I, 100/4)

2. TEXT

The present translation is made from the text in *Works*, 1944–51, vol. ix, itself based on that of Chekhov's *Collected Works* (1906), vol. xi.

There is one previous recension: that published by the magazine *Zhizn*, vol. i, January 1900.

3. VARIANTS

When preparing the *Zhizn* text for his *Collected Works* Chekhov made four minor changes in the wording.

APPENDIX XIII

THE BISHOP

1. Composition
2. Text
3. Variants

1. COMPOSITION

The birth-pangs of *The Bishop* were unusually protracted.

According to Chekhov's own testimony, his conception of the story goes back as far as the year 1886: in a letter, dated 16 March 1901, to his wife, he writes of *The Bishop* as embodying 'a theme which I've had in mind for about the last fifteen years'. This claim accords with information supplied by Chekhov's brother Michael: that a real-life Bishop Sergius helped to inspire the story. Born in 1864, the bishop had been called Stephen Alekseyevich Petrov before changing his name on becoming a monk. As a student at Moscow University during the late 1880s he had had rooms in the same house (Korneyev's, on Kudrinsky-Sadovy Street) as the Chekhov family, and had been a welcome guest in their home. The acquaintanceship was renewed ten years later in Yalta when Petrov, now Bishop Sergius, visited the town in order to obtain treatment for a nervous ailment, and became a frequent visitor at Chekhov's villa (W., ix, 617; xvii, 536–7).

Michael Chekhov claims that a Father Ananias of St. David's Monastery (about three miles from Melikhovo, Chekhov's residence in 1892–9) was the prototype of 'Father Sisoy' in *The Bishop* (W., ix, 617).

An episode of February or March 1899 also contributed to the conception of Chekhov's Bishop. It was then that he chanced to see, in a photographer's shop in Yalta, a picture of Michael Gribanovsky, Bishop of the Crimea, taken with his aged mother. So impressed was Chekhov that he purchased the picture, also acquiring a book by the same Bishop, and asking questions about him of S. N. Shchukin (who was later to publish his memoirs of Chekhov). But Chekhov never actually met Bishop Gribanovsky—who, incidentally, died of tuberculosis in Yalta (W., ix, 617; Gitovich, p. 551).

Shchukin also states that: 'after publication of *The Bishop*, Chekhov used to say that this was an old story of his, written earlier and now remodelled.' Shchukin quotes Chekhov as saying: 'Here's an excellent subject for a story. A Bishop holds morning service on Maundy Thursday. He's ill. There is a full congregation. The choir sings. The Bishop reads the lesson on Christ's Passion.

He is deeply saturated in that lesson—obsessed with pity for Christ, for himself and for other people. He suddenly feels downhearted, feels he's soon going to die—may die this very moment. This feeling—whether through the sound of his voice, through the general tension or through other channels invisible and unintelligible—is communicated to those who are officiating with him, and then to the worshippers: first one, then another and finally to all. Sensing the approach of death, the Bishop himself weeps and his whole church weeps with him' (W., ix, 616–17).

The first mention of *The Bishop* in Chekhov's correspondence occurs in a letter of 6 December 1899 to V. S. Mirolyubov, editor of *Zhurnal dlya vsekh* [*Everybody's Magazine*]: 'I'll send you a story without fail, only don't hurry me. I'm suffering from piles and eye strain, and a lot of work has accumulated at the end of the year. . . . The story I shall send you is *The Bishop*. Should there be any misunderstanding, should it turn out to present your magazine with censorship problems, I shall send you something else.' Not until more than a year later does Chekhov claim (in a letter of 16 March 1901) to be at work on *The Bishop*, after which we hear nothing of it for several months. On 3 August Chekhov tells Mirolyubov that: 'The first thing I write will be a story for *Zhurnal dlya vsekh*. I'll send it to you personally, and you must send me the proofs . . . without fail.' But by 31 August Chekhov has only got as far as 'taking *The Bishop* out of my trunk' (W., xix, 126). On 19 October we find him apologizing to Mirolyubov from Moscow: 'Sorry I haven't yet sent you that story, old man. The reason is: I stopped working on it—and I've always found it hard to finish work which has been interrupted. As soon as I'm home [in Yalta] I'll begin it again, and send you it—don't worry.'

On 9 November Chekhov informs his wife (from Yalta), and probably with reference to *The Bishop*, that 'I am writing but I can't say I'm enjoying it much.' Three days later, in response to a request to send material for a public reading in aid of charity, Chekhov says that: 'The writing which I am now engaged on isn't very likely to get past the censorship: i.e. it's not likely to be acceptable for public recital.' On 27 November we find Chekhov speaking disparagingly of *The Bishop*: 'You write [he tells his wife] of your yearning to read my new story. But in my present mood and in a lousy dump like Yalta I can't write anything capable of satisfying . . . such a yearning.' On 17 December Chekhov informs the long-suffering Mirolyubov that he feels unwell and cannot write. 'I have been spitting blood, and now I feel weak and bad-tempered. I sit with a warm compress on my side, I'm taking creosote and all sorts of rubbish. Be that as it may, I shan't let you down over *The Bishop*—I shall send it you sooner or later.'

It is on 20 February 1902 that Chekhov at last sends the story to Mirolyubov. He writes that he had it finished long ago, 'but found it rather hard to make a fair copy, being unwell all the time. . . . Send me proofs without fail. I'll add a couple of sentences at the end. I'm not going to yield a single word to the censor, so bear that in mind. If the censor should reject so much as a word, please return the story to me and I'll send you another one in May.' On 8 March Chekhov receives proofs and writes to Mirolyubov that he 'had wished to correct them and send them off today. But, firstly, your reader has turned all the full stops into exclamation marks, and has put inverted commas where there shouldn't be any ("Syntax"). And, secondly, there are many omissions (e.g. "Snake-Eye Demyan") which I have to make good. In addition I also want to make a few insertions. So you'll receive the proofs the day after this letter, or on the same day if I manage to get finished by seven o'clock this evening. Excuse my repeating the following request, my dear fellow, which is: not to publish the story at all if the censor should strike out one single word. In that case I'll send you another story. While actually writing I had already made cuts and discarded a lot of things with the censorship in mind.' On the same day Chekhov writes somewhat mysteriously to his wife: 'I've had proofs of my story from Mirolyubov and am now trying to ensure that it won't be published, as the censor has very much spoilt it.' *The Bishop* did, nevertheless, appear in the April issue of Mirolyubov's magazine, and we know nothing of any cuts imposed by the censor.

The entries in Chekhov's *Notebooks* bearing on *The Bishop* go back to 1891 (Gitovich, p. 300). They include the following items:

'The deacon's son's dog—was called Syntax.' (N. I, 11/5)

'Cyprian: "The Japanese are just the same as the Montenegrins." ' (N. I, 72/5)

'A blind beggarwoman was singing about love.' (N. I, 81/10)

'Boy, laundrywoman's son, asks clerk in post-office: "Do they pay you by the day or by the month?"' (N. I, 99/2)

'"Katya, who is it keeps opening and shutting the door down there? What's that creaking and groaning?"
"I can't hear anything, Grandfather."
"But someone just went past. Can't you hear?"
"But that's your tummy, Grandfather."' (N. I, 105/3)

'Bish weeps—as when ill in childhood with his mother caring for him—weeps just because of general nervous prostration. . . . He has kept his faith, he has achieved everything possible for a man in his position, but he remains ill at ease: not everything has been clear to him, there has been something missing, he doesn't want to die.

'Soon a new bishop is appointed, the old one is forgotten—no one remembers him, except for the deacon's widow. Walking to the pasture with other women to fetch her cow, she speaks of having had a son who was a bishop. They don't believe her.

'Conversation between Bishop and mother about nephew: "Does Stephen believe in God?" The housekeeper is preparing to go to Moscow—the Holy Synod has given him permission to sell some old things, but this isn't to the present bishop's liking.' (N. I, 106/2)

'A schoolmaster, a former theological student and drunkard, used to beat his pupils. Had a birch hanging on the wall with a notice under it: BETULA KINDERBALSAMICA SECUTA.' (N. I, 108/2)

'The priest's son lost his temper. "Oh, thou ass of Jehudiel!" he said to the hired woman. But the priest said not a word, ashamed of having forgotten where such an ass is mentioned in the Bible.' (N. I, 109/9)

'The Bishop remembers having been archimandrite at the embassy chapel when a blind beggarwoman used to sing about love beneath his window every day.' (N. I, 110/6)

'The superintendent priest gives the other priests and the entire clergy—and after that even their wives and children—conduct marks.' (N. I, 120/18)

2. TEXT

The present translation is based on the text in *Works*, 1944–51, vol. ix, itself based on that of Chekhov's *Collected Works* (1906), vol. xi.

There is one previous recension: that published in the magazine *Zhurnal dlya vsekh*, no. 4, April 1902.

3. VARIANTS

When preparing the *Zhurnal dlya vsekh* text for his *Collected Works* Chekhov made three insignificant changes in the wording.

APPENDIX XIV

A MARRIAGEABLE GIRL

1. Composition
2. Text
3. Variants

1. COMPOSITION

The first mention of the story occurs in a letter of 20 October 1902 from Chekhov to V. S. Mirolyubov, editor and publisher of the magazine *Zhurnal dlya vsekh* [*Everybody's Journal*]: 'if you need a title for the story—one we can change later—here it is: *A Marriageable Girl.*' On 6 December of the same year Chekhov informs his wife that he has settled down to work and is writing 'a story' (probably *A Marriageable Girl*). On 14 December Chekhov tells his wife that he is working at a story which he describes as 'rather uninteresting—to me, at any rate. I'm bored with it.' On 30 December Chekhov informs Mirolyubov that he will be sending him the story 'shortly': a somewhat over-optimistic prediction.

Other passages from Chekhov's correspondence shed further light on the composition of *A Marriageable Girl*, as follows:

'I am writing a story in the old-fashioned style of the 1870s for *Zhurnal dlya vsekh*. How it will turn out I don't know.' (*Letter to O. L. Knipper, 26 Jan. 1903.*)

'As the years go by, I become more and more prone to fatigue. I *am* writing a story—but slowly, in dribs and drabs: perhaps because there are so many characters, or perhaps because I've lost the knack and must pick it up again.' (*Letter to O. L. Knipper, 30 Jan. 1903.*)

'I am writing *A Marriageable Girl*. I reckon on finishing it by 20 February, give or take a day or two, depending on health and so on and so forth. Don't worry, anyway—you *will* get it. My only fear is that my marriageable young lady may find herself in trouble with those marriageable young men who stand guard over the chastity of your magazine.' (*Letter to V. S. Mirolyubov, 9 Feb. 1903.*)

'The story's finished. I'll spend about five days copying it, while also revising it at the same time. So I'll send it you on 25 February and you'll receive it on 2 March.' (*Letter to V. S. Mirolyubov, 20 Feb. 1903.*)

'I'm two days in arrears, dear Victor Sergeyevich: not having finished until the evening of the 27th—and not on the 25th, as I promised. My health isn't what it was and I can't write as I used to—I tire so quickly. Send me proofs because I must revise it and deal with the ending. I always write my endings in proof.' (*Letter to V. S. Mirolyubov, 27 Feb. 1903.*)

'I can't send you my *Marriageable Girl* because I haven't got her. You can soon read about her in *Zhurnal dlya vsekh*. I've written such stories umpteen times before, so you won't find anything new there.' (*Letter to O. L. Knipper, 23 March 1903.*)

In March 1903 Chekhov reads the first galley proofs of the story and makes extensive alterations in the customary wide margins. At some time in April he receives a second set of wide-margined galley proofs incorporating his corrections to the first set. In May and early June he works on the second galleys, making further extensive alterations. On 5 June he informs V. V. Veresayev (like Chekhov himself, both an author and a doctor) that he has 'hacked the *Marriageable Girl* about and altered her in proof'. On 2 July Chekhov asks Mirolyubov for yet another set of proofs. He wants 'one more glance: not to correct but for the sake of the punctuation'. On 10 July page proofs are sent to him, and are returned to Mirolyubov with certain further corrections, probably in September. By contrast with the two sets of galleys, these corrected page proofs have not survived.

Eventually *A Marriageable Girl* is published by *Zhurnal dlya vsekh* in December 1903. Its labour pangs had—like those of the preceding *Bishop*—been unusually protracted. As for the amount of surviving evidence bearing on the various stages of composition (see further, *Text*, below), *A Marriageable Girl* remains unique in this respect among Chekhov's stories (*Literaturnoye nasledstvo: Chekhov*, p. 88).

Some preliminary notes (of unknown date, in Chekhov's hand, on a single sheet of paper) are preserved in the Lenin State Library of the USSR. They provide the earliest evidence on his conception of the story and of the roles projected for Sasha, Nadya and Nadya's fiancé Andrew (here designated as 'A. A.'). In the translation which follows (made from the text in W., ix, 528) material crossed out by Chekhov is included without being typographically differentiated.

Whatever the results might or might not be, her life now seemed to have been transformed and turned topsy turvy. Come what might, wherever fate might lead, it would be nothing but worry, now, till the end of her days.

VI. She to Sasha: 'You're ill. My only feeling for you is annoyance. You're ill, aren't you—so why don't you see a doctor? (Meanwhile you go out without wearing a hat.) Why don't you take account of your illness? And why haven't you studied—why *don't* you study? Oh, it really is wrong of you—it's disreputable, actually, I'm sorry—to spend all day drinking tea. It's what I call being thoroughly dissipated!'

Away, away from this place! One neither can nor should live here.

And he (A. A.) kept waiting for her to tell him something.

She strolled about the garden, amazed that she could ever have lived in this town without any hope of escaping from it.

'When you twist your thin fingers in front of me, my only reaction is annoyance [when] I look at you,' she said.

A. A. fell on his knees before her. In another era, twenty years or so, this (love affair, perhaps) would have seemed moving perhaps (would have aroused sympathy) but now, in this day and age, A. A. seemed so pathetic and bewildered. He was an extinct species: a piteous sight, nothing more.

Still, your conscience is clear your life will be pure and your conscience clear.

So insignificant did she find A. A., so (trivial) petty did his grief seem that she was at a loss for words—she just shrugged her shoulders and went away.

'Oh, it's a wonderful life, mine is! The wretched Fuss-pot is always watching to see I don't—. God, why am I still alive?'

'Just one single word, dear. Is there any hope for me? Oh, I'll wait, I don't mind waiting.'

When she went in the garden two boys were sitting on the fence.
'Who thought she was going to get married?' some urchins shouted from next door.
Everyone in the place teased her about being engaged to be married.

A shout came from the kitchen. 'Run along, Marina—Old Fuss-pot wants you.'

Chekhov's *Notebooks* contain only one item bearing on *A Marriageable Girl*:

'"Slow harnessing, but fast driving ... such is their national character," said Bismarck.' (N. I, 118/5)

2. TEXT

The present translation is made from the text in *Works*, 1944–51, vol. ix, itself based on that of Chekhov's *Collected Works* (1906), vol. xi.

There are five previous recensions:

(*a*) a rough manuscript draft in Chekhov's hand, preserved in the Lenin State Library of the USSR;

(*b*) a revised fair copy of the above, also in Chekhov's hand, which came to light in 1957 and is also preserved in the Lenin State Library of the USSR;

(*c*) and (*d*) first and second galley proofs of the story, both extensively corrected in Chekhov's hand and preserved in the Institute of Literature (Pushkin House) of the Academy of Sciences of the USSR in Leningrad;

(*e*) the text published in *Zhurnal dlya vsekh*, no. 12, December 1903.

3. VARIANTS

No other story of Chekhov's provides such a rich array of variants, as emerges from a study of the various early recensions (listed under *Text*, above) taken in conjunction with the numerous erased passages which remain legible in these recensions despite Chekhov's crossings-out. All the above variants have been comprehensively described by comparatively recent Russian editors (W., ix, 617–78; *Literaturnoye nasledstvo: Chekhov*, pp. 87–108).

It is neither practicable nor desirable to reproduce all this material in translation. A clear idea of the revision process as a whole can, however, be obtained by studying Chekhov's rough draft as it appears in W., ix, 505–27. This draft —the first coherent extant form of the story—has been translated *in toto* and is given below. But variants *preceding* this rough draft (i.e. material which, though crossed out by Chekhov in that draft, yet remains legible) are not accounted for here. Nor are the various revisions subsequent to the rough draft, as evidenced in items (*b*), (*c*) and (*d*) listed under *Text*, above. Item (*e*) (the *Zhurnal dlya vsekh* text) is identical with that of the final version with the exception of a single word only.

A MARRIAGEABLE GIRL

[*The Rough Draft*]

I

'Go upstairs. Hurry up—Old Fuss-pot wants you,' shouted a maid angrily.

Through the open window came the sound of people scurrying in the kitchen, which was in the basement. A door banged on its block and pulley. There was a smell of roast turkey in the garden near the house. It was ten o'clock in the evening and a full moon shone above the garden. At the Shumins' home a prayer meeting—arranged by the grandmother—had just ended. Nadya had gone into the garden for a minute. She could see them laying the dining-room table for supper while Grandmother bustled about, resplendent in her silk dress. Father Andrew, a canon from the cathedral, was talking to Nadya's mother Nina, who somehow looked very young when seen through the window in the evening light. Father Andrew's son—himself an Andrew—stood by listening attentively.

All was quiet and cool in the garden. Tranquil black shadows lay across the ground, while far, far away—out of town, no doubt—frogs croaked. May, lovely May, was in the air. How she would have liked to think that under this sky and these trees, on these shadows and far beyond town, in fields and woods, Springtime had generated a life of its own, a life wonderful, rich, mysterious: a life wholly ignored, probably, by Grandmother, Father Andrew and Mother as being of no interest to them.

Nadya reflected that she was twenty-three, had longed to be married since she was sixteen, and was engaged at last to this Andrew who could be seen through the window. Though she liked him, and though the wedding was to be on the twenty-second of July, yet there was no joy in her heart, she was sleeping badly and her spirits were low.

Somehow everything seemed so obscure and incomplete these days. She had forgotten her father, but today she somehow kept remembering him carrying her in his arms long, long ago. No sooner did she start thinking about her marriage than her father at once came to mind for some reason.

'If only he was alive!' she thought.

Then someone came out of the house and stood on the steps. This was Sasha Gerasimov, who was staying with them, having arrived from Moscow about ten days earlier. At one time, long ago, a seamstress, a Mary Petrovna, had resided with Grandmother: a small, thin, ailing, angry woman who was always on her dignity.

'I may be a poor widow,' she would say, 'but I *am* a gentlewoman, not one of your common herd.'

Sasha was her son: a big boy who had been making poor progress at his high school. Of Sasha it was said for some reason that he would make an excellent artist if he was taught painting. But it was hard, now, to see why Grandmother had sent him to Moscow, where he had entered the Komissarov School and had then moved on to the School of Fine Art and taken a diploma in architecture. He hadn't practised architecture, though, but had taken a job with a Moscow lithographic firm, drawing wall-paper patterns at home. He would come and stay with Grandmother almost every summer. Very sick, almost on the point of death, he never stayed long there—only a couple of days before vanishing and leaving town, sometimes without saying good-bye. Last year, just as now, he had worn an unbuttoned black frock-coat and shabby canvas trousers frayed at the bottoms. His shirt was unironed. He looked rather frowsty, by and large. Very lean, with big eyes and long, thin fingers, he was bearded and swarthy. His mother had long since died. He treated the Shumins as his kinsfolk, feeling completely at home with them. The room in which he stayed was called Sasha's.

While standing in the porch he spotted Nadya and went up to her.

'Isn't this nice?' he asked, standing near her and not sitting down. 'I do feel much stronger after a week here.'

'That's all very well, but you'll run away, won't you Sasha? You're sure to. You should stay on till autumn.'

'Yes, I expect it will come to that. I dare say I'll stay till September. I like it here, it's marvellous.'

He laughed for no reason and sat down by her side.

'I've been sitting looking at Mother,' said Nadya. 'She seems so young from here. And young she actually is. Mother does have her foibles, of course, but she is someone rather special.'

'Yes, she's a good sort,' Sasha agreed. 'Everyone thinks his mother's someone special: look at various authors' memoirs. In her own way,' he went on after a moment's thought, 'your mother's a very kind and charming woman, of course, but—I happened to go into the kitchen early this morning and four of your servants were asleep on the bare floor. They have no beds or bedding: only rags, stink, bugs, filth, cockroaches. That's treating people like pigs! Nothing's changed in twenty years, nothing at all. Never mind your grandmother, now—she can't help it. But your mother's still young, you know, isn't she? She does speak French, she acts in private theatricals. Fancy living in such filth!'

'This is boring,' sighed Nadya with a sudden laugh. '*My* mother . . . filthy!'

They were silent for a while. Then Sasha spoke, his large eyes unwinking—spoke convincingly in a quiet, pleasant, deep voice which soon tired with use and began to sound rough.

'How you people can just do nothing . . . that's what amazes me!' He shrugged his shoulders. 'You and your mother do absolutely nothing. It may sound funny, but I feel as if I was in some Turkish or Persian harem, I honestly do! It does seem rather barbarous if you're not used to it. Your fiancé Andrew, your grandmother . . . they're both idle. What in heaven's name are you all recovering from?'

'My fiancé isn't idle,' said Nadya. 'But what it is he does I just can't make out.'

'He does nothing. He *is* a very nice man indeed, granted. Oh, he's bright enough too. The thing is, though, no one in Russia needs such people.'

Nadya had heard all this last year. That Sasha was incapable of thinking in any other way she knew. It was all a joke, really, but somehow her spirits suddenly drooped—she felt bored and cold.

Again a cry was heard from the kitchen. 'Go on, I tell you, Old Fuss-pot's asking for you.'

There was a resounding crash—some plates must have fallen on the floor.

'Oh, really!' laughed Sasha.

Both stood up and made for the house. Near the porch, with two lamps burning and light coming from the hall, Sasha looked very thin and exhausted, somehow, as though he had recently suffered from an illness which had also made his eyes seem so large.

Nadya paused. 'Excuse my asking, Sasha, but have you been drinking in your room?'

'No, I haven't, honestly—not a drop. Not one blessed drop.'

A diamond gleamed on her breast. Tall and good-looking, she stood and waited for him to say something else, looking graceful and fresh by his side— younger than her years. Then she suddenly felt sorry for him—so sorry that she just couldn't think what to say. But she had to say something, so she told him that he obviously didn't know 'my Andrew'.

'*My* Andrew! Your wasted youth . . . that's what I deplore.'

They went into the dining-room as everyone was just sitting down to supper.

'One should study in youth,' said Sasha quietly, sitting down at table with Nadya. 'Yes, yes, study one must. To St. Petersburg with you! Yes, yes,' he repeated with a laugh.

Grandmother—'Gran' to the family—a very stout, ugly, bushy-browed, bewhiskered old woman—spoke loudly: unmistakably the head of the household in her voice and manner. She owned rows of stalls in the market and this period house with its columns and garden which gave on the river, but every morning she prayed to be preserved from bankruptcy, weeping as she did so. Then there was her daughter-in-law Nina—Nadya's mother: a fair-haired, tightly corseted woman sporting a pince-nez and diamonds on every finger. There was old Father Andrew—thin, toothless, looking poised to tell a very funny story. And there was his son: Andrew Junior, Nadya's thirty-three-year-old fiancé—stout, handsome, curly-haired, looking like a musician or artist. All three were discussing hypnotism. Also at the table were two lady guests and a deacon.

'How much milk did you drink this morning, Sasha?' asked Grandmother loudly.

'About five glasses,' Sasha replied.

'One week in my house and you'll be well again. But you must eat more— just look at you,' sighed Gran. 'Dreadful you look. Good grief—a regular Prodigal Son, I call you.'

'He wasted his substance with riotous living,' said Father Andrew slowly, with laughter in his eyes. 'He filled his belly with the husks that the swine did eat.'

'I'm so fond of my old man,' said Andrew, touching his father's shoulder. 'A wonderful old chap, he is—such a dear old boy.'

No one spoke. Then Sasha suddenly laughed and pressed a napkin to his mouth to stop himself exploding with mirth.

'Our Prodigal Son is always laughing,' said Grandmother, looking at Sasha affectionately and laughing herself. 'You *are* funny, confound you.'

'So you believe in hypnotism, do you?' Father Andrew asked Nina.

'The fact is, I once spent a long time studying hypnotism,' Nina answered, assuming an earnest—not to say severe—expression. 'That I believe in it I cannot, of course, asseverate. But that many things in Nature are mysterious and incomprehensible I must own.'

'I quite agree—while adding, however, that religion does materially diminish the bounds of the Unknown.'

A large, exceedingly plump turkey was served. Father Andrew and Nina went on talking. Diamonds sparkled on Nina's fingers, after which tears sparkled in her eyes. She was excited.

'I don't dare argue with you,' she said. 'But there are plenty of insoluble problems in life, grant me that.'

'Not one, I venture to assure you.'

Grandmother sighed. 'I can't understand a word you say,' she loudly observed.

After supper Andrew played the violin, accompanied by Nina on the piano. Ten years ago he had taken an arts degree, but he had never done a job and had no fixed occupation apart from an occasional appearance at charity concerts. They called him a 'musician' in town.

Andrew played while everyone listened in silence. The samovar quietly bubbled on the table, but only Sasha drank tea. Then, after twelve o'clock had struck, a violin string suddenly snapped. They all laughed, bestirred themselves and began to say good night. Stirred into melancholy by the music, young Andrew put his overcoat on in the hall, and then kissed both Nadya's hands, wanting to embrace her and say how much he loved her. But his father was in the hall and a maid came in.

'See you tomorrow,' said the young man.

Nadya brushed past Sasha and wished him good night.

'One must study in youth,' he said. 'Yes—to St. Petersburg with you!'

She went upstairs where she and her mother both had their rooms, Grandmother occupying the lower floor.

Down in the dining-room they had started putting out the lights, but Sasha sat on drinking his tea. He always spent a long time over his tea, Moscow fashion, drinking seven glasses at a sitting. Long after Nadya had undressed and gone to bed she could hear the servants clearing away downstairs and Gran's angry voice. In the end all was quiet except for the occasional deep cough proceeding from Sasha's room.

II

It must have been about two o'clock when Nadya woke. Dawn was breaking, and a watchman was making his banging noises somewhere far away. She wasn't sleepy. It was uncomfortable lying there: too soft, with the bed creaking at her slightest movement. As always on past May nights, she sat up in bed, put her arms round her knees, leant her head on them and thought, thought, thought.

Monotonous, futile, obsessive thoughts they were, the same as those of the night before: about Andrew paying his addresses and proposing—and that at a time when she was beginning to think she was an old maid, when she'd begun to lose hope, for she *was* twenty-three now, wasn't she? She had accepted him and had come to appreciate this handsome, kind, intelligent man. But now that the wedding was less than a month away she felt vaguely scared and troubled. If only the ceremony had been put off for some reason till autumn, or even till winter, she would have had time to think things over—might even have fallen more in love with her fiancé, perhaps.

A desultory clicking thud was heard: that watchman again.

Through the large old-fashioned window she could see the garden and distant bushes of burgeoning lilac beyond it—drowsy and lifeless in the cold. A thick white mist slowly bore down on that lilac, wanting to submerge it. On far-away trees, by the river, tired rooks cawed.

'God, why am I so depressed?'

Perhaps—who knows—every young girl felt like this before her wedding. Or was it Sasha's influence? He was always running down marriage and talking about Andrew in that off-hand way—could that be it? But Sasha had been on and on about all this for several years now, hadn't he? His talk sounded so eccentric and peculiar. If she wasn't bored with him yet the reason might be that she rather pitied him: so much that it brought tears to her eyes.

The watchman had long stopped his din. Birds started singing beneath the window and in the garden the mist vanished, everything was a-glow and a-gleam. Soon the whole garden, warmed and caressed by the sun, came to life, with dew-drops glittering on the leaves like diamonds. That old garden . . . it seemed so fresh this morning, so free and healthy.

But Nadya still sat up in bed worrying, as if she was ill. Strange thoughts went through her mind. Everything was, it seemed, perfectly all right. Wasn't there something missing, though—something crucial which remained unsaid, undone, unprepared? But what precisely? She feared, she shunned the thought.

Downstairs Gran was already awake. There was a sound like the babbling of a brook down there—the old woman was nagging the servants as usual. Sasha was coughing his deep cough. Nadya heard the servants putting on the samovar and moving chairs downstairs. An out-of-breath maid dashed past

Nadya's room calling down some enraged and tearful imprecation on 'that wretched old Fuss-pot'.

Nadya slowly washed, dressed and went down to breakfast. Ever since leaving school she had spent the mornings after breakfast in total idleness, not knowing what to do. The hours seemed to pass slowly, but why did the days and years seem to flash by in such rapid sequence, disappearing without trace?

Here was Nina, her mother—in a loose blouse, tears in her eyes—carrying the glass of mineral water which she drank each morning to cure some mysterious disease. Nina was fascinated by the mystery of life after death, she practised spiritualism and homoeopathy, she read books all day—even at meals—she was a keen theatre-goer and concert-goer, she attended charity balls. She was always arguing about whether the stage did any good. She actually appeared in a performance herself on one occasion, after which she breathed heavily all through the night and following day. She liked discussing the doubts which assailed her.

'Apathy . . . it will be the ruin of us,' she was always saying.

To these words Nadya attributed a mysterious hidden meaning. The daughter loved her mother—rating her as someone special, seeing in her tears a quality significant, enigmatic and melancholy.

Nadya kissed her mother on the cheek and fell in by her side.

'Why am I so miserable, Mother darling?' she asked a little later, tears showing in her eyes. 'It must be because I never do anything.'

'But how *can* one do anything in this place?' the mother asked heatedly. 'Your charming grandmother has taken charge of every blessed thing—I don't even dare pour the tea. I know you're bored with nothing to do. But you'll never change Grandmother, you know.'

Nadya put her arms round her mother as they strolled along without speaking.

'How about sketching?' asked Nina. 'Or take up embroidery.'

'Embroidery? Sketching? What's the point?'

Her mother did not answer, and Nadya—feeling rather annoyed—suddenly burst into tears.

'Oh, do forgive me, Mother,' she said. 'I'm just in a bad mood today.'

They were called to lunch at two. As it was a Wednesday—a Church fast—Grandmother was served with beetroot soup, the smell of which depressed them from then until evening. As an invalid Nina was given beef tea, while Sasha and Nadya had gherkin soup with meat in it. Sasha was in a bad mood. To tease Grandmother he spoke of rumours that the local market was to be shut down, with the result that its buildings—which included Grandmother's stalls—would none of them be needed any more.

'We're to be a county town, they say.'

'I know you're only joking,' said Grandmother. 'But one thing's certain—

things are going from bad to worse. One fine day I'll come a cropper over my shops if I don't mind out.'

'Yes, they want to make a metropolis out of you,' Sasha goaded her. 'You haven't one shop where they don't give short measure—not one official who doesn't play cards and knock back his vodka day in day out. The streets are nothing but mud, filth, stink. Does anyone in your town ever repay a loan? If someone borrows a book you'll never get it back, you can bank on that! And these gentry in their club, at their name-day parties and things ... hark at them! All they talk about is pessimism and having no joy or pleasure in life. B-b-bastards!'

'How he does go on!' Grandmother sighed. 'But what he's talking about he has no idea.'

She saw Sasha as a kind, intelligent but wayward lad, and was very fond of him. She suspected him of drinking too much in Moscow—of playing cards and of bad behaviour in general. Whatever he said, it always made her sigh.

'This town's dead, and so are the people in it,' Sasha went on. 'If the earth swallowed it up it would only rate three lines in the newspapers. No one would care. It's a backward town, this is. "Slow to harness, quick to drive" ... such, according to Bismarck, is the Russian national character. But this fair city hasn't even got to the harnessing stage, quite frankly—let alone being ready to drive!'

'Ours *is* a provincial town, very true,' said Nina, looking extremely earnest and displaying the diamonds on all her fingers. 'But it does have forty-seven thousand inhabitants according to the latest census, it has gas lighting and a theatre. I'm very fond of our town, frankly—actually, I love it.'

'Well, I shan't start loving it until I see it in ruins.'

'Don't talk nonsense, darling, please!' There were tears in Nadya's voice. 'Do talk like a human being.'

Having finished his gherkin broth, Sasha moved on to the beetroot soup to annoy Grandmother. His jokes all had some laboured moral and fell flat. It was particularly boring when he introduced a witticism by uplifting his long, wasted, corpse-like fingers, and when you noticed how ill he was—that he wasn't long for this world, perhaps. He made a disagreeable spectacle at times, especially when he told a funny story and roared with laughter till he cried, but that laughter gradually infected all the others and made them chuckle too.

'Oh, if you would only listen to me, dear girl, if only you'd go away and study,' began Sasha when Grandmother and Nina had gone to their rooms after lunch. 'Educated, dedicated people ... they're the interesting ones, we don't need any other kind. The rest of them are just a mob like any other mob throughout the ages: an undifferentiated lump. It's only the others who have a real life which distinguishes them from the animals. A time will come when their name shall be legion. Bit by bit, you'll find, there won't be one stone left on another in your town. The place will turn topsy-turvy, change as if by magic. Perhaps—who knows?—there will be splendid great mansions, marvellous gardens and wonderful people. The poor, the sick, the miserable . . . they won't exist any more because there's no room for them in a civilized environment. Not that any of that matters. The point is, there will be no rabble as it exists today. Do leave this place, Nadya darling. Do show them all that this stagnant, drab, reprehensible existence disgusts you. Show your own self!'

'I can't. I'm getting married.'

'Oh, really! What nonsense! However successful or unsuccessful your studies may be, you'll see a different way of life anyway, you will learn a thing or two, and you will make one or two discoveries.'

Andrew arrived late in the afternoon and played his violin for hours. Never a talkative man, he perhaps liked this fiddling because it gave him an excuse to say nothing. He started leaving for home at about half-past ten, and already had his overcoat on when he embraced Nadya, greedily kissing her face, shoulders, hands.

There was no one in the hall apart from him and Nadya.

'My dear, my darling, my beautiful one,' he muttered. 'If you only realized how happy I am. I'm in a sort of mad ecstasy.'

But it sounded like something she had heard long, long ago or read about somewhere.

He said good-bye and left in the end. Sasha sat at the dining-room table drinking tea and balancing the saucer on his five long fingers. Gran played patience, Nina read. The icon-lamp sputtered, all was quiet and—it seemed—well.

Nadya went to her room, lay in bed and fell asleep at once. But she woke early, as on the previous night with the first glimmer of dawn. She wasn't sleepy, she felt troubled and depressed. She sat with her head on her knees thinking about her fiancé, about falling in love with him, about her wedding. She remembered Nina crying in the mornings, remembered how that crying led to spasms in her arms and legs. Then Nadya suddenly felt rather annoyed. Why had she always regarded her mother's weeping as something special and out of the ordinary? She had no idea. And why, indeed, had she even seen in it some lofty, enigmatic quality beyond her comprehension?

Sasha couldn't sleep either—she heard him coughing down below. Now, there's a man with firm convictions and firm principles, thought Nadya. No dreamer, he—he has absolute confidence in the justice of everything he says. He does repeat himself, and he is becoming a tiresome bore, obviously. And yet there was something so fine, so marvellous, so bewitching about his talk that the very thought of going away and studying flooded her, body and soul, with joy and hope.

'But it's far, far better not to think about it, I mustn't,' she whispered.

The watchman's clicking thuds echoed from somewhere far away.

III

Sasha seemed to have cheered up and recovered, but in mid-June he suddenly felt bored and prepared to leave for Moscow.

'I can't stand this town,' said he gloomily. 'No water supply! No drains! It's not a very nice place to eat your meals—that kitchen's filthy beyond description. Above all, I'm bored, I must work.'

He frowned squeamishly and began seeing dirt everywhere.

'Not so fast, Prodigal Son,' Grandmother urged him, in a whisper for some reason. 'The wedding's on the seventh.'

'I don't care.'

'But weren't you going to stay till September?'

'Well, I don't want to now, I have work to do.'

The summer had turned out damp and cold, the trees were sodden, everything in the garden looked dejected and uninviting—it really did make you feel like working. All over the house, upstairs and downstairs, strange women's voices sounded, and the sewing-machine rattled away in Grandmother's room. Boxes, crates and bundles were being constantly fetched from the shops. Exhausted and keyed up, Grandmother told everyone that she had lost her memory.

Nadya's trousseau was hurriedly made up. There were no fewer than six fur coats and the cheapest of them was costing seven hundred roubles, said Gran. All this pre-wedding fuss ... it irritated Sasha. He sat fuming in his room. Still, they did persuade him to stay on—he had promised not to leave before the first of July.

Time passed quickly. After lunch on St. Peter's Day, Andrew took Nadya to Moscow Street for another look at the house which had been rented and made ready for the young couple some time ago. It was of two storeys, but so far only the upper floor had been decorated. The drawing room had a gleaming floor painted to look like parquet, Viennese chairs, a grand piano and a violin-stand, not a single rug and a feeling of emptiness. There was a smell of paint. On the wall hung a large gilt-framed painting of a naked lady with a broken-handled mauve vase by her side.

'Exquisite!' said Andrew, standing silently in front of it for a minute out of respect. 'A Shishmachevsky!'

Then came a parlour with a round table, a sofa and arm-chairs upholstered in bright blue. Above the sofa hung a large photograph of Father Andrew complete with purple hat and decorations. They entered a dining-room with a sideboard, and then the bedroom. Here two beds stood side by side in the murk, together with a wash-basin and a large shiny-framed mirror. It looked as though that room had been furnished with the idea that nothing either would, or possibly could, ever go wrong in the place. Andrew led Nadya through the house, clutching her waist all the time. But she felt weak and guilty, she hated all these rooms, these beds, these arm-chairs. And that naked lady made her feel sick.

She was no longer in love with Andrew, that was obvious—perhaps she had never loved him. But how she could say it, who she could say it to, what the point would be ... that she neither did nor could understand, though she thought about it all day and night.

Andrew held her by the waist, he spoke so affectionately and modestly, he was so happy striding about these rooms, whereas she could see nothing in all this but sheer complacency: horrible, mindless, stupid smugness. All she noticed about her future husband were his very soft hands with stubby fingers and the new, well-pressed trousers which he wore.

Every minute she was on the point of running away, sobbing or throwing herself out of a window. Andrew took her to the bathroom, reached for a tap in the wall—and suddenly water flowed.

'How about that!' he laughed. 'I had a two-hundred-gallon tank put in the loft, so we shall have water now, you and I. Pretty cunning, eh?'

They walked round the yard, then into the street and took a cab. It looked like rain, dust blew about the streets.

'Aren't you cold?' asked Andrew, squinting in the dust.

She said nothing.

'Remember yesterday—Sasha criticizing me for never doing anything?' he asked after a brief pause. 'It was less of a criticism than just a hint, though. Well, he's right, absolutely right! I don't do anything, I can't. Now, why is that, my dear? The mere thought of ever sticking a cockade on my cap and going into government service ... why does it so repel me? Why am I so put off when I see a lawyer, a Latin master, a county councillor? Oh, Russia, Russia—what a lot of useless loafers you do support, my poor long-suffering motherland!'

He had even built a theory round his own idleness, seeing it as a sign of the times.

Then he went on to say that 'when we're married, my dear girl—we'll live in the country together. We're going to work! We'll buy a small plot of land with a garden and river, we shall toil, we shall watch the world go by. Now, won't that be nice?'

He took off his hat and his hair streamed in the wind.

'God, God, I want to go home!' she thought as she listened.

They had nearly reached the house when they overtook Father Andrew.

'Ah, there's Father,' rejoiced Andrew Junior with a wave of the hat. 'I'm so fond of my old man, honestly,' he said, paying the cabby. 'A wonderful chap he is, such a dear old boy.'

He loved his father and was always saying how wonderful he was. This puzzled Nadya. That everyone in town rated Father Andrew as a very rich, mean, cunning fellow, that no one had a good word to say for him ... could the son really fail to realize these things? Didn't he know that his father never paid cab drivers—something which was quite the talk of the town? No, he knew nothing!

As Nadya went into the house she felt cross and unwell. There would be guests to entertain all evening, she reflected. She must chat, smile, listen to music, talk of nothing but her wedding.

Grandmother, magnificently dignified in her silk dress, and haughty—as she always seemed with visitors—sat by the samovar. Only now, oddly enough, did Nadya realize as she looked at the old lady that it was her grandmother whom everyone in the house called Old Fuss-pot.

Father Andrew came in.

'I have the pleasure and blissful gratification of seeing you in good health,' he told Grandmother—seriously or in jest, it was hard to tell which.

IV

The wind beat on shutters and roof, there was a whistling. A grim, invisible something chanted piteously, or rushed and roared round the garden. It was turned midnight, and everyone in the house had gone to bed, but no one could sleep, and Nadya had an impression of someone playing a violin downstairs or of Father Andrew laughing. There was a loud bang in a distant part of the house —and it struck her that one of the upstairs shutters must have snapped off. A minute later steps were heard. In came Nina in her nightgown, with a candle, and asked Nadya what 'that bang' was.

'I don't know.'

'It sounded like one of the iron sheets falling off the roof. What a storm, I'm quite frightened.'

Mother—big-eyed, pale, with her hair in a single plait, with her nervous smile—looked older, uglier, shorter on this stormy night. Nadya remembered how recently she had thought of her mother as someone rather special. How proudly she had listened to her mother's words, whereas now she simply couldn't recall those words—all that came to mind was so feeble and futile.

Nadya sat up in bed, suddenly clutched her hair and burst into tears.

'Mother, Mother,' she said quietly, under her breath. 'Save me, darling, Mother, save me! Please, I beseech you, let me leave this place! Please!'

'What's that?' Nina asked, not understanding, and sat down on the bed. 'Where is it you want to go?'

Nadya wept, couldn't utter one word.

'Let me leave this town!' she went on in a whisper, fearing to look at her mother. 'There can't be any wedding—there shan't be. I don't love that man, I can't talk about him.' She sobbed.

Nina embraced Nadya and began kissing her.

'No, no, no darling,' she said quickly and burst into tears herself.

'Do calm yourself. You're just upset—it will pass. These things happen. Go to sleep.'

'I can't sleep, Mother. I'm so depressed, did you but know it. Do, do, for God's sake let me go.'

Nina stood up and took her candle.

'How you torment me, Nadya!' she gulped. 'You'll be the death of me, I tell you, that you will.'

She quickly left the room.

'Yes,' said Nina after a pause. 'You were a child, just a little girl not so long ago—and now you're engaged to be married. It's a law of Nature, this is: the transmutation of matter. You'll be a mother yourself before you know where you are—and you'll have a naughty little daughter just like mine. Shall I live to see that day? I doubt it. I shall be dead, you see: from my aneurism.'

Nadya turned towards the wall and made no reply, while Nina just sat there.

'Why don't you speak?' she asked.

After a minute she stood up.

'All right then, so you don't want to talk to me.' She sounded insulted. 'God, I only wish I could hurry up and die! And die I shall, I tell you, that I shall.'

She burst into tears and went to her room. Nadya got out of bed and followed her. On reaching her room, Nina had quickly got into bed and covered herself with a light-blue quilt.

'Do listen, Mother,' said Nadya, kissing her hands. 'I'll explain everything— but do, for God's sake, listen.' She spoke rapidly without even knowing what she was saying. 'I don't—I can't, I can't, I really can't—love Andrew, so get that into your head. All right, I did once find him attractive. But now my eyes are open. Oh, I see through *him* all right. Lord, he's not all that bright, you know, Mother. God, he's so stupid, Mother—can't you see that?'

Nina sat up abruptly, her bare feet thudding on to the floor.

'You and your grandmother are torturing me,' she said, flaring up. 'I want a bit of life—yes, life!' she repeated, twice striking her chest with her fist. 'So give me my freedom. I'm still young, and you two have made an old woman out of me!'

She burst into tears and curled up under the quilt, seeming oh so small and pathetic. Nadya went to her room, dressed, and sat by the window to wait for morning. Someone seemed to be banging on the shutters and whistling.

In the morning Grandmother complained that the wind had blown all the apples off in the orchard during the night and had broken an old plum-tree. No longer was that wind roaring as it had in the night, but everyone complained of the cold. It was raining: a grey, dim, cheerless morning, dark enough for the lamps. After breakfast Nadya went to Sasha's room, knelt down without a word in the corner by his arm-chair and laid her head on it.

Sasha asked what the matter was.

'It's too much,' she said and sobbed quietly, her shoulders shaking. 'How I could live here before I don't understand, I simply don't.' She gazed at Sasha with tearful eyes, wringing her hands. 'Oh God, I'm going out of my mind, I'm at the end of my tether.'

She leant her head on the arm-chair and went on, trying to speak quietly so as not to be heard in the dining-room.

'I despise the man I'm engaged to, I despise myself, I despise Grandmother, I despise Mother. I'm finished!'

'Well, that's all right then, isn't it?' said Sasha quietly, and laughed. 'Now, don't cry or they'll hear you and interrupt us. Very well, you leave with me tomorrow. I'll take you to Moscow, and you can go on to St. Petersburg on your own. Splendid!'

Sasha laughed again, gleefully doing a sort of tap-dance in his slippers.

'Splendid!' he repeated, rubbing his hands. 'Tomorrow you come to the station to see me off, then you get in the train and that will be that! I'll also take your luggage and get you your ticket—you can set your mind at rest. Have you your identity documents?'

'Yes,' she smiled and again burst into tears. 'I've had them for ages.'

'Now, I have something serious to say.' He frowned. 'I'm convinced, I profoundly believe, that Russia needs only two kinds of people: the dedicated and the educated. That is my deeply held faith, and I conceive it my duty to convert such as you to it. This is a crude and ignorant epoch, so we must side with the minority. You'll have no regrets, I swear—no second thoughts. You'll even get married, you'll find a splendid husband.' He laughed again. 'Just go away and study—then let your destiny take over. Do we leave tomorrow, then?'

'Yes, yes, for God's sake yes!'

Nadya felt that she was greatly agitated, that she had never been so depressed before, that she was faced with misery and agony of mind from now till the moment of her departure. But no sooner had she gone up to her room and lain down than she immediately dropped off and slept soundly—with tears in her eyes and a smile on her face—right up to evening.

V

It was morning. A cab had been sent for. Nadya went upstairs in hat and coat for one more look at her mother and everything that had been home. She stood in her own room near the still warm bed, looked about her, then went softly to her mother's room. Nina was asleep and it was quiet, very quiet in the room. Nadya kissed her mother, patted her hair, stood for a couple of minutes. Then she started back downstairs.

'Now, why don't I cry?' she wondered.

Then she went downstairs.

It was raining hard. The cabby had put the top up and stood by the porch, wet through.

'There's no room for you, Nadya,' said Grandmother as the servants began loading the luggage. 'You should stay at home—goodness me, what rain!'

Nadya wanted to speak, but couldn't. Sasha said something to Grandmother who stood tearfully in the doorway, making the sign of the cross over the traveller. He helped Nadya in, covered her legs with a rug and settled down by her side.

'Good luck and God bless you,' Grandmother shouted. 'Now, you be sure you don't start drinking in Moscow, Sasha darling.'

'But I don't drink, Gran.'

'No one can help drinking in Moscow. Heaven protect you.'

They left.

'Confound this weather.' said Sasha.

Only now did Nadya start weeping. Now she realized that she was definitely leaving—she still hadn't believed it when saying good-bye to Grandmother and looking at Mother. Farewell, old town! Everything suddenly came back to her: Andrew, his father, the new house, that naked lady with vase—but none of it scared or terrified her any longer, it was all so inoffensively trivial and seemed to be receding further and further into the past.

They got into their carriage, the train started, and all her past life—which had once loomed so large and serious—now shrank into the compass of a man's hand, and a vast, broad future unfurled before her . . . a future hitherto barely conceivable. Rain drummed on the carriage windows and nothing was seen but green fields with glimpses of telegraph-posts and birds sitting on the wires. She suddenly caught her breath out of sheer joy: remembered that she was on her way to freedom, that she was going to study—it was just like running away to join the Cossacks in the old days. She laughed and wept, she knelt and prayed.

Three stations down the line they sent a telegram home. Then Sasha drank tea and spoke non-stop during the rest of the journey.

'One must work,' said he. 'Whether it's Man's duty to achieve anything or not I have no idea, generally speaking. But that he must work to avoid being a parasite who exploits others . . . that's crystal clear to me.'

He kept on and on like this, which was boring. But when he had finished his tea and was clearing away the glasses he had some amusing ideas, and that made things more cheerful.

In Moscow next day Sasha quarrelled with a cab-driver near the station and had a violent bout of coughing. For a long time that cough 'had him beat', as the saying is, and Nadya realized that, far from recovering, he was as ill as ever. He stayed in Moscow while Nadya went on to St. Petersburg.

VI

Nadya received telegrams and letters every day in St. Petersburg. Money arrived and a parcel of clothes. Nina paid her a visit in October. She looked guilty and nervous, as if expecting Nadya to be rude to her or ask what she was doing here.

'I'd never been in St. Petersburg before. What a nice town!' It was as if she wished to make it clear that the worst and most terrible part of the ordeal was over, and that it was better not to talk about such things.

Smiling guiltily, looking overwrought and somewhat unwashed, she finished her tea and explained what had happened on the morning in question: how they had waited until lunch time without worrying, but had realized exactly what had happened when the telegram came. Grandmother had collapsed and lain motionless for three days, just groaning, after which she had prayed and wept all the time, lifting up her hands—even the maids had laughed to see her. Since then she had looked all peaky, somehow. She had quietened down and started pronouncing words incorrectly, saying things like 'wash' instead of 'watch'.

'She isn't angry with you, she's fonder of you than ever,' Nina said. 'She keeps going to your room and making the sign of the cross over walls and bed. Now, I was dumbfounded, of course—felt so low at the time that I couldn't bear to see anyone. It was my own fault, after all—it was I insulted you that night, I realized that later and I kept praying that God would punish me and take away every single thing I had. Oh, I can't tell you what it was like, even now—no one should suffer like that!'

She had eyes for nothing but Nadya. She didn't eat much lunch, and she couldn't sleep at night, but just lay there quietly.

After spending five days in this way she left.

Sasha sent letters addressed to SAINT (spelt in full) PETERSBURG in handwriting so cheerful that it seemed to dance. Autumn passed, then winter. Nadya was very homesick, now, she thought of Mother and Grandmother every day—thought of her own room and sleeping in her own bed. The letters which reached her from home were gentle and kind, and all seemed to have been forgiven and forgotten. She set off after her examinations at the beginning of May, finding it odd to think that she was on her way home and had nothing to hide from anyone. In Moscow she saw Sasha. He hadn't changed since last summer. He still had that beard and dishevelled hair, still wore the same frock-coat and canvas trousers, but he looked bedraggled and worn out, he had aged, he was thinner, he kept coughing.

'Aha—someone from *Saint* Petersburg!' said he cheerfully. He was delighted to see her. 'Well, what's the news from that remarkable and sainted capital?'

They sat and talked, then lunched in a restaurant. He ate and spoke, coughing all the time, while she couldn't eat but just looked at him in terror—scared of him collapsing and dying here in the restaurant.

'Sasha, dear,' she said, placing her hand on his. 'You *are* ill, as you know perfectly well yourself.'

'I'm not, I'm well.'

'Come home with me. I'll look after you—nurse you as a good friend, as a sister'—she burst into tears—'as one who's beholden—infinitely grateful—to you. Do come with me.'

'God forbid,' laughed Sasha. 'I've seen enough of that town with its provincial bores and its Andrews, I can tell you that! No, thank you very much—I leave for the Volga tomorrow.'

'Do, do come with me,' she besought him—her face wet with tears, which fell on to her plate. 'Please.'

'No, Nadya, don't ask me—your town bores me so. Besides, I'm well, I've nothing to complain of. I leave for the Volga tomorrow with a young fellow. He's a good enough chap—the only snag is, he's from *Saint* Petersburg. You tell him you're hungry, say, or deeply insulted, or oppressed by tyranny, you tell him we're all degenerating . . . and he answers with talk of Dostoyevsky's Grand Inquisitor and Father Zosima. This stuff about "mystical moods" and "zig-zagging into the future" . . . it comes from being afraid to answer questions straight out. Giving a straight answer is a terrifying thing, isn't it? It's the confounding of languages in the Tower of Babel all over again. You ask someone for an axe and he tells you to go to blazes!'

'Listen, Sasha, I'm going to repeat myself. I owe you so much, and I really would like to take you away from here and talk to you, I'd like to give you a gentler, more broad-minded attitude towards life and people. I do so want you to have peace of mind.'

'Well, I'm not going. Your place bores me.'

He paid the bill in the restaurant. 'I earn three hundred roubles a month now.' He laughed and slapped his wallet. 'What do you say to that?'

He saw her to the station, treated her to tea and apples. When the train started he smiled and waved his handkerchief, the very shape of his legs indicating that he was extremely ill and not long for this world.

It was noon when Nadya reached her native town. As she was driven home from the station the streets seemed very wide, the houses small and squat. There was no one about except for the piano tuner Schwabe in his brown overcoat. A skinny black dog munched grass. Grandmother—a really old woman now, as stout and ugly as ever—flung her arms round Nadya, pressed her face against the girl's shoulder and cried for some time, unable to break away. Nina looked ten years older. She gazed at her daughter.

'Darling, darling, darling!' she kept saying.

Then all three sat silently weeping. That the past was utterly lost and gone for ever, Grandmother and Mother both obviously sensed. Their social position, their former prestige, their right to entertain guests . . . all were gone. It was as if the police had suddenly raided and searched their house at night, and the head of the household had turned out to be an embezzler and forger.

Nadya went upstairs and saw the same old bed, the same old windows with their unpretentious white curtains, and through those windows the same old garden: now cheerful, noisy, drenched with sunlight. She touched the bed, sat by her table and wept.

Then they had lunch. That night Nadya went to bed and pulled the blankets over her, smiling all the time. She felt so good! Would that watchman bang in the night? Then Nina came into her room.

They said nothing for a while.

'Well, how are things, Nadya?' asked Nina. 'Happy, are you? Very happy?'

'Yes, Mother. When I started my course I naturally thought I'd achieved everything—attained my heart's desire. But when I'd been around a bit and learnt a little, new perspectives opened before me—followed by other, yet newer, yet broader horizons. My toils and cares . . . no limit is, or ever will be, set to them, it seems.'

Nina stood up and made the sign of the cross over Nadya and the windows. 'I've taken up religion, you see. And I don't read those books any more, you know.'

'Why not?'

'I don't really know—I can't read any more. My life is already over, as I see it. Now you sleep, God bless you.'

She went out.

The watchman's tapping sounded in the night.

Next evening Andrew Junior came and played his violin for hours, looking as if he had no other function in life but fiddling.

'Father Andrew hasn't been to see us, though,' whispered Grandmother. 'He hasn't been since that time.'

May passed, June began.

Nadya had grown used to being at home. Grandmother's fussings over the samovar, her tear-stained face, her deep sighs, Andrew Junior, the evening fiddlings . . . they became boring. How anyone could lounge around all day doing nothing she failed to understand. It depressed her. She strolled in the garden, looked at other houses through windows, looked at the orchard. The whole town was so outmoded and antiquated, she felt. Was it awaiting its own end? Or expecting something fresh and original to begin? Oh, if it *would* but hurry up and begin . . . that brave new world which you can look straight in the eyes, knowing that you're in the right. Oh, to be cheerful and free! A time would surely come when Grandmother's house—so arranged, now, that four servants are forced to share a single room . . . a time would surely come when that house would fade away, disintegrate and give way to a new house in which the old one would be forgotten—no one would have time for memories of it.

Grandmother beckoned Nadya. 'My dear, darling little granddaughter,' she said with an ingratiating, pseudo-jocular smile. 'Don't desert me and your mother! You do what you want, you live as you like—only don't abandon us completely!'

She burst into tears and Nadya didn't know what to answer.

'Nowadays the kitchen-maids call me Old Fuss-pot to my face. I don't care, though—I don't mind, confound them. I'm old, I'll soon be dead. Do set an old woman's mind at rest, darling.' Grandmother wept. 'Don't refuse Andrew. Wait a while, you may change your mind. He says it's all right with him, he doesn't mind waiting—he told me so yesterday, darling. He will forgive everything. But do set my mind at rest.'

'Oh, why talk about it, Grandmother?' asked Nadya, and went up to her room.

When she was getting into bed Nina came into her room and sat on the bed as usual for a little chat before saying good night.

'Look here, Nadya,' said she. 'There's one thing I don't understand, I'm sorry. I know I'm only a provincial and I've never been abroad. Still, I do have an idea or two, I do keep in touch with things. And what puzzles me is how you can live in a small room in St. Petersburg in the middle of strangers, meeting strangers every day—and with *men* in the rooms next to you! If it was anything else I wouldn't mind, Nadya. But that I can't accept.'

A letter came from Sasha in Saratov. In his sprightly, smiling hand he wrote that his Volga trip had been a complete success, that he had contracted some minor ailment in Saratov—a cough, fever and other trivialities. He was now in bed in an hotel, but would return to Moscow in a week when he felt better. Instead of a signature he had drawn a smiling face with shaggy beard and long nose. It was inscribed THIS IS ME.

Three mornings later Nadya went downstairs and found Grandmother in a terrible pother. She was crying so much that she couldn't say a word. On her lap was a telegram. Nadya guessed what was in it and asked no questions. Saddened, she paced the room for a while before taking and reading that telegram. It was just as she thought: Alexander Timofeyevich or Sasha for short had perished of tuberculosis in Saratov on the previous evening. She imagined Sasha lying there dead with that kind, sly smile on his face.

'Lord, rest his soul,' their servants said.

She walked up and down in Sasha's room.

Grandmother, Nina and the maids went to church to arrange a memorial service while Nadya continued to pace the house, musing. She suddenly felt bored, bored stiff. She couldn't stay on in this town, she felt. She was so lonely here, she was a stranger. All her past life had been ripped away as if burnt to ashes scattered in the breeze.

'Farewell, Sasha darling!' she thought.

She went up to her room to pack, and as she left next morning she took with her the prospect of a life of broad, unsullied horizons, a life of hard work.

APPENDIX XV

ALL FRIENDS TOGETHER

1. Composition
2. Text
3. Variants

1. COMPOSITION

The story was written in response to an invitation—soliciting contributions and dated 16 April 1897—from F. D. Batyushkov, editor of the Russian section of *Cosmopolis*: a magazine published in four languages. On 21 April Chekhov replied favourably, but said that he would be unable to send any contribution until the autumn. On 15 December Chekhov wrote to Batyushkov from Nice, informing him that he was 'writing a story for *Cosmopolis*, writing with difficulty, in fits and starts. I normally do write slowly and with a feeling of strain, but here—in a hotel room, at a table not my own, on a fine day when I feel the urge to go outside—writing conditions are even worse. So I can't promise you the story in under a fortnight. I'll send it by 1 January. Will you then very kindly send me proofs—I shan't hang on to them for more than a day. So you can reckon on publishing in your February issue, but no earlier. . . . In one of your letters you expressed the wish that I should send an "international" story, taking my theme from life in these parts. But I can only write such a story in Russia and in retrospect. That's the only way I can write: from memory. I've never done live portraits from nature. I need my memory to sieve the subject, leaving behind—as on a filter-paper—only what is essential and typical.'

On 3 January 1898 Chekhov dispatched the manuscript and wrote asking Batyushkov to send him proofs, 'as the story is unfinished and unpolished. It will be ready only when I've scrawled all over the proofs longways and sideways. I can only polish in proof—I never see anything in manuscript.' Proofs were dispatched to Nice on 15 January, received by Chekhov on 19 January and returned to Batyushkov on 23 January.

On 6 February 1898 Chekhov wrote a letter of complaint to A. S. Suvorin, proprietor of the newspaper *Novoye vremya* [*New Time*]: 'The other day I read on page one of *N.V.* an eye-catching advertisement for the issue of *Cosmopolis* containing my story *A Guest*. Now, firstly my title is not *A Guest*, but *All Friends Together*. And secondly, such advertisements grate on me. Besides, the story isn't all that sensational—it's the kind you churn out at the rate of one a day.'

Chekhov's *Notebooks* include the following entries bearing on *All Friends Together*:

'A plump little girl resembling a bun.' (N. I, 70/5)

'He had once encountered her husband at a whore's, since when he had ceased visiting her—it was awkward because knowledge of the husband's secret made him a participant in the betrayal.' (N. I, 79/3)

'What can one do about a man who behaves like an utter swine and then bursts into tears?' (N. I, 80/3)

'He—the husband, that is—has enjoyed, and still enjoys, success with women. They ascribe his improvidence and lack of practicality to kindness, they call him an idealist. And they (the wife and the lady doctor) can't resist being cruel to the young man in a small way by reproaching him with "your generation's quite different, George." What have generations got to do with it? Why, there's only eight or ten years difference between them, they're practically the same age.' (N. I, 80/5)

'The husband kept slobbering and calling his guest "my dear, good fellow". He knew a lady doctor who had been very clever as a little girl, but had since grown old and was lacking in perception.

'The husband's short, single-breasted jacket was buttoned up in such a way that it seemed likely to burst under the pressure of his fat chest.

'The lady doctor wears a corset and large sleeves.

'The husband's sole concern is to satisfy his animal instincts.' (N. II, 46/7)

'He is successful with women—they call him an idealist.' (N. III, 17)

2. TEXT

The present translation is made from the text in *Works*, 1944–51, vol. ix, itself based on that published in the magazine *Cosmopolis*, vol. ix, no. 2, February 1898.

There is one previous recension: a corrected fair copy of the manuscript in the author's hand, preserved in the Institute of Literature of the Academy of Sciences of the USSR (Pushkin House).

3. VARIANTS

The variants are fairly numerous, including (a comparatively small number) certain brief passages erased by Chekhov—but still legible—in the manuscript fair copy.

The only alterations of any substance involved insertions—rather than the excisions more typical of Chekhov—made at the proof stage. These insertions include the entire sequence in which parts of Nekrasov's poem *The Railway* is recited: from '*Along the railway line . . .*' (p. 232) to '*. . . will see that brave new world before we die.*'

Among the remaining insertions the most substantial are the following:

'He disliked Losev . . .' (pp. 228–9) to '. . . found his company rather off-putting.'

' "Oh, how little you know me . . ." ' (p. 239) to ' ". . . you *are* such a stupefying bore!" '

'. . . or who—had she indeed spoken of love . . .' (p. 241) to '. . . already sometimes anticipate.'

' "Please don't detain me . . ." ' (p. 242) to ' ". . . most frightfully sorry——" '

APPENDIX XVI

MANUSCRIPT FRAGMENTS

1. The Cripple
2. Poor Compensation
3. A Letter

These three fragments, none of which can be dated with certainty, consist of unfinished stories left in manuscript by Chekhov and all belonging (to judge from evidence quoted below) to the last years of his life.

1. THE CRIPPLE

The text in *Works*, 1944–51, vol. ix, on which the present translation is based, is in turn based on a manuscript, in the author's hand, preserved in the Lenin State Library of the USSR. A letter to Chekhov, dated 12 August 1900, from the journalist and editor M. O. Menshikov suggests that the story was intended for the magazine *Knizhki nedeli* [*Books of the Week*], and that it may have been written in 1900. The manuscript contains variants in the form of legible erasures, but these are not recorded here.

2. POOR COMPENSATION

The text in *Works*, 1944–51, vol. ix, on which the present translation is based, is in turn based on a manuscript in the author's hand, preserved in the Lenin State Library of the USSR. This unfinished story was probably written in 1902–3, being presumably intended by Chekhov for the magazine *Zhurnal dlya vsekh* [*Everybody's Journal*], where it was published in no. 2 of 1905 (the year following Chekhov's death) and in a form bearing signs of editing (presumably posthumous) in a hand other than Chekhov's. The numerous variants in the form of legible erasures are not recorded here.

3. A LETTER

The text in *Works*, 1944–51, vol. ix, on which the present translation is based, is itself based on a manuscript in the author's hand, preserved in the Institute of Literature of the Academy of Sciences of the USSR (Pushkin House) in Leningrad. The story was evidently intended for the magazine *Zhurnal dlya vsekh*

[*Everybody's Journal*]. It would, indeed, have appeared there posthumously late in 1906—had the periodical not ceased publication in September of that year. It was presumably written in 1902–3.

The remarks made at the beginning of *A Letter* (about the work of an unnamed author) strongly resemble a comment made by Chekhov on Tolstoy, as recorded in the memoirs of S. N. Shchukin: 'Have you noticed Tolstoy's language? Its huge periods, its sentences piled one on top of the other? This is no accident or defect, believe me. It is art, and is the result of effort. These periods produce the impression of strength' (W., ix, 703).

It was probably with reference to *A Letter* that Chekhov informed his wife (on 12 December 1902) that he was writing a story which would 'even put Leonid Andreyev's nose out of joint'. The mention, in *A Letter*, of two 'brothers'—one mad, the other a convict—suggests that Chekhov had in mind Andreyev's penchant for stories hinging on crime and mental illness.

NOTES

The following notes, which have been kept as brief as possible, are designed to explain references in the text which might be obscure to English-speaking readers and to point out certain difficulties which have occurred in the translation.

Page

15 ‘the village elder's barn.’ It was the practice for the heads of households in a village to elect an elder who became the head of the *mir* or village commune. He presided over and summoned its meetings, and was in charge of village administration.

17 ‘their Turgenev and their Shchedrin.’ Reference is to the novelist I. S. Turgenev (1818–83), a well-known liberal; and to the satirist M. Ye. Saltykov (1826–89), a well-known radical (who wrote under the pseudonym ‘Shchedrin’, and is often known as Saltykov-Shchedrin).

17 ‘Henry Buckles.’ Reference is to Henry Thomas Buckle (1821–62), the English social historian and author of *History of Civilization* (1857–61), which enjoyed a great vogue in Russia.

18 ‘“Where Southern Breezes Blow”.’ A popular Ukrainian folk-song.

19 ‘Gadyach.’ A small town in the Ukraine about 150 miles east of Kiev.

21 ‘Master Creepy Crawly.’ See Preface, above, pp. xii–xiii.

32 ‘six foot of earth.’ Reference is to the short story *Does a Man Need much Earth?* (1886) by L. N. Tolstoy (1828–1910).

35 ‘To hosts of petty truths. . . .’ From the poem *A Hero* (1830) by A. S. Pushkin (1799–1837).

41 ‘“this is a great mystery”.’ Ephesians 5:32.

42 ‘*European Herald.*’ *Vestnik Yevropy*—a historico-political and literary monthly of liberal complexion published in St. Petersburg/Petrograd, 1866–1918.

51 ‘“Ere from the Cup of Life I yet had Drunk the Tears”.’ From the poem *An Elegy* by A. A. Delvig (1798–1831).

53 ‘“Rushlight”.’ A well-known folk-song.

53 ‘“A thing of beauty is a joy for ever”.’ Literally: ‘Die, Denis, you'll not write better!’ This remark was made to the eighteenth-century Russian playwright D. I. Fonvizin by Catherine the Great's favourite Potemkin after a performance of Fonvizin's play *The Brigadier.*

Page

54 ' "Your Voice, to me both Languorous and Tender".' The first lines of Pushkin's lyric *Night* (1823) read: 'My voice, to you both languorous and tender.'

56 'Pisemsky . . . *A Thousand Souls*.' Reference is to the novel *A Thousand Souls* (1858) by Alexis Feofilaktovich Pisemsky (1820–81).

57 'The hour cometh when—.' John 4:23.

72 'a baggy uniform.' Uniforms being very much in vogue in Imperial Russia, even non-governmental organizations such as the merchants' guilds tended to devise their own.

72 'a medal and Red Cross badge.' An indication that Lyalikov may have been decorated for doing charitable work.

72 'certain noises.' Russian night-watchmen were detailed to improvise banging noises to warn thieves, to prove that they had not fallen asleep, or—in the present case—to strike the hours.

73 'Polyanka Street.' In the merchant quarter in the south of Moscow.

77 'Lermontov's Tamara.' Reference is to the long poem *The Demon* (1839) by M. Yu. Lermontov (1814–41), in which the devil's kiss destroys Tamara, the girl whom he loves.

82 'Bryansk.' Town about 250 miles south-west of Moscow.

82 '*Faust Inside Out*.' Perhaps a burlesque of the opera *Faust* (1859) by Charles Gounod (1818–93).

82 '*Orpheus in the Underworld*.' The operetta *Orfée aux enfers* (1858, revised 1874) by Jacques Offenbach (1819–80).

84 'Mogilyov.' Town about 350 miles west-south-west of Moscow.

89 'Kharkov.' Large city in the Ukraine.

112 'The Nevsky Prospekt.' The main thoroughfare of St. Petersburg.

112 'Petrovka Street.' A street running north from central Moscow.

113 'the gaffer on the parish council.' Literally, the cantonal elder: a peasant elected to perform certain administrative duties within a *volost* (group of villages or canton).

113 'Five years after the serfs were freed.' Loshadin is saying that his appointment dates from 1866: i.e. five years after the Emancipation of the Serfs.

116 'Fell off me perch, I did—came down with a bump: it was king of the castle one day and dirty rascal the next.' A literal translation would be: 'Mokey had four lackeys, but now Mokey is himself a lackey. Petrak had four men working for him, but now Petrak himself is working for some-one else.'

Page

119 'Pushkin's "He clove the snow in powdered furrows".' The quotation is of line 5, verse II, Canto Five of Pushkin's verse novel *Eugene Onegin* (1823–31).

120 '*The Queen of Spades*.' Reference is to the opera *The Queen of Spades* (1890) by P. I. Tchaikovsky (1840–93), based on Pushkin's short story with the same title.

127 'Yalta.' Town and seaside resort on the Crimean coast, where Chekhov built a villa in 1899, and which was his main residence from then until his death in 1904; Vernet's café is mentioned in Baedeker's *Russia* (1914), p. 417.

128 'Belyov.' Small town about 150 miles south of Moscow.

128 'Zhizdra.' Small town about 200 miles south-west of Moscow.

128 'sunny Spain.' The text has 'Grenada' (an island in the West Indies), but it seems more likely that Chekhov had the Spanish 'Granada' in mind.

132 'Oreanda.' On the coast about five miles south-west of Yalta, Oreanda contained a park which extended down to the sea.

132 'Feodosiya.' Resort on the Crimean coast, about 70 miles north-east of Yalta.

133 'the waterfall.' The waterfall of Uchan-Su, about six miles from Yalta, was a favourite target for excursions.

136 '*The Geisha*.' The operetta by Sidney Jones, first produced in London (1896).

138 'The Slav Fair.' A large hotel in central Moscow, at which Chekhov himself sometimes stayed.

149 'Charcot.' Jean Martin Charcot (1825–93), the French physician and pioneer of psychotherapy.

153 'Yepifan.' Village about 150 miles south of Moscow.

162 'Yegoryevsk.' Town about 80 miles south-east of Moscow.

170 'a member of the Chamber of Commerce.' Literally, 'a merchant of the First Guild': i.e. the more prosperous of the two (at one time three) associations in which Russian businessmen and merchants were enrolled.

182 'Amur.' River in far eastern Siberia. Its first 800 miles form the frontier with China.

182 'Altay.' Mountainous region of southern Siberia and Mongolia.

199 'bridegroom who cometh at midnight.' Matthew 25:1–6.

202 ' "Now is the Son of Man glorified".' John 13:31.

202 'since Christianity had first come to Russia.' In about A.D. 988 with the conversion of Vladimir, Grand Prince of Kiev.

Page

209 '"He wasted his substance . . . filled his belly. . . .".' Luke 15:13–16.

211 'Anna Karenin.' Reference is to the heroine of the novel *Anna Karenin* (1875–7) by L. N. Tolstoy.

214 'St. Peter's Day.' 29 June.

214 'A Shishmachevsky.' The name appears to be an invention of Chekhov's.

218 '. . . your identity documents.' A Russian citizen was required to possess a 'passport' for purposes of internal as well as external travel.

219 'to join the Cossacks.' A reference to the custom of escaping from the centralized Muscovite state to lead a wild, free life among the Cossacks of the periphery, especially before they were brought under tighter control by Catherine the Great in the eighteenth century.

220 'koumiss.' A fermented liquor prepared from mare's milk. A koumiss diet was prescribed as a cure for tuberculosis, and Chekhov himself went on such a diet in 1901.

222 'Saratov.' Town on the Volga, about 500 miles south-east of Moscow.

227 'Tula.' Provincial capital about 120 miles south of Moscow, an old centre of the metal-working industry.

228 'Brest Station.' On the western side of Moscow, for trains to Smolensk, Brest-Litovsk, Warsaw etc.

228 'The Hermitage.' A restaurant on Trubny Square in Moscow.

228 'Little Bronny Road.' In north-west Moscow.

231 'Ufa.' Town near the Urals, now capital of the Bashkir Autonomous Republic.

231 'Perm.' Town about 800 miles east of Moscow.

232 '*Through narrow cuttings.* . . .' This and the quotations which follow come from the poem *The Railway* (1864) by N. A. Nekrasov (1821–78).

234 'Before he'd time to turn a hair. . . .' The lines come from the fable *The Peasant and the Workman* by I. A. Krylov (1769–1844).

237 'Thou sha-alt be quee-een of all the world.' The line is from Lermontov's poem *The Demon* (1839).

240 'in the days of serfdom.' Dating from before 1861, the year in which the serfs were emancipated.

249 'a gentleman of some note in the county.' Literally 'an *uyezd* marshal' (of nobility): that is, the elected representative of the local gentry in an *uyezd*, the administrative district below province (*guberniya*).

260 'Byron's *Cain*.' Reference is to *Cain* (1821) by the English poet Byron (1788–1824).

SELECT BIBLIOGRAPHY

I. BIBLIOGRAPHIES IN ENGLISH

Two most useful bibliographies, published by the New York Public Library and containing in all nearly five hundred items, give a comprehensive picture of the literature relating to Chekhov published in English—translations of his writings, biographical and critical studies, memoirs, essays, articles etc. They are:

> *Chekhov in English: a List of Works by and about him.* Compiled by Anna Heifetz. Ed. and with a Foreword by Avrahm Yarmolinsky (New York, 1949) and
>
> *The Chekhov Centennial Chekhov in English: a Selective List of Works by and about him, 1949–60.* Compiled by Rissa Yachnin (New York, 1960).

Bibliographies in English will also be found in the books by David Magarshack (*Chekhov: a Life*), Ernest J. Simmons and Ronald Hingley mentioned in Section III, below. Magarshack provides a bibliographical index of Chekhov's writings in alphabetical order of their English titles, Simmons includes a list of bibliographies in Russian, and Hingley gives a list of Chekhov's translated stories in chronological order.

II. TRANSLATIONS INTO ENGLISH OF THE STORIES IN THIS VOLUME

(Where the titles of translated stories differ from those in the present volume, the title adopted here is given in square brackets if the difference is so great as to make it difficult to identify the story.)

(a) TR. BY CONSTANCE GARNETT

The Darling, and Other Stories (London, 1916).

Includes: *The Darling [Angel]*.

The Lady with the Dog, and Other Stories (London, 1917).

Includes: *The Lady with the Dog, A Doctor's Visit [A Case History], Ionitch [Doctor Startsev]*.

The Wife, and Other Stories (London, 1918).

Includes: *The Man in a Case [A Hard Case], Gooseberries, About Love [Concerning Love]*.

The Witch, and Other Stories (London, 1918).

Includes: *The New Villa, At Christmas Time, In the Ravine [In the Hollow]*.

The Bishop, and Other Stories (London, 1919).
Includes: *The Bishop.*

The Schoolmistress, and Other Stories (London, 1920).
Includes: *On Official Duty* [*On Official Business*].

The Schoolmaster, and Other Stories (London, 1921).
Includes: *Betrothed* [*A Marriageable Girl*].

(b) BY OTHER TRANSLATORS

The Steppe, and Other Stories. Tr. Adeline Lister Kaye (London, 1915).
Includes: *The Hollow* [*In the Hollow*], *He who Wore a Husk* [*A Hard Case*], *The Gooseberry-Bush* [*Gooseberries*], *Of Love* [*Concerning Love*].

Stories of Russian Life. Tr. Marian Fell (New York, 1915).
Includes: *The Man in a Case* [*A Hard Case*], *In the Ravine* [*In the Hollow*].

The House with the Mezzanine, and Other Stories. Tr. S. S. Koteliansky and Gilbert Cannon (New York, 1917).
Includes: *Gooseberries, The Lady with the Toy Dog* [*A Lady with a Dog*].

The Masterpiece Library of Short Stories. Ed. J. A. Hammerton (London, 1920).
Includes: *Darling* [*Angel*], *The Encased Man* [*A Hard Case*]. Tr. by Rochelle Townsend(?).

The Short Story's Mutations from Petronius to Paul Morand (New York, 1925).
Includes: *The Darling* [*Angel*]. Tr. Frances Newman.

The Grasshopper, and Other Stories. Tr. with Introduction by A. E. Chamot (London, 1926).
Includes: *In the Ravine* [*In the Hollow*].

Great Russian Stories. Ed. Stephen Graham (New York, 1929).
Includes: *Dusechka* [*Angel*], tr. Rosa Graham.

The Heritage of European Literature. Ed. Edward H. Weatherly and others (Boston, Mass., 1948–9).
Includes: *The Darling* [*Angel*], *On Official Business*. Tr. Avrahm Yarmolinsky.

The Unknown Chekhov: Stories and Other Writings. Tr. with Introduction by Avrahm Yarmolinsky (London, 1949).
Includes: *A Visit to Friends* [*All Friends Together*], *Decompensation* [*Poor Compensation*].

The Woman in the Case, and Other Stories. Tr. April FitzLyon and Kyril Zinovieff (London, 1953).
Includes: *A Visit to Friends* [*All Friends Together*].

Anton Chekhov: Selected Stories. Tr. with Introduction by Jessie Coulson (London, 1963).
Includes: *A Visit to Friends* [*All Friends Together*], *On Love* [*Concerning Love*], *From a Case-Book* [*A Case History*], *The Darling* [*Angel*], *The Lady with the Little Dog* [*A Lady with a Dog*], *In the Ravine* [*In the Hollow*], *The Bishop*.

326 SELECT BIBLIOGRAPHY

Seven Short Novels by Chekhov. Tr. Barbara Makanowitzky with Introduction and Prefaces by Gleb Struve (New York, 1963).

Includes: *In the Ravine* [*In the Hollow*].

The Image of Chekhov: Forty Stories by Anton Chekhov in the Order in Which they were Written. Tr. with Introduction by Robert Payne (New York, 1963).

Includes: *On Love* [*Concerning Love*], *The Lady with the Pet Dog* [*A Lady with a Dog*], *The Bishop, The Bride* [*A Marriageable Girl*].

Ward Six, and Other Stories. Tr. Ann Dunnigan. With Afterword by Rufus W. Mathewson (New York, 1965).

Includes: *In the Ravine* [*In the Hollow*].

III. BIOGRAPHICAL AND CRITICAL STUDIES

Leon Shestov, *Anton Tchekhov and Other Essays* (Dublin and London, 1916).

William Gerhardi, *Anton Chekhov: a Critical Study* (London, 1923).

Oliver Elton, *Chekhov* (The Taylorian Lecture, 1929; Oxford, 1929).

Nina Andronikova Toumanova, *Anton Chekhov: the Voice of Twilight Russia* (London, 1937).

W. H. Bruford, *Chekhov and his Russia: a Sociological Study* (London, 1948).

Ronald Hingley, *Chekhov: a Biographical and Critical Study* (London, 1950).

Irene Nemirovsky, *A Life of Chekhov.* Tr. from the French by Erik de Mauny (London, 1950).

David Magarshack, *Chekhov: a Life* (London, 1952).

David Magarshack, *Chekhov the Dramatist* (London, 1952).

Vladimir Yermilov [Ermilov], *Anton Pavlovich Chekhov, 1860–1904.* Tr. Ivy Litvinov (Moscow, 1956; London, 1957).

W. H. Bruford, *Anton Chekhov* (London, 1957).

T. Eekman, ed., *Anton Chekhov, 1860–1960* (Leiden, 1960).

Beatrice Saunders, *Tchehov the Man* (London, 1960).

Ernest J. Simmons, *Chekhov: a Biography* (Boston, Toronto, 1962; London, 1963).

Maurice Valency, *The Breaking String: the Plays of Anton Chekhov* (New York, 1966).

Thomas Winner, *Chekhov and his Prose* (New York, 1966).

Robert Louis Jackson, ed., *Chekhov: a Collection of Critical Essays* (Englewood Cliffs, N. J., 1967).

Nils Åke Nilsson, *Studies in Čechov's Narrative Technique: The Steppe and The Bishop* (Stockholm, 1968).

Karl D. Kramer, *The Chameleon and the Dream: the Image of Reality in Čexov's Stories* (The Hague, 1970).

J. L. Styan, *Chekhov in Performance: a Commentary on the Major Plays* (Cambridge, 1971).

Virginia Llewellyn Smith, *Anton Chekhov and the Lady with the Dog*. Foreword by Ronald Hingley (London, 1973).

Harvey Pitcher, *The Chekhov Play: a New Interpretation* (London, 1973).

Sophie Laffitte, *Chekhov, 1860–1904*. Tr. from the French by Moura Budberg and Gordon Latta (London, 1974).

Kornei Chukovsky, *Chekhov the Man*. Tr. Pauline Rose (London, n.d.).

IV. LETTERS AND MEMOIR MATERIAL, ETC.

Letters of Anton Tchehov to his Family and Friends. Tr. Constance Garnett (London, 1920).

The Note-books of Anton Tchekhov together with Reminiscences of Tchekhov by Maxim Gorky. Tr. S. S. Koteliansky and Leonard Woolf (Richmond, Surrey, 1921).

Letters on the Short Story, the Drama and other Literary Topics. By Anton Chekhov. Selected and ed. Louis S. Friedland (New York, 1924).

Konstantin Stanislavsky, *My Life in Art*. Tr. J. J. Robbins (London, 1924; New York, 1956).

The Life and Letters of Anton Tchekhov. Tr. and ed. S. S. Koteliansky and Philip Tomlinson (London, 1925).

The Letters of Anton Pavlovitch Tchehov to Olga Leonardovna Knipper. Tr. Constance Garnett (London, 1926).

Anton Tchekhov: Literary and Theatrical Reminiscences. Tr. and ed. S. S. Koteliansky (London, 1927).

Vladimir Nemirovitch-Dantchenko, *My Life in the Russian Theatre*. Tr. John Cournos (London, 1937).

The Personal Papers of Anton Chekhov. Introduction by Matthew Josephson (New York, 1948).

Lydia Avilov, *Chekhov in my Life: a Love Story*. Tr. with an Introduction by David Magarshack (London, 1950).

Konstantin Stanislavsky, *Stanislavsky on the Art of the Stage*. Tr. with an introductory essay on Stanislavsky's 'System' by David Magarshack (London, 1950).

The Selected Letters of Anton Chekhov. Ed. Lillian Hellman, tr. Sidonie Lederer (New York, 1955).

Letters of Anton Chekhov. Tr. Michael Henry Heim in collaboration with Simon Karlinsky. Selection, Commentary and Introduction by Simon Karlinsky (New York, 1973).

Letters of Anton Chekhov. Selected and edited by Avrahm Yarmolinsky (New York, 1973).

V. OTHER WORKS USED IN THE PREPARATION OF THIS VOLUME

P. Semyonov (compiler), *Geografichesko-istorichesky slovar Rossiskoy imperii* (St. Petersburg, 1862–85).

Karl Baedeker, *Russia with Teheran, Port Arthur and Peking: Handbook for Travellers* (Leipzig, 1914).

Polnoye sobraniye sochineny i pisem A. P. Chekhova, ed. S. D. Balukhaty, V. P. Potyomkin, N. S. Tikhonov, A. M. Yegolin, 20 vols. (Moscow, 1944–51).

Chekhov v vospominaniyakh sovremennikov: vtoroye, dopolnennoye izdaniye, ed. N. L. Brodsky and others (Moscow, 1954).

N. I. Gitovich, *Letopis zhizni i tvorchestva A. P. Chekhova* (Moscow, 1955).

Literaturnoye nasledstvo: Chekhov, ed. V. V. Vinogradov and others (Moscow, 1960).